TANGLED WEBS

Center Point
Large Print

Also by Irene Hannon and available from Center Point Large Print:

Deceived
Thin Ice
Hope Harbor
Sea Rose Lane

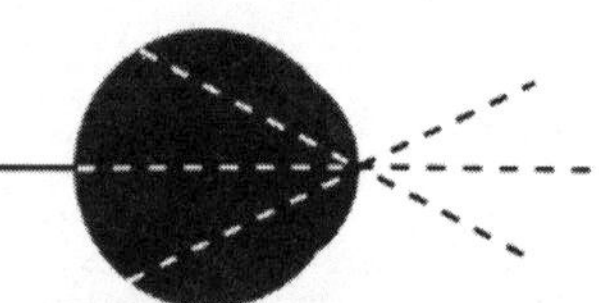

This Large Print Book carries the Seal of Approval of N.A.V.H.

Men of Valor #3

TANGLED WEBS

Irene Hannon

CENTER POINT LARGE PRINT
THORNDIKE, MAINE

This Center Point Large Print edition is published
in the year 2016 by arrangement with Revell,
a division of Baker Publishing Group.

The text of this Large Print edition is unabridged.
In other aspects, this book may vary
from the original edition.
Printed in the United States of America
on permanent paper.
Set in 16-point Times New Roman type.

ISBN: 978-1-68324-170-6

Library of Congress Cataloging-in-Publication Data

Names: Hannon, Irene, author.
Title: Tangled webs / Irene Hannon.
Description: Center Point Large Print edition. | Thorndike, Maine :
Center Point Large Print, 2016.
Identifiers: LCCN 2016033918 | ISBN 9781683241706
(hardcover : alk. paper)
Subjects: LCSH: Large type books. | GSAFD: Mystery fiction. |
Christian fiction.
Classification: LCC PS3558.A4793 T36 2016b | DDC 813/.54—dc23
LC record available at https://lccn.loc.gov/2016033918

To my father, James Hannon—
the most unselfish man I've ever met.

As I conclude my Men of Valor series,
thank you for reminding me by example
that valor isn't found only in
grand, sweeping gestures,
but in quietly doing—day after day, with
kindness, grace, humility, and love—
what needs to be done.

You will always be my hero.

—Prologue—

It was a terrible night to die.

Father Daniel Pruitt cringed as another boom of thunder shook the ground beneath his older-model Taurus. This weather wasn't fit for man nor beast.

Priests, however—different story. Being available 24/7, no matter the whims of Mother Nature, was part of the job description. That's why the archdiocese paid him the big bucks.

Right.

Setting his brake, he peered through the pelting rain toward the hospital. In better days, Joe Larson would have offered one of his quiet smiles at that wry joke. He knew, as did all the parishioners at St. Michael's, that priesthood was a vocation, not a job, for their pastor. That Father Pruitt considered it a sacred privilege to be there for his flock during life's biggest transitions.

And death was a huge transition.

Especially when the person dying was alone—except for God.

Father Pruitt gauged the distance from the car to the front door of Faith Regional and sized up the black umbrella on the seat beside him. The folding model was better suited to fending off April showers than April monsoons.

No way around it—he was going to be uncomfortably damp for hours.

With a resigned sigh, he tucked his book of prayers inside the inner pocket of his raincoat. Positioned the umbrella. Opened the door.

His pants legs were soaked before his feet hit the ground.

Ducking his head—and keeping a firm grip on the umbrella as the blustery wind tried to wrench it from his grasp—he jogged toward the entrance as fast as his sixty-five-year-old arthritic knees allowed.

The door whooshed open as he approached, and he scurried inside, moving from darkness to the perennial day of the rarefied hospital world.

At this late hour, the reception desk was deserted, all the volunteers long gone and in bed—the very place he'd been until the urgent call came in sixty minutes ago.

And based on what the nurse had said, there would be no more sleep for him this night.

He continued to the bank of elevators. One opened the instant he pressed the up button, and ten seconds later the doors parted on Joe's floor.

A woman at the nurses' station looked up as he approached. Holly, according to the ID pinned to her scrub top. The nurse who'd summoned him.

"Father Pruitt?"

"Yes." He halted across the counter from her, his

sodden umbrella shedding drops of water on the floor.

"Sorry to make you come out on such an awful night, but after Mr. Larson took a sudden turn for the worse, he insisted. In fact, he became quite agitated about it. Since he's left directions for no mechanical ventilation and it's hard to predict timing with end-stage COPD, I thought it best to call you. I hope you didn't have a long drive."

"Twenty-five miles."

She winced. "Too long on a night like this."

True. Motoring through the Nebraska cornfields from Linden to Norfolk was pleasant enough on a sunny day, but the trek across dark countryside while battling wind and rain had seemed endless.

The nurse pulled out her cell, checked the window, and exhaled. "It's going to be one of those nights. Thunder has a way of unsettling patients." Finger hovering over the talk button, she nodded down the hall. "Last door on the right. Mr. Larson asked us to hold off on morphine until after he spoke with you, so just press the call button once you're finished."

"Thanks. I will."

She was already talking on her cell, heading the opposite direction from Joe's room.

Trying to ignore the wet fabric clinging to his legs, Father Pruitt made his way down the corridor. Most of the rooms he passed were dark; Joe's was dimly lit. Hand on the knob, he paused for a moment of prayer, then entered and closed the door behind him.

As he approached the bed, his rubber-soled shoes silent on the floor, Joe didn't stir. Hard to believe this gaunt figure was the same man he'd visited here three days ago, when they'd both assumed his lung infection would follow previous patterns and clear up.

But it didn't take a medical professional to know there would be no reprieve this time. Above the nasal cannula delivering oxygen to lungs that had finally succumbed to the man's sole vice—chain-smoking—Joe's cheeks were sunken and shriveled. His disease had followed the classic pattern: shortness of breath, fatigue, weight loss, infections, heart failure . . . and now his uneven respiration completed the pattern, affirming the truth of the nurse's comment.

The end was, indeed, near.

Father Pruitt hung his coat over a chair and moved beside the bed.

"Joe."

No response.

Perhaps his faithful parishioner hadn't been able to hang on to consciousness after all.

Vision misting, he touched the dying man's hand. During the dozen years he'd tended parishes in three small towns that dotted the cornfield-quilted land, he'd never met a kinder, more humble person. Joe might not have much in a material sense to show for a lifetime of labor in the corn processing facility, but he'd always given generously to his church and to those in need. And along the way, he'd also become a trusted friend.

Saying good-bye wouldn't be easy.

All of a sudden, Joe's eyelids flickered open. "Father." The greeting was no more than a wisp of air.

Father Pruitt grasped the gnarled fingers that had seen more than their share of hard work over the past seventy-two years. "I'm here, Joe."

"I . . . need you . . . to do . . . a favor . . . for me." Each gasping word was a struggle, pain contorting the man's features.

"Anything."

"After I'm . . . gone . . . letter in my . . . night-stand . . . at home . . . will you . . . mail it?" He tightened his grip, his gaze intent.

"Of course."

An odd request, though. Joe had lived alone in his tiny, two-bedroom bungalow for decades—and despite their friendship, he'd never mentioned relatives or talked about anyone with whom he might have corresponded.

"Need to . . . confess something."

"You did that on my last visit, Joe. Three days ago."

"There's . . . more."

More?

What possible transgression could he have committed while flat on his back in a hospital bed?

"I'm sure you and God are on solid ground, my friend."

"No." He clenched his fingers. "Need . . . to confess."

"All right." If talking about some minor sin eased his mind, there was no harm in repeating the ritual. Gently Father Pruitt retracted his hand, lowered himself into a bedside chair. "Whenever you're ready."

The room fell silent save for the other man's labored breathing, and at last he lifted his chin. Joe was watching him, eyes filmed with moisture.

"This is . . . bad . . . Father." Anguish darkened his blue irises.

Father Pruitt touched the fingers Joe had clamped around the edge of the sheet. "When we approach God with a contrite and sincere heart, no sin is too great to be forgiven. And both I and God have heard it all. Nothing you can say will shock either of us."

But as it turned out, that was a lie.

Because as Joe recited his confession in a halting, thready voice . . . as the meaning of the letter the dying man had asked him to mail became clear . . . Father Pruitt wasn't just shocked.

He was stunned.

Somehow he managed to complete the rite. But as he spoke the final prayer, as Joe drifted out of consciousness for the last time, his mind was spinning.

How could you know a man for years and never suspect he carried such a devastating secret?

He pondered that through the long hours of darkness as he kept vigil beside the bed—and was still pondering it as faint lines of pink streaked the horizon and Joe's breathing slowed. Stopped.

For several minutes, he remained seated . . . in case Joe's spirit hadn't yet departed the earthly realm.

But at last, filling his own lungs with air, Father Pruitt pulled himself to his feet and rested his hand once more on Joe's motionless fingers. Studied the kindly face, now at rest, all lines of pain erased. Bowed his head and uttered one final prayer.

"May God have mercy on your soul."

—1—

Maybe his brothers were right.

Maybe this was a mistake.

Gripping his mug of coffee, Finn McGregor pushed through the door of the cabin, into middle-of-the-night darkness. The April air was chilly, but the brush of coolness against his clammy skin eased his jitters a tad.

Funny how the notion of spending four quiet weeks in a secluded cabin had seemed inspired ten days ago but now felt so wrong.

Just as Mac and Lance had predicted.

He huffed out a breath. Okay . . . staying in St. Louis until he'd fully wrestled his demons into submission might have been smarter—except he had a decision to make, and trying to do that with his two overprotective big brothers in hover mode had been impossible.

Melting into the shadows of the rustic porch, he took a sip of the strong brew and did a sweep of woods unbrightened by even a sliver of moon. The blackness was absolute . . . yet it didn't raise his anxiety level one iota. Darkness had often been his friend. A significant tactical advantage in certain circumstances, in fact. Like the night his unit . . .

Hoo. Hoo.

His hand jerked, and hot coffee sloshed over the rim of the mug, burning his fingers.

Shaking off the liquid, he gritted his teeth.

Spooked by an owl.

How dumb was that?

Good thing Mac and Lance weren't here. He could picture them, arms folded in that intimidating pose all the McGregor men had mastered, reminding him that hanging out alone in the middle of nowhere might not be the best game plan at this stage of his recovery.

Too bad.

He was here now, and he wasn't going back—not yet, anyway. Not after two nights. His McGregor ego would never let him admit defeat this fast.

However . . . if the quiet and solitude were still too oppressive in a few days, he might make the hour-and-a-half drive back to St. Louis. Despite its remote feel, this part of the Mark Twain National Forest wasn't all that far from the bright lights of the big city he'd called home for the past nine months.

More than likely, though, he just needed a few days to acclimate. The stack of books he'd brought with him should keep him occupied. And he might chop some wood with that ax he'd found in the shed. Nothing beat manual labor for exorcising restless energy.

He lifted the mug and took a swig. Once he settled in, adjusted to the slower pace, and—

"AAAAHHHHH!"

Finn choked on the coffee as a woman's distant scream ripped through the night.

What the . . . ?!

Still sputtering, he pushed off from the wall, adrenaline surging, every muscle taut.

Five seconds passed.

Ten.

Fifteen.

The owl hooted again.

Twenty.

Yards from where he stood, the underbrush rustled—a foraging rodent or raccoon, no doubt. Nothing sinister.

Thirty seconds.

The forest remained quiet.

Throttling his paranoia, he exhaled and forced his brain to shift into analytical mode.

Fact one: The sound had been distant, and somewhat indistinct.

Fact two: His cabin was surrounded by a national forest more populated by deer than people. As far as he could tell—based on the single narrow gravel lane off the main drag he'd passed before turning onto his own access road—he had only one relatively close human neighbor.

Fact three: This was rural Missouri, not downtown St. Louis or some crime-ridden—

"AAAAHHHH!"

His hand jerked again, sloshing more coffee.

It *was* a woman's scream. He was *not* being paranoid. This was *not* a tray dropping in the base cafeteria that just *sounded* like an explosion.

This was the real deal.

Another scream propelled him into action. Moving on autopilot, he grabbed his compact Beretta, Ka-Bar knife, and a flashlight from the cabin, left behind the cell phone that didn't work around here anyway, and raced through the woods, every ounce of his dormant training kicking back in.

Several more terrified screams kept his direction true as he zigzagged through trees in early leaf-out stage, the winter-scoured forest floor hosting little undergrowth that would impede his progress.

When he at last emerged into a clearing, breathing harder than he should be after a quarter-mile run, a large, meandering lake stretched before him.

A scream to his right directed his attention to a small cabin perched on a slight rise above the water, a hundred yards away.

Ignoring the protests of his left leg, he sprinted toward the log structure, where light shone from behind curtains in several windows. Not helpful. The element of surprise worked best if you entered in an optimal spot. If he could determine the woman's location . . .

As if on cue, another scream pierced the air.

She was in the back of the cabin, left side.

Beretta in hand, he raced toward the log structure, staying in the shadows at the edge of the woods. Too bad he didn't have his trusty M4—but that kind of equipment wasn't part of his standard issue anymore. Nor would it be again. He might be unclear about a lot of stuff, but that much he knew.

Still, a Beretta could be as deadly as an

assault rifle in a shootout, if it came to that.

He hoped it didn't. He wasn't up for a life-and-death battle . . . physically or emotionally.

But that was a moot point.

Something bad was going down in this cabin, and ducking out when things got dicey wasn't part of the McGregor DNA.

Bending low, he dashed from the cover of the woods to the structure. Flattening his back against the rough-hewn logs, he eased around the corner, to the rear wall.

All clear.

He crouched lower and edged close to the dim light shining from the window of the room he'd pinpointed. It was open halfway—no wonder the scream had carried in the quiet country air. But the shade was pulled all the way down, and a screen stood between it and him.

Might there be a window open somewhere else that would allow less obvious access?

Circling back to the front of the cabin, he checked every window.

Bingo.

One was cracked.

He pulled his knife out of its sheath, dispensed with the screen, and worked the sash up. A slight tip of the shade revealed that the space on the other side was clear, and he slipped inside—just as another high-pitched scream ricocheted through the house.

Sheathing the blade, he flexed his fingers on the Beretta and slipped noiselessly through the cabin, ticking through the factors in his favor as he psyched himself up for a confrontation that was liable to become violent.

The element of surprise was on his side.

He was armed.

He'd led dozens of successful assault and rescue missions.

No matter what he found on the other side of the door where the woman was being held, he could handle the situation. *Would* handle it.

Whatever it took.

Finn stopped outside the door. Angled sideways. Smashed his heel below the lock.

The door flew back.

Another scream sliced through the air as he tucked himself beside the frame, pistol in the ready position. He ducked down, muscles coiled as he prepared to spring into action, and looked around the edge.

Froze.

A thirtyish woman with tousled light brown hair was sitting bolt upright in bed, clutching a blanket against her, blinking as if she'd been abruptly awakened from a peaceful slumber and was trying to figure out what was going on.

There was no one else in the room.

She squinted at him, and despite the dim light he knew the instant full consciousness returned.

Stark terror widened her eyes, and she shot to her feet, grabbed a cell phone off her nightstand, and dashed for the door in the corner. It banged behind her. A moment later, the lock slammed into place.

Regroup, McGregor.

Sucking in a lungful of air, Finn gave the room a fast sweep. The covers were jumbled. The pillow was scrunched up. A glass of water and a bottle of aspirin rested on the nightstand.

Conclusion?

There was no emergency here. This woman had simply been having a nightmare.

To make matters worse, he'd broken into her house wielding a gun, exacerbating whatever trauma she was already dealing with.

Stomach clenching, he closed his eyes.

What a colossal mess-up.

And now she was barricaded in the bathroom, calling the cops. Or trying to.

If he was lucky, her cell would be as useless as his was out here.

But whether she got through or not, he had some serious explaining to do.

He holstered his pistol and crossed to the bolted door. "Ma'am?"

No response.

Of course not. She thought he was some thug, up to no good.

Would telling her the simple, honest truth convince her otherwise?

Unlikely—but that was the only strategy that came to mind.

"Ma'am? I'm sorry about frightening you. I'm actually your neighbor, Finn McGregor. I heard screams coming from your cabin and thought you might need help, but it appears you were just having a bad dream. Mark Busch, who owns the adjacent property, can confirm my identity if you want to contact him. In the meantime, I'll take the screen I destroyed getting in, have it fixed in town, and return it tomorrow. I'll also repair your bedroom door. I'm leaving now—but I'll come around back first to let you verify I've left the house. Again . . . I apologize."

Beating a hasty retreat, he escaped through the window, unclipping the slashed screen first. Man, he'd done a number on it. If there wasn't a hardware store in Beaumont, he'd have to drive into Potosi to get it fixed.

At least tomorrow was Monday, and the local businesses should be open bright and early.

He circled the cabin, screen in hand, and stopped a few feet away from the bathroom window in the back. She hadn't flipped on the light. Smart. Staying in the dark would allow her to crack the shade and see the exterior without being seen.

"Ma'am? I'm outside now." He set the screen on the ground, pulled the flashlight out of his back pocket, and shined the light on his face, making it easy for her to identify him. That should help calm her.

Or would it?

He hadn't shaved in two days, and while the stubbled bad-boy look might be popular in Hollywood, it could have a negative connotation in this situation. In real life, true bad boys often sported this look too.

He flicked off the light.

"Again, it's Finn McGregor. I'll return your repaired screen tomorrow."

With that, he turned away from the window and trudged back toward his cabin—berating himself every step of the way.

Way to go, buddy. Freak out a woman who's already on edge—and who isn't going to sleep another wink tonight, thanks to you.

But what else could he have done? She *had* been screaming. And if she *had* been in trouble, politely knocking on the door and alerting the perpetrator to his presence would have been stupid.

He'd explain that to her tomorrow when he returned her screen—unless she'd locked herself in the house . . . or summoned reinforcements . . . or hightailed it out of here.

He pushed past a cedar tree, the distinctive scent reminding him of the old chest his mom had inherited from her grandmother. She'd always said the treasured heirloom was a reminder of the importance of family—a value she'd passed on to her three sons. The McGregors always stood shoulder to shoulder in times of trauma or trouble.

The woman in that cabin was obviously in the midst of some kind of trauma too—yet she appeared to be alone.

Had she left a caring family behind, as he had—or did she lack a support system?

And what sort of demons would produce such anguished screams?

He increased his pace as the wind picked up, the chilled air sending a shiver rippling through him.

Neither of those questions would be answered tonight.

But perhaps on his return visit tomorrow, in the safety of daylight and after another sincere apology, he might get a few clues about the background of his young, attractive—and traumatized—neighbor.

Assuming she was still around.

Dana Lewis lifted her shaking hand and checked her cell again.

No signal.

Raking her fingers through her tangled hair, she huddled on the toilet seat lid. What did she expect? In the four weeks she'd been here, how often had she managed to get a signal in the cabin? Never. Just on the dock down by the lake.

No way was she venturing out there tonight,

though. The guy who'd burst into the cabin could be lurking in the shadows, waiting to pounce.

Not likely, Dana. He was in your bedroom. If he'd wanted to get to you, he could have.

Yes . . . that was true. Plus, he'd made a point of letting her see his face. The light he'd flashed on hadn't illuminated it long, and the shadows had distorted his features, but there'd been no missing the dark auburn hair and wide, muscular shoulders.

Her pulse slowed as the left side of her brain continued to process the situation. He'd told her his name too. And Mark Busch did own the adjacent property. First senior, now junior. A quick call to him would confirm the man's identity.

As for the excuse the intruder had offered for breaking in—it was credible. The nightmares plagued her less often now, but they cropped up on occasion . . . and the one tonight had been bad. It was very possible she'd screamed. Hadn't her big-city neighbors told her they'd heard her cry out on several occasions, despite the sound-proofing in the high-rise walls?

But given her remote location, who'd have guessed someone out here would not only hear her but respond?

Clutching her dead phone, she stood and sidled up to the window. A quick crack of the shade confirmed the man was gone.

And unless she wanted to cower in the bathroom all night, she needed to open the door and do a walk-through of the house.

Gathering her courage, she slid the bolt back and pushed the door open.

The room was just as she'd left it—bedclothes disheveled, dim light burning, purse untouched on the chair beside the door. She moved to the window and shut it, flipping the lock.

Then she crossed to the hall door that was hanging on one hinge. Peeked out.

The corridor was deserted.

There was no one in the rest of the house, either. When she came to the screenless window in the living room, she closed and locked it too.

She was as safe as she could be for the rest of the night.

Rotating her stiff shoulders, she returned to the kitchen and peered at the tacky fish-shaped clock that had hung on the wall for as long as she could remember. Two-forty-nine.

Daylight was more than three sleepless hours away.

But between the nightmare and her unexpected visitor, there would be no more slumber for her this night.

Stifling a yawn, she filled a mug with water, added a bag of English breakfast tea, and slid it into the microwave. Might as well get some work done if she was going to be up anyway. She could always take a nap tomorrow if her short night caught up with her.

While she waited for the water to heat, she booted up her laptop, flipped on the adjacent monitor, and padded back down the hall in search of her slippers and the oversized cardigan sweater Pops had always worn.

She found both at the foot of her bed. After shoving her feet into the slippers, she pushed her arms through the rolled-up sleeves of the sweater, fingering a spot that was beginning to unravel.

Kind of like her life of late.

Wrapping her arms around herself, she did a slow pivot in the room, with its knotty pine paneling, handmade log bed crafted from trees grown on this property, and framed serenity prayer attributed to Francis of Assisi that sat on the doily-bedecked pine dresser. At least here, in her refuge, life felt more stable.

Or it had until tonight.

Spirits drooping, she returned to the kitchen as the microwave emitted a high-pitched summons. A soothing cup of hot tea was the perfect antidote to whatever ailed you. That and a warm hug. Or so Mags and Pops used to tell her.

She retrieved the mug from the turntable, dunking the tea bag as she wandered toward her computer. The tea, she had. Warm hugs? In short supply.

Instead of the discouragement that usually

accompanied such melancholy thoughts, however, an image of auburn hair and broad shoulders zipped across her mind.

Dana stopped in front of the laptop, frowning. How bizarre was that? She'd seen the man for less than ten seconds and could call up nothing more than a vague impression of him. Plus, he'd broken into her house. With a gun.

Taking a sip of tea, she lowered herself into the chair, for once barely noticing the baby giraffe in her screensaver, neck straining to reach a leafy branch just out of grasp.

The man hadn't seemed to be a criminal, however. He'd had a logical explanation for his appearance, offered a heartfelt apology, and left fast once he realized his mistake. Plus, he had a nice voice. Deep and resonant and . . . caring. It was the voice of someone who'd come to help, not hurt.

In fact, if everything the man told her was true, his behavior tonight was downright heroic. He'd been willing to put himself in danger to rescue her.

Dana opened the document she'd been working on earlier and scrolled through to where she'd left off. This author was talented—but her work needed a lot of polishing. The perfect project to occupy her mind until dawn chased away the darkness.

Yet as she dived into the task, she found herself

thinking ahead to tomorrow—and looking forward to Finn McGregor's return visit.

Which was silly.

The man was a stranger to her. He might be her temporary neighbor, living within shouting—or screaming—distance, but once he returned her repaired window screen, there would be no reason for their paths to intersect.

Besides, for all she knew, he had a wife and children staying with him at Mark's place. That would put the kibosh on any dreamy-eyed fantasies.

Rolling her eyes, she picked up her glasses, slid them on, and leaned toward the screen. She'd been editing too many romances recently—like this one. Maybe she should take on a literary novel next. No need to worry about optimistic, happy endings with those.

Yet the whole notion of heroes and heroines overcoming great odds to find a future together was a lot more uplifting.

Even if it didn't often happen in real life.

—2—

"Good morning, Chief Burnett. I'm glad I caught you."

At the comment from behind him, Roger Burnett tightened his grip on the arms of his chair.

He knew that voice—too well. Alan Landis had cornered him twice in the past month . . . but always during normal business hours.

If the finance manager for Woodside Gardens long-term care facility was here this early on a Monday morning, he was getting ready to play hardball about the overdue bill. This wasn't a casual meeting, as his greeting implied; he must have told the staff to let him know if Leah's husband showed up during off hours.

The sheets rustled. His wife stirred and peered at the man in the doorway.

"Are you from the nursery? Did you bring the impatiens I ordered? I'm not paying you until they're all planted, you know. And I don't want any half-dead ones, like you brought last summer."

"Honey." Roger pushed himself to his feet and moved beside the bed. "This is Mr. Landis. He works here. He came to see me."

His wife glowered at the finance manager. "I don't like him."

Neither did he . . . but his reasons weren't delusional, like his wife's. They were all too real.

Landis wanted money he didn't have . . . and he wasn't going to be able to put him off much longer.

Roger tried to contain the wave of panic that crashed over him. He had to find a way to pay this bill. Leah deserved the best possible treatment—

and he'd promised to provide it. Going back on his word wasn't an option. He owed her this.

"You . . ." Leah poked him in the arm and pointed toward Landis. "Make him go away."

"I'd appreciate it if you'd stop by my office before you leave." The man spoke in the sotto tone he'd no doubt perfected as a result of dealing with dementia-plagued residents like Leah.

"I'll do that."

Landis dipped his chin and disappeared from the doorway.

Leah pulled a tissue from the box on her bedside table and began to shred it, her head whipping back and forth on the pillow. "Where am I?"

"Woodside Gardens. In Potosi."

"I live in Beaumont."

A rare moment of lucidity. The kind that used to give him hope.

But hope was a rare commodity in his life these days.

"That's right. You're staying here until you get better."

"Am I sick?"

Very—and there was no cure for early onset Alzheimer's. The woman he loved had been slipping away day by day for the past seven years. She didn't even remember his name anymore.

"You'll get better soon." It was the same lie he told her whenever this subject came up.

She gave him a hard stare. "I think you're

keeping me here! You don't want me to leave! You don't want me to go home!" Her pitch rose with each word. "You get out! Get out *now!* I hate you!"

Her tirade ended in a screech that brought one of the aides hurrying in.

Roger backed away. He knew the drill by now. Leave it to the experts to calm her. When she got like this, his presence only upset her more.

Once in the hall, he ran a hand down his face while his wife continued to rant. There was so little left of the vivacious woman he'd exchanged vows with thirty-five years ago. So little. In fact, with every passing day, it was getting harder and harder to recognize this shrieking shrew as the bright-eyed, happy-go-lucky girl who'd stolen his heart.

But she was there, trapped somewhere in the recesses of her deteriorating mind . . . and he wasn't going to let her down.

Hand resting on the gun at his hip, he straightened up, smoothed a hand down the front of his navy blue uniform shirt, and set out for Landis's office.

The man was waiting for him, mug of coffee at hand. No surprise he was loading up on caffeine, given the early post-dawn hour. He must have rushed into work after receiving the call from a staff member.

"Would you like some?" Landis lifted his mug.

"Yes. Thanks." An infusion of java might help him get through this meeting.

The man disappeared out the door, and Roger sank into the seat across from the desk. The same seat he'd occupied during their previous two meetings. Landis had been sympathetic and polite at the first one, concerned and a bit cooler at the second.

If the pattern of deteriorating civility continued, today wasn't going to be pleasant.

He'd stall again, of course. Make more promises he couldn't keep. What else could he do? The well was dry. The equity loan he'd taken on the house was gone, since there hadn't been much equity to tap. The family jewelry Leah had inherited had been sold. He owned nothing else of value. And no bank would give him a loan he couldn't repay.

At least no one knew about his dire financial straits. Not a single person in Beaumont, and certainly not Alan Landis. If the finance manager had the slightest inkling how tapped out he was, Woodside Gardens would throw Leah out on her ear, despite their "Where every guest is treated with dignity" marketing slogan.

Landis reentered, set the coffee on the desk, and circled back to his seat. "I'm sure you know why I asked you to stop by."

"Yes." Roger lifted the disposable cup and took a sip. "I appreciate your patience these past few weeks."

"We try to give the families of our guests as much consideration as we can. Illness creates a great deal of stress, and we all want the best possible situation for our loved ones. But care at a top-notch facility like Woodside Gardens isn't inexpensive, and sometimes, if a guest is here for an extended period, it becomes burdensome." He shuffled some papers and extracted a sheet. "According to our records, your wife was admitted twenty-eight months ago."

"Yes." The day was seared in his memory. She'd clung to him—sobbing, begging, making promises she couldn't keep—when he had to leave.

He hadn't clocked more than two hours' sleep a night for the next two weeks.

"And you've always been prompt with your payments—until last month. Now you're two months in arrears. That's a lot of money, Chief Burnett."

"I know . . . and I'm working on it."

"That's what you said two weeks ago."

"It's still true." Roger took another sip of the unsweetened coffee and set the cup back on the desk. "Look, I've had difficulty liquidating some assets. I expect to have this resolved very soon." He maintained eye contact with the finance manager, hoping the man wouldn't see through his lie.

Landis tapped a finger on the polished surface of his desk. "I'd like to help you out—but I have to report to the Woodside board, and they expect our guests to pay their bills."

"I realize that, and I'm doing my best to rectify the situation as fast as possible." He hated the pleading note that crept into his voice, but desperation was beginning to undermine his usual composure. He'd been short-tempered with his staff too—not his usual style, either. Thankfully, they attributed his grouchiness to his wife's declining health and were cutting him some slack.

"I'm confident you are." The man's tone remained cordial, but there was a steel edge to it. "However, we need to begin looking at alternative arrangements."

A wave of nausea rolled through him. Like what? That seedy facility on the edge of town that charged half as much and had been cited more than once for resident abuse?

No way.

Trouble was, at this point he couldn't even afford that place.

"Will you give me a little more time?"

"How much?"

"The end of the month. If I haven't paid my bill in full by then, I'll move Leah."

The man let an uncomfortable five seconds drag by. "All right. We'll expect the balance by April 30."

"Thank you." Roger rose and picked up his cup. "I'll work toward the deadline."

Without waiting for a reply, he left the office.

Once outside, he drew in a lungful of the fresh spring air. No matter how high-end these places were, all of them had the same distinctive odor. They reeked of advanced age. Lingering illness. Imminent death.

After taking another swallow of the bitter coffee, he pitched the rest in a trash container in the parking lot.

The only positive outcome from today's meeting was the temporary reprieve. He'd bought himself twenty-three days to come up with almost twenty thousand dollars for the March, April, and May bills.

A fortune, when your checking account was on fumes and you had zilch in savings.

Only one thing would allow him to raise that kind of money by the deadline.

A miracle.

He unlocked the police cruiser, slid inside, and gripped the wheel.

Please, God—help me find a way to get through this crisis. Leah has been your faithful servant all her life. She doesn't have much time left . . . help me make her last few months comfortable. Please.

A drop of rain splashed onto the windshield. Another followed. Several more splattered on the glass. Then the skies opened. Driving back to Beaumont on the rural roads would be tricky.

But he could handle this kind of storm.

It was the storm in his life that sent his blood pressure soaring.

And as he put the car in gear and aimed it toward Beaumont, he hoped the good Lord had heard his plea.

Because if God ignored him, he didn't have a clue what he was going to do next.

This had to be it.

Finn slowed as he approached the gravel road that veered off the main drag. A rusted wagon wheel was propped against a rock, but no mailbox stood at the entrance.

Since there were no other driveways anywhere close to the entrance to Mark Busch's place on this side of the two-lane highway, the screaming woman's cabin must be down here.

Twisting the wheel, Finn maneuvered the SUV through a ditch that would no doubt be impassable in a downpour and drove down a narrow, woods-bordered track that barely accommodated his vehicle.

After a few hundred yards, he emerged into a small clearing behind the cabin he'd invaded last night. A parking pad large enough to hold two cars was off to the side of the structure, but it was empty.

Had the woman fled rather than wait for him to appear today?

Only one way to find out.

He parked the SUV, retrieved the repaired screen and the toolbox he'd found in Mark's shed, and circled around to the front of the house.

Pausing, he took in the scene.

What a difference from the sinister mood of last night.

With sunshine spilling through the new green sprouts on the trees and sprinkling the blue water of the lake below with diamonds, the tidy cabin looked more like a peaceful retreat than a house of terror.

Hopefully some of that peace had seeped into the occupant in the past few hours.

Ascending the steps to a porch furnished with two caned-seat rocking chairs separated by a table topped with a pot of geraniums, Finn prepared to issue another apology.

Once at the door, he set down the toolbox, leaned the screen against the wall, and ran a hand over his smooth jaw. Dispensing with the stubble had gone a long way toward giving him an air of respectability. Exchanging last night's sweatpants and plain white T-shirt for jeans and a real shirt should work to his advantage too.

He hoped.

After wiping his palms down the denim covering his thighs, he lifted his hand and knocked.

Fifteen silent seconds passed.

He tried again.

Zilch.

Propping his hands on his hips, he examined the screenless window. He couldn't put the screen back in from the outside—but the woman could do it herself when she returned. It wasn't a difficult job.

Assuming she *did* return.

This could be a vacation rental. In that case, after what had happened last night, she might have decided to cut her visit short and . . .

"Sorry. I was taking a break for a few minutes down near the dock."

Pulse vaulting into overdrive, he whirled around, every muscle taut and poised for action.

The woman from last night stood twenty feet away.

"Sorry again. I didn't mean to startle you."

He squinted against the glare of the sun and gave her a discreet once-over. The longish brown hair was familiar, though the copper highlights sparked by the sun were new—but man, did she look different in the daylight, long legs encased in snug jeans, red Stanford sweatshirt hinting at enticing curves.

Too bad dark glasses hid her eyes. Based on her model-like cheekbones and lush lips, they were probably—

"Are you okay?"

He did his best to rein in his wandering thoughts

and relax his posture. “Yes. I, uh, didn’t expect to find you outside.”

“And I didn’t expect to find you in my cabin last night. Shall we call it even?”

“That would be far too generous on your part.” Her stark terror as he crashed through her bedroom door would be etched in his memory for the foreseeable future. “But I hope to make amends.” He indicated the screen and tool kit.

She inspected them, then shoved her hands in her pockets. “The door’s open.”

After retrieving both items, he twisted the knob and entered.

She didn’t follow.

Who could blame her after last night? She might have accepted his story—or perhaps done as he’d suggested and checked it out—but he was still a stranger. In her place, he’d be cautious too.

Within two minutes, the screen was locked back into place. Tool kit in hand, he walked down the hall toward the bedroom, surveying the kitchen as he passed. The room was cheery, if dated, with knotty pine cabinets, white porcelain sink, faded checkered yellow curtains, and a wooden dinette set that appeared to be used more for work than eating. Half of the space was taken up with a laptop and a large monitor displaying grossly oversized text.

Curious.

Ten minutes later, he finished securing the door.

The bedroom was much neater today than it had been last night, a quilt covering the double bed, pillow plumped, the water and aspirin gone. Had she straightened up in anticipation of his visit—or was she simply a neat person?

Based on the spotless, clutter-free house he passed through en route to the front door, it was the latter.

She was sitting on the porch steps as he exited, but she rose the instant he appeared and backed off, putting distance between them.

"All finished." Finn sent her his warmest smile. The one most women found irresistible.

She didn't return it.

"Thanks. And thanks, too, for responding last night to what you thought was an emergency. A lot of people wouldn't have bothered."

"That's not how I was raised."

"Kudos to your parents."

"I'll pass that on."

Silence.

Finn transferred the toolbox to his other hand. The lady hadn't offered any explanation about the nightmare . . . or the reason for her visit here . . . or why she was alone. Nor had she given him her name.

If he wanted more information, he was going to have to prolong this conversation and work in a few subtle questions.

"Nice lake." He surveyed the glistening expanse

at the base of the gentle slope that led from the house to the water.

"Yeah." She cast a lingering glance in that direction, giving him an excellent view of her perfect profile. "Great fishing too."

Not what he'd expected. Despite her casual attire, she exuded a certain polish that suggested she'd be more at home juggling a latte and briefcase than worms and a fishing pole.

"You fish?"

"Not much these days—but Pops taught me to bait a hook with the best of them right there on that dock." She gestured to a listing wooden structure in obvious need of repair.

He took his best guess. "Your dad?"

"Grandfather. This was my grandparents' weekend place. After Pops retired, they spent their summers here."

So she wasn't a renter.

But where were her grandparents?

And how long was she going to be here?

"Nice spot for a vacation."

"Yes."

"Do you come often?"

She focused again on the lake, and her throat contracted. "I haven't been here in several years. Not since Pops got sick. I hoped we might make another trip here together before he died, but . . ." Her words choked, and she lifted one shoulder.

"I'm sorry."

"Thanks." She swallowed again. "It's been six months, but it's still hard. Pops and I had a special bond that grew even stronger after my grandmother died twelve years ago. When I inherited the place, I couldn't bring myself to come here at first. But after—" She stopped abruptly.

After what?

Not much chance his curiosity was going to be satisfied, based on the firm clamp of her jaw.

Move on to a new topic, McGregor.

"Your dock needs some work." He surveyed it again. Several of the wooden planks were missing or rotted.

"I know."

"I'd be happy to replace the boards for you."

She studied him from behind her sunglasses. At last she reached up and removed them.

Warm, intelligent—gorgeous—hazel eyes regarded him. She didn't seem to be wearing a speck of makeup . . . meaning those thick, sweeping lashes were all hers.

He forced himself to pay attention to her words as she spoke.

"I don't want to interrupt your vacation. Besides, you've already repaid last night's debt."

Maybe—but he wanted another excuse to call again.

Needed another excuse.

He'd figure out why later.

"I'll be here a month. I have plenty of time on my hands. Unless you're leaving soon?"

"No. I'm here . . . indefinitely."

He flicked a glance at her ring finger. Empty. So a husband wasn't financing her extended sojourn in the country. She could be independently wealthy. Or she might have inherited a lot of money from her grandfather, along with the cabin. Or maybe she was between jobs and living off her savings.

Whatever the reason for her protracted stay, he'd take it.

"Why don't I give it a quick look?" He inclined his head toward the dock.

After a slight hesitation, she motioned for him to precede her and slid her glasses back onto her nose.

They walked down in silence, and he did a quick inspection. If he paced himself, he ought to be able to stretch the job out over a couple of days.

"This won't be too difficult to fix." He stood to face her. "And there's a hardware store in town."

"I know. I have an account there—and at the general store. If you put together a list of what you need, I'll call and order it. They deliver twice a week. I can have everything by Wednesday."

"Or I could load it in my SUV and get started sooner."

"No sense making a special trip into town. I don't want to inconvenience you."

“It’s not a . . .” The phone on his hip began to vibrate, and he pulled it out. “Huh. This worked in town this morning, but I haven’t been able to get a signal anywhere out here.”

“Mine works down here too.”

He skimmed the screen. Mac. Between his two brothers, they’d left four messages since he’d arrived Friday night—and neither had picked \up when he’d tried to return their calls while he was in Beaumont.

Better take this, or they were likely to send in the cavalry.

“Do you mind if I answer? It’s my brother, and I doubt I’ll have a signal again today.”

“Sure. Go ahead.” She strolled away, along the edge of the lake.

He put the phone to his ear, keeping her in his line of sight. “Hey.”

“Finally.”

“There’s not much cell service out here.”

“That’s what we figured. Listen, you need to call us every couple of days.”

The same instruction his mom had given him.

“It’s not that easy. I don’t want to drive into town just to make a phone call.”

“Then we’ll be trekking your direction on a regular basis.”

“Not necessary.”

“It is if you won’t call.”

He angled away and lowered his voice, reining in his temper. “I’m fine.”

“Define fine.”

Leave it to Mac to detect an exaggeration and give him the third degree.

“Better than I was.”

His brother expelled a breath, accepting the amended version. “I still don’t get what you’re going to do down there for a month. You’re not an assume-the-lotus-position-and-contemplate-mother-nature kind of guy.”

“There’s stuff to do here.”

“Like what?”

“Read books. Take walks. Chop wood.” And fix a dock.

“You’ll be bored with all that in three days—and I don’t like the idea of you being there all alone once that happens.”

He shifted again toward his neighbor. She’d bent down to examine some kind of flower at water’s edge, her hair sleek and shiny in the sun.

Bored?

All alone?

Not if he could help it.

“Finn?”

“Yeah.” He watched the woman pluck the flower and finger the petals. “I’m not bored—and I need to go.” If nothing else, maybe he could finagle ongoing visits to the lake by asking to take advantage of the cell service sweet spot.

"What's your hurry? You have a hot date waiting?"

He gave his neighbor's lithe figure a once-over. Hot was a perfect adjective to describe her.

"Right. In the middle of a national forest."

"As I recall, you always managed to scrounge up dates wherever you were."

"Not on my priority list at the moment."

"Which tells me you're nowhere close to fine yet."

"I'm getting there."

"You know you can call me anytime, right?"

His throat tightened. "Yeah. I'll be in touch later in the week."

"I'll hold you to that—and take care of yourself in the meantime."

The line went dead, and Finn slipped the phone back onto his belt.

His neighbor twirled the flower between her fingers and wandered back toward him, her demeanor wistful. "It must be nice to have family who cares enough to keep tabs on you."

"You don't?"

She shrugged, lifting the posy toward her nose—to smell it or to hide her expression?—and changed the subject. "Did you want to measure the boards?"

"Yeah." He dug a retractable steel measuring tape out of the toolbox, along with a pencil, and went to work.

After taking all the measurements and jotting them down on the back of his receipt from the general store in town, he held up the slip of paper. "Would you like me to leave this on the table on the porch?"

She hesitated . . . but in the end, she approached him and took it from his fingers.

Progress—even if she did back off a few steps again.

"I'll call the order in this morning."

"And I'll pick it up tomorrow." He closed the toolbox and stood. "What name will it be under?"

Pushing, perhaps—but since she hadn't offered . . .

She bit her lip. "I never introduced myself, did I?"

"Nope." He smiled to make certain she knew he didn't hold the lapse against her.

"Dana Lewis." No offer of a hand.

"And I'm Finn McGregor, as I mentioned last night. Feel free to verify that with Mark."

"I did."

In other words, she knew he was legit.

Then why was she still wary?

Not an answer he was going to get today.

"Well . . ." He hefted the tool kit. "I'll be on my way—but I'll be back tomorrow morning."

"Thanks again."

She stayed where she was as he ascended the small hill. When he turned at the top, she was where he'd left her. Watching him.

He lifted his hand.

No response.

The lady was playing her cards close to her vest.

But that was okay. He'd have other opportunities to see her—and try to find the answers to some of his questions.

Once behind the wheel, he put the SUV into drive, crunched over the loose rock toward the state highway—and felt the corners of his mouth tug up.

Odd.

Spontaneous smiles hadn't been part of his world for quite a while.

Even more surprising?

For the first time in almost two years, he found himself looking forward to tomorrow.

—3—

"Mail call."

Roger turned from hunting-and-pecking a fender bender report as Lynette Jackson dumped a bunch of paperwork in his in-box.

"Anything urgent?"

The fortyish Beaumont Police Department office manager set a square Styrofoam container on his desk. "Not unless another complaint from our resident atheist about the church bells ringing too early on Sunday merits that description."

"It doesn't. What's this?" He tapped the carton with the Walleye Café sticker plastered to the top.

"Lunch. I didn't have any decent leftovers from last night to bring."

"You don't have to feed me, Lynette."

"If I don't, you're going to waste away. You're too thin already—and I bet you've dropped another ten pounds in the past six weeks."

More like fifteen . . . but worry had always killed his appetite.

"You're going to spoil me."

"You could use some spoiling. You've had a tough row to hoe. And for the record, we're all with you. I bend the good Lord's ear about you and the missus every day. Lee and I put in a word for you every night during our blessing before dinner too."

"I appreciate that. A person can't have too many prayers. What's on the menu?" He tapped the container of food he didn't want.

"Meatloaf. Hazel said it was extra tasty today. The sides are garlic whipped potatoes and string beans. You eat every bite."

"I'll do my best."

"Why don't you take your lunch out to the patio? The fresh air might perk you up. Bill's out there."

Spending a half hour making conversation with one of his three full-time officers was the last thing he wanted to do. Too much effort.

"I think I'll go through the mail while I eat. Cross one item off my to-do list for the afternoon."

"Suit yourself." She started to walk out but stopped at the door. "Oh, there *was* one unusual piece of mail. I didn't open it, because it was addressed to you and marked personal and confidential. From someplace in Nebraska."

"That's a little outside our jurisdiction."

"More than. I thought it might be from a friend or relative instead of official business."

"I don't know a soul in that part of the world."

"Could be an old college pal or Army buddy who wants to get back in touch."

"Or a clever marketing ploy that's a sales pitch for some new gadget we don't need and can't afford."

"Yeah. Like the letter we got last year from that company trying to convince us the department needed hazmat suits." Lynette hooted. "About the only noxious material we deal with in Beaumont is Tinkerbell's poop."

One side of Roger's mouth quirked up. "How many citations have we issued to Sarah Clay for ignoring the clean-up-after-your-dog ordinance?"

"I've lost count. But she's paid enough of those twenty-five-dollar tickets to buy a bench or two for the town square, I can tell you that. Poop for benches—not a bad trade, if you ask me. And on that appetizing note, I'll leave you to enjoy your lunch." She exited, closing the door behind her.

As the brief moment of levity faded, Roger sighed. Hungry or not, he had to eat. Might as well get it over with.

Flipping up the lid of the container with one hand, he reached for the stack of mail with the other.

A third of the way through his meal, he found the letter Lynette had mentioned, postmarked on Saturday in Linden, Nebraska. Not an ad or solicitation, based on the address that had been written in a slightly shaky hand—unless this was some new marketing gimmick.

Curious.

He set his fork down, slid the letter opener under the flap, and extracted two sheets of paper, also handwritten.

The first line told him this wasn't junk mail.

Dear Chief Burnett:

My name is Len White—and by the time you receive this, I will be dead.

Meatloaf forgotten, he leaned back and read every word.

Reread them.

As he finished his second pass, his adrenaline was pinging. Could this be for real?

Setting the letter on his desk, he scooted over to the keyboard and began googling.

Less than ten minutes later, he closed his browser, sank back in his chair, and stared at his screen.

Everything fit.

Unless someone had gone to a great deal of trouble to concoct an elaborate practical joke, the letter was real.

And if it was . . .

Another surge of adrenaline shot through him.

If it was . . . it could solve all his problems.

Was it possible this was the answer to his prayer?

No!

As the booming denial from his conscience reverberated through his mind, Roger crimped the edges of the stationery between his fingers and acknowledged the truth. God had no hand in this. It wasn't an opportunity but a temptation—and those came from a far different source.

Yet how could he pass up this chance to help Leah?

Tossing the letter on the desk, he rose and began to pace.

It was wrong to even consider reneging on the principles he'd followed since the day he pinned on his first badge. The author of this letter expected him to abide by the law and do the honest thing.

But maybe you don't have to do it right away.

He tried to tamp down the voice of temptation . . . but it was loud. Insistent. And there *was* some logic to it. After all, the incident described in this letter was ancient history. The course he was contemplating might not be honorable, but no one would get hurt. He could always leave this letter, with a note of his own, for someone else to address after he was gone.

It's still wrong, Burnett. A betrayal of public trust. You know that.

Yeah. He did.

The aroma of the cooling meatloaf roiled his stomach, and he strode over to his desk, shut the lid on the container, and shoved the food to the far side.

He was a law-upholding public servant with a spotless reputation. No whiff of scandal had ever tainted him in his two decades as chief here. He always took the honorable course, did what was right.

But . . . what *was* right in this case? Which was the greater good—helping Leah or taking immediate action on this letter?

A knock sounded on his door, and his heart stumbled. Shoving the letter and envelope under the stack of unopened mail, he retook his seat and folded his hands on the desk. "Yes?"

Lynette cracked the door and stuck her head inside. "Sorry to interrupt your lunch, but you asked me to let you know when the mayor had a few minutes. He can meet with you in ten, if that works."

"It works. I'll walk down to his office."

She inspected the takeout container. "Tell me you ate that."

"Some of it. I'll have the rest for dinner."

"You want me to put it in the fridge?"

"Yeah. Thanks." He passed the food over.

She weighed it in her hand. "You didn't put much of a dent in this."

"I wasn't too hungry."

Her features softened. "Worry can do that to a body. Not this body, mind you. I keep Hershey in business when I've got a load on my mind, as this proves." She patted her generous hip. "I'll say this, though. Leah's blessed to have you. Not many men would make that long drive day after day, month after month, to keep an eye on the situation and be certain she's getting the best of care."

"Thanks." The word scratched past his throat.

"I'll let the mayor know you're about to pay him a visit." She retreated, the remains of his lunch in hand.

As her heels tapped down the hall, he dug the letter out from under the pile, guilt gnawing at his gut. Unless he found a way to pay the bill at Woodside Gardens, Leah wasn't going to be getting the best of care for much longer.

But if the information in this letter panned out, he'd be able to not only pay the overdue bill but all the bills to come—with plenty left over once

Leah was gone to let Len White repay his debt to society . . . or most of it.

Assuming, of course, that he was willing to compromise his principles and ignore everything he'd always professed to believe about obeying the law.

He rose again, stuffed the letter back in the envelope, and tucked it in his pocket. After all these years, a day or two delay wouldn't make any difference in the big scheme of things. He didn't have to decide now.

So he'd sleep on it. Do some research. Think the situation—and the ramifications—through in detail.

And in the end, whatever he decided, he'd follow through without a backward glance.

Finn McGregor was a hard worker.

Mug of tea in hand, Dana watched from behind the repaired screen in her living room as he hoisted another rotten plank and tossed it on top of the others he'd ripped off the dock. He'd been at it for an hour and a half, moving at a steady, measured pace since he'd pulled in and unloaded the supplies from his SUV.

And the reason she knew that?

She'd taken far too many breaks to peek out at her volunteer handyman.

Dana blew out a breath. This was *not* the best use of her time. She'd promised to have the manuscript on her computer finished by the end of the week, and she needed to hunker down if she wanted to meet that deadline.

But Finn McGregor was one big distraction, with those alluring green eyes, biceps that spoke of long hours in the gym or physical labor, and proven heroic qualities.

Go back to work, Dana.

Right.

She started to turn away . . . only to have the gray skies that had threatened rain all morning suddenly open.

Her gaze flicked back to the figure on the dock. He stopped, scooped up his tools and jacket, and sprinted up the hill.

Directly toward her porch.

Lungs stalling, she backed away from the window. Watching him from a distance was fine. Up close and personal . . . much more unsettling.

Once he clambered onto the porch, she lost sight of him—but wherever he was, he was going to get drenched. The rain was coming down in sheets, and the gusty wind was blowing it his direction.

Ask the man in, Dana. You know he's safe. You've listened to Mark's voicemail three times.

Except there were different kinds of safe.

She might be physically safe with Finn McGregor, but she wasn't as sure about her heart. The man exuded an action-figure magnetism that appealed to her.

Which made no sense.

If she'd come here to get away from action and excitement, to seek a quieter life, why was she attracted to a guy who radiated energy and a subtle, coiled tension that suggested he was always on high alert?

No answer came to mind—but much as she might prefer to keep her distance, letting him get drenched by a cold rain was downright uncharitable.

Shoring up her defenses, she marched to the door, flipped the lock, and pulled it open.

He was standing a few feet away, back against the wall of the cabin, jacket zipped to his neck, auburn air glistening with moisture.

"It got a little wet out there." He gave her a half-hitch grin as he nodded toward the dock.

"I noticed. Would you like to come in?"

A glimmer of surprise, along with some emotion she couldn't identify, flickered in his irises. "Yeah. Thanks."

Finn pushed off from the wall and she retreated into the house.

He followed her, filling the cozy living room with a powerful presence that dominated the space.

She moistened her lips. "Would you . . . uh . . . like something to drink?"

"That would be great." He eyed her half-empty mug. "Is that coffee?"

"No. I'm partial to tea." She shifted from one foot to the other. "But I have soda and orange juice and hot chocolate and milk . . ."

Milk?

Sheesh!

Like this guy was a milk drinker.

"I can do tea."

But not by choice, based on his stoic tone. A gun-brandishing man who kicked down doors to save a woman in distress probably drank black coffee with grounds in the bottom.

"I . . . uh . . . can offer you several choices." She walked toward the back of the cabin.

Though his sport shoes were noiseless on the floor, she knew he was following her. His presence in her wake was almost palpable.

She kept her back to him as she retrieved a mug, set the kettle on the stove, pulled out the basket of tea . . . and did her best to regulate her respiration.

When she at last faced him, he was standing beside the kitchen table, looking at the computer monitor. She read the words on the screen.

Cindy touched his face. "That's one of the nicest things anyone has ever done for me."

"It was my pleasure. And so is this."

He grasped her hand, pulled her close, and lowered his head until their lips . . .

Dana cringed.

Why, oh why, had she stopped editing in the

middle of a romantic scene, when there was much, much more to that book?

Finn transferred his attention to her, his expression speculative.

She thrust the basket of tea toward him. “Help yourself.”

As he took it, she leaned over, shut off the monitor, and lowered the screen on her laptop. “I’m a book editor. That’s one of my projects.” As the explanation popped out, she frowned. Why had she felt the need to clarify?

“Really?” He selected a bag of caffeinated black tea. “That sounds interesting. Do you work for a publisher?”

“Not anymore. I used to be a senior editor, but after I came here I started freelancing.”

“Who did you work for before?” He pulled the string loose and let the bag dangle.

She watched the hypnotic sway of the tea bag as it swung below his lean fingers—until the kettle began to whistle, yanking her back to reality. “Let me . . . uh . . . get your hot water.”

Pivoting away, she busied herself with the mug and the kettle, taking as long as she dared. Hoping he’d let the subject of her work history drop. She didn’t want to talk about her recent past. With him—or anyone.

Yet if this man . . . this mesmerizing stranger who’d invaded her house and her life . . . pushed, she had a sinking feeling she might spill her guts.

And unless Finn McGregor was as adept at handling teary-eyed women as he was at confronting would-be bad guys, he might find more than his tea bag in hot water.

Finn took the steaming mug Dana held out to him and gave her trembling fingers a discreet perusal.

Strange.

Was she still spooked from Sunday night? Uncomfortable talking about her background? Freaked out by his presence in her house?

All of the above?

He dropped his tea bag into the water, swirling it around, giving her a chance to answer the question about her publisher as the liquid darkened.

"I have some cookies, if you'd like a snack."

She was changing the subject . . . but who was he to question her dodge? There was plenty of stuff in his own background that was off-limits too.

"I never turn down cookies."

"Have a seat." She gathered up some papers at the far end of the table, tapped them into a neat stack, and pulled a package of Oreos out of the cabinet. "Sorry I can't offer homemade."

"No worries." He claimed a chair. "I grew up on store-bought. My mom was too busy raising three rambunctious boys and running a graphic design business from the various far-flung outposts where my dad was stationed to do much baking."

"Was your dad military?" She perched on a chair at a right angle to him.

"State Department."

"Oh." She took a sip of her tea. "In his voicemail, Mark said you had a military background. I thought it might be a family tradition."

Narrowing his eyes, Finn wrapped his hands around his mug. How much did Mark know about his career—and recent history?

Very little, if Mac had been his usual discreet self.

As logic kicked in, he relaxed. His oldest brother wasn't the type to run off at the mouth about family business. In all likelihood he'd offered his college buddy no more than a topline explanation—a fact Finn intended to verify during his next conversation with his brother.

"It's a family tradition in the sense that both my brothers were military too."

Her eyebrows rose. "That's unusual. Did you serve together?"

"No. We're competitive enough without going head-to-head in the same outfit."

"Were you deployed overseas?"

His stomach tightened. *Deflect. Deflect.* "Yes. So you never told me what publisher you worked for."

She stalled by taking a sip of tea, but in the end

she answered with a name even a nonliterary type like him would recognize.

"Impressive. Does that mean you lived in New York?"

"Yes."

No wonder he'd picked up a touch of big-city polish.

But why had she ditched the bright lights and what must have been a coveted job for an indefinite stay in a cabin in the middle of a national forest in Missouri?

Before he could figure out how to diplomatically pose that question, she finished off her tea in a couple of long gulps and sprang up. "I think I'll get a refill. Would you like . . ."

All at once she swayed and groped for the back of her chair.

Finn vaulted to his feet and grabbed her shoulders. "Whoa. Steady there. Are you okay?"

Those big hazel eyes blinked at him. Once. Twice. As if his neighbor was having difficulty focusing on him.

When she didn't respond, he gently pressed her back into her chair. "Look . . . why don't you sit again for a minute?"

She didn't resist.

"Would you like me to make you another cup of tea?"

"No, thanks."

He retook his seat, watching her. Twin creases

had appeared above her nose, and she was shaking again. Not visibly, but he'd felt the tremors running through her.

What was going on with this woman? Surely today's nervousness couldn't still be a reaction to his break-in.

Was it somehow connected to her reason for hiding away in a secluded cabin in the woods?

Tempted as he was to explore the second question, probing could shut her down. Better to start with the first one and hope it opened the door to further discussion.

"Listen . . . if I upset you enough the other night to cause repercussions like that, I apologize again—and repairing your dock doesn't come anywhere close to making amends."

"No. That had nothing to do with you." She exhaled and laced her fingers into a tight knot on the worn surface of the table. "I suffered a concussion three months ago that left me with some lingering issues—headaches, occasional dizziness, sensitivity to light, blurred vision. The fancy name is post-concussion syndrome. The worst side effect at this stage is that I can't stare at a screen for extended periods and have to take lots of breaks from my work."

Ah.

Now the large type on her monitor made sense.

"Was it an accident?"

Her throat worked. "No. I got hurt in . . . in a fall."

She offered nothing more; no explanation about why she'd left her job . . . or retreated to the woods . . . or was plagued by scream-worthy nightmares.

"Are you all right here by yourself?"

"I thought I was . . . until someone barged into my room in the middle of the night." The subtle quiver in her words undermined her wry attempt at humor.

"I can guarantee that will never happen again." He flashed her a brief grin. Man, this woman needed to chill out. Waves of tension were rippling off her. "But I was talking more about day-to-day stuff. Is it safe for you to be alone while you're dealing with those kinds of medical issues?"

"Safe is a relative term."

What was that supposed to mean?

She continued without giving him a chance to ponder her comment. "I manage fine around here. My problems aren't life-threatening, and other than a few bumps and bruises from running into furniture, I'm coping fine. The only thing I can't do is drive. But this is all temporary. I've made a lot of progress, and my doctor tells me my physical complaints should go away within the next few weeks."

What about the nightmares? Did she expect those to go away too?

A topic for another day, perhaps. He had a feeling she'd already shared more than she'd intended.

"I'm glad to hear that. You picked a nice spot to recuperate."

"Yes." Her lips softened. "I spent a month here every summer for many years with Mags—my grandmother—and Pops. It's always been a haven for me."

From what?

Another question she didn't seem inclined to expound on.

She pushed the bag of cookies toward him. "Have a few more. My waistline will thank you."

There wasn't a thing wrong with her waistline as far as he could see, but he helped himself to three more. "These are a particular favorite of mine."

"Mine too. So what brings you out here for a whole month?"

He shoved a cookie in his mouth, buying himself a few seconds to compose a response as he chewed, took a swig of tea—and tried not to grimace. Oh, for a cup of high-octane java!

"I needed a vacation . . . and I have some decisions to make. I was looking for a quiet place without a bunch of distractions. My brother Mac knows Mark, and he set this up for me."

"Then we have something in common. I'm in decision-making mode too."

She stopped. Waiting, by chance, to see if he'd

offer her a few more details about *his* decision?

Not happening. If he talked about that, he'd also have to share background—and he wasn't ready to do that with a woman he'd just met, no matter how captivating she was.

It seemed she wasn't inclined to offer more, either. She stood again—this time more carefully—and picked up her mug. "I'm not certain the rain is going to let up for a while. You might have to defer work on the dock until tomorrow. And I have an aggressive deadline to meet on that book." She waved a hand toward the computer monitor.

Nothing subtle about that send-off.

He polished off the last cookie, washed it down with a scant sip of tea, and rose too. "I'll get out of your hair."

"You can leave your tools on the porch, if you like, and go out the back. It's closer to your car. Can I lend you an umbrella?"

"No, thanks. I'll run for it."

She led the way toward the rear door and flipped the lock. "Sorry Mother Nature didn't cooperate."

"The dock will keep until tomorrow."

Easing past her, he caught a faint whiff of some fragrance that evoked fresh air and spring rain and quiet evenings near a lake, watching fireflies play hide-and-seek.

Finn rolled his eyes. If Mac or Lance ever knew

he'd waxed poetic, they'd rib him for the rest of his life.

"I'll see you tomorrow." Ducking his head, he sprinted toward the SUV.

Once behind the wheel, he looked back at the cabin through the steady curtain of rain. Dana remained at the door, and he lifted his hand in farewell.

She didn't respond.

But as he backed up and executed a quick turn toward the narrow rocky lane that would lead him back to the main road, she fluttered her fingers.

Ah.

The reason she hadn't responded to his wave the other day or just now was different than he'd assumed. She hadn't *seen* him wave, thanks to her compromised vision. It hadn't been a snub.

His spirits took an uptick.

And as he drove between the overhanging trees, their new leaves glistening with moisture, he found himself wishing tomorrow would hurry up and get here.

Because Dana Lewis was a puzzle waiting to be solved—the exact kind of challenge a McGregor found hard to resist.

Especially when that challenge was drop-dead gorgeous.

—4—

Somewhere far away a phone was ringing.

Roger tried to pull himself back to consciousness. But after thrashing until the predawn hours, he'd fallen too deep into a dark well of slumber to surface quickly.

The phone rang again.

Answer it, Burnett. You're a police chief—24/7 availability goes with the job.

Summoning up every ounce of his willpower, he rolled over and fumbled for his cell on the nightstand. Eyes still closed, he felt for the talk button.

"Burnett."

"Chief Burnett, this is Meg at Woodside Gardens. I'm the night nurse this week. I wanted to let you know your wife had a little accident."

The fog in his mind vaporized as he shot to a sitting position. "What kind of accident?" He peered at the digital alarm clock as he spoke. Seven-ten. If he threw on his clothes and skipped shaving, he could be in Potosi by—

"She got out of bed and walked as far as the lounge before we spotted her. When she saw us coming, she tried to run and slipped. The doctor's already been in to examine her, and other than a bruised knee, she's fine. We've given her a sedative, and she's drifting back to sleep. We just wanted to alert you to what happened and assure you we're keeping her under observation."

"Should I come in?"

"There's no need. I expect she'll sleep for several hours. We like to inform families about any incidents ASAP, though."

"I appreciate that. Thank you."

"Call us if you have other questions—but there's no need to worry. The situation is under control."

Roger broke the connection, dropped back onto the pillow, and crumpled the sheet in his fists.

This was why he had to find a way for Leah to stay where she was. Alzheimer's patients could be difficult to control. Accidents happened, even at the best places. But the staff at Woodside Gardens was responsive and diligent. If she was at a low-end facility, who knew how a scenario like this might escalate? What if she managed to get outside, God forbid? The rigorous security measures at Woodside were designed to prevent that, but a lot of places ran a much looser ship.

He reached up to massage his temple, where a headache was beginning to throb. No sense staying in bed. Two hours' sleep wasn't adequate to keep him at the top of his game, but it was all he was going to get this night.

After swinging his legs to the floor, he leaned over and picked up the glass of water on the nightstand beside his cell. Took a long swallow. It eased his parched throat—but he needed a hefty dose of caffeine to jump-start his morning.

Fifteen minutes later, dressed for work, a mug of fresh-brewed coffee in hand, he eyed the letter from Nebraska on the kitchen table. The solution it offered had become more and more tempting with every sleepless hour that crept by last night —and this morning's call heightened its allure.

He crossed to the table where he and Leah and John had shared thousands of breakfasts. Sank into his usual chair and surveyed the empty seats.

A solitary breakfast table was a lonely place.

It had been hard enough to carry on after they lost John. There'd been no laughter at this table for many months.

Now, there would never be any again.

Quashing his self-pity, Roger pulled the hand-written pages from the envelope and flipped them open. Not much chance another reading would offer any new insights or direction, but what else did he have to do at this hour of the morning?

After a fortifying swig of coffee, he skimmed the sheets again.

Dear Chief Burnett:

My name is Len White—and by the time you receive this, I will be dead.

For the past forty-nine years, I have gone by the name of Joe Larson. I took a new identity when I was twenty-three, after an acquaintance, Deke Nichols, and I robbed a Brinks armored car in rural Missouri. The gold bars we stole have a current value of more than one million dollars.

After the robbery, Deke and I agreed to temporarily ditch the gold, split up, and stay under the radar until interest in the case waned. We purchased two ammo cans from an Army surplus store and put half of the ten-ounce bars in each. Deke grew up in your jurisdiction and knew about a lake on some wooded, unoccupied property. In those days it was owned by a man named Jacob Powers. We dropped the cans in the middle of the lake for later retrieval.

Within days, however, our plans fell apart. The authorities realized we'd had inside information and nailed Deke's cousin, who worked for Brinks. He didn't know my name, but the police tracked Deke down. He was killed in a shootout.

During the next few weeks, I secured a new identity and put as much distance between me and Missouri as I could.

One night, a kind priest here in Linden found me digging through a dumpster for food. He offered me a handyman job and a cot in the church basement. I didn't tell him my story, but as I talked with him over the next few days, I began to realize how badly I'd messed up my life.

In the weeks that followed, guilt began to

weigh heavy on my heart for the evil things I'd done . . . from minor truancy, vandalism, and petty theft as a teen up to the Brinks robbery—and possibly murder. One of the guards managed to pull a gun on us during the incident, and both of us shot at him. I have no idea whose gun delivered the fatal bullet.

After many talks with the priest who took me in and eventually got me a job at the corn processing plant, I vowed to spend the rest of my days living a modest, lawful, and charitable life.

I kept that vow, as Father Daniel Pruitt in Linden, who mailed this letter for me, will attest. He knew me for the last dozen years of my life, and his predecessors before that.

I've often come close to turning myself in, but in the end I couldn't bear the thought of living behind bars—and as you know, there is no statute of limitations on murder. So I prepared this letter to be sent upon my death.

These events happened long ago, Chief Burnett. I doubt there is anyone left who will remember the players or the details. But the gold, which is in your jurisdiction, needs to be returned to its owner. I've read about you online, and as far as I can tell, you are an honorable public servant. I trust you will be able to locate the gold and see that justice is done at last.

Father Pruitt does not know the contents of this letter, but I did share my story with him shortly before I died. I encourage you to contact him if you have any questions about anything I have told you.

Thank you for your help in righting this wrong, and may God bless you.

Roger read the man's shaky signature, refolded the letter, and weighed it in his hand.

More than one million dollars in gold sitting at the bottom of a lake.

Leo Lewis's lake.

Everyone in town knew Leo had bought Jacob Powers's three hundred acres more than thirty years ago.

Roger took a sip of his cooling coffee. How many hours had he spent on that lake with Leo, fishing pole in hand, never knowing the water held a much bigger treasure than the five-pound bass he'd once caught?

And even a small portion of that treasure would be sufficient to secure Leah's care until the not-too-distant day God called her home. Plus, given the wealth in Leah's background, he'd be able to sell a few bars with no questions asked. Everyone in town thought they were loaded.

But could he find the treasure—and do it without being detected?

The sweet trill of a cardinal sounded in the

backyard, announcing a new day, and he rose to top off his coffee.

From what he'd gathered in talking to Leo, the original lake on the property had been quite small. He'd enlarged it several times during his first decade of ownership, creating a more meandering, natural shape.

Bottom line? There was no way to determine the original location of the middle.

In terms of detection—that was a definite risk, with Leo's granddaughter in residence. He might not have seen her himself, but he'd heard plenty through the grapevine, especially from Sam at the general mercantile and Marv at the hardware store, where she'd opened accounts. Hazel at the café had mentioned her too. Although she was keeping a low profile, talk on the street was that Dana Lewis had left her job in New York and was planning an extended stay.

He shook his head and took a tentative sip of the steaming brew. Could her timing be any worse? The place had been unoccupied for what . . . two, three years now? Ever since Leo became too feeble to make the trip down from St. Louis. Why couldn't it have stayed unoccupied a few more weeks? Early morning or twilight trips out there wouldn't have attracted any attention. The lake was well hidden from the road.

But the cabin offered its occupant a view that encompassed most of the shoreline.

However . . . if he confined his search to the night hours while Leo's heir was asleep, that should mitigate the risk. The lake wasn't more than ten or fifteen feet deep, from what he could remember, and he and Leah had been proficient scuba divers in their day. The equipment was still in the basement. All he needed to do was refresh his memory about the sport and buy an underwater metal detector.

A ray of sun streaked in the window, illuminating the letter on the table—like a beacon pointing him toward the solution to his quandary.

Roger let out a slow breath as he regarded the handwritten envelope and faced the truth.

He wouldn't be thinking about scuba equipment and metal detectors and optimal search windows if he hadn't already made his decision.

His fingers warmed as they tightened on the ceramic mug, and he transferred it from one hand to the other. Getting burned wasn't on his agenda for the day.

Yet as he finished his coffee and prepared to drive to his office, he had a sinking feeling that getting burned in a much more serious way was a distinct possibility in the days to come.

Someone was hammering.

Stretching, Dana reluctantly pulled herself out of a sound sleep. Squinted at the oversized LED display on her bedside clock. Froze.

Nine in the morning?!

It couldn't be that late . . . could it?

Maybe.

For the first night in months, she'd had eight full hours of uninterrupted sleep. No nightmares. No tossing. No staring at the ceiling as the minutes ticked by in slow motion.

And the only change in her life during the past seventy-two hours was the appearance of the hammer-wielding man outside.

Meaning that for whatever reason—and despite their less-than-auspicious meeting—knowing Finn McGregor was nearby gave her peace of mind.

Go figure.

Rather than try to decipher that puzzle, she swung her feet to the floor and stood, spirits rising. This would be a productive day. Her energy was rebounding, and her vision seemed a tiny bit clearer.

After tugging on jeans and Pops's sweater, she detoured to the living room for a peek at the auburn-haired man on her dock. One quick glimpse, that's all she'd allow herself.

But as she positioned herself in the shadows beside the window, her good intentions dissolved. She watched as he hoisted a plank, his legs encased in slim jeans, a sweatshirt stretched over his broad chest. Leaned sideways to keep him in sight once he edged out of range. Sighed.

All those years she'd spent in New York, editing more than her share of romantic novels, hoping to meet Mr. Right—yet she'd never found one single man in the big city who'd captured her attention as much as Finn McGregor had here, miles from so-called civilization.

Letting herself get carried away, however, was nuts. He wasn't planning to stay around long enough for anything to develop . . . even if he was interested in her. And that was a big if. She might be able to discern his trim, muscular physique and pick up the color of his eyes, but the subtle nuances of expression and body language that provided cues about attraction were beyond her compromised vision—unless she got up close and personal for longer than the handoff of a mug or a slip of paper.

Not likely to happen.

Besides, at age thirty, she should be beyond romantic fantasies. Those happened in the pages of the books she edited, not in real life. It was wiser to leave the rose-colored glasses in the . . .

The sound of an approaching vehicle interrupted her musings, and she cocked her ear. Must be the delivery from the general mercantile.

As she started to turn toward the back of the house, a movement on the dock caught her eye.

Finn had dropped the plank he was holding and was jogging toward the porch. He must have heard the vehicle pulling in too.

Though his features were blurry, his determined stride told her he'd morphed into protective mode. The same mode he'd been in the night he'd raced through the woods after he'd heard her screams.

Better nip this in the bud.

She pushed through the front door as he approached and called out, "It's a grocery delivery from town."

He halted thirty feet away, his taut posture easing. "Oh. Sorry. I didn't mean to overreact . . . but your place is pretty isolated, and I didn't get the impression you had a lot of invited guests."

"None. Thank you for . . ." What? Caring? That would be a stretch. They were nothing more than acquaintances—and new ones, at that. Given his military background, the man was probably wired to go into defensive mode at the merest hint of a threat. "For being tuned into your surroundings. That's a useful skill, I'm sure."

"Sometimes."

His one-word response held a curious undertone—but she had no chance to dwell on it. The delivery person rapped on her back door.

"I need to get that."

"Right. And I need to get back to work before those clouds hovering on the horizon move in and cause another rain delay."

With that, he turned and retraced his steps.

Dana watched him—until another, more

insistent knock spurred her into action. If she didn't answer fast, her groceries would end up making a return trip to town.

Besides, she had work to do . . . and while reading stories about make-believe heroes wasn't nearly as interesting as interacting with a real live one, it paid the bills.

Finn secured the second-to-last plank, sat back on his heels, and inspected the dock. The job was almost finished.

Bummer.

This was his excuse to hang around . . . but unless he shifted into slow motion, it would be impossible to stretch the task out another day—and he'd been working at half speed as it was.

At least he could kill a few minutes by giving Mac a ring, as he'd promised—though if his brother was hip-deep in some homicide investigation, he'd no doubt let the call roll.

Dropping onto the deck, he dangled his legs over the edge and pulled out his cell. Yep, this was the sweet spot. The signal was strong.

He tapped in Mac's speed-dial number and watched a blue heron swoop in for a landing near the edge of the water.

"You actually called."

Leave it to Mac to dispense with the niceties and get straight to the point. "You asked me to."

"Since when can I count on you to do what I ask?"

"Very funny. Let's just say I didn't want to run the risk of you and Lance barging in on me with no warning."

"Why not?" Mac's voice sharpened.

Finn watched the heron stalk some prey in the shallow water with slow, careful, deliberate steps—as intent on its mission as Mac always was.

And both Mac and Lance had made him their mission of late.

"I'm fine, Mac. Chill out."

"You didn't answer my question."

"Okay. How's this? Because I might be entertaining."

Dead silence.

"That's a joke, right?"

Finn's mouth twitched at his brother's cautious tone. "Why would you think I'm joking?"

"You don't know anybody down there."

"Hey—I got the charm gene in this family, remember? I know how to make friends."

"With who? The deer and raccoons?"

"Actually, there's a squirrel I'm partial to. He was searching for another nut, and there I was. It was the beginning of a beautiful friendship."

Mac exhaled. "Man, it's good to hear you kidding around. It's been too long."

Yeah, it had been. Since before . . .

He cut off that train of thought and watched the heron. The bird was moving at a careful, methodical pace through the shallow water, searching the depths for lunch, letting time and patience work to his advantage.

Perhaps they were working to his too, as the doctors had promised they would.

"I think my kidding gene is kicking back in."

"I guess Lance and I will have to eat crow if this trip ends up being a turning point for you. I never expected hiding away alone in the woods would be a positive experience."

It might not have been—if he hadn't crossed paths with an intriguing neighbor.

Not that he intended to tell his brothers about Dana.

"Maybe you'll trust my judgment in the future." A fish jumped a few feet from shore, leaving nothing but ripples behind as it disappeared below the surface.

"Don't get your hopes up. So did you drive into town to call?"

"No. I discovered a spot near a lake not far from Mark's cabin where I can get reception."

"He doesn't have a lake."

"It's on the adjacent property. Say . . . how much did you tell him about me, anyway?"

"Why?" Caution colored Mac's query.

"The owner of the property next door knew about my military background."

"That's all I told him. I said you'd been in the Army, had mustered out, and needed someplace to decompress. You know I don't share persona information outside the family."

"Okay. Just checking. The comment about the military threw me."

A screen door banged behind him, and he anglec sideways. Dana crossed the porch, descendec the steps . . . and began walking down the hil toward him.

He scrambled to his feet. "Listen, I need to run Tell Lance I called or he'll leave me a dozer messages."

"What's your hurry?"

Finn dropped his voice. "My neighbor's coming down to the lake."

"So? Are you trespassing?"

"No. But I need to say hi."

"I didn't think you went down there tc socialize."

"I can be friendly if it saves me driving intc town to make phone calls." He lifted his hand a Dana and sent her an encouraging smile as her step faltered. "I'll call you or Lance again in twc or three days."

"We'll hold you to that. Talk to you soon."

The phone went dead, and Finn slipped it back on his belt, his pulse accelerating as Dana once again picked up her pace.

Odd.

Once upon a time, he'd gravitated toward glitzy, glamorous women. Dana might have a touch of big-city polish, and at some point she could also have had glitz and glamor, but not anymore. She was beautiful, no question about it, but her hair was pulled back in a haphazard ponytail, no makeup disguised the faint sprinkle of freckles across her nose, and her oversized sweater that could at best be called ratty was more thrift shop than Saks.

She was nothing like the women he'd dated in the past.

So why did a buzz of attraction thrum through his veins whenever she got close?

She stopped a few feet away and held out a mug. "I thought you might be ready for some coffee. I have sugar and creamer packets in my pocket if you need them."

Dana had coffee in the cabin? Then why hadn't she offered it to him yester . . . ?

Wait. The grocery delivery this morning.

She'd ordered coffee for him.

A gentle rush of warmth infiltrated his heart as he closed the distance between them and took it. "Thank you."

"Sugar? Cream?" She patted her pocket.

"Black is fine."

"I didn't mean to interrupt your phone conversation."

"We were finished." He took a tentative sip of the coffee. Not bad, considering it had been made by a tea sipper.

She spoke as if she'd read his mind. "Pops was a big coffee drinker. He taught me to make it, then put me in charge of the daily ritual. I used to grumble, but he said the skill would come in useful someday. He was right, as usual." Her tone grew wistful.

"Sounds like he was a great guy." He took another sip of the potent brew.

"The best."

"So you and your parents came here to visit every summer?"

"No. Just me. Sometimes my dad joined us for a week. Never my mom."

There was a story there, based on the edge in her voice . . . but would she share it?

"Not an outdoor woman?" He kept his stance casual, his inflection conversational.

Dana gave an unladylike snort. "That's putting it mildly."

When she offered nothing more, he swept a hand over the dock. "I've got a few minutes left on my break, and this is the best seat in the house. Would you like to join me? There's a blue heron on the right providing entertainment."

She hesitated, but only for a moment—then lowered herself to the dock. "I can spare a couple of minutes. You'll have to give me a play-by-play of the heron's antics, though."

Right. The lady had vision issues.

So much for being Mr. Sensitivity.

"Sorry about that." He dropped down beside her, balancing his coffee. "I keep forgetting about the eye situation. You seem fine."

"No need to apologize. As Pops used to say, 'Taking offense when none is intended says more about the offendee than the offender.' I got comfortable in my skin long ago, thanks in large part to the vacations I spent here."

Another opening—but best to proceed with caution.

"The other day you referred to it as a haven."

"Yes." She leaned back on her palms, lifted her face to the sun, and closed her eyes, giving him a perfect view of her long, slender neck. "I was a late-in-life only child. My dad was excited about my arrival, my mom—not so much. They didn't agree on much of anything else, either. My dad worked in the aerospace industry, same department, same company his whole career. He was content to be an engineer, but Mom always thought he could do better, rise higher, make bigger money, gain more prestige. With the constant tension in our house, coming here every summer was my great escape."

"Are they still together?"

"No. They divorced when I was eighteen. Dad died ten years ago, far too young, and Mom married a senior executive at a Fortune 500 company who gave her the kind of life she'd always wanted. We don't talk all that often. I take after my dad, and Mom and I tend to clash." She looked over at him. "By contrast, I get the feeling you're close to your family and had an ideal childhood."

Better than hers, at any rate.

"No complaints—but we had our challenges, relocating every few years all over the world, changing schools, living in foreign countries, making new friends. I think that's one of the reasons my brothers and I are tight. We were the one constant in each others' lives. And despite our globe-hopping, my mom and dad managed to create a sense of stability and an all-for-one/one-for-all bedrock foundation for the family."

"Kudos to them. Is your dad still with the State Department?"

"No. He retired a few years ago and started a personal security business in Atlanta, my mom's hometown."

"Now I see the source of your excellent manners. You're the son of a Southern belle."

He grinned as he imagined his mother's unladylike reaction to that label. "I don't think Mom ever thought of herself in those terms—though I have to admit, she does have Scarlett O'Hara's determination."

"Southern women can be very strong and resilient. That's experience speaking, by the way. I grew up in Raleigh, North Carolina."

"Ah. That explains the slight drawl I detect in a few of your words."

"I lost that long ago."

"Nope. It's subtle, but I've spent enough time in the South to pick it up."

"Where?"

"Georgia."

"Which part?"

He hesitated—but the facility supported more than a hundred thousand people. Not much chance she'd be able to single out his particular job. "Fort Benning."

"The Army base."

"Yes."

She ran her fingers over the rough edge of a board he'd secured but hadn't yet sanded. "You were a Ranger, weren't you?"

It was hard to maintain a neutral expression after that out-of-the-blue insight. "A lot of people are affiliated with Benning."

"Only one special forces unit, though. A co-worker in New York dated a guy who was a SEAL, and I got the lowdown on special forces from her."

"Why do you think I was special forces?"

"Mark mentioned that the brother who called to arrange the cabin for you was a former SEAL. You told me all three of you were in different branches of the service but very competitive . . . seems logical you might try to make

your mark in a different but equally prestigiou
outfit."

The lady had some serious smarts.

"We could have used your critical thinkin
abilities on a few of our more dicey missions."

"Does that mean I'm right?"

"Yeah."

"Are you still in?"

"No." He turned away, toward the heron tha
continued to pursue its prey, forcing his lungs t
inflate and deflate at a normal rate. "An injur
sidelined me."

"Combat?"

"Yeah."

He braced, waiting for the next question.

It never came.

Using his mug as cover, he risked a glance a
her as he took a sip.

She was looking straight ahead, out over th
water—but turned her head toward him, as if sh
felt his scrutiny. "I'm sorry your career ende
that way. Are you doing okay?"

"Improving every day."

"That's good." She peered toward the vicinit
of the heron. "What's our blue-feathered frien
doing now?"

He exhaled. Dana must have sensed hi
reluctance to talk about the injury.

The lady had great intuitive ability as well a
smarts.

He shifted his gaze to the shoreline. It took him a few seconds to spot the heron, which was standing motionless, blending into his environment. A great skill for a heron—or special forces soldier. "Waiting for an opportunity to make his move."

A spasm passed over her features—one that suggested pain and bad memories. It came and went so fast he almost missed it.

"Speaking of making a move . . . I need to get back to work. The book on my computer won't edit itself." She swung her legs around and rose without giving him a chance to stand and offer her a hand.

She'd already retreated a few paces before he got to his feet.

"Thanks for the coffee." He drained the mug and held it out.

"There's more in the pot if you want to keep that."

An excuse to knock on her door later. Excellent.

"I'll do that."

"Well . . ." She withdrew a few more feet. "I'll let you go back to work too."

"I expect to finish up within the hour. Too bad you don't have a boat to go with the dock."

"I do. Or Pops did, anyway. A rowboat. It may be in the shed. I haven't poked around in there on this trip."

"Want me to get it out for you if it's in decent shape?"

"Sure. Thanks. I used to like rowing out to the middle of the lake in the evening, as the sun set. I'll peek into the shed and leave the door unlocked if the boat's there. See you later."

With that, she swung around and hurried up the hill.

Finn watched her until she disappeared around the corner of the house. He'd made a little progress today putting together the Dana puzzle, but as soon as one question got answered, a new one popped up. Like her troubled expression after his innocuous comment about the heron waiting to make his move.

One thing for sure. His stay in the woods wasn't going to be one bit boring as long as he kept talking to his neighbor.

And with every encounter, getting to know the book editor next door rose higher on his priority list.

—5—

Why hadn't Finn stopped by today?

Dana adjusted her pillow, squinted through the darkness at the digital display on the clock, and sighed. She should be asleep instead of staring at the ceiling as the minutes flicked toward midnight, thinking about her neighbor . . . and asking the wrong question.

The real question was why *should* Finn stop by? He'd finished the dock yesterday; hauled the rowboat out of mothballs, cleaned it up, and secured it to a mooring post; and bid her farewell after she'd refused his offer of a test spin around the lake.

You haven't exactly been Miss Congeniality, Dana. What did you expect? A man like Finn could have his pick of women. Why should he bother with one who keeps her distance? Gives him no encouragement? Cuts every conversation short?

And why do you care, anyway?

Excellent questions—and the last one deserved serious consideration.

Surrendering to insomnia, Dana sat up and bunched the pillow behind her head. Yes, Finn was nice. Handsome. Thoughtful. Exciting. The kind of guy she'd have drooled over six months ago.

But the exciting part wasn't a draw anymore—and with his special forces background, Finn McGregor wouldn't be satisfied living in a cabin in the woods for the rest of his life. He might not even last the month he'd allotted.

Whatever injury had taken him out of action, he was a fast-lane kind of guy who wouldn't slow down for long. He might be content to hang out fixing docks and retrieving boats and watching blue herons for a few days, but he'd soon get bored and start searching for a more exhilarating way to channel his energy and adrenaline.

And the fast lane wasn't for her anymore.

Besides, her neighbor had secrets. Traumatic ones. Sitting beside him on the dock yesterday at close range, she'd been able to pick up a subtle underlying tension in his body language and facial expressions. Six months ago, that wouldn't have been as big a deal. Now . . . different story. She needed to deal with her own baggage before she took on anyone else's.

So while it was perfectly normal to find a man with his many attractive attributes, it was important to keep his downsides top of mind—and stay cool.

Dana twisted her neck toward the clock again. Eleven-forty-seven . . . and she was as wide awake as if it was noon.

Grabbing Pops's sweater from the foot of the bed, she swung her legs to the floor and shoved her feet into her slippers. If sleep was going to play hide-and-seek, she ought to make up some of the ground she'd lost on the manuscript today while distracting thoughts of Finn played havoc with her concentration. And why not build a cozy fire? There was plenty of well-seasoned wood on the porch, and the April nights were chilly. With a crackling blaze in the hearth, a cup of hot chocolate by her side, and a compelling story awaiting her fine-tuning, she might actually make some headway during the middle-of-the-night hours.

It was worth a try, at any rate.

Because thinking about a certain former special forces soldier while sleep eluded her was *not* a productive—or relaxing—way to spend the rest of the night.

The bulky diving suit was hot as blazes.

Roger paused, perspiration dripping off his forehead. Donning the getup at the car had been a bad idea. The dry suit had been designed for diving in water temperatures below sixty, not hiking in fifty-degree weather.

Too bad it wasn't midsummer. In warm weather, all he would have needed for the shallow lake dive was his breathing equipment. No dry suit, no gloves, no hood. He could have traveled a lot lighter.

At this time of year, though, spending more than a few minutes in Leo's lake without protective gear would put him at serious risk of hypothermia.

But next visit, he was changing a lot closer to the lake—even if that meant he'd have more paraphernalia to lug through the woods.

He swiped a hand across his brow. If only Dana Lewis hadn't shown up. It would be so much simpler to drive up Leo's road and park by the cabin. Having to find an isolated spot to hide the car on the adjacent national forest land, then trek in from the back of the property, doubled the difficulty of the task.

On the plus side, however, he'd had most of the proper equipment on hand from when he and Leah had taken those scuba classes and practiced at Bonne Terre mine. Compared to that location, diving in Leo's lake should be a piece of cake.

The real challenge was getting there in a dry suit with an air tank strapped to his back while he juggled the metal detector he'd bought yesterday in St. Louis in one hand and an oversized duffel bag with the rest of his gear in the other. A third hand to push through the brush would have come in handy.

But lamenting the situation wasn't going to change it.

At least tonight's clear weather and full moon eliminated the need for a flashlight. There wasn't much chance Dana Lewis was up and about at this hour, but why draw attention to a bobbing beam in the woods just in case?

He rested a shoulder against the nearest tree and glanced around, his eyes fully adjusted now to the dimness. He'd never been on this part of Leo's property. The older man hadn't been inclined to wander too far from the house in recent years, and while Leo's open invitation to hunt on the land had been gracious, the appeal of shooting innocent birds and animals had always eluded him.

Roger surveyed the trees and scrubby brush. Everything was beginning to leaf out, which would make this trek tougher on every subsequent trip. If lady luck smiled on him, he'd hit pay dirt in the lake after a search or two and . . .

His gaze homed in on a small white box a few feet away, and he bent down for a closer inspection. As the familiar design registered, he set the metal detector on the ground and picked up the container, angling it toward the light of the moon.

Sudafed—and of recent vintage, given the like-new condition of the cardboard.

He bowed the package. An empty blister pack was inside.

Odd place for a package of cold medicine. Of course, it could belong to Dana. If she'd gone exploring, it might have fallen out of her pocket. Or someone hiking in the national forest could have wandered onto her land by accident and dropped it.

Or it might belong to someone using Sudafed for an illegal purpose. There was a lot of that going around these days.

Roger dug out his watch. Twelve-thirty. The dry suit might be uncomfortable, but it hadn't slowed him down. He could spare ten minutes to nose around, see if there was anything else suspicious in the vicinity.

It took him less than five minutes to find a crude

outbuilding that had been designed to blend into its wooded surroundings. The padlock barred him from entry, but an empty box of matches near the corner and a sniff test at the crack in the door that offered a whiff of cat urine verified his suspicions.

There was a meth lab on Leo's property—and from all indications, it had been here awhile. A daylight search would no doubt turn up a nasty trove of toxic waste as well. It appeared to be a small operation . . . but no matter the size, it was big-time illegal.

He sighed. This wasn't the first meth lab he'd dealt with, and it wouldn't be the last. Missouri had been the meth capital of the US for years. The state might have given up that dubious honor, but the drug remained a huge challenge for law enforcement . . . and the isolation of national forests earned those locations favored status among cookers.

This guy—and possibly a partner—were smart, however. By using tricky-to-access national forest as insulation, they'd reduced the chance that some unwary hiker would stumble onto the lab. And doing their cooking on private land that, until the past few weeks, had been unoccupied for an extended period, had given them complete privacy.

Conclusion? There was a high probability he was dealing with a local who knew the area, was clued into the town grapevine—and couldn't be happy about Dana Lewis's arrival.

Yet based on the pristine package of Sudafed, the owner of this lab wasn't letting her presence slow him down.

Another trickle of sweat rolled down his temple, and he wiped it away. He'd have to bust this, of course. Meth was a dirty, destructive drug that needed to be wiped off the face of the earth. And it would be a straightforward investigation. An "anonymous" tip about an illegal activity was common in law enforcement, and Dana Lewis wasn't likely to balk if he stopped by and asked if he and his officers could poke around. It wouldn't take long for one of them to stumble across this lab, and setting up a stakeout wouldn't be difficult. The highway patrol was always happy to send a few reinforcements to help in a situation like this.

That, however, was a chore for tomorrow. Tonight, he had a higher-priority task.

Leaving the makeshift lab behind, he continued toward the lake, compass in hand to guide him.

But as he drew close to his destination, he didn't need any navigational assistance. Light was shining from several windows in the cabin on the far side of the water.

He halted, his heart missing a beat. Why would Dana be up at this hour of the night?

Could be lots of reasons, Burnett. Stay cool.

He forced the left side of his brain to engage. She might suffer from insomnia, as he did. Or perhaps she was a night person who went to bed late and slept in every morning. Or a cold or upset stomach could be disrupting her sleep.

No matter. Whatever the explanation for her nocturnal activity, there wasn't much chance she was wandering around outside in the dark. He'd be fine as long as he entered the water from this side of the lake.

Roger continued to the bank and finished donning the rest of his equipment, hands fumbling despite his practice session at home. Suiting up in your basement was a lot different than suiting up in the woods beside a body of very dark intimidating water.

A shiver snaked through him despite the sweat trickling down the sides of his face. Maybe this was a bad idea after all. It wasn't too late to change his mind. He could retrace his steps through the woods, dump all his gear back in the basement, and return the metal detector tomorrow.

But if he did, Woodside Gardens was going to throw Leah out.

No.

He had to do this. And he *could* do this. He might prefer the clear, blue waters of the Caribbean, but he'd dived in caves. This was no different. Plus, the payoff could be huge—in both dollars and peace of mind about Leah.

Squaring his shoulders, he finished his preparations and picked up his brand-new VLF metal detector. Weighed it in his hands. There had been cheaper models in the store, but the sales guy had steered him away from those. For fresh water, it seemed he needed the very low frequency version —and this one could detect objects almost two feet underground. That was important. After fifty years, it was very possible the ammo cans were buried under layers of silt.

The more expensive model was worth the extra couple hundred bucks if it led him to the gold—and now was the time to put it to the test.

Roger eased into the water . . . stretched out . . . and let himself sink into the murky depths as he flipped on his dive light.

Praying the lake would give up the treasure that would solve all his problems.

Someone was driving up the road to her cabin.

As the crunch of gravel penetrated Dana's consciousness, she scrambled up from the couch in front of the fireplace where she'd fallen asleep around four.

It wasn't a delivery. She hadn't called in a new order to either the general mercantile or the hardware store. Nor had she invited anyone to visit.

Her pulse picked up. All her life this had been a peaceful, safe refuge—but Pops had always been with her. What would she do if someone with bad intentions showed up? Look how easily Finn had gotten in last Sund—

Finn.

Could *he* be her visitor?

Draping the afghan Mags had knitted two decades ago around her, she padded back to the kitchen, lifted a shade an inch, and peered out.

She saw the SUV before she spotted the driver.

It was Finn.

Relief—and another, sweeter emotion—washed over her.

A moment later, he appeared from behind the vehicle carrying . . . She strained to identify the object, but her eyes wouldn't cooperate.

He disappeared as he circled to the front of the cabin. Clutching the afghan, she moved toward the living room to follow his progress. Glanced in the hall mirror as she passed. Stopped.

Her vision might be blurry, but even she could tell the fuzzy woman in the reflection was a mess. Hair sticking up, smudges under her lower lashes, disheveled clothing.

She looked like a refugee from one of those Halloween haunted houses.

And Finn was going to knock on her door any minute!

Running her fingers through her hair, she dashed for the bedroom to grab her robe, waiting for his summons.

It never came.

Huh.

Wrapping her robe around her, she returned to the living room and peeked out the window.

He was down at the dock. While she watched, he boarded the rowboat and sat on the seat.

Had her neighbor come to take a solo spin around the lake?

No.

He bent down, as if he was working on something.

A reprieve!

Dana dashed back to the bedroom, and in short order had pulled on her jeans, slipped on her Stanford sweatshirt, and run a brush over her hair. The biggest tangles would have to wait until later.

The knock sounded on her door as she applied a touch of lipstick—and her hand jerked, creating a pink slash under her nose. She grabbed for a tissue to wipe it off.

So much for cool and composed.

Finn knocked again.

Rubbing at the spot, she dashed out of the bedroom, halting for a second at the hall mirror to finish the lipstick removal job before pulling open the door.

He smiled, giving her a quick, appreciative once-over that made her toes tingle. "Good morning."

"Good mor . . ." Her voice rasped, and she cleared her throat. "Morning."

"I noticed the other day that two of the screws in the oarlocks were loose. I didn't have the right size bit with me, so I came back to fix them." He held up a power drill. "I hope I didn't interrupt your concentration."

"No. I . . . uh . . . worked late last night and fell asleep on the couch. I hadn't gotten rolling for the day yet."

Faint creases appeared above his nose. "Did I wake you?"

"I needed to get up anyway."

"Does that mean you haven't eaten yet?"

She blinked. "Yes."

"Then join me for breakfast at the Walleye Café in town. I stopped in there the other day for pie and coffee, and from my spot at the counter I had a bird's-eye view of the orders as they came up. The food looks great."

Finn wanted to take her to town for breakfast.

While she tried to wrap her mind around that, he continued.

"Nice as this spot is, it might be good to get out and see a bit of the world once in a while. And my chariot is at your service."

It was hard not to respond to his engaging grin. Plus, she'd made serious progress on the book in the wee hours of the morning. She ought to be able to meet her end-of-day deadline even if she took an hour or two off this morning for a trip into town. What harm could there be in an innocent little outing like that?

Ha. As if you don't know.

She throttled the little voice in her head.

"Okay. Thanks. I love their cinnamon rolls."

"Great. Are you ready now, or do you need a few minutes?"

"Can you give me five?"

"I could be persuaded to go as high as ten. Beyond that, my rumbling stomach will begin to make very loud protests—and it won't be pretty."

Her mouth twitched. "I'll rush."

"I'll wait." He strolled over to one of the rocking chairs and sat.

Dana closed the door. Five minutes. She'd have to prioritize. Mascara . . . hair . . . a nicer blouse—those were the essentials.

Because despite the caution signs hovering around Finn, as long as she didn't let the buzz of attraction short-circuit her brain, there was no reason she shouldn't primp a little or enjoy a simple meal in the company of an attractive man.

You're playing with fire, Dana.

She moved into the bathroom, picked up her mascara wand—and tried again to muzzle the nagging voice in her mind.

It refused to be silenced.

And maybe the warning was sound.

But she'd be careful. She was a thirty-year-old woman, not a teenager with raging hormones. She could recognize Finn's charm without succumbing to it.

Of course she could.

Besides, how much could happen over bacon and eggs in the folksy ambiance of the Walleye Café?

Roger rubbed a hand down his face and regarded the gaunt, bleary-eyed stranger in the bathroom mirror.

He looked like . . . a word Leah preferred he not use.

But the term was accurate.

Dark circles hung under his bloodshot eyes and the creases around his mouth and nose seemed to have deepened overnight.

His trek through the woods weighed down with equipment, his forty-five-minute dive in a cold dark lake until his air tank gave out, and the worry about those burning lights in Dana Lewis's cabin had all taken a toll.

To make matters worse, he had nothing to show for his effort. The metal detector hadn't registered anything that could be an ammo can containing gold. Plus, he'd covered far less of the lake bottom than he'd hoped.

This could be a long, slow search.

And he didn't have the luxury of time.

His cell began to vibrate, and he pulled it off his belt, fighting back a wave of panic. He needed to stay calm, continue to go about his daily routine as if nothing was wrong. Letting nerves rattle him would be counterproductive.

"Good morning, Lynette."

"Morning, Chief. I didn't wake you, did I?"

"No. I'm up and dressed and getting ready to come in."

"I thought you were under the weather."

"I was when I left the message last night. Must have been the four-day-old leftovers I had for dinner." *Lie.* "But I'm feeling better now." *Double lie.* "What's up?"

"The mayor stopped in. He wanted to talk to you about the vandalism at the picnic grounds you two discussed a few days ago. There was another incident last night. Bill went out as soon as we got the report from Hazel. She saw the damage as she drove by on her way to work."

Roger turned his back on the mirror and rested a hip on the vanity. "What happened?"

"More graffiti spray-painted on the bleachers and picnic tables. Nasty stuff, according to her report. It also appears someone drove an ATV over the ball field. You can imagine what that did with all the rain we've had."

Yeah, he could. What he *couldn't* imagine, despite all his years in law enforcement, was why some people got a kick out of destroying property.

"Tell the mayor I'll pay him a visit after I drive out and take a look at the damage."

"Be prepared for him to bring up surveillance again. He mentioned it when he dropped in."

Like they had the staffing for that.

"Thanks for the heads-up."

"We'll see you later."

As the line went dead, Roger twisted his wrist. Nine-seventeen. A much later start than usual to his day—but he'd already been operating on fumes before last night, and a three-thirty turn-in hadn't helped. Buying himself a few extra hours of sleep with an upset stomach excuse had been a necessity, not a luxury.

And truth be told, while bad food wasn't the cause, his stomach *was* churning. Had been for days. He'd have to stock up on some antacids at the mercantile if the indigestion became chronic.

Pushing himself to his feet, he risked one more glimpse in the mirror. At least no one would question his complaint about feeling poorly, given his haggard appearance.

But there was work to do, and wallowing in self-pity wasn't going to improve the situation. Maybe once he drove out to the picnic grounds and met with the mayor, he'd stop at the Walleye for a cup of coffee and a dose of Hazel's good humor to perk up his spirits.

He left the house through the front door, locked it behind him, and trudged down the path to the patrol car in his driveway. The daffodils that rimmed the walkway, planted by Leah and tended with her loving hands each spring, were once again in full bloom, as dependable as the cardinal's trill that serenaded him each morning.

If only life in general could be that predictable.

After unlocking the car, he slid behind the wheel, put the key in the ignition—and frowned. What was with the envelope stuck under his windshield wiper? If someone wanted to talk to him, all they had to do was pick up the phone, knock on his door, or drop into his office.

He was *not* in the mood for games this morning.

Temper spiking, he opened the door, stood, and grabbed the envelope. There was no name on it, but the missive was obviously meant for him.

Once back in the driver's seat, he ripped open the flap, extracted a single sheet of paper, and skimmed the brief, typed message.

I saw you scuba diving on the Lewis property in the middle of the night. I doubt it was official business. I also saw you poking around my "office." Plus, you parked in my reserved spot. So let's make a deal. You ignore what you saw, I'll ignore what I saw. If you don't . . . I have photos—and video. The moon was bright. Lucky—for me, anyway.

Roger's lungs locked, and a wave of nausea rolled through him.

The meth cooker had witnessed his late-night visit to the Lewis place—and was blackmailing him to ensure his operation didn't get shut down.

Breathe, Burnett. Think!

He tried to follow that advice, but his brain was stuck in neutral.

One minute passed.

Two.

Three.

At last he sucked in a lungful of air, ran a shaky hand through his hair, and faced the truth.

He'd been busted—and whoever was running that meth lab held all the cards. If he had pictures and video—and given today's cell phone capabilities, that was a very real possibility—there was no credible explanation for a midnight dive on Dana Lewis's property. This guy could have been smart enough to pan up and take footage of her cabin, too, to identify the location.

If the blackmailer was also a user—another very real possibility—this was a powder keg. Meth could make people volatile, anxious, paranoid, moody, violent. In other words, he might be dealing with a loose cannon. The note had sounded rational, but that could be misleading.

So what was he supposed to do? Ignoring a crime happening right under his nose went against everything he believed.

And keeping Len White's letter a secret while you try to find stolen gold to use for your own illegal purposes doesn't?

An ache began to pound in his temple, and he lifted a shaky hand to massage it.

This was spinning out of control, tangling

him in a sticky web and shrinking his options.

If he pulled back on his search, took the appropriate action with Len White's letter, and shut down the meth lab, the guy could produce the photos and video he claimed to have. No matter how murky they were, a competent lab would be able to brighten up the images, identify him. And how would he explain his midnight excursion? There was no rational reason for him to be diving in the dark in a lake on private property.

Besides . . . he needed that gold. Needed to get Leah the care her trust fund would have paid for if he hadn't lost every dime of it in that can't-miss speculative investment an old college buddy had told him about. A scheme that had gone belly-up twenty-four months later.

Leah, bless her soul, had never held that mistake against him. In fact, she'd tried to console him afterward. He could still hear her sweet voice after he delivered the bad news.

"It's okay, Rog. Your job provides us with a steady income, our house is paid for, and we're debt-free. Best of all, we have each other. That's the most important thing. It's love, not money, that makes life worth living."

She'd been right—and he'd allowed himself to be soothed by her words and her forgiveness.

But love wasn't going to pay the bill at Woodside Gardens.

He needed that gold.

Meaning he was once again going to have to compromise his principles—and let a meth lab remain in business.

Roger refolded the note. Slid it back in the envelope. Tried to control the tremble in his hands as he put the patrol car in gear. All his life, he'd been repulsed by civil servants who violated public trust, who circumvented legalities, who broke their vows to enforce—and abide by—laws they'd sworn to protect.

Now he was one of them.

A criminal.

His gut churned, and a sour taste filled his mouth as the offensive word echoed in his mind.

But like it or not, the label was accurate.

He'd just have to find a way to live with it—and make sure he didn't get caught.

—6—

"Well, aren't you a sight for sore eyes! Let me give you a big hug."

As the greeting boomed across the Walleye Café, the stocky bleached-blonde waitress Finn had noticed on his first visit came flying across the room, beaming a smile at Dana. She pulled the younger woman into an enthusiastic embrace and held tight, mashing in part of a bouffant hairstyle long out of fashion.

Just as he began to wonder if the waitress was cutting off Dana's air supply, she released her, the teased do instantly popping back into shape.

Dana's answering smile lit up her face, animating it with a radiance that vaulted her from pretty to stunning in a heartbeat.

Finn tried not to stare.

"It's wonderful to see you too, Hazel."

"I heard you were in town and kept wondering when you'd stop in. How are those eyes doing, anyway? Marv told me you were having some issues." Hands on her padded hips, the blonde inspected Dana.

"Improving—but not enough yet to drive. I'm cabin-bound unless I have a chauffeur, like today." Dana shifted toward him.

Picking up the cue, Finn moved forward and held out his hand as Dana introduced them.

"Very nice to meet you." Hazel gave his arm a vigorous pump. "You were in here the other day, weren't you? At the counter. Let me think . . ." She pursed her lips as she scrutinized him. "Apple pie and coffee, right?"

"I'm impressed."

"Don't be. I've been waitressing since you were in diapers. Besides, we don't get many handsome strangers in here. You kinda stood out." She gave him a nudge with her elbow, along with a good-natured grin. "I'll say this—you know how to pick your chauffeurs, Dana. How'd you find a Hollywood hunk like this out here in the boonies?"

Dana looked like she wanted to sink through the floor. "He's . . . uh . . . staying in Mark Busch's cabin."

"Neighbor, huh. Some people have all the luck. I've got the town crank on one side and an empty lot full of weeds on the other. What can you do?" She stepped back and gave Dana a thorough perusal. "My, but you've grown into a beauty. I remember when you used to come in here with Leo, all gangly arms and legs." Her demeanor softened. "I sure was sorry to hear about his passing. He was a fine man."

"Yes, he was." Dana's voice choked.

Hazel patted her shoulder and motioned them toward the dining area. "You two find yourselves a spot and I'll be over to take your order in a few minutes. I can recommend the Denver omelet if you have a hearty appetite. We use free-range eggs, and the ham is cured here in Washington County, a few miles down the road."

"You sold me." Finn rested his hand in the small of Dana's back and guided her out of the way as the door opened behind him to admit another diner. "But we're in no rush to order." Or he wasn't, anyway. Dana no doubt had work waiting for her . . . yet she didn't correct him.

He followed her across the room, weaving in

and out of tables, toward a booth for two in the far corner. Once she was seated, he slid in opposite her.

"This was where Pops and I always sat if it was available." She ran her fingers over the scarred wooden surface. "It's out of the line of traffic but lets you keep tabs on who's coming and going."

"Did you two come here often?"

"Two or three times a week after Mags died. When she was alive, we usually ate at the cabin. But the three of us always managed to get in here once a week for pie. Hazel's been a fixture at the Walleye for as long as I can remember."

"I got that feeling. Need a menu?" He indicated the holder on the wall.

"Nope. Hazel's never steered me wrong. I'm going with the omelet—and a cinnamon roll." Her lips curved as she surveyed the homey restaurant. "This place brings back a lot of happy memories. I've been wanting to stop in, but without wheels, I've been cabin-bound."

"Speaking of that—how did you get here?" Finn unwrapped his silverware and spread the paper napkin on his lap.

"After I flew in from New York, I spent two weeks in St. Louis, at Pops's house. The couple next door offered to drive me down. They were his neighbors for forty years."

"How long have you been here?"

"A little over a month."

"And today is the first time you've ventured out?" He didn't try to disguise his surprise.

"Yours is the first chariot to come along."

At the glint of humor in her irises, he hitched up one side of his mouth. "For the record, it's at your disposal."

"I appreciate that . . . but I'm content at the cabin."

"Forever?"

She hesitated. "For now, anyway."

Before he could pursue that topic, Hazel hustled over, order pad in hand. "Have you two decided?"

Finn looked at Dana, and she gestured for him to order. "Two of the omelets you recommended and two cinnamon rolls."

"Coffee?" She continued to scribble on her pad.

"For me. Tea for the lady."

"Lipton okay?"

"Fine." Dana extracted her own silverware from the napkin, her expression poignant. "It's nice to know some things never change. This place is exactly the same as I remember."

"Oh, we've done an update or two." Hazel tucked the order pad in the pocket of her apron. "A few new trophy fish on the walls, chairs with cushions for the tables, different lighting fixtures. But the biggest change . . . we have Wi-Fi."

"No kidding." Dana surveyed the patrons, who were all focused on their food or the newspaper. "Anyone use it?"

"Teenagers, mostly. We've become quite the hangout for the afterschool crowd, since there's no Starbucks for miles. Now let me get these orders in to Chuck or you'll be having your breakfast during the lunch rush."

"Would you give him my best?"

"Happy to."

As the woman hurried off, Dana folded her hands on the table. "Chuck's been the cook here for years."

"A diner with minimal turnover. Unusual."

"Not around here. There aren't a lot of jobs close by. People tend to stick with the ones they have."

"Speaking of jobs . . . you're fortunate to have one that allows you to work wherever you want."

"I agree. My work is very portable."

"But how do you function here, without internet or email?"

"Phone conversations can replace email—and UPS delivers manuscripts and flash drives anywhere."

"You don't get cabin fever?"

"Not yet—though I would like to do some hiking around the place. That's on my agenda once my vision improves a bit more."

"If you don't want to wait that long, I'd be happy to go with you."

She sent him a speculative look. "Thanks. I'll think about that."

Not the answer he'd hoped for . . . but at least she hadn't said no.

The bell on the front door jingled, and Dana glanced over as Hazel delivered their beverages. Squinted.

"Hazel . . . is that Chief Burnett?"

The waitress angled sideways. Sighed. "Yes."

"Is he okay? He was never heavy, but . . . wow. He's lost a ton of weight."

"Yep—and no matter how much food Lynette, his office manager, or I shove at him, he keeps getting skinnier." She leaned down and dropped her volume. "That man's had a passel of tribulations in the past ten years. You knew about his son, right?"

"No. What happened?"

"Got killed over in the Middle East. He was a marine."

Shock flattened Dana's features. "I had no idea."

"The chief never talked about it much—but it took a toll on him and Leah. A few years after that, she was diagnosed with Alzheimer's. He kept her at home as long as he could, but after she got away from the caretaker he hired and was found walking down the street in her underwear, he had to put her in one of those homes. A fine place—Woodside Gardens—over in Potosi. First class all the way . . . but it's been real hard on him emotionally."

Finn watched the man slide onto a stool at the

counter. "Not to mention financially, I expect. The tab for those kinds of places can be off the charts."

"That's one worry he doesn't have, thank the Lord." Hazel swiped at a stray crumb on the table. "Leah's parents left her a sizeable trust fund and a safe-deposit box chock-full of goodies, according to town scuttlebutt. Her father was some honcho at a big company in KC."

"I didn't realize she came from wealth." Dana took a sip of her water.

"She never flaunted her money. Nicest woman you'd ever want to meet, and she and Roger always lived a modest life. Still, he hit the jackpot the day he pulled her over for speeding back when he was a street cop in KC. Not only did he find the love of his life, he never had to worry about money again. Sad to see such a happy marriage come to this end."

"I might stop by and say hello before he leaves." Sympathy softened Dana's eyes.

"He'd like that. Your granddad and Roger spent many an hour fishing on that lake at your place. Now I better go see what I can offer from the menu to tempt his taste buds."

Dana watched her hurry over, shaking her head. "You never know what life is going to—"

A loud crash from the kitchen cut her off.

Every muscle in Finn's body went rigid, and he half rose. His hand jerked, sending coffee spewing toward Dana. She yelped as it seared her forearm.

Her cry of pain yanked him back to the present as Hazel came rushing over, dishcloth in hand.

"Oh, goodness. I'm sorry about that noise." She sopped up the spreading puddle of dark liquid. "I don't know what's gotten into Chuck these days. Banging pots, spilling half the profits on the floor." She homed in on Dana's arm. "You need some ice. Let me grab some from the kitchen." She took off again.

As Dana studied him, heat surged up Finn's neck. Based on her expression, he'd overreacted—big-time.

Just like he had in the base cafeteria.

Maybe he hadn't made as much progress as he'd thought.

"Sorry about this." He rested his fingertips lightly on her red skin. The injury wasn't bad and it would heal in a few days—but it shouldn't have happened.

"I'm fine. I've gotten worse burns making popcorn. That kind of crash could startle anyone."

Not true. No one else in the café had reacted as he had . . . including the woman across from him.

Hazel returned with some ice in a plastic bag plus a new mug of coffee for him. "You sure you're all right, honey?" She touched Dana's shoulder.

"Fine." She balanced the ice on the burn and offered them both a reassuring smile. "It will take more than a splash of coffee to kill my appetite for that omelet and cinnamon roll."

"They'll be up soon. You wave at me if you need anything else before then."

Quiet fell between them as Hazel departed, and Finn tried to come up with some lighthearted remark that would dispel the tension lingering in the air.

But Dana spoke first, her comment carefully phrased. "I imagine a combat injury—or just living in a combat zone—can leave scars of many kinds."

She was giving him an opening to explain his reaction to the dropped pot.

Taking a slow sip from his mug, he did a discreet sweep of the café. Other than the police chief gabbing with Hazel at the far end of the counter and a guy with his nose in the newspaper at a table by the window on the other side of the room, the place had cleared out. They had privacy.

But he needed one other ingredient before he could open the can of worms that had upended his life.

Courage.

And his was shaky when it came to revealing the demons that haunted him.

However . . . if he dug deep and managed to summon up enough nerve to share his story, might she open up to him too?

Possibly—but was it worth the risk?

Yet what did he have to lose? Dana Lewis didn'
strike him as the type who would violat
confidences even if she didn't reciprocate b
sharing some of her own.

"That's true. Scars linger." In his periphera
vision, he saw Hazel pick up their orders from th
window and head their direction. "But our food'
on the way, and I don't want to ruin you
appetite." Nor did he want to make a ras
decision. Better to mull this over while he ate.

Hazel bustled up to their booth. "Here you go.
She slid a brimming platter in front of each o
them. "Dig in. I'll wait till you put a dent in tha
before I warm up your cinnamon rolls. You tw
need anything else right now?"

"I think we're set." Finn picked up his fork.

"Enjoy." She set a bottle of Tabasco sauce on th
table and returned to her conversation with th
police chief.

Dana waited to speak until the woman wa
out of earshot. "If that's a brush-off, no problem.
get that some topics are personal and off-limits
But if you need a friendly ear while you're here
I've been told I'm a good listener." She speare
a bite of her omelet and motioned to his. "G
ahead and eat. Egg dishes are best consumed hot
Likewise for cinnamon rolls."

She dived in, and he followed her lead. N
way would he enjoy his food if he launched int
his story while they were chowing down. Bette

to keep the conversation light during the meal.

Twenty-five minutes later, Finn tried not to let his jaw drop as Dana washed down the last bite of a huge cinnamon roll . . . *after* scarfing up every morsel of her omelet and hash browns.

A woman who liked to eat instead of push her food around and complain about the calories.

One more check in her positive column—and one more reason to tell her his story.

Except just as he began to psych himself up to launch into his tale, the front door opened and a half dozen older gents entered and claimed the large round table beside their booth. The ensuing noisy banter and laughter was definitely not conducive to an intimate tête-a-tête.

A lost opportunity.

Or could it be a chance to rethink his approach?

Finn tapped a finger on the table. Maybe this wasn't the ideal place to initiate an intense dialogue. There were better settings—one in particular.

"You two ready for your check?" Hazel stopped beside their booth after exchanging a few words with the new arrivals.

"Yes." They spoke simultaneously as Finn held out his hand.

Dana frowned. "No—let me pay. I owe you for fixing my dock."

"Nope. That was part of my debt repayment to *you*."

"What kind of debt?" Hazel looked from one t the other, interest sparking in her eyes.

"Long story." Finn snagged the bill, gave it cursory scan, and handed over his credit carc "And I've got to get Dana home. She's on a stric deadline with one of her work projects."

"You're working? I thought you were here on a extended vacation."

As the older woman addressed Dana, Fin flashed his breakfast partner a silent apology. I was possible she didn't want to talk about her job

But the question didn't appear to bother her.

"I'm doing a lot of freelance editing whil I'm here. Let me tell you, it beats the rush-hou commute in New York—and the view is much better."

"That's a fact. I'll run this for you and you twc can be on your way."

When she returned a few minutes later, Dana motioned toward the empty counter. "It appears I missed the chief."

"Yeah. I mentioned to him you wanted to say hello, but he had to leave and he didn't want tc interrupt your breakfast."

"I'll have to stop by the station and say hi on my next visit to town."

"I bet your friend would be happy to bring you in again." Hazel winked at him.

"I've already made the offer."

"Good man." She gave an approving nod, then

transferred her attention back to Dana. "And you, young woman, take him up on it. No reason to be a stranger now that—"

"Hey, Hazel, where's our coffee?"

"Hold your horses, Harvey." She tossed the remark over her shoulder. "I'm brewing a new pot."

"We're ready to order too."

She rolled her eyes. "Some of our patrons would try the patience of a saint."

"I heard that," the older man announced.

Her mouth twitched. "Good."

Finn edged toward the end of the seat. "We'll get out of your hair so you can take care of your new customers."

"Don't rush out on their account."

"We really do need to leave. The UPS truck will be at my cabin bright and early tomorrow for a pickup." Dana slid out too.

Hazel engulfed her in another hug after she stood. "You come back real soon."

"I'll do my best."

She started toward the door, and Finn fell in behind her. If she was super busy, as she claimed, his plan might have to wait for another day.

But if she was willing to give him an extra twenty or thirty minutes, this could end up being the day he broke radio silence and spilled his guts.

Assuming, of course, that his wobbly courage held.

—7—

You shouldn't have pressed, Dana.

As Finn swung onto the road that led to her cabin, she risked a peek at him. He'd been quiet during the ten-minute ride from town, responding to her comments but offering few of his own. Her fault. She, of all people, should understand turf boundaries. Why, oh why, had she mentioned combat scars? And pushed him to open up with that good-listener comment?

At this stage, she wouldn't blame him if he dumped her at the door and took off in a spray of rock.

"How's the burn?" Finn kept his eyes aimed at the rutted road as his SUV jounced over the bumpy surface.

She glanced down at the reddish splotch on her skin. "It'll fade in a day or two."

The cabin came into view as they emerged from the woods. He pulled up close to the back door and offered her a smile that seemed forced. "Home safe and sound."

"Yes." She picked up her purse from the floor. "Thanks for taking me to town—and for breakfast. It was a nice change of pace." She fumbled for her door handle.

"Wait."

As the single, strained word cut through the silence, she turned back. One of his hands had a death grip on the wheel, the other lay balled in his lap.

"If you have time, we could take a spin around the lake. I know you have work to do, but I . . . I wouldn't mind taking advantage of those listening skills you mentioned."

Dana's pulse hitched. Finn hadn't been subdued on their drive back to the cabin because he'd been offended by her comments; he'd been mulling over her offer.

Her spirits soared. Who cared if she had to work late tonight to have the book ready for the UPS driver tomorrow? No way was she passing up this opportunity to learn more about an ex–special forces soldier who rushed to the aid of women in distress in the middle of the night.

"I can spare thirty or forty minutes." Or however many it took.

"Great." Based on the uncertainty in his inflection, he was already having second thoughts . . . but all at once his jaw firmed and he shut off the engine. "Let me get your door."

She waited while he circled the vehicle. Too bad she had to make a pit stop—but it would be a quick one. The longer she was gone, the greater the risk he'd get cold feet and back off.

"Let me run inside and put on some sunscreen."

She slid out of the SUV. “I’ll meet you on the dock in five minutes.”

“I’ll be there.”

She hoped that was true.

He stayed by the SUV until she opened the cabin door, then disappeared around the side of the structure.

Dana did apply some sunscreen—and a touch of lipstick for good measure—but in less time than she’d allotted, she joined him on the dock.

“Our friendly heron is back.” Finn nodded toward the same spot the bird had claimed on his last visit.

She peered that direction, trying to distinguish his long neck in the tall grass growing in the shallow water near the bank, but finally gave up. “My vision isn’t there yet.”

He dropped into the center of the rowboat and held out a hand. “Shouldn’t you be getting your eyes examined on a regular basis?”

Instead of responding at once, she put her fingers in his and stepped down. The boat rocked, and his grasp tightened, steadying her as she caught her balance.

Except she lost it again when she lifted her head. At five-seven, she was tall, but he topped her by at least five or six inches. And he filled the small boat, his broad shoulders blocking her view of the cabin behind him, his solid chest inches away. As for those jade green irises—whoa!

"Dana?"

"What?"

"I asked about your eyes."

"Oh. Right." She fumbled behind her, feeling for the seat, and lowered herself to the bench. *Real smooth, Dana.* "Yes. My, uh, doctor in New York suggested that . . . but he also told me what to expect as I healed, and up to this point everything is textbook. I have the name of someone in St. Louis I can see if that changes."

"Mmm." He leaned toward the dock and slipped the mooring rope off the post.

She had no idea what that enigmatic comment meant—but as he settled into place, she had a feeling her answer hadn't satisfied him.

"Do you think this is seaworthy?" Dumb question. The boat had sat at her dock since he'd pulled it out of mothballs two days ago, and there wasn't a drop of water in the hull. But it moved the conversation to a more neutral topic.

"We're about to find out. Can you swim?" He pulled a pair of shades out of his pocket and slid them over his nose, flashing her a quick grin.

"Yes. Pops taught me—here in this lake, as a matter of fact."

"Then we're set. Prepare to cast off."

With that, he put the oars to work . . . giving her an excellent view of bulging biceps below the sleeves of his snug black T-shirt.

Whew.

She slipped on her sunglasses too, and forced herself to watch the rippling water, sneaking an occasional peek at her companion as she explained how Pops had enlarged and stocked the original pond through the years.

Finn did a complete circuit, his pace steady and unhurried, listening to her guided tour. Then he aimed for the center of the lake, finally pausing there.

She sent him an admiring look. "Despite all that exertion, you aren't even breathing hard."

His lips flexed. "I try to stay in shape."

"A successful quest, based on today's performance. Rowing the perimeter of the lake is taxing. I used to do it, and by the end I was always gasping. You make it seem easy."

The corners of his mouth flattened. "It is now. It wouldn't have been a few months ago."

"After your injury?" She asked the question cautiously. It wasn't too late for him to change his mind about sharing his history—and if he decided to back off, she needed to let him.

"Yeah."

The silence that followed was broken only by the call of a cardinal and a distant rumble of thunder suggesting a storm was brewing somewhere beyond the horizon.

Dana waited, giving him a chance to collect his thoughts . . . or reconsider.

Just when she began to think he'd chosen the

latter option, he released the oars. "If you still want to hear my story, I'll tell you—but I need to warn you . . . it isn't like those novels you edit."

"You might be surprised what's in a lot of romances. Overcoming serious obstacles is often a major theme. And I edit a lot of other stuff too. Some of it can get very dark."

"Dark about sums up what I'm going to tell you."

"I'd still like to hear it."

"Okay." His Adam's apple bobbed. "Fifteen months ago, during an insertion into hostile territory, our helo was hit by an RPG. It went down while I was fast-roping to the ground. I had a lot of damage—shrapnel, second-degree burns, internal injuries. The fall also did a number on my right leg. Several bones were broken, and the lower tibia was shattered. I've been in surgery and rehab ever since. But I was one of the lucky ones. Only two guys from that mission survived." His voice hoarsened, and the skin over his cheekbones grew taut.

Dana was tempted to reach over, lay her hand on his knee, make a physical connection that would communicate more clearly than words how much she cared . . . and that she understood his pain as well as anyone could who hadn't lived through combat trauma.

But his rigid posture said "keep your distance."

So instead, she laced her fingers on her lap. "I'm

so sorry, Finn." The hushed words were inadequate . . . but what else was there to say in the face of such heartbreak?

"Yeah. I was too. About a lot of stuff."

Like what?

A number of possibilities raced through her mind. He could be dealing with survivor's guilt. Or regretting the sudden and unexpected end to his career as a Ranger. Or trying to cope with any number of other traumas she couldn't begin to imagine.

He spoke again before she could think of a discreet follow-up question. "For the record, the helo crash wasn't what ended my career. I'd already decided I wasn't going to re-up."

Not what she'd expected.

"May I ask why?" *Please, don't let me be over-stepping!*

He wrapped his hands around the edge of the seat. "I had PTSD. Or a variation of it."

Post-traumatic stress disorder.

The air whooshed out of her lungs. Stories about that devastating affliction were all over the media these days.

Again, she reined in the impulse to touch the white-knuckled fingers clenching the seat, homing in instead on the second part of his explanation. "What do you mean, a variation?"

"I had—and continue to have, to a minor degree—typical PTSD symptoms. Insomnia, anxiety, withdrawal . . . plus the exaggerated response to everyday events that you saw in the café today. The same thing happened in the mess hall a month before the crash—except that time I dived for the floor and yelled for everyone to take cover. So I've made progress. But I also have symptoms of what the shrinks call moral injury or traumatic loss, which was intensified by the helo crash. All of that started before I was injured, though."

"When?"

"When I realized how hard it was to distinguish between the people we were supposed to kill and the people we were supposed to protect." A bitter thread wove through his words. "Conflicts in the Middle East are . . . complicated, to put it in language suitable for polite company."

"But there was a particular incident that pushed you over the line, wasn't there?" Although Dana had no idea where that insight had come from, she knew it was true.

"Yeah. It happened on a recon mission, two years ago this month. Someone got wind of our presence and alerted the local villagers. They were waiting for us with all the firepower they could muster. One of them came rushing straight at me, his rifle aimed at my chest. I took him out. After the fight was over, we checked on the casualties. Turns out the guy gunning for me wasn't a guy after all. I'd shot a little boy who couldn't have been more than twelve." His voice cracked.

Squelching any lingering qualms, Dana followed her instincts and laid her hand over his knotted fist.

He dropped his gaze to her fingers. Drew a ragged breath. "Something in me snapped that night. I couldn't make sense of a war that asked me to kill children."

Pressure built in Dana's throat. Her own story might be traumatic, but it paled in comparison to the soul-wrenching choices this man had faced day in and day out.

A tear trailed down her cheek and dropped onto her jeans, leaving a dark splotch.

Finn lifted his chin and slowly removed his glasses, his eyes awash with pain—and remorse. "I'm sorry, Dana. I didn't mean to make you cry."

"No." She shook her head as she choked out the response. "Don't apologize. There aren't any words to express how much my heart aches for you. Maybe tears can communicate it better."

His own irises began to shimmer. "No one except my mother has ever cried for me."

Oh, mercy!

Another tear welled up and spilled out.

He reached over with an unsteady hand to brush it away, his fingertips lingering a moment longer than necessary against her skin.

Keep breathing, Dana.

The advice was sound—but hard to follow as they sat knee-to-knee in the gently rocking boat, under the spring sun on the diamond-sprinkled lake. The temptation to lean close . . . stroke his face . . . press her lips to his was fierce.

But that would be crazy. Despite the fact that emotions were running high, nerves were raw, and trauma was too close to the surface, they were just getting to know each other. Moving too fast would be a mistake. She needed to get a grip. Ramp things down. Restore some rationality to the situation.

Fast.

"So . . . are you doing okay now?" Her question came out shaky. "Aside from the incident at the Walleye, I mean?"

He grasped her hand and twined his fingers with hers when she tried to break the connection between them. "Better. The insomnia isn't as bad, the anxiety has diminished, I'm more social, and I rarely have an incident like today. I'm also off most of my meds and no longer have regular appointments with a shrink. Having a great family support system sped up the recovery process."

"And your leg?"

"Also improving. Not quite like new . . . but close enough. The only unresolved issue on my plate is what to do with the rest of my life. That's why I came down to the cabin. I needed some space, away from everything and everyone, to think."

"Has it helped?"

One side of his mouth lifted. "I haven't had as much solitude as I expected."

"Should I apologize for that?"

"No. Having you next door has been a plus—and I've had plenty of opportunity to think. My dad's been pushing for me to join his personal security firm, and I'm leaning that direction. He had a heart attack a couple of years ago and wants to cut back. Since my brothers went into law enforcement after they left the service—FBI agent and police detective—I'm his heir apparent."

"I expect your skills would be an asset in that kind of work."

"They would. And I like Atlanta. It wouldn't be a bad fit. I told him I'd let him know at the end of the month." He cocked his head. "Didn't you tell me you're in decision-making mode too?"

As he swung the spotlight to her, she tugged her fingers free and trailed them through the water. "Yes. But the longer I'm here, the more certain I am that I don't want to go back to the life I led in New York, where career was always front and center, the hours were long, and the pace was frenetic. I took a leave of absence after the . . ."

Uh-oh. It was way too easy to talk to this man. If she wasn't careful, she'd end up spilling her sad tale too.

She cleared her throat. "Anyway, my leave is winding down, and much as my bank account liked the steady paycheck and my ego liked the prestige, I don't think I'm going back. I can generate a decent income doing freelance editing."

"I hear you about getting tired of the rat race—but it sounds like there was also a precipitating incident."

Of course he'd picked up her slip. This man was trained to notice every detail. Lives had depended on his astute observation skills.

Besides, he'd heard her screaming in the middle of the night. He knew there was trauma in her past.

She shifted on the seat, setting the boat into a gentle rock, wishing now he'd left his sunglasses on. Those penetrating, perceptive eyes were difficult to avoid.

"Yes, there was . . . and it was one of those events that forces a person to step back and take inventory." Perhaps if she emphasized the aftereffects rather than the incident, he wouldn't push for details. "I realized that much as I loved my work, I didn't love big-city life with its smog and congestion, or living in a cramped one-bedroom apartment with exorbitant rent and no green space, or big-company politics that favored a chosen few and required a lot of game playing. I started thinking about my summers here, about how happy I'd been in this cottage, and decided this would be a perfect place to regroup."

He studied her, and she held her breath. She wasn't ready to talk about what had happened in

New York—but she was closer to sharing her trauma than she'd ever been . . . thanks to the man sitting across from her. One day soon, if he continued to come around, she had a feeling the story would come out.

But not today.

As if he'd read her mind, Finn set the oars back into position. "Shall we head for dry land? I don't want to be the one responsible for keeping you up till all hours tonight trying to meet your deadline."

She exhaled. "Yes. I think I've played hooky long enough."

He rowed them toward the cottage with strong, solid pulls on the oars, his muscles bunching and releasing with each stroke.

Once back at the dock, he secured the boat, then extended a hand back down to her. His grasp was firm and sure as he drew her up beside him.

When he loosened his grip, however, she held fast—startling both of them, based on the flicker of surprise that darted across his face and short-circuited her lungs.

Yet she couldn't let him walk away without acknowledging how profoundly moved she was by his willingness to share his painful history with her.

"I want to thank you for telling me your story." She removed her glasses too. "I work with words every day, but none come close to expressing how honored . . . and touched . . . I am." Her voice quivered, and she swallowed.

He held her gaze, his eyes warm and serene. "Thank you. I thought it would be hard, but you made it as easy as possible." Thunder rumbled again. Closer now. "Looks like we could be in for a storm."

Not trusting herself to speak, she nodded.

With one final squeeze of her fingers, he released them. "I'll stop by again in a day or two, if that's okay."

"Please."

"Count on it—and don't work too late." With that, he strode up the hill and around the cabin. Less than three minutes later, she heard the SUV engine come to life. Gravel crunched, the sound receding as he drove away.

Dana let out a slow sigh and wandered toward the house. Working late tonight was a given—but her book deadline wasn't what would keep her awake until the wee hours.

The blame for that rested squarely on the shoulders of an ex–Army Ranger who was fast making himself at home in her life . . . and her heart.

—8—

Know your enemy.

As Roger adjusted his black balaclava and shifted into a more comfortable position behind a clump of brush on Dana Lewis's property, the admonition from *The Art of War* flashed through his mind. Sun Tzu might have written the tome hundreds of years before Christ, but it had been studied by military strategists ever since. And the ancient general was right. To most effectively fight, you had to know your opponent.

A spurt of irritation surged through him as he trained his night-vision binoculars on the meth lab in the distance. The quiet, moon-washed Friday night was perfect for diving—the very thing he'd be doing if the scumbag who ran this illegal operation wasn't blackmailing him. But he needed to deal with this complication first.

On the plus side, IDing the guy shouldn't delay his diving plans too long. The size of the lab suggested the cooker was making and selling meth for profit, not just feeding his own habit. Otherwise, the one-pot shake-and-bake method would have sufficed—and required far less equipment and risk. This lab was a business. The guy no doubt employed smurfers to collect the raw material, and possibly a dealer to sell the product. There would be regular customers to satisfy and—

A rustle sounded, and Roger froze. An animal on the prowl—or his target?

More rustling.

Something . . . or someone . . . was on the prowl.

He swung his binoculars toward the disturbance. Detected movement. Picked up a shadowy figure.

It was human.

Pulse accelerating, he exchanged his binoculars for the police department's sophisticated digital camera and zoomed in. The images would be grainy, but with a little tinkering, they should contain sufficient detail to allow him to make an ID.

He located the backpack-toting hooded figure again. Followed his progress, willing him to step out of the shadows. Even a few moments in brighter light would produce shots with better clarity.

Fifteen seconds later, the figure separated from the trees fifty feet away and strode toward the lab.

Roger began snapping.

Before ducking inside, the cooker stopped, turned, and surveyed his surroundings. Then he unlocked the door and disappeared.

Roger lowered the camera, hoping his hands hadn't been shaking as badly while he'd been shooting as they were now. He needed to get home, download these photos, see if he knew his blackmailer.

And if he did, this guy wouldn't be the only one with pictures—and leverage.

"So am I off your call list or what? And how come you answered? Mac said you don't have cell service."

As Lance gave him an earful through the cell, Finn pulled into a parking space at the Walleye and set the brake. "You caught me on a trip to town—but I was going to call you today or tomorrow."

"Right."

"True."

"Whatever. All I know is every scrap of intel I've gotten up to this point is secondhand from Mac. I want to hear your version."

"Of what?" Finn grabbed his laptop off the seat beside him and opened his door.

"Your wilderness experience."

"I'm not in the wilderness."

"Is there a Starbucks anywhere close?"

"No."

"I rest my case. So how goes it?"

Finn slid out from behind the wheel and set the locks. "It's been . . . worthwhile."

"Yeah?"

"Yeah."

"Mac said you're socializing with the neighbors."

"Neighbor. Singular. I only have one. Since I can get cell reception at the lake over there, I'm trying to maintain cordial relations. It's a lot faster to run next door for phone calls than to drive into town."

"In that case, why make the trip to town at all?"

"The café here's not half bad, and it has Wi-Fi. I thought I'd catch up on email. How are things at the FBI?"

"Busy."

"How's Christy?"

"Busy."

"That must be why you're calling me on a Saturday. New wife unavailable?"

"She's at the rink with two skating students this morning—but you were on my call list in any case. So . . . everything else okay? You're not wigging out down there, are you?"

Lips twitching, Finn leaned back against the SUV and lifted his face to the blue sky, letting the spring sun warm his skin. "And to think they passed you by for the Most Tactful award senior year in high school. Go figure."

Silence.

"You're joking." Lance sounded surprised.

"No. I'm serious. You don't remember? Some kid named—"

"That's not what I meant. I meant, you're joking around. Mac said you sounded more like your old wisecracking self, but I didn't believe him."

"Mac never lies."

"He's been known to stretch the truth if it keeps someone he cares about from worrying. I'm glad this was on the level. You staying down there the full month?"

"That's the plan." No sense telling him he'd seriously considered bailing after the first couple of days. That was ancient history now.

"Well . . . whatever works. You talked to Mom and Dad since you been down there?"

"Yes. I'm going to touch base with them again before I head back to the cabin."

"Good. Maybe they'll stop calling us for updates—like we hear from you any more often than they do. What do you do with yourself every day, anyway?"

"I've got my PT routine, and there's always wood to chop. I brought books too."

Lance snorted. "Since when have you been a reader?"

"People can change."

"Uh-huh. You sure you're not bored?"

With Dana next door? No way.

"Nope."

"And you have everything you need? I could always do a supply run."

"I'm fine, Lance." He pushed off from the SUV. "I'll call you or Mac again in a few days—and thanks for checking in."

"Sure. Can't let the runt get himself into

trouble now that he's back on home turf. Stay cool."

"Will do." Finn broke the connection, slid the phone onto his belt, and crossed the crushed-stone parking lot to the café. Lance didn't exactly wear his emotions on his sleeve, but he knew his brother well enough to pick up the concern in his voice. And while he didn't want his family worrying about him, he had to admit—as he'd told Dana—that having them in his corner had made all the difference during his recovery.

The instant he stepped through the door, Hazel wiggled her fingers at him from across the room and wove through the tables. "Well, look who's back." She craned her neck to see past him. "Is Dana with you?"

"Not today."

The woman's face fell. "Next time, I hope. You here for breakfast?"

"Yes. Any recommendations?"

"Chuck makes Belgian waffles on Saturday. Light as a feather. Today's flavor is pecan—but he can do a plain one if you prefer. Some people think nuts are too fattening."

"I'll risk the calories and go with the pecans."

"I like a man who lives on the edge." She chuckled and gave him a nudge with her elbow. "Pick yourself out a table while I get you some coffee. The Saturday early birds get the best choice. In another hour, this place will be packed to the gills. Pardon the pun—but it's hard to resist when you work at a place called the Walleye." She grinned and hustled toward the coffee station.

Finn skimmed the diner and zeroed in on a private booth in the far corner, tucked in a small alcove away from the hustle and bustle of the main room. Once he claimed it, he booted up his laptop.

"Business or pleasure?" Hazel dipped her head toward the laptop as she deposited a mug of java on the table—black, just the way he liked it.

"A little of both."

"What's your line of work?"

"Security." Close enough. He'd done plenty of that in the military, and it was likely he'd end up doing it as a civilian too, if he joined his father's firm.

"Oh." She lowered her voice and cast a furtive glance over her shoulder. "Hush-hush stuff, huh?"

"A lot of it."

"Then I won't ask another question. You want me to order that waffle for you now, or wait a bit? It'll come up fast."

"Why don't you give me fifteen minutes to knock out a few emails and enjoy my coffee?"

"You got it. I'll catch your eye about then and you can wave at me if you're ready."

She moved off to greet some new arrivals, and Finn went to work on his email—not that many had come in over the past week. Three from his dad, all dangling interesting cases as bait to sway his decision to join the firm; two chatty ones from his mom, both ending with the assurance they wanted him to make his own career decision but reminding him how blessed they'd feel if he settled down in Atlanta; and a couple from military buddies.

Lucky the Walleye was an easy drive. It wouldn't have been worth the trip to Potosi to find Wi-Fi for these.

In less than the fifteen minutes he'd requested from Hazel, he was done and ready to order. But by then, the waitress was deep in conversation with two older women who'd claimed the booth he and Dana had occupied on their last visit.

Finn leaned back. Stretched. No hurry on his end. What else did he have to do—except maybe pay a visit to his neighbor later this afternoon?

As he waited to catch Hazel's eye, he took a sip of coffee and opened his browser. Dana hadn't said a lot about her publishing career in New York, but that senior editor title had been impressive. It sounded like a responsible, higher-level position. A quick search of the net might turn up a few details about her job. An old news release announcing a promotion, perhaps.

He typed in her name—and a bunch of hits popped up. One, from two years ago, was an item in *Publishers Weekly* about her advancement to the senior editor position.

But that wasn't the first hit . . . or the second . . . or the third.

The top hits were on a different subject altogether.

He skimmed the first headline, from a *New York Times* article dated three months ago.

Bank Robbery Foiled,
Armed Thieves Take Hostage

It was the first two paragraphs of the news item, however, that kept him riveted to the screen.

> A dramatic daylight robbery attempt yesterday at Smithfield Bank in Manhattan left one NYPD SWAT team member dead after two armed men took a hostage and tried to make off with twenty-five thousand dollars in cash. Both of the perpetrators were also killed.
>
> Police officer Carlos Perez, a fifteen-year veteran of the force, was fatally shot during the attempt to free hostage Dana Lewis, a publishing professional. Lewis was also injured during the rescue.

Finn sucked in a sharp breath.

Someone had taken Dana hostage.

At gunpoint.

No wonder she woke up screaming in the middle of the night—and slept with all the lights on.

Finn read the rest of the article. It described the robbery and rescue, provided background on the two thieves and the slain police officer, quoted bank and police officials—but offered no additional information about Dana.

He moved on to the other articles about the robbery. No more mentions of Dana.

"Can I interrupt?"

At Hazel's question, Finn quickly lowered his laptop screen. "Sure."

"I've been waiting for your high sign, but I thought I better come over. We passed the fifteen-minute mark a while back. You sure were caught up in whatever you were doing."

"Just email—and some research."

"Security business, I bet." She reduced her volume. "I noticed how you picked this out-of-the-way booth . . . and you closed that up real fast when I walked over." She dipped her chin toward the laptop. "You don't work for the government, do you?"

"Not anymore."

"Ah. One of those private contractors with a high-level security clearance, I bet. I've seen TV shows about stuff like that. Well, my lips are sealed. Your secret is safe with me."

Finn let that pass. If the woman wanted to make assumptions, why correct her? This way she wouldn't ask too many personal questions. "I think I'm ready for that waffle now."

"Coming right up." She scribbled on the orde pad and stuck the pen into her beehive hairdo i the vicinity of her ear. "Now I'll let you get bac to whatever you were doing." With a conspira torial wink, she took off for the kitchen.

Finn lifted the screen of his laptop agair Tapped a finger against the edge of the keyboarc Powered down.

Dana would *not* appreciate him snooping int her business—but how could he have known simple search for career information would lea to this?

And what was he supposed to do now that he' stumbled onto a minefield?

Tell her you know, McGregor. It's the hones thing to do.

True. Coming clean would be the honorabl course.

But what if she accused him of prying and tol him to get lost?

His stomach bottomed out at that very rea possibility. Everything he'd read might be publi information . . . but if she'd wanted to share al that stuff with him, she would have. It was goin to look like he'd been sneaking around behin her back.

Sighing, Finn shoved his laptop aside, makin space for the breakfast he no longer wanted.

Why did life always have to be complicated?

Rhetorical question aside, before this day wa

over he was going to have to decide on a plan of action with Dana . . . and pray that if he took the high road and spilled what he'd learned, she'd cut him some slack instead of cutting him off.

Wayne Phelps?!

Roger leaned closer to the screen and squinted at the photo. Only three of the shots he'd taken last night were clear enough without sophisticated enhancement to discern the shadowed features under the man's hood, and this grainy image was the best of the bunch.

Yet there was no question about the identity of his blackmailer.

Slumping back in his chair, he kneaded the knot at the back of his neck.

Why on earth would Wayne Phelps be involved in a dirty business like this? His family had lived in Beaumont for generations, and all of his relations had been upstanding folks. Sure, Wayne had faced some setbacks a few years ago when the smelter closed and he lost his job, but he'd done okay. Better than most of the other folks who'd found themselves out of work. That market garden of his brought in top dollar at those hoity-toity gourmet food stores in the city, where people were willing to pay an arm and a leg for organic, natural stuff.

What had possessed him to go over to the dark side?

And now that he had a name, what was he going to do about it?

Stomach twisting, Roger pushed himself to his feet and grasped his middle. Maybe some food would help . . . though nothing much coaxed the pain to go away these days. Not even the antacids he chugged. Chronic stress could tear a man's insides to pieces.

But until he found that gold—and decided how he was going to deal with Wayne and his meth lab—there wasn't much chance his stress level was going to diminish one iota.

"Would you like a visitor?"

At the familiar voice, Dana sat back on her heels beside Mags's overgrown perennial garden, angled toward the lake, and shaded her eyes.

"I took the shortcut." Finn waved toward the woods but remained by the dock . . . waiting for an invitation to join her, perhaps?

She pulled off her garden gloves and stood. "Come on up. I was just getting ready to take a break."

As he ascended the small incline, she brushed off the knees of her jeans, tugged down her sweatshirt—and reminded her heart to behave. Thank goodness she'd had the foresight to put on some makeup.

Finn stopped a few feet away, surveying the ground at her feet. "Is that a garden?"

"Used to be. My grandmother planted it years ago. Pops kept up with it until his health declined. Pathetic, isn't it?" She inspected the weed-infested five-by-ten-foot patch. The irises were valiantly trying to poke through the tangle of noxious interlopers, and a few hardy phlox had triumphed on one end. But even the stone border had been overgrown in spots by rampaging weeds.

"Nothing some elbow grease won't fix. Could you use another pair of elbows?"

A flush of pleasure warmed her. "You don't have to work every time you stop by."

"I like being busy. I'm not used to sitting around." He toed a hand trowel at her feet. "Do you have any more garden tools?"

"Yes. In the shed where the rowboat was stored. I was about to go get a small spade. Some of these dandelion roots are deep. You want to sit for a while first, have some lemonade and cookies after your trek over?"

"Not unless you do. The snack will taste better if I invest some sweat equity."

"Fine by me. I never turn down free labor."

"I'll be back in three minutes, equipped to dig."

Once he was out of sight, Dana smiled and knelt back down. It didn't get much better than spending a beautiful spring day in the garden—especially if a handsome man was by your side.

It took Finn more like five minutes to collect the tools he wanted. He set them on the ground and gave the garden another once-over. "What would you like me to do?"

"How much do you know about flowers?"

"My mom always had a garden, and as the youngest, I often got recruited to help when my brothers bailed. So I know more than they do." He gave her a crooked grin. "Which, to be honest, isn't saying much."

She motioned toward the irises. "See those spiky leaves coming up over there?"

"Yeah."

"They're flowers. Anything else in that section is a weed and needs to be yanked."

"Got it."

He dropped down a few feet away from her and went to work.

Over the next twenty minutes, as they focused on their tasks, Dana gave her volunteer a few surreptitious peeks. The faint furrows on his brow suggested he was concentrating on distinguishing weeds from iris . . . or did he have more serious concerns on his mind?

A ripple of unease told her it was the latter. Something was up with the subdued man beside her.

Trowel in hand, she attacked the roots of a stubborn cedar sapling that had sprouted amid the daisies. Had he come to kiss her off? Tell her it had been nice meeting her, but he needed more time alone . . . or was cutting his stay short . . .

or didn't think they had all that much in common?

Perhaps she ought to initiate a conversation and see if she could ferret out whatever was troubling him.

"So . . ." *Keep it conversational, Dana.* "Did you do anything interesting this morning?"

Out of the corner of her eye, she caught his almost indiscernible pause as he worked to free a captive iris. "I had breakfast at the Walleye, answered email, and touched base with one of my brothers. What about you? Did you meet your deadline?"

"Yes. I was ready for the UPS truck bright and early this morning." She stifled her irrational disappointment at being left out of his trip to town. The man was under no obligation to invite her to accompany him for another meal at the café. Hadn't she told him she was content being here at the cabin? "But I'm paying the price today for my late night."

"How late?"

"After midnight." Thanks to disruptive thoughts about her companion, not the volume of work.

"Long day."

"I've had longer."

Silence.

Man, he was *not* in a talkative mood today.

She renewed her attack on the cedar, until it at last gave up the fight and relinquished its hold on the garden.

"Success." She held up the sapling.

He inspected it. "Those have deep roots."

"Yeah." She set her trowel down. If he wasn't going to talk while they gardened, he might be more inclined to converse over a glass of lemonade. "Are you ready for those cookies?"

"Anytime you are."

"Those rockers have our names on them." She motioned toward the porch and stood. "Meet you there in five."

"It's a date." His lighthearted tone sounded forced.

Once inside, she corralled the butterflies in her stomach as she filled two glasses with lemonade, arranged some cookies on a plate, and grabbed several napkins. There was no better place for a heart-to-heart than on the porch of the cabin. She and Pops had spent many a twilight evening there talking about the important stuff in life. If Finn didn't open up out there, it was a lost cause.

He was waiting as she pushed through the door, leaning against the rail, his back to the lake. Taking the tray from her, he stepped aside to let her precede him to the rockers. She moved the pot of geraniums to the floor, and he set the tray on top of the small table between the chairs.

"Those don't look store-bought." Finn eyed the cookies.

"They're not. Those are my grandmother's chocolate chunk pecan cookies, which were a staple at the cabin and one of the few recipes of hers I still make on a regular basis—when I'm not eating Oreos." She smiled. "I have no idea how many of those I've ingested through the years . . . nor do I want to know. Some questions are better left unexplored."

His mouth flattened, and a muscle flicked in his jaw.

The man was seriously stressed.

Could this odd mood somehow be related to his PTSD?

The only way to find out was to ask—and accept the consequences. She couldn't just sit here and ignore the tension emanating from him.

Angling toward him, she spoke quietly. "Do you want to talk about it?"

His head jerked toward her. "What do you mean?"

She handed him a napkin. Picked up one for herself as she formulated her response. "I don't mean to intrude on your personal space, but I can tell you're worried. Is there a family problem?"

"No." He folded his napkin in half. Pressed the crease. "This is about you."

She blinked. "Me?"

He gripped the arm of his chair, his troubled gaze capturing hers. "I know about the bank robbery in New York, Dana."

Her lungs froze, and the world around her went silent.

"I took my laptop to the Walleye this morning to check email. That didn't take as long as I expected, and while I was waiting to place my order, I googled you." He leaned closer, his posture taut. "I was only trying to find some career background. Senior editor at age thirty sounded impressive. I had a feeling you'd downplayed your accomplishments, and I wanted to know more. I had no idea those news stories would pop up when I typed in your name."

"How much do . . . do you know?" Her hollow words seemed to come from a distance. As if someone else was talking.

"Very little. The stories were short on detail where you were concerned. All I know is you were taken hostage and injured during the rescue."

Dana looked down at the cookies. A fly had landed on one, tainting the sweet treat—just like talking about her experience in New York here, in her special haven, tainted the one place where life had always been happy and safe and unblemished.

"There's a lot more to the story."

"I thought there might be." Finn reached across the table, chasing away the fly before touching her arm. "Sometimes it helps to talk about difficult periods in our lives. I speak from experience on that score—thanks to you."

She shifted her attention to his strong, lean fingers. Through the fabric of her sweatshirt, she could feel the warmth of his hand.

His offer was tempting. Bottling everything up inside wasn't healthy, and despite their short acquaintance she trusted this man. Besides, like it or not, Pops's place was already tainted by her memories. Why else would she wake up screaming in the room that had always been her refuge? Why else would she leave every light on at night while she slept? Why else had she had new locks installed on all the doors after she arrived?

Yet putting everything into words as Finn had about his traumatic experience overseas . . . that took a lot of guts.

Somehow, he'd managed to summon up the courage to bare his soul.

But could she do the same?

—9—

Finn squirmed as he read the emotions tumbling across Dana's face—shock . . . distress . . . disappointment.

She was going to toss him out on his ear.

"How much do you . . . did you read?" Her expression was wary as she balled her napkin in her fingers.

Tempted as he was to lie, he stuck to the truth. "Too much. I could have stopped as soon as I saw your name mentioned in the first article about the robbery. *Should* have stopped. If you'd wante me to know about it, you would have shared you story. I'm sorry I didn't wait and give you th chance to tell me on your own, if you chose to."

She gazed out over the lake. Exhaled. "Th funny thing is, I was considering doing exactl that."

But now I'm glad I didn't.

She didn't have to say the words for him to hea the caveat. She'd trusted him up to this point, tol him a lot of personal information about he family and her summers here at the cabin. Bu unless he did some fast damage control, dug dee and found the words to express feelings he didn yet fully understand, she was going to shut down

And he did *not* want that to happen.

"Dana." He leaned over the platter of cookie that separated them and touched her arm again.

She stiffened but turned toward him.

"I didn't intend to pry. Please believe that. Bu once I saw your name, once I got the gist of th story, I couldn't stop reading, because . . . I car about you. I've watched you struggle to see Sensed the fear lurking just below the surface Heard you scream in the middle of the night. knew something bad had happened, and I wante to understand so I could try to help. I know how hard it is to get past trauma." He pausec Swallowed. *Just spit it out, McGregor.* "The trutl is, despite our short acquaintance, you've becom very special to me. More special than any woman I've ever met."

He heard her breath hitch. Watched as a pulse began to throb in the hollow of her throat. Felt her tremble beneath his fingertips.

"It's too soon for . . . to say stuff like that."

"Maybe. But when something feels right, there's no sense dancing around the truth. And this feels right—on my end, at least."

She caught her lower lip between her teeth. Brushed back a few stray, breeze-tossed strands of hair that had escaped her ponytail. Whispered her response. "It feels right to me too."

Lightness filled him, as effervescent—and heady—as bubbles in a glass of champagne.

And that's when it hit him, the impact as potent and earth-shaking as the shock wave from an IED explosion.

Dana could be The One.

Yet even as he tried to wrap his mind around that blinding insight, he knew one thing with absolute certainty: it was far too early to put that into words.

Ignoring the giddy buzz in his nerve endings, he squeezed her arm. "That's good to know. Does that also mean you'll forgive me for prying?"

"Can I be honest? In your place, I have a feeling I'd have done the same thing."

"I don't know if I buy that. You strike me as a very disciplined person."

"And an Army Ranger isn't?"

"About most things. You aren't one of them."

She swallowed. "In light of that admission . . . would you like to know my side of what happened at that bank?"

Absolutely! Every detail.

But he tempered that response.

"If you'd like to tell me. But hang on a minute." He rose, picked up his rocker, and set it beside her chair. Then he folded her cold fingers in his and gave her his full attention. "Whenever you're ready."

She leaned back and looked at the blue sky where a hawk she probably couldn't see circled overhead, drifting to and fro at the whim of the air currents.

"It started off as a normal day. A busy morning with typical, routine tasks at work. On my lunch hour, I ran out to the bank to cash a check. After I'd taken care of my business and was walking back down the street, I heard someone shout. There are lots of shouts on New York streets, but this one was different. More like a barked order, though I couldn't make out the words." She groped for her lemonade. Almost knocked it over.

"Here. Let me." Finn leaned past her and picked it up, pressing the glass into her hand.

She took a long drink, then rested the tumbler on her jeans-clad leg. "Turns out an off-duty police officer had spotted the robbers and was chasing them on foot. I didn't know that at the time. All I knew was that two guys wearing ski masks were bearing down on me. I tried to move out of their way, but one of them grabbed me. He had a g-gun."

Finn's stomach contracted, and he squeezed her fingers.

When she picked up the story, her words were shakier. "He said he'd shoot me if I resisted. They ducked into the lobby of an office building a few doors away. A security guard approached them, and they fired at him as they headed for the mezzanine. The place cleared out fast after that and the building went into lockdown. The guard disabled the elevators, and there was no way off the mezzanine except through the lobby."

Finn's jaw tightened. In a desperate scenario like that, the situation often went south very, very fast.

Dana could have been killed.

He tried to push that stomach-churning thought aside as she continued.

"Once emergency vehicles began to arrive, the robbers knew they were trapped—and that I was their only bargaining chip. So they called 911 on their cell. A hostage negotiator called back in five minutes. They demanded a car and safe exit in exchange for my l-life."

Her voice hitched, and Finn stroked his thumb over the back of her hand in a soothing, rhythmic pattern.

"I knew I might d-die." Beads of sweat broke out above Dana's upper lip, despite the mild spring temperature. "The two guys didn't sound all that balanced—nor were they in agreement about how to proceed, especially when the negotiator didn't come through fast enough to suit them. Accusations were thrown back and forth. Tempers flared. I began to think they might be high . . . and that scared me even more. People on drugs aren't rational."

Neither were robbers who thought they could pull off a daylight robbery in Manhattan, doped up or not—but Finn left that unsaid.

"I assumed the police were hatching some sort of rescue plan, but I also knew there was a good chance these guys would crack before it could be implemented—or if not, that I could get caught in the cross fire once the police rushed in. In light of all that, I decided to take the first opportunity I got to break free. They weren't paying all that much attention to me anyway, since they were blocking the stairway they assumed was my only way out."

But it wasn't.

I got hurt in a fall.

As Dana's explanation of her concussion from earlier in the week echoed in his mind, he curled the fingers of his free hand. "You jumped from the mezzanine, didn't you?"

"Yes. It was about t-twenty feet high. I knew I'd

be injured . . . but I decided injured was better than d-dead."

Except she could have died from that fall as easily as she could have died from a gunshot.

"Is that how you escaped?"

"Partly." Her throat worked, and a shiver rolled through her. "The police were monitoring the lobby from the security camera feed, and once they saw me jump, the SWAT team went into action—before they'd planned to. I managed to roll under the mezzanine, out of the line of fire, but one of the robbers got off a shot. A SWAT team member died."

"I read that part." Finn continued to stroke her hand.

She lifted the glass of lemonade from her leg and stared at the dark round spot the condensation had left on her jeans.

It looked like blood.

The ice in her glass began to rattle, and she set the tumbler back on the table. "The whole experience was t-terrifying. But the ongoing nightmares are almost worse. They force me to relive every awful moment. No matter how hard I try, I can't shake the m-memories—or the guilt."

Finn frowned. "Why should you feel guilty?"

She turned to him, her hazel eyes anguished. "Because I keep thinking that if I'd w-waited for the SWAT team to make its move instead of forcing their hand, that police officer might not have d-died."

Without a word, he stood and pulled her into his arms. "You can't blame yourself for being proactive, Dana. You assessed the risk based on what you observed and took action that seemed appropriate under the circumstances. That's the same technique I used every day as a Ranger. Don't beat yourself up about that. If you'd stayed where you were, you might not have survived—and that SWAT team member could still have been killed."

A muffled sob shuddered against his chest. "That's what I keep telling myself . . . but I can't shake the feeling that if I'd waited, he might be alive today."

Finn stroked her back, searching for words of comfort. They hadn't ever talked about faith, but based on what he'd learned about her, he had a feeling hers was strong. "Have you tried praying about it?"

"Yes . . . but there are days God feels far away."

"Yeah. I know what you mean." Not an admission he'd make to most people—neither the fact that he talked to God nor that the attempt to connect wasn't always successful. The subject was too personal. Yet he'd had no difficulty sharing it with Dana.

One more sign she was special.

"Really?" She eased back to search his face. "I didn't peg you as a praying kind of guy."

He lifted one shoulder. "I was raised in a faith-centered home. I can't say I've been diligent in recent years about communicating with the Almighty, but I've been bending his ear a lot since the accident. I agree with you, though—he's not always easy to hear."

"That's where trust comes in, I guess. You just have to keep believing he's there, watching and listening."

"True. But sometimes it's also helpful to talk to a person you can see—assuming it's the right person." He locked gazes with her, willing her to understand more than he was ready to put into words.

"I agree." Her response came out in a whoosh of breath. "As a matter of fact, since you . . . since we met, my nightmares have gone away."

"Mine too."

She swayed toward him a fraction, the movement so subtle he doubted she was aware of her unconscious invitation.

He, by contrast, was super aware—and a powerful urge to lean down and claim her lips swept over him.

But she wasn't ready for that. Nor was he. When he kissed Dana—and it was definitely a matter of when, not if—he wanted the moment unencumbered by the trauma of their pasts.

However—if she stayed in his arms three more seconds, it was going to happen now. Ready or not.

Summoning up every scrap of his willpower, he gave her a final squeeze and stepped back. “We better have our snack or the flies will take over.”

She blinked, and her expression morphed from yearning to puzzled to wary. “Yes. We should do that.” She turned away.

Great job, McGregor. The lady pours out her heart, and you bring up food. Real sensitive.

“Dana.” He touched her arm, and she sent a cautious look over her shoulder.

His pulse began to pound. All his life he’d played his cards close to his vest with women. It was too easy to create unrealistic expectations, fuel false hopes, get finagled into unwanted commitments. As a result, his rules had always been simple: choose your words with care, stay in the moment, keep the atmosphere light, make no promises.

Trouble was, he’d already broken most of those with Dana.

Might as well break the last one.

“Look . . . if I’d followed my instincts a minute ago, I’d be kissing you. With any other woman, I wouldn’t have hesitated. But I don’t want to risk derailing this by rushing you. Nor do I intend to do anything that could possibly hurt you. That’s a promise you can count on.”

She let out a slow breath. "Thanks for telling me that. And for caring about protecting me. It kind of goes with that hero-to-the-rescue image you established the first night."

"As long as you don't expect me to wear a white hat."

"I was thinking more along the lines of armor and a white charger."

His mouth quirked. "Not my style, either. This is more my speed." He waved a hand over his jeans and T-shirt.

"Works for me. Ready for that snack now?"

"Yes."

He sat back in the rocker he'd placed beside hers, and the conversation shifted to innocuous topics while they ate their cookies, finished up for the day in the garden, and said their good-byes.

"Thanks for all your help. Mags would be pleased." Dana wiped her hands on her jeans and surveyed the plot of ground, where two-thirds of the flowers now swayed unfettered in the spring breeze.

"There's more work to be done."

"But we made great progress."

"I could come back tomorrow to help you finish up."

"I'd like that." She transferred her weight from one foot to the other and scrubbed at a streak of dirt on the back of her hand. "As long as you brought up God . . . do you have any interest in attending services in town? I haven't been able to get there, and I've missed it. You'd like the church; the congregation is very welcoming, and the pastor gives a great sermon. He's been there for years."

Finn hesitated. While he *was* talking to God again, he hadn't set foot in a church since his last trip to Atlanta to visit the folks.

But maybe it was time to get back into that habit too.

"Sounds like a plan. When should I pick you up?"

She smiled up at him. "The service is at ten . . . does twenty till work?"

"I'll be here." He bent to collect the garden tools.

"Let me do that." She restrained him with a hand on his arm. "You've more than earned those cookies I fed you."

"You sure?"

"Yes. Go home and have a nice, relaxing evening."

"I'll try." He gave a mock salute and headed for the path through the woods, determined to do his best to abide by that promise.

But truth be told, no matter how hard he tried, his evening would be a lot nicer if he could spend it with the girl next door.

"Roger?"

As the sweet, familiar voice he'd loved for more

than thirty-five years drifted toward him from a distance, Roger sighed, savoring the tender, gentle lilt he missed with an ache that never went away.

"Rog, honey . . . are you asleep?" A hand came to rest on his shoulder.

He furrowed his brow. This *was* a dream, wasn't it?

No.

He was sitting upright, not lying in bed.

As consciousness fought its way back through a cloaking fog of fatigue, he struggled to orient himself. After stopping at the office for his standard Saturday morning check-in, he'd driven to Potosi. Once in Leah's room, he'd sat in the recliner while she slept—and promptly fallen into a heavy slumber himself. No surprise there, given his sleepless nights of late.

But the hand on his shoulder was real—and when he opened his eyes, he *was* surprised.

Leah was standing beside him. The *real* Leah, not the shrew who had taken over her body. Her eyes were soft and warm and loving, just as he remembered them.

Gratitude welled up inside him, tightening his throat.

Lord, thank you for this interlude of lucidity, no matter how brief. You know these rare moments are what keep me going—and I appreciate every one.

"Good morning, sweetheart." He pushed himself to his feet and wrapped her in his arms, relishing every millisecond of the hug she gave him in return.

As they held each other, the soft music playing in the background suddenly registered.

It was their song. The one they'd danced to at their wedding.

"Longer" by Dan Fogelberg.

He glanced toward the small CD player on the nightstand, the one he'd brought months ago after reading that favorite music could trigger episodes of clarity. It had worked in the beginning . . . but for weeks, the player had been silent. Why she'd fiddled with it this morning, and why that song had come up on the CD he'd burned, was one of life's small miracles.

When she at last pulled back, concern creased her forehead. "You look tired, honey. Are you having trouble sleeping? Are there problems at work? Are you worried about me?"

Yes to all of the above.

"It's been busy, that's all. Would you like to take a walk with me in the garden? All the spring flowers are coming up—and the daffodils are blooming."

"That would be lovely."

"Let me get your robe."

He retrieved it from the closet, guided her arms inside, and fastened it down the front.

She stroked his cheek as he fumbled with the

buttons. “You’re a good man, Roger Burnett. Through all these years, you’ve taken wonderful care of me. I’m sorry to be such a burden to you now.”

“You’re not a burden, Leah. Don’t ever think that. I love you. Always have. Always will.” His voice rasped, and he swallowed.

“I love you too.” She smiled, a teasing light adding a sparkle to her eyes. “And my father said it would never last.” She tucked her hand in his arm.

Once more his throat clogged. Oh, how he’d missed these small exchanges of shared history and humor!

He led her outside, where the well-tended gardens were in full spring display, pointing out all her favorite flowers as they walked.

They strolled for ten glorious minutes before he picked up the familiar, subtle tension in her posture that intensified with each step.

He was losing her.

And no matter how desperately he wanted to hold on to her, to make her remember him, there was nothing he could do to stop her free fall back into oblivion.

As moisture clouded his vision, he guided her back toward the facility.

By the time they reached the door, his loving wife had slipped away.

Yanking her hand from his arm, Leah peered at

him through glazed, confused eyes. "Why are you taking me into this place? That isn't where I live. I want to go home."

He opened the door and signaled to an aide. "It's too cool out here, sweetheart. I don't want you to catch a chill."

"You're keeping me here, aren't you?" She backed away from him. "You get away from me!"

The staff member he'd beckoned edged past him and approached Leah, another aide on her heels. As the two women tried to calm his wife, he retreated inside. Leaned against the wall. Choked back a sob. He needed to leave. Seeing him again would only agitate her further.

Pulling out his keys, he trudged toward the exit, blocking out the image of the shrieking woman he'd left, recalling instead the feel of his wife's hand in his, her caring eyes, her tender voice. That was the woman he loved. The woman he intended to take care of, as he'd promised long ago. He wasn't going to let her down.

Meaning tonight he was going diving.

—10—

As the final organ notes of the closing hymn reverberated through the small church in Beaumont, Dana risked a peek at her companion. In his dress shirt and slacks, the morning sun streaming through the windows behind him setting off glints in his auburn hair, Finn could be a hero from the cover of one of the romance novels she edited.

On top of that, the man could sing. He'd joined in on every hymn, and his resonant baritone had drawn more than a few admiring glances.

As if sensing her scrutiny, he looked down. "Shall we?" He gestured to the crowd surging toward the back of the church.

Taking his cue, she edged into the aisle. He joined her—and the proprietary hand he placed in the small of her back sent a thrill zipping through her. How ridiculous was that? His touch was nothing more than a simple courtesy his mother had probably taught him as a teen that had become an ingrained habit. There was nothing personal about it.

Yet the warmth of his fingers seeping through her silk blouse was playing havoc with her respiration—and no matter how hard she tried to rein in the delicious tingle in her spine, it refused to be subdued.

Once they shook hands with the minister at the door, Hazel waved them over from a small cluster of people under a redbud tree in full bloom.

"You game?" Finn hesitated, letting her make the call.

"Yes. I've been wanting to talk to Chief Burnett

since Hazel told us about his wife, and he's in that group."

They picked up their pace again, and Hazel reached for her as they drew close. "It's good to see you again, Dana." The waitress dispensed a hearty hug. "And your friend too." She beamed at Finn.

"Thanks. I'm glad I was able to get to church this week." Dana surveyed the group of six. There were a couple of new faces, but most were familiar from past trips—including the chief of police, who took her hand as she greeted him.

He returned her smile, but the weariness in his demeanor didn't dissipate. "I heard you were back in town. Are you comfortable by yourself out at the cabin? It's kind of isolated."

"I'm fine." She kept her own smile pasted in place as she surveyed him. She'd noticed his weight loss from a distance last week at the café, but up close the man's pallor was alarming, as were the dark shadows under his lower lashes and the network of deep lines etched around his mouth. "And I have a very nice neighbor who volunteered to be my chauffeur today." She motioned to Finn as she did the introductions.

After the two men shook hands, the police chief angled toward her while the rest of the group carried on a separate conversation. "I want to offer you my sympathy on your loss. Leo was a great guy—and a first-class fishing buddy. He'll be missed around here."

"Thank you. I think his happiest spot on earth was sitting in a boat in the middle of his lake . . . and I know he enjoyed the hours he spent fishing with you." She laid her hand on his arm. "Hazel told me about your wife. I'm so sorry to hear about her illness. I can't begin to imagine how difficult it must be—for both of you."

His Adam's apple bobbed. "It's been a challenge, no question about it." He shifted toward Finn. "How long will you be staying in Beaumont?"

Obviously the man didn't want to dwell on personal topics.

"About three more weeks."

"Where do you call home?"

Finn hesitated. "For the past few months, St. Louis. But I'll be moving on soon."

"We'll be seeing more of you before you leave, I hope." Hazel rejoined the conversation.

"Oh, I expect I'll work in a few more trips to the Walleye. The food's great, and the service is excellent."

"Such a flatterer." She waved him off, but her cheeks pinkened. "You bring your neighbor with you next visit. She needs to get out once in a while." Hazel turned to the police chief. "Dana's been having some eye issues, so she's not driving."

"Nothing serious, I hope."

"Not anymore. My vision is improving every day. I'll be back behind the wheel soon."

"Glad to hear that. I imagine an impediment like that could put a serious crimp in your activities."

"It has until now. But I'm about ready to wander a bit farther afield—on the property, at least. I used to like to hike around Pops's land."

"You might want to wait until you're fully recovered to tackle a hike." Creases appeared above the chief's nose as his gaze flicked to a thirtyish man standing nearby, whose attention was on the screen of his cell. He was vaguely familiar, but no name came to Dana's mind. "You could trip and fall, or get disoriented. Leo owns a fair amount of property, and you might stray onto national forest land. Once you do that, it would be easy to get lost."

"Believe me, I don't intend to take chances . . . or go alone." She sent Finn a smile.

Her reply didn't seem to reassure the chief. In fact, if anything he appeared to be *more* worried. "Well . . . use caution. There's plenty to enjoy on Leo's property without venturing far from the cabin or lake."

As another member of the congregation stopped to chat with the chief, Dana stepped back and angled toward Finn. "Ready to hit the road?"

"Yes. We have a garden to finish."

"You still up for that?"

"Are there any of those great cookies left?"

"Yes."

"Then I'm up for it. Let's go."

Once again, his hand came to rest in the small of her back as they wove through the clusters of people on the church lawn. And once again, her heart gave a happy skip.

Yet as they drove back to her place and he dropped her off with a promise to return as soon as he changed into his work clothes, Dana sternly reminded herself not to get carried away. Finn had been clear on more than one occasion that his stay here was short. A job was waiting for him in Atlanta, and if he decided to pass on that one, there would be countless other opportunities for a man with his skills. He wasn't going to hang around Beaumont long enough for anything serious to develop, no matter how much electricity was zipping between them.

Those were the facts.

Of course, a long-distance courtship was possible—*if* Finn was interested in pursuing one—but those relationships often fell apart. Absence typically didn't make the heart grow fonder, no matter what the novels said.

On the flip side, rushing would also be a mistake.

Still . . . as many of the happy-ending books she edited pointed out, nothing could keep two people apart if they were supposed to end up together.

She'd just have to put her trust in God and hope for the best.

But in the meantime, she had two and a half more weeks to get to know her ex–Army Ranger neighbor—and she intended to make the most of them.

Exhaling a slow, contented breath, Finn propped his feet on the back porch railing of his cabin and wrapped his fingers around a mug of high-octane coffee.

Yesterday had been as close to perfect as any day in his life had been since his world collapsed overseas. Church in the morning—with a beautiful woman by his side. Working outdoors, under a warm spring sun—with a beautiful woman by his side. An impromptu dinner of chips and hot dogs on the dock—with a beautiful woman by his side.

It didn't get much better than that.

Well . . . actually, it did. There was a nicer way to end an evening with a beautiful woman than exchanging smiles and simple good-byes . . . but it was too soon to be thinking along those lines with Dana.

Down the road, however . . . a distinct possibility.

Stretching, he checked his watch and shook his head. When had he last slept in until ten in the morning? Too long to remember, after rising at dawn for years and being wired to wake at the slightest noise. Eleven hours of sound, nightmare-free slumber had been exactly what the doctor ordered.

He could get used to this.

Especially with a great-looking neighbor a short hike away.

He took a sip of his coffee. Too bad she had to work today. He was in the mood for a lazy row around the lake. Maybe he could convince her to take a break around noon—or better yet, join him for a moonlight spin across the water.

In the interim, he had PT to do, a loose hinge to fix on the door, and a book to read.

Two hours later, as he tested the repaired hinge, the sound of tires crushing rocks alerted him to approaching company.

Uninvited company.

Letting the door swing shut behind him, he strode toward his room to retrieve his compact Beretta. Not much chance someone with nefarious intent would blatantly announce his arrival . . . but in an isolated place like this, it never hurt to be prepared for trouble.

Pistol in hand, he watched from inside the window as a black Chevy Cruze with dark-tinted windows rolled up the drive.

Was that Lance's FBI duty car?

But what would his brother be doing down here at noon on a Monday?

Sixty seconds later, the car stopped and Lance emerged from behind the wheel.

Five seconds after that, Mac slid out of the passenger seat, toting a white bag.

Both of his brothers had come to call on a workday?

Pulse accelerating, he pushed through the door as they walked across the gravel toward the cabin. There would be no reason for them to show up together on a weekday unless they'd come to deliver bad news.

"Is Dad okay?"

Lance and Mac froze, both of them eying the Beretta in his hand.

"What's with the gun?" Lance's focus remained riveted on the weapon.

"Dad's fine. Mom is too." Mac shifted his attention to their middle brother. "Wouldn't you be packing too, if you were living in the middle of nowhere?"

"I guess. You want to put that away now?" Lance gestured to the Beretta.

Finn let out the breath he'd been holding and stuck the Beretta in his pocket. "If the folks are okay, why are you guys here instead of working?"

"I *am* working. I need to meet our agent in Rolla, and Mac came along for the ride." Lance elbowed the eldest McGregor sibling.

"I worked a double homicide all weekend.

Comp time." Mac lifted the white bag. "We come bearing gifts."

"Why?"

"Because we like you." Lance smirked at him.

"Besides that, we thought after more than a week here all by yourself, you might be ready for some company other than squirrels, raccoons, and deer. Plus we have Ted Drewes." Mac dangled the bag again.

"You brought me a concrete?" Finn's salivary glands kicked into high gear as he inspected the bag.

"Only the world's best frozen custard for the runt. You going to ask us in?" Lance nodded toward the cabin.

"Yeah. Sure." He opened the door.

His brothers filed past him, their large frames dominating the kitchen in the small, two-bedroom cabin.

"Not bad, if you like rustic." Lance poked his head into one of the bedrooms.

"It suits me."

"If we don't eat these soon, we'll have to drink them." Mac plopped the bag on the table and uncrimped the top. "They put some dry ice in here, but we've been on the road awhile." He sat and pulled out four lidded containers, four spoons, and a handful of napkins.

"Why'd you bring four?" Finn took a seat at the small table.

Lance joined them, backing up a chair fo
legroom. "Mac thought your favorite was straw
berry. I voted for mint chocolate chip. Since w
couldn't come to a consensus, we brought one o
each."

"I like them both."

"Good. Pick one for now and put the other i
the freezer for later." Mac popped off the lid o
his custard. Blueberry, naturally.

Lance opened his. The usual butterscotch.

His brothers were nothing if not predictable—i
some things, anyway.

Finn stashed the chocolate chip for late
consumption and opened his strawberry as h
retook his seat. No sense beating around the bush
"So do I pass?"

Lance slanted a glance at Mac and kept eating.

"What do you mean?" Mac dug his spoon int
the blueberry concrete, avoiding eye contact.

"Oh, come on. You guys came down to check u
on me. And you know what? I'm cool with that. I
you want the truth, it kind of warms my heart."

"Warms your heart?" Spoon poised in midair
Lance gaped at him. "Is that on the level?"

"Yeah."

"I told you he wouldn't be upset." Mac dive
into his concrete, eating with gusto.

Lance squinted at him. "What have you bee
doing down here, getting in touch with you
feminine side?"

"Hey . . . it's okay to have feelings. Ask your new wife." Finn took a heaping spoonful of the creamy strawberry confection.

Bliss.

"That's different."

"Doesn't have to be."

"What kind of books have you been reading out here, anyway?" Lance was staring at him as if he suspected an alien had taken over his kid brother's body.

"Your concrete is melting." Finn waved his spoon at the dissolving custard in Lance's cup.

His brother dived back in, duly distracted.

Perfect.

"How's the leg?" Mac wiped a drip of custard off the table with one of the napkins.

"Ninety-five percent. This might be as good as it gets."

"Better than the alternative."

"Yeah." His oldest brother didn't need to remind him how close he'd come to losing his leg. Once in a while he still woke up in a cold sweat, thinking about it. "I'm not complaining. And I'm working with it. I might eke out another percent or two improvement."

"Hold that thought."

Lance scraped up the last dregs of his concrete and licked the plastic spoon clean. "That is great stuff."

"No kidding." Mac finished his too. "I hope we

didn't ruin Finn's lunch, though. You know what a stickler Mom always was about meal first, dessert second."

"Don't worry about it. I slept late today. Lunch is an hour or two away." Finn set his empty cup on the table.

"Did it take you awhile to fall asleep last night?" Mac's question sounded casual, but Finn heard the underlying thread of concern.

"No. I slept like a log for eleven hours."

"No nightmares?" Mac gave him his don't-lie-to-a-police-detective stare.

"Nope. I haven't had one in almost a week."

"Yeah?" Lance propped an ankle on his knee and leaned back. "Who would've expected playing Thoreau would be therapeutic? But better you than me. If I was stuck in a place like this with no one to talk to 24/7, I'd probably be climbing the—"

A knock sounded on the back door, and Lance quirked an eyebrow.

Finn shoved his chair away from the table and stood. Weird to have two sets of visitors in the space of an hour after more than a week of solo living—and if the latest arrival was who he suspected it might be, the timing couldn't have been worse.

"Hang on a minute while I see who that is."

Without giving his brothers a chance to respond, he crossed to the door and peeked out the window that offered a view of the back porch.

It was Dana—also bearing gifts, if that plastic-wrap-covered plate of cookies was any indication.

He stifled a groan. Any other time, he'd have welcomed her with open arms . . . literally.

As it was, no matter how hard he tried to keep their exchange polite and hands-off, his brothers were going to have a field day with this.

Scrambling to come up with a strategy, he twisted the knob, pulled it back, and smiled at Dana through the screen door. "Hi."

"Hi back." She hefted the plate of cookies. "Since we demolished the last batch, I made some more. I thought you might like a midday snack . . . and I also wanted to thank you for taking me to services yesterday and helping with the garden."

As Finn pushed open the door, took the cookies, and ushered her in, Lance spoke from behind him.

"Aren't you going to introduce us?"

Dana hesitated halfway over the threshold, her gaze darting past his shoulder. "Oh! I'm sorry. I didn't know you had company."

"We're not company." Lance moved forward, Mac on his heels, and held out his hand. "We're his brothers. Lance McGregor."

Dana returned the shake. "Nice to meet you."

"And this is Mac." Lance eased aside while Mac greeted her. "And you are?"

"Dana Lewis." Finn muscled back into the conversation. "My next-door neighbor."

"Ah." Lance's eyes sparked with humor. "The one you maintain cordial relations with."

Heat crept across Finn's cheeks—and there wasn't a thing he could do to stop it, thanks to his stupid red hair. "We've become acquainted over the past few days."

"I can see why." Lance gave Dana an appreciative scan.

Man, his brother was a flirt, newly married or not.

"I just didn't realize you had such good taste." The corners of Lance's lips tipped up.

"I'll be sure to tell Christy you said that." Finn gave him the evil eye.

Lance ignored it. "So how did you two meet?"

Dana sent him a panicked look.

Great. Now she was upset.

As soon as she left, he was going to seriously hurt his brother for causing her distress.

"I was walking through the woods, emerged at Dana's lake . . . and the rest is history." He locked gazes with her as he spoke, trying to communicate that he would never share the real story of their first encounter without her permission.

Her shoulders relaxed.

Mac regarded the three of them, picked up on the subtle undercurrents that always eluded Lance, and stepped in. "However you met, it's a pleasure to meet you. And I'm glad to know Finn has a neighbor close at hand."

"Thank you." Dana moistened her lips and backed toward the door. "I, uh, need to get back to work. I'll let you all finish up your visit without further interruption."

"I'll see you out." Finn shoved the plate of cookies against Lance's chest and followed Dana to the porch, shutting the door firmly behind him. "Sorry about that. My brothers—Lance in particular—can be a little in-your-face."

She stopped at the railing. "No kidding. But they seem like . . . solid guys. And it's nice that they drove all the way down from St. Louis to visit."

"Yeah." Or it would have been, any other time. "Thanks for the cookies."

"It was no big deal. I appreciate all the help you've given me over the past week."

"It's been my pleasure." He shoved his hands in his pockets. "You're welcome to stay for a while if you can put up with my siblings." It was the polite thing to say, though it would be much nicer—and safer—to have her to himself.

"I can't. I really do have to get back to work."

He tried not to let his relief show. "I could drop by later, if you'd like. Maybe we could take a hike around your place or a row on the lake."

"I'd like that."

"About six? That should give us about an hour of daylight."

“Perfect. I’ll see you then.”

He watched as she walked through the small clearing behind the cabin. Once she disappeared into the woods, he braced himself.

His brothers were waiting in the living room. Lance draped in the easy chair, Mac on the sofa with his feet propped on the polished-log coffee table.

“You’ve been holding out on us.” Mac folded his arms.

“No wonder you haven’t been lonely, with a hot chick like that bringing you cookies.” Lance grinned.

“She’s never been over here before.”

“Yeah?” Mac helped himself to one of the cookies from the plate Lance had set on the end table.

“Yeah.”

“But you’ve been over there. A lot, I bet.” Lance waggled his eyebrows. “And what’s this about taking her into town to *services?* Mac and I couldn’t get you within a hundred yards of a church while you were in St. Louis.”

“I wasn’t ready then.”

“Uh-huh.” Lance snagged a cookie.

Finn grabbed the depleted plate and moved it out of his reach. “How many of these did you guys eat already?”

“A few.” Mac brushed the crumbs off his fingers. “What else did we have to do while you two said your good-byes?”

"At least I didn't spy on you through the curtains. Mac wouldn't let me." Lance stood. "So who is this mystery woman? And does she actually live around here?"

Finn gave them a topline—not by choice, but if he didn't, they'd never stop bugging him.

"So she inherited her grandparents' farm, huh? Lucky timing for you, me thinks." Lance winked at him. "New York City book editor meets ex–Army Ranger in the middle of the Mark Twain National Forest. What are the odds of that?"

"Sounds like a match that was meant to be. Don't knock fate." Mac rose and tapped his watch in front of Lance. "Don't you have an appointment?"

"Yeah." Lance snatched another cookie before Finn could jerk the plate away. "The lady knows how to cook. Another check in her pro column."

"I'm not keeping score."

"Start. She could be a keeper. Classy *and* beautiful. Wonder what she sees in you?" Lance chomped on the cookie.

"We just met. I barely know her." He forced the reply through gritted teeth.

"Yeah?" Lance finished off the cookie. "You two acted like old friends—and there was some serious electricity pinging around the room. Plus, you had a goofy grin while she was here. Right, Mac?"

"In the interest of family harmony, I'll plead

the Fifth.” The corners of his mouth twitched

Great.

His brothers were on to him.

“Guess we don’t need to worry about checking in on you quite as often.” Lance strolled toward the door, and Mac fell in behind him.

Finn followed them out, depositing what was left of the cookies on the kitchen table. “I told you I was fine.”

“There’s fine, and there’s *real* fine. You, runt, are in real fine territory.” Lance gave him an exaggerated leer.

“All kidding aside”—Mac sent a “can it” look to his wise-cracking sibling—“we’re glad things are improving. Whatever the reason.”

“Thanks. And thanks for stopping by with the Ted Drewes. That was a treat.”

“Not as much of a treat as the one you have in your backyard.” Lance tossed his keys in the air.

Mac caught them. “Get in the car. We’re leaving.”

“Aye, aye.” Lance gave a jaunty salute. “Be good, kid. Call us if you need anything.”

“Call us even if you don’t.” Mac put a hand on his shoulder. “I want you to stay in touch. Got it?”

“Yeah.”

“And in the future, we’ll call before we drop in.” Mac gave him a one-sided grin and joined Lance at the car.

Two minutes later, the Cruze had disappeared

down the drive in a cloud of dust, Lance waving out the window.

Hands in his pockets, Finn ambled back inside. His brothers might like to give him a hard time, but the McGregor bond was strong. The Ted Drewes run was evidence of that—but best of all, they'd be there for him in a heartbeat if he needed them. All he had to do was pick up the phone.

A week ago, he might have considered using that lifeline. Now . . . not so much.

Because Lance was right.

He *was* in real fine territory. With his neighbor to keep him company, he doubted there'd be any need to send out a distress signal. For the duration of his stay, Dana Lewis was all the companionship he needed. She was smart, kind, an excellent listener, empathetic—and much easier on the eyes than his brothers.

So come six o'clock, he'd mosey on over to her place and spend as long as she'd give him enjoying the view.

He needed her gone.

From the cover of heavy underbrush, Wayne Phelps watched through binoculars while Dana Lewis and her new friend rowed around the lake at sunset. They'd been at it for forty-five minutes, and with the light diminishing, there wasn't much chance they'd venture any farther tonight.

But based on what he'd overheard at church

yesterday, the impaired vision Marv at the hardware store had mentioned was improving, and she was getting ready to start hiking around the property.

That could be very dangerous—for him *and* for her. An able-bodied neighbor who appeared to be hanging around way too much and could provide escort service to the more remote parts of Leo's land didn't help, either. His presence would dramatically up the odds she'd stumble onto something best kept hidden.

Lowering the binoculars, he leaned a shoulder against an oak tree. Who could have predicted she'd hang around this long? A quick visit to take a cursory look before putting the place up for sale—no sweat. With the rural real estate market what it was, that could have bought him the ten or twelve more months he needed to hit his nest-egg goal. Property in these parts was moving about as fast as the trickle in Clear Creek after a summer of Midwest heat.

Now his perfect setup was on the cusp of exposure.

Unless he convinced Leo's granddaughter to hightail it out of here and leave him in peace.

Wayne lifted the binoculars again, watching as Dana and her neighbor pulled up to the dock. The guy helped her out of the boat, and the two of them stood there for a few minutes . . . close, but not touching. Then he took off in the direction of

Mark Busch's place, following the edge of the lake. After he disappeared through an opening in the trees, Dana wandered toward the cabin.

He was safe for tonight.

And he intended to stay safe in the nights to come.

It was time to launch a get-rid-of-Dana campaign.

—11—

Roger swung onto the road that wound through the woods to Leo's place. Drove fifty yards. Stopped.

This was going to be very, very awkward.

Maybe he should have sent one of his officers to respond to Dana's call about vandalism on her property. Pretending not to know who'd drilled holes in the bottom of her rowboat and sprayed orange paint on her dock would require some serious playacting when he was certain of the culprit.

Wayne Phelps.

It had to be him.

The man had been standing within spitting distance after church on Sunday while Dana talked about exploring Leo's property, perhaps with her muscled neighbor in tow.

Roger exhaled and massaged his temple, his annoyance diminishing slightly. Truth be told, in Wayne's shoes he'd be running scared too. If Dana stumbled upon the lab, his convenient setup would be history.

Besides—while he might not like the man's methods, he had to admit he wanted Dana gone too. Trying to search for the gold right under her nose was one stressor he could do without. And he needed to spend a lot more time doing it, since his dives to date had yielded zilch . . . and the clock was ticking at Woodside Gardens.

Straightening up, he flexed his fingers on the wheel. He might officially be responding to a vandalism call, but his real job in the next few minutes suddenly clicked into crystal clear focus.

He had to convince Leo's granddaughter to leave.

Clenching his jaw, he depressed the accelerator again.

As he pulled in behind the cabin and got out of the car, Dana opened the back door. "Thanks for coming so fast, Chief."

"That's what we're here for. Shall we go down to the dock?"

"I'll meet you in front." She reentered the house and closed the door.

He circled the cabin, and she joined him as they walked down the slope toward the lake. "I don't recall Pops ever saying he had any vandalism here." Her words wobbled slightly.

"He didn't. Or none I knew of. But those kinds of crimes have picked up in recent years. The world we live in, I suppose. Even quiet little Beaumont isn't immune anymore."

"Have you had other reports of vandalism?"

"Yes. The picnic grounds have been a recent target. Someone—or multiple someones—spray-painted graffiti on the tables and bleachers and left ATV ruts on the ball field. The culprits are still at large."

They continued in silence until they reached the dock. The orange paint had been sprayed at random. No message. The rowboat was pulled halfway up the bank, the bottom peppered with sizeable holes a hand-held, battery-powered drill could produce with little effort or noise.

"The boat was tied to the dock when I discovered it, but it was taking on water and beginning to sink so I pulled it out as much as I could." Dana crossed her arms and gripped her elbows.

"When did you notice it?"

"This morning. I saw the paint on the dock first. After I came down to investigate, I spotted the holes in the boat. Everything was fine last evening. Finn—my neighbor—and I went out for a row around twilight."

"Did you hear anything during the night?"

"No. I only crack one window in the bedroom, and that's at the back of the house." She rubbed her arms, as if a chill had passed over her despite the warm spring sun. "What do you think?"

I think Wayne is trying to make you so nervous about staying out here by yourself that you'll leave.

Roger pretended to mull over her question. "It could be the same no-accounts who are messing with the picnic grounds." He framed his next comment with care. "So far, we haven't seen any violence in connection with the vandalism. They appear to be targeting property rather than people. That could change, though." He gave her a few seconds to digest that. "Do you have adequate locks on your doors?"

"Yes. I changed them after I arrived."

"Smart move. But you don't have phone service on the property, do you?"

"Only here, by the dock." A flicker of fear ignited in her eyes.

"Not in the house?"

"No."

"Hmm." Again, he let the implications sink in, then walked around the dock area, inspecting the ground. "It doesn't appear your visitor—or visitors—left anything behind . . . including footprints."

"What about fingerprints?"

"I doubt they touched the dock or the boat. Or

if they did, they probably wore gloves. Even the most amateur lawbreakers are too savvy to leave behind obvious incriminating evidence now, thanks to TV and movies." He bent down, examined the holes in the boat, and stood. "I'll take a few photos with my cell for the police report, and we'll beef up patrols in this area, but with you being so far off the main road . . ."

Her complexion lost a few shades of color. "I don't understand why someone would do this."

"Vandalism is often hard to explain. Sometimes people do it for no other reason than the adrenaline rush. In any case, you should notify your insurance company. I'll file a report by this afternoon, and we'll be happy to provide a copy."

"Do you think . . . is there any chance they could . . . come back?"

"The picnic grounds have been hit several times." At least he could be truthful about that.

"Not the best news I've heard today."

He didn't try to reassure her.

After snapping a few photos, he slid the phone back on his belt. "May I ask how long you're planning to stay at the cabin?"

"I don't know. I was thinking indefinitely, but with this kind of stuff going on . . ."

He tried to maintain a neutral demeanor despite the sudden uptick in his spirits. If she got spooked and left, he might even be able to pull off a few daytime dives instead of skulking around at midnight. Visibility would be a lot higher too.

"I'd hate to think an incident like this would chase you away." He tried for a commiserating tone. "On the other hand, a single woman alone in an isolated spot, with limited ability to contact anyone in case of emergency . . . I can see how that would be a cause for concern. We'll be keeping our eyes and ears open, though. It's possible we could get a lead on this." He infused the last sentence with a hefty dose of skepticism.

She chewed on her lower lip. "It would help if they'd left a clue or two."

"Yes, it would have." He surveyed the woods surrounding the lake. "I'm assuming they arrived on foot—unless you might have slept through the approach of a car on your drive?"

"No. I'm a light sleeper. The sound would have roused me."

"Well, I'll poke around for a few minutes, see if I can spot anything helpful."

"I'll wait on the porch."

She retreated up the hill and took a seat in one of the rocking chairs.

For the next ten minutes, he pretended to examine the ground around the dock and along the edge of the lake. Finally, hat in hand, he joined her, pausing at the bottom of the steps that led to the porch.

"Nothing?" She remained in her chair, fingers clenched together in her lap.

"No. As I said, we'll stay alert, ask a few questions around town. In the meantime, use some extra caution. Stay close to the house and don't wander around at night."

Distress tightened her features. "I can't believe this is happening here. It's the one place I always felt safe and protected."

"And I'm sure you always were . . . while Leo was here. I know he doted on you."

"The feeling was mutual." A sudden sheen appeared in her eyes, and her throat worked. "Thank you for coming out personally, Chief."

"I was happy to do it. Let me know if you have any more trouble."

"I will."

He touched the brim of his cap and circled around to the back of the house.

Two minutes later, as he rolled down the drive toward the state road, he glanced in his rear-view mirror at Leo's receding cabin. He'd accomplished his goal. Dana was shaken. Second-guessing her decision to stay at the cabin. Afraid.

But scaring women was wrong. As a law enforcement officer, he was supposed to help people, not cause them physical—or mental—harm.

All at once, the bagel he'd eaten for breakfast congealed into a hard lump in his stomach, and the trees on either side of the road blurred. Gripping the wheel with one hand, he swiped the back of the other across his lashes. The view cleared.

If only he could as easily chase away the mist obscuring the personal road ahead for him. A road that grew more rocky and twisty with each passing day.

One thing for certain—the route he was traveling was leading him into enemy territory.

And there was no going back.

Dana watched Finn assess the dock and rowboat, jaw tight, mouth flattened into a thin line, twin crevices creasing his brow, eyes narrowed.

It wasn't difficult to discern his mood.

He was mad.

Yet when he angled toward her, she picked up another emotion in those jade-colored irises.

Concern.

He was worried about her.

Which only ratcheted up *her* concern.

If an ex–Army Ranger thought there was reason for continued apprehension, the anxiety she hadn't been able to shake since Chief Burnett's visit earlier this morning seemed more than justified.

"What did the police say?" Finn hooked the earpiece of his sunglasses over the neck of his black T-shirt, letting the shades dangle against his chest.

"He said they'd ask a few questions around town and patrol more in this area. He also said there have been other vandalism incidents in town recently and suggested I be careful." Her voice hitched on the last word, despite her attempt to sound calm.

His frown deepened. "Did he search for clues?"

"Yes—and took some pictures. But he didn't find anything." She twisted her fingers together. "Do you think whoever did this might come back?"

He hesitated.

Her pulse kicked up another notch.

"I don't see why, unless you're being targeted for some reason." His words were measured. Careful. "But you don't know that many people in town . . . unless you've made an enemy you haven't mentioned."

"No."

"Then it could be a random crime. But I want to look around a bit." The smile he offered seemed forced. "I wouldn't mind a glass of lemonade and a few cookies after I'm finished, if you have some on hand."

"Always."

"I'll join you on the porch in a few minutes."

"Okay." She ascended the hill, stopping at the bottom of the steps. Finn was already prowling around the dock, bending here and there to examine anything that caught his attention.

But there wasn't much chance he'd turn up a significant clue. The chief was a pro. He'd been at this business for decades, was well respected in town—and he'd come up empty. If there'd been anything to find, he'd have discovered it.

Yet Finn was still down by the boat when she emerged from the house a few minutes later with the tray of cookies and lemonade.

"Do you have a ziplock bag and a couple of tissues?" He called the question up to her.

"Sure." She set the tray on the table between the rockers as he started up the hill toward her. "Give me a sec."

She retrieved the items and handed them over. "Did you find something?"

"I'll show you in a minute."

He returned to the dock, plucked some object from the rowboat with the tissues, and dropped it into the plastic bag.

Two minutes later, he rejoined her and held it up. A dark gray button was inside, thread dangling from the holes. "Does this belong to you?"

"No."

"Me neither."

"How did Chief Burnett miss it?"

"It was wedged between the seat and the side of the boat."

"Could it have been there for a while?"

"It's possible—but the thread isn't dirty, and I didn't see it while I was cleaning up the boat after I pulled it out of the shed. How long did Burnett look around?"

"Five, ten minutes. I don't think small-scale vandalism is a high-priority crime."

His features hardened. “A crime’s a crime.”

“Are you going to give him that?” She motioned toward the button.

“I’ll show it to him next time I’m in town. I doubt it will be of much help—but you never know.”

“Mmm.” She studied the button and shoved her hands in her pockets. “It’s kind of creepy to know someone was sneaking around out here last night while I was sleeping.” Again she tried for a casual tone. Again, a slight tremor ran through her words.

Based on his keen gaze, Finn noticed. “Yeah, it is. Do you mind if I check out your locks?”

“No.” She edged aside to allow him access to the cabin, then followed him around in silence as he inspected them, ending in the living room.

“They’re not bad—and the doors are sturdy. Under normal circumstances, your security should be sufficient . . . but I don’t like the fact you’re isolated here and the only place you get cell service is outside, by the lake.”

“The chief commented on that too.”

“You don’t by any chance have a gun, do you?”

Her heart stuttered. “Do you think I need one?”

“Not necessarily, but I’d be happier if you had a weapon.”

She swallowed. “As a matter of fact, Pops’s hunting rifle is in the back bedroom, along with some ammunition.”

“Do you know how to use it?”

"Yes. He taught me when I got older. He said it was important to be comfortable around guns if I was going to hang out in the country. He used to set up empty soda cans down by the lake and we'd have shooting matches. I was an excellent shot, by the way."

"You remember how to load it?"

"I think so. It's been awhile—and I haven't had much interest in guns since the incident in New York." The mere mention of that trauma sent a cold chill through her.

"Why don't you go get it and let me take a look?"

It was on her lips to refuse . . . but she could almost hear Pops's voice encouraging her to do what Finn suggested.

The man's right, sweetie. After all that's happened, it won't hurt to refresh your memory. Preparation averts a lot of disasters.

Without a word, she rose and retrieved the Winchester, along with a box of cartridges.

He examined the gun, then handed it back. "Go ahead and load it."

Calling up all that Pops had told her, she accomplished the task much faster than she expected, despite the quiver in her fingers.

"Okay. I'm satisfied. Keep it loaded and handy. Just make sure the safety's on."

"You know . . . none of this is making me feel real warm and fuzzy." She double-checked the safety and rested the gun against the wall, near the door.

"It doesn't hurt to be prepared for any contingency." He smiled, but it came across as a mite strained. "Why don't we have those cookies and lemonade now?"

She slipped past him as he held the door. Once seated, she inspected the vandalized dock and broke off a piece of cookie she didn't want.

"Hey."

At his soft summons, she turned.

"I'm sorry this happened. I know this place has always been your refuge."

Her eyes prickled, and a tear welled on her lower lid.

No! She was not going to cry! She was stronger than that.

Mustering her self-control, she nodded. "Thanks. I guess it's unrealistic to expect perfect things to always stay the same. Nothing good lasts forever."

"Nothing bad, either." His gaze held hers.

"I suppose that's true." Case in point—the nightmare of the New York bank robbery. Since Finn had come into her life, memories of the terror had begun to dissipate.

"But nothing can alter the perfect memories you have of your visits here with your grandparents. This vandalism incident can't change those. And there's no reason you can't make more great memories here in the future."

She gave him a tentative smile, ignored the voice in her head reminding her she wasn't the impulsive type, and took a scary leap. "I've already made some new ones I'll always treasure."

For a moment, he seemed taken aback by her frankness—but he recovered fast.

"Recently, I hope." He smiled back with no uncertainty at all.

"Very."

"Me too."

She took a long drink of her cold lemonade, eying him over the rim of her glass. Was that on the level? Her admission had been sincere—but all three of the handsome McGregor siblings were chick magnets. They were probably used to flirting with women, had learned all the smooth moves, knew just what to say to . . .

"I meant that, Dana."

She flushed as he pinned her with an intent look. The man was a mind reader too?

"And for the record, I don't go around saying stuff like that to every woman I meet."

Her doubts evaporated—yet there was still a snag. "I appreciate that. But I also know our situation here is temporary. You'll be leaving in a couple of weeks, and my own plans are in limbo. Especially now." She surveyed the dock and damaged boat again.

"That doesn't mean we have to lose touch. In fact, I hope we don't. In case you haven't noticed, there's some high-wattage electricity between us."

"I noticed."

"So did my brothers." He gave her a half-hitch grin and took another cookie.

Wonderful.

"I bet they gave you a boatload of grief about it too."

"Yeah, but I'm used to their ribbing. It's the fate of a kid brother. We're easy targets."

She nibbled on her cookie. "Why do I think you can hold your own?"

"Simple. You're a smart, intuitive woman." He polished off his cookie and brushed the crumbs from his fingers.

"Thanks for the compliment—but it's pretty obvious you're not the kind of guy who puts up with a lot of guff."

"True. I also give as good as I get."

Amusement tickled the corners of her mouth. "It must be lively when the three of you get together."

"That's one word for it." He checked his watch. "And now, while I hate to end this party, I bet your lunch break is about over."

"Unfortunately, it is. I'd invite you back later for another cruise on the lake, but I think we're out of luck on that score."

"The boat should be salvageable—and with some elbow grease I might be able to get rid of some of that orange paint. I'll add it to my to-do list for tomorrow. In the meantime . . . could I interest you in a trip to town for a piece of pie at the Walleye tonight?"

"You could."

"Seven?"

"Perfect."

He stood, and she followed him across the porch. At the top of the steps, he turned back to her. "If you need anything, remember I'm not far away. Sound carries out here. All you have to do is yell. I leave my windows open day and night, and except for an occasional trip to town, I'm nearby."

Her throat constricted. "I appreciate that."

Instead of continuing down the steps, he lifted his hand with slow, deliberate intent and smoothed the hair back from her face. "You don't need to be afraid, okay? I can get here fast. If anything at all scares you, don't hesitate to scream. I'll hear you."

He was so close she could see the jagged edges of the thin white scar near the hairline on his temple. Smell his subtle, musky aftershave. Sense the steady cadence of his breathing.

All at once, an absurd longing surged through her, short-circuiting her respiration.

She wanted to throw herself into those strong arms . . . rise on tiptoe . . . and press her lips to his.

His green eyes darkened, and a spark began to sizzle in their depths. "You've done this to me before, you know." His familiar baritone had dropped a few pitches.

She swallowed. “W-what?”

“Sent a message that’s very hard to resist.” He eased closer.

The warmth of his breath feathered against her forehead—and a red alert began to strobe across her mind.

Step back, Dana! Be prudent! Don’t rush the relationship, remember?

She heard the warning clearly.

Ignored it.

“What message?” As if she didn’t know.

So much for thinking *he* might be a flirt!

He slowly trailed his fingertips down her cheek and across her lips, his touch whisper soft.

Her eyelids drifted closed.

Oh. My. Word.

A shudder rippled through her.

“Dana?”

At his husky question, she forced her eyes open.

“I’m not in the habit of asking permission to kiss a woman . . . but I’m also not in the habit of caring a whole lot whether my impulsiveness might shoot me in the foot. Are you okay with this?”

She tried to consider his question rationally . . . but only one fact was super clear—if she kissed him, her plan to play this cautious and safe would crumble.

Because she had a feeling one kiss from Finn was all it would take for her to fall.

Hard.

Yet as she stared up at him, there was no way she could refuse.

"Yes." Her acquiescence came out in a croak.

He didn't give her a chance for second thoughts. Moving in, he cupped the back of her head with one hand, wrapped his other arm around her, and pulled her into the shelter of his arms.

The instant his lips met hers, Dana's lungs stalled. She'd suspected Finn would be an excellent kisser, but this . . . this was magic.

By the time he released her, she had to cling to him to maintain her balance.

"Not bad for a first kiss." His tone was teasing, but the rough timbre of his voice suggested he was as shaken as she was.

"Yeah." She kept a tight grip on his arms. "Let me know when the earthquake is over."

He chuckled, a low, sensual rumble that shifted the ground beneath her feet again. "For what it's worth, that registered at about a nine on my personal Richter scale."

"Same here. I definitely sustained some permanent changes in ground topography."

"At the risk of stating the obvious, I think this calls for further exploration. How do you feel about long-distance relationships?"

A euphoric warmth filled her. "I think they can be difficult to sustain. But a few more kisses like that could persuade me to give one a try."

"Happy to oblige."

He attempted to tug her close again, but prudence finally triumphed and she pressed her hands against his chest. "Not back-to-back. I don't think my heart could take it."

Several charged seconds ticked by. Then, with a sigh, he released her. "I suppose one of us has to be practical."

"This *is* moving kind of fast."

He gave her an unrepentant grin. "Isn't that how things work in those books you edit?"

"This is real life, not fiction."

"And I thought women were supposed to be the romantics."

"I *am* romantic."

"Yeah?" He tipped his head. "I bet I'm more romantic than you."

"A tough, hard-driving Army Ranger romantic? Not a chance."

He folded his arms and propped a shoulder against the porch support. "What's the most romantic thing you've ever done for a guy you were dating?"

It took her a moment to dredge up an answer. "I planned a private picnic for his birthday, with music and homemade cake and sparklers for after it got dark."

"Not bad."

But not great, based on his smug expression.

"What's the most romantic thing *you've* ever done for someone you were dating?"

"I hired a violinist, ordered a gourmet meal—complete with waiter—from the best restaurant in town, and rented a cabana on the beach for our dinner. And it wasn't even her birthday."

Wow.

"Surprised you, didn't I?" His grin broadened.

Uh . . . yeah.

"A little."

"A lot. Come on . . . admit it."

She held up her hands in surrender. "Fine. A lot. She must have been someone special."

"Not as special as you—and definitely not special enough to consider taking on the hassles of a long-distance relationship."

Double wow.

"I'll give you this, Finn McGregor. You're a man of surprises."

"With more to come." He winked. "Now I'll let you get back to work." With that, he descended the steps and set off toward the woods, whistling some peppy tune she didn't recognize.

Once he disappeared, his whistle floated back for several more minutes. A purposeful reminder that sound carried?

Perhaps.

But she already knew that from the night he'd raced to her rescue after hearing her scream.

Hopefully, it wouldn't come to that again.

In the meantime, though, it was comforting to know she wasn't quite as alone in the woods as she'd been before Finn charged into her life and changed everything.

Including her work ethic.

Dana sighed. It would be so much more fun to sit on the porch and daydream about the future and the man and that kiss.

Too bad her aggressive deadlines were locked in stone.

Turning away from the sparkling lake at last, she returned to her computer, took her seat . . . and decreased the magnification yet again. Her vision was improving as quickly as her love life.

Plus, she had tonight to anticipate. Since her first trip there with Pops and Mags, pie at the café in town had always been a happy event. And while much had changed over the past few weeks, it appeared that tradition would continue—albeit with a new cast.

Best of all, she had a feeling Pops would approve of the man who'd stepped in to take his place across the table at the Walleye.

She opened the document she was editing, pushing the vandalism incident to the back of her mind. Upsetting as it had been, it was history. Finn had even promised to try to fix the row-boat. She needed to focus on the future, not the past.

Because there was no reason to think anything but blue skies and smooth sailing lay ahead.

—12—

She was still here—and that neighbor of hers was hanging around more than ever.

Wayne lowered his binoculars and spat out a word that would have earned him a whipping in his younger years. He needed to get cooking again if he wanted to stay on track with his savings plan—but wandering around on the property was getting dicey. Just because Leo's granddaughter and her new friend hadn't strayed too far from the lake didn't mean she'd given up on the idea of taking a hike around the place, despite his attempt to scare her off three days ago.

And that would be dangerous. Getting caught was unthinkable . . . but having the operation shut down would be almost as bad. If the lab was discovered, his plan to ditch this place and have a real life would be history.

He couldn't let that happen, not this close to achieving his goal.

The two figures in the distance got into the boat someone had obviously repaired and pushed off from the dock that bore faint orange marks.

Dana—perhaps with the help of her friend—had tried to erase all evidence of his warning.

He lifted the binoculars again and homed in on the cozy twosome. The man leaned close to speak, and the woman's laugh carried across the water.

His mouth tightened as the muscled dude rowed the boat with smooth, powerful strokes while the woman trailed her fingers in the water. Must be nice to have a gorgeous babe look at you like you were some kind of superhero.

But maybe he'd get lucky too, once he left Beaumont behind and had a few bucks to throw around. Rich guys always got the girl—and based on town scuttlebutt, the guy in the boat had some high-paying, top-secret government gig.

Getting those extra bucks, however, meant he needed to start cooking again. Soon.

As the boat approached the edge of the lake closest to him, he melted back into the underbrush. Not that there was much chance he'd be spotted; those two had eyes only for each other.

The guy maneuvered the boat around and rowed back toward the cabin, biceps bulging as he displayed some serious muscle power. The kind best given a wide berth.

Yet as long as the girl was in the cabin, her friend would be around—meaning there was a definite possibility he and the muscleman might tangle.

Which brought him back to square one.

He needed Dana Lewis gone.

Compressing his lips, Wayne gripped the binoculars. Too bad she hadn't left after his first warning. Now he'd have to ratchet up the attacks.

And while he didn't intend her any harm, the more she dug in her heels, the greater the chance she was going to get hurt.

Someone was watching them.

Finn didn't break rhythm as he rowed Dana back toward the cabin, nor did he alter his expression . . . but the reflective shimmer in the woods at the far end of the lake spiked his adrenaline.

Thank goodness he was able to contain his immediate, over-the-top impulse to grab her and dive into the water, where they'd be less exposed. Instead, he listened to the left side of his brain reminding him this wasn't a combat situation. She might have had some vandalism on her place, but there was no evidence anyone wanted to harm her. The gleam could be some sort of metallic object that had gotten caught in a tree. It didn't have to be from binoculars . . . or a rifle barrel.

". . . working on Friday night."

He pulled himself back to their conversation. "Sorry. I drifted for a minute. What did you say?"

She flicked some water at him. "Am I losing my luster already?"

"Hardly. Shall I stop rowing and prove it?"

"You did that already, on the dock."

"It bears repeating."

She laughed—an enchanting musical sound

he'd been hearing more and more often in the past few days.

"When we say good night."

He put some extra muscle into the oars, sending the boat zipping across the water.

"Anxious?" Grinning, she flicked more water at him.

"Anticipating."

As he pulled up to the dock a few minutes later, his arm muscles were feeling the strain . . . not that he intended to share that with Dana and ruin his hero image. Vaulting onto the wooden planks, he leaned down and extended a hand, drawing her up—and straight into his arms.

She sighed and nestled against him. "Man, I *so* don't want to have to work tonight."

"I can think of more pleasant activities too."

"Hmm." She raised her chin and appraised him. "Come to think of it, it might be safer if I go back to work."

"But not nearly as much fun."

She opened her mouth to respond—but he put it to better use.

By the time they both came up for air, she was pressed tight against his chest, their heartbeats mingling.

"Go home, Finn." She wriggled free, pushing at her rumpled hair.

Much as he wanted to stay, it *was* time to go. She had work to do, the electricity between them was approaching the danger level—and he needed to do a little reconnaissance.

"Are we still on for breakfast at the Walleye tomorrow?"

"Nine o'clock. It will be the highlight of my Saturday."

"The food or the company?"

"Hmm. They do have great cinnamon rolls."

"So much for my ego." He brushed another kiss over her forehead. "Where's the whistle I gave you?"

"In the house. I knew I wouldn't need it while I was with you."

"True. But keep it with you otherwise, okay?" The piercing, hundred-decibel safety model he'd purchased at the general mercantile wasn't a great security system—but it was better than nothing.

Plus, she had her grandfather's gun.

"I do. In fact, if you want the truth, I wear it around my neck."

In other words, she continued to be spooked by the vandalism incident.

Not a bad thing in light of that glint he'd spotted in the woods, perhaps. It might end up being nothing more than a discarded fast-food wrapper that had blown into the branches . . . but the vandals *could* still be roaming around.

"Good. I'll wait until you get to the porch."

He stayed by the dock until she waved him off

from behind the railing, then set off around the lake.

Once in the woods, he veered off course the instant he lost sight of her and moved in the direction of the reflection. It was slower going compared to two weeks ago now that everything had leafed out, and brambles snagged his jeans at every step.

Following the perimeter of the lake from the cover of the woods, he approached the approximate location of the reflective glimmer, slowing to a quiet skulk as he drew close.

But after a thorough search, it was clear stealth wasn't necessary. There was no sign of anything metallic in the trees, nor was anyone lurking in the brush.

Yet someone had been there very recently.

Finn paused beside some trampled greenery in the approximate spot he'd placed the glare. In other circumstances, he might attribute the matted ground cover to an animal—but today it was too coincidental.

A quiver of unease spiraled down his spine.

Someone *had* been watching them.

He leaned down, doing an inch-by-inch search of the ground, broadening the radius in increments.

Nothing.

Nor was there a pattern of footprints or broken branches to indicate the direction their clandestine watcher had taken.

Finn raked his fingers through his hair and did a final three-sixty of the area.

Zilch.

Giving up, he hiked back toward his cabin, alert to his surroundings even as he mulled over his discovery. The vandalism incident had been disturbing, but based on what Dana had said about other such episodes in town, not necessarily an indication she was in physical danger.

This was different.

Spying on someone was more personal. More targeted.

More sinister.

Making a trip into Beaumont vaulted to the top of his priority list. He needed to show the button he'd found to Chief Burnett—and tell the man about today's incident. Neither would help him solve the crime, but they might light a fire under him about asking questions around town and beefing up patrols in this area.

Finn pushed through a dense patch of thorny vines, trying to elude the prickly tentacles. They might not have a clue yet about who was taking a special interest in Dana, but he knew one thing.

He'd be sleeping with all of his windows wide open in the future.

Something was burning.

Dana pulled herself out of a deep slumber, rubbed the grit from her eyes, and got up close and personal with the digital clock on her nightstand.

Twelve-ten.

She frowned. Why would she smell smoke at this late hour? Pops's fireplace liked to puff a little, but she'd extinguished the embers hours ago, before she went to bed.

Yet the smell was distinct, if faint.

After grabbing the oversized cardigan from the foot of the bed, she swung her feet to the floor and snatched Finn's whistle from the nightstand.

Wincing as her toes hit the cold floor, she crept to the door, eased it slightly open, and sniffed.

The smoke smell wasn't as strong in the hall.

She padded toward the living room, the smell dissipating as she left her room behind. That must mean it was wafting in from outside, through the bedroom window she'd cracked open an inch.

Tucking her hair behind her ear, she crossed to the kitchen, flipped open the blinds—and froze.

The shed was on fire!

Pulse hammering, she raced for her purse. Dug out her cell phone. Started for the front door.

Stopped.

What if the vandals were back, and the fire was a ploy to lure her outside?

What if they were lying in wait for her?

Think, Dana!

Heart pounding, she forced her lungs to inflate.

If she didn't call 911, the shed was going to be a total loss. She had to get to the lake.

But first she'd whistle for Finn. If whoever had done this was hanging around, her Army Ranger neighbor would be here within minutes.

Besides, based on what the chief had said, the town vandals had never done any bodily harm. There wasn't any personal danger.

She hoped.

Whistle at the ready, she edged the front door open, verified that the porch was empty—and blew as hard as she could.

Then, grabbing Pops's Winchester and praying no one was lurking in the shadows, she dashed for the lake.

Dana was in trouble.

The shrill, urgent screech of the whistle brought Finn instantly awake, no vestiges of sleep slowing his reaction time—a life-saving talent cultivated by every one of his combat buddies.

Thirty seconds later, gun and knife in hand, he was out the door.

Chest heaving, he closed the distance between his cabin and Dana's as fast as his less-than-one-hundred-percent leg allowed. Not fast enough to suit him . . . but a vast improvement over a few months ago.

Halfway there, he smelled the smoke.

Another surge of adrenaline propelled him

forward at hyperspeed along the familiar path.

As he at last broke through the tree cover near the lake, the flames came into view.

The shed—not the house—was on fire.

Good news . . . except the gusty wind was blowing burning fragments of the outbuilding toward the house.

He sprinted toward the cabin, following the curve of the lake as the distant wail of a siren drifted through the chilly night air, searching in the dark for Dana.

There.

She was huddled on the dock with her grandfather's Winchester.

He altered his course.

The instant she spotted him, she laid the rifle on the planks, flew his direction, and launched herself into his arms.

"Are you okay?" He held her tight, his lips against her hair as tremors coursed through her. From fear . . . cold . . . both?

"Y-yes."

A lie, based on her shaky response.

"What happened?"

"I woke up. Smelled that." She directed a quick glance toward the shed, which was glowing against the night sky, the acrid scent of billowing smoke polluting the fresh spring air. "The vandals came b-back."

The sirens got louder.

"You called 911?"

"Yes. After I whistled for you." She shivered again.

"Let's get you back in the house, where it's warmer. Your feet must be freezing."

She studied her bare toes. "I didn't stop for shoes."

"We'll find you some socks too. Come on." Keeping one arm around her shoulders, he retrieved the rifle and guided her toward the cabin.

As they reached the porch, flashing lights began bobbing through the trees rimming the access road. A few moments later, a Beaumont police car pulled in behind the cabin. An officer emerged, surveyed the burning shed, and circled around to join them.

"Officer Bill Waters, ma'am. The fire truck should be here soon. It takes a few minutes for the volunteers to assemble." He gave the shed a dubious perusal as part of one wall collapsed, sending a pyre of fiery sparks swirling toward the black sky. "She's burning really hot, though. They may not be able to do much. Any injuries?"

"No—but she's cold. We're going inside." Finn kept walking, urging Dana toward the door.

"Right. I'll stay out here until the truck arrives, keep an eye on the fire. You folks go on in. We can talk in a few minutes."

Finn guided her through the door and toward the couch. "Socks?"

"There's a pair of slippers Mags knitted for me on the floor in my room."

"Sit tight."

He found them at once, the yarn faded and patched. They weren't in any better shape than that oversized sweater she favored.

The one that must have belonged to her beloved Pops.

Throat tightening, he retraced his steps down the hall and joined her on the couch, the flicker of the flames casting eerie shadows on the drawn shades. After flipping on a light, he sat beside her.

She held out her hand for the slippers, but he set them on the floor. "Let's warm your feet up first."

He bent down, lifted her legs into his lap, and began to massage her ice-cold toes.

"You don't have to do that." Her protest was lame, and she made no attempt to pull free.

"I don't mind." Vast understatement. Giving this woman a foot massage any time of the day or night would be no hardship. "Any idea what happened out there?"

"No. I didn't hear a sound, just smelled the smoke. It was a full-out blaze when I called 911. The shed's been there forever. The wood has to be dry as kindling."

Another siren pierced the silence.

"Sounds like the volunteer fire department has

arrived." He kept working on her feet. "Was there anything of value in there?" As far as he could tell from his few forays inside, it didn't hold much besides a few dusty tools.

"No. The rowboat was all I cared about, and you salvaged that."

Except it was punctured with plugged-up holes.

A knock sounded on the door. Finn released her feet and tugged on her slippers. "Stay put."

He twisted the knob and found the police officer on the porch.

"The fire department thinks it would be safer if you came outside until they have this under control. The wind is blowing a lot of burning debris toward the cabin, and the wood in most of these old buildings is dried out. They're watching it, but they'd feel better if you were farther away."

"We'll be out in a minute."

Finn explained the situation to Dana, downplaying the danger to her cherished cabin, then helped her into a fleece jacket and sturdier footwear.

Officer Waters was waiting for them on the porch. "Why don't you sit in my car while I ask a few questions? It's warmer there."

They followed the man to his vehicle. Finn tracked the blowing debris, the heat from the fire warming him despite the distance. No way around it—the shed was going to be a total loss.

The officer went through a short list of questions

as he stood beside the open back door, but Dana could offer no clues about the culprit.

At last the man closed his notebook. “The fire people will go over the scene in the light of day. We might even contact the state fire marshal’s office if it seems suspicious.”

“I don’t think the fire started on its own.” Dana stared through the window at the raging inferno located much too close to the cabin.

“I’m inclined to agree this wasn’t an accident.” The man’s radio crackled to life, and he pulled it off his belt. “Excuse me a minute.” He walked far enough away that only his end of the conversation was clear. “Chief . . . Yes, I’m there now . . . No . . . Pretty bad.” The man’s gaze shifted to the cabin. “It’s fine, and they’re watching the blowing sparks . . . Yeah, I will . . . Got it.” He rejoined them. “You folks feel free to wait here while I have a word with the fire captain.”

As he strode away, Finn turned to Dana. “You holding up?”

“Yes. But I’m not liking that this person—or persons—came back so soon after the boat and dock incident.”

“Me neither.” Much as he hated further disrupting her peace of mind, he wasn’t going to lie.

She pulled her jacket closer around her. “So what do you think is going on?”

“I wish I knew. Are you certain you haven’t made any enemies in town?”

"Yes. I haven't been to town *often* enough to make any on this trip."

"What about in the past?"

"No. On previous trips I always stuck close to Pops. I've met a lot of the Beaumont residents, but I never got chummy with any of them or did anything to offend anyone. And Pops was well liked."

"Has anyone approached you about selling the place?"

"No. I understand the market for rural property is very slow. And I haven't said anything to anyone about selling, either." She burrowed deeper into her jacket. "Did you ever give that button to Chief Burnett?"

"Not yet. I didn't think it was that urgent. My plan was to swing by his office Monday—that would be tomorrow at this point." Finn hesitated. Should he tell Dana about his discovery of trampled brush in the woods on Friday night, after their boat ride? Or would that spook her more?

"What's wrong?" She peered at him through the darkness, posture stiffening.

The woman had great intuition.

Better to brief her. Forewarned was forearmed.

As he told her what he'd found, she listened in silence. It was impossible to read her face with only the distant, flickering flames illuminating the interior of the car.

After he finished, she let out a slow breath. "I don't get any of this. Why would someone be spying on me?"

"I have no idea—but this whole thing is beginning to smell bad. Two incidents in the space of a few days is suspicious. It's almost like someone is targeting you."

"But the vandals hit the picnic grounds more than once too."

"This close together?"

"I don't know."

"One more question to ask the chief when I hand over the button."

"I'd like to come with you—and I'd prefer to do it today rather than wait until Monday."

"Fine with me. I'm sure the officer here tonight can pass on a message that we'd like to see him."

Another shower of sparks billowed into the night sky as the roof of the shed collapsed. Finn took her hand as she cringed.

"Pops built that himself, not long after he and Mags bought this place." The light from the roaring fire flickered over her features, illuminating a demeanor that was more pensive than sad. "He wasn't the handiest guy with a hammer and saw, though. The shed always listed to one side."

"I noticed. I assumed it was from age."

"No. It was like that from the beginning. Mags was always afraid it would collapse someday while he was inside. Ironically, she was always threatening to burn it down."

Was that a touch of . . . humor . . . in her voice?

As if sensing his scrutiny, she looked over at him. "I'm sorry it happened this way, but Mags would be happy to see it gone. To be honest, I am too. I always worried it would fall down and kill someone. And I never liked the spiders that lurked in the dark corners, either." She shuddered.

He squeezed her fingers. "That's one way to put a positive spin on this."

"Better than crying over things you can't change, as Pops would say if he was here."

"Okay, folks, they've got the fire under control now." The officer pulled open the back door of the squad car. "You can go back inside the cabin if you like."

While they slid out, Finn passed on their request to the officer.

"Sure thing. I'll leave a message for the chief to swing by here after he visits his wife in Potosi. He always runs over there after services on Sunday, but he'll be back by noon. Not much sense hanging around all day anymore now that she doesn't recognize him." The man shook his head. "Sad situation. They had such a great marriage. An inspiration to all of us."

They shook the man's hand, and Finn walked Dana to her door. "Will you be all right the rest of the night by yourself?"

She motioned toward the fire crew. “I think I’m going to have company for a while. I’ll be fine.”

“You sure? I could sleep on your couch if that would make you more comfortable.”

A weary smile lifted the corners of her mouth. “That wouldn’t make *you* more comfortable. Your feet would hang over the edge.”

“I’ve bunked in worse places. I wouldn’t mind.”

“I would. Go home and get some sleep during what’s left of this night. We both need to be alert for our conversation with Chief Burnett tomorrow.”

He could argue . . . but Dana was right. There would be activity here for an hour or two, and it wasn’t likely whoever had done this would try another stunt tonight—or after daylight began to brighten the sky.

“I’ll see you about noon, then.” Angling his body to shield them from view, he leaned down and brushed his lips over hers.

“Mmm.” She rose on tiptoe to meet him. “Not a bad end to this night, after all.”

More like perfect, as far as he was concerned.

As a matter of fact, he wouldn’t mind ending *every* night like this.

But Dana was smart to be cautious about rushing their relationship. Being impulsive in any aspect of life—from a Ranger mission to a romantic commitment—was dangerous.

Yet as he set off back through the woods to try

to clock a few hours of shut-eye, he was more certain than ever that while he might be saying good-bye to Beaumont in ten days, his relationship with Dana was just beginning.

—13—

Wayne Phelps's place was in dire need of a hefty dose of TLC.

Setting the brake on the squad car, Roger surveyed the overgrown yard, the drooping gutter, the peeling paint. Jackson would turn over in his grave if he could see how his son had let the place fall apart. The Beaumont native might not have had a lot of money, but he'd taken great pride in the house he'd built for his bride forty years ago, God rest their souls.

Maybe the market garden business wasn't as successful as Wayne had always let on.

With a glance at the brooding clouds massing overhead, Roger swung his legs out of the car and pulled himself to his feet. Listened.

The buzzing drone of cicadas and the distant woof of an angry dog were the only sounds of life on this quiet Sunday evening.

He circled around to the back of the house, wove through some rusty lawn furniture, and walked to the edge of the garden at the end of the backyard, where Wayne grew his organic produce and herbs.

The two-acre plot was in slightly better condition than the house and front yard . . . but not by much. While the rows of produce were distinguishable, weeds were making serious inroads.

It, too, was deserted.

Either Wayne wasn't home, or he was inside. Hard to tell, since the door was closed on the detached garage.

Didn't matter, though. The man would be back at some point. And Roger wasn't leaving until they had a long talk about the fire this morning at Leo's place—and the subsequent conversation he'd had with Dana and her neighbor. Neither of them had been happy . . . and he couldn't blame them.

He shoved his fingers through his hair. What in the world had Wayne been thinking? If a gust of wind had blown some of that burning debris onto the roof of the cabin, the place could have caught fire. Dana might have succumbed to smoke inhalation before she could get out.

If that had happened, Leo's granddaughter would be dead.

Roger rubbed at the gnawing pain in his belly. It was bad enough to ignore a meth lab in his backyard, but to stand by and let Wayne take chances that could have fatal . . .

"Evening, Chief. Need some produce?"

Roger swiveled toward the house. Wayne stood on the back porch, wearing worn jeans, a Red Hot Chili Peppers T-shirt—and a less-than-welcoming expression.

"Not today." He walked toward the man, hooking a thumb toward the garden. "But how's business?"

"Could be better, thanks to the punk economy." He folded his arms and leaned a shoulder against a weathered upright beam on the porch. "If you aren't in search of the world's best organic arugula, what can I do for you?"

"We need to talk."

"About what?"

"I think you know."

Wayne's eyes narrowed. "I'm not sure I do. Why don't you tell me?"

"Let's go inside. I don't like discussing private matters in public."

"You know . . . you caught me at a bad time. I was just getting ready to go out."

Roger straightened up and rested his hand on his pistol. "That wasn't a request."

The other man's gaze dropped to the gun. Rose. Met his square on. His jaw took on a slight, defiant tilt. "Fine." He spun around and disappeared inside, letting the screen door slam behind him.

Roger followed him into the living room.

The inside of the house was even less well kept than the outside. Empty bags of chips lay crumpled on the couch. A few beer bottles decorated the end tables. Kernels of popcorn dotted the carpet.

"Okay, I'm listening."

No invitation to sit—not that he'd have accepted one. This was a conversation better held standing.

"I know you're the one running the lab on Leo's property, Wayne."

The man's face went blank. "What are you talking about?"

"Cut the games. I have pictures."

"Of what?"

"You. Wearing a black hoodie and carrying a backpack. The images are stored in a very safe place—as I'm certain yours are."

A few beats ticked by. Then Wayne shrugged. "So what? You can't do anything with them or I'll produce mine. It's a stalemate."

"It was . . . until you set fire to the shed on Leo's property."

"You don't have any proof of that."

"Not yet . . . but the state fire marshal's office will be investigating. Are you that certain you didn't leave any incriminating evidence behind?"

"Yeah." A touch of uncertainty undercut his attempt at bravado.

"I hope you're right . . . because I can't look the other way if they find any real evidence. Like this." He pulled out the ziplock bag containing the button and dangled it from his fingers. "Familiar?"

Wayne's complexion lost some of its color. "Where'd you get that?"

"Dana Lewis's neighbor found it wedged beside the seat in the rowboat. I'm thinking a search of this house might turn up a match."

"You'd need a warrant for that—and you don't have grounds to get one."

"That's true. But if you keep pulling stunts like last night's fire and this"—he swung the bag back and forth before tucking it back in his pocket—"someone else could find incriminating evidence that links you to one."

"You better not let that happen."

"Another threat?"

"Let's call it a warning."

"You can't reveal what you know any more than I can."

"So what's the point of your visit?" He picked up a hunting knife from the end table and weighed it in his hand.

A sharp pain beat a throbbing rhythm in Roger's temples. "To let you know two can play this game you started. And that you're not as invincible as you seem to think." He tapped the pocket holding the button.

"So I'll be more careful in the future."

Roger blew out a breath. Wiped a hand down

his face. "What in blazes is going on with you, anyway? Getting involved in drugs is crazy."

The man's dark eyes began to smolder, and his knuckles whitened around the carved handle of the knife. "No, it's not. It's my ticket out of this dead-end town. I'm tired of spending my days digging in the dirt. Of counting every penny and wondering if I'll have enough to pay the bills at the end of the month. Of watching from the sidelines while other people live real lives. I want out—and that takes a lot more money than I'll ever make putzing around with a stupid market garden."

"I thought it brought in a decent income."

"Only if I work sunup to sundown every day of the week . . . and the weather cooperates . . . and the aphids and mites stay away . . . and the plants don't get black spot or mildew . . . and the rabbits and deer don't get hungry. Meth is a lot easier—and a lot more profitable. Forty thousand dollars street value per pound versus twelve bucks retail for a pound of organic arugula. Do the math."

Roger rested one hand on the back of a chair, a sudden weariness draining his meager reserves of energy. "Are you using too?"

"No!" The man grimaced. "You think I'm stupid? I've seen what meth does to people. I want no part of that."

That was probably the truth. He didn't exhibit any of the typical signs of meth use. No paranoia, dramatic mood swings, or hallucinations. No premature aging, open sores, or rotting teeth. He was in this strictly for the money, not to get high.

At least that meant they could have a rational discussion.

"There has to be another option to earn the kind of money you need, Wayne."

"Like what? You try getting a decent-paying job with only a high school education and no experience except working in a lead smelter. I'm not flipping burgers for the rest of my life."

"So you're going to make meth forever?"

"No. I've been working this gig for two years; ten, twelve more months, I'm out of here. Once I hit my target amount, I'm going to live on easy street for the rest of my life. But I need more time." His features hardened. "And I'm not going to let anyone stop me from getting what I want."

Acid gurgled in Roger's stomach. It was hard to believe the stony-faced man standing across from him was the same kid who used to hang around the station and dream about being a big-city detective someday.

"What happened to you, Wayne? You used to be better than this."

The man gave a bitter laugh. "Life happened, Chief. The cold, hard realities of being under-educated, out of work, scrabbling for every dollar —and knowing nothing is ever going to change if I just sit here. That this"—he swept a hand over the room—"is my future. Let me tell you, that is real depressing. So I finally took some initiative."

"Turning to crime isn't the answer."

"Easy for you to say. You've always had a cushy job, made a generous salary. Plus, you married into dough. You've never had to spend a single minute worrying about money."

He stared at the man in silence. If only he knew.

All at once, Wayne's expression turned speculative. "You know . . . there might be an easier way to fix this."

"Like what?"

"You dig into that family stash of yours. If you pay me what I need to reach my goal, I'll shut down the lab tomorrow and disappear from your life."

"How much are we talking?" Not that it mattered. Until he had the gold in hand, he had zero cash to spare.

"Let's see . . ." Wayne sized him up and offered a number.

A big number.

Roger shook his head. "I don't have that kind of money. People around here have an overinflated opinion of my net worth."

"Then we're back to square one." Wayne rested a hip on the back of the couch and crossed his arms. "But let's talk some more about you. What were you doing at the lake in all that scuba gear?"

"I didn't come out here to discuss my business.

I came to warn you to watch your step. I won't stand by and let you put anyone's life in danger."

Wayne barked out a laugh. "And what do you plan to do about it?"

"I haven't decided yet. I'm hoping you don't force me to make a choice we could both live to regret."

For a long moment, the man studied him. "You're bluffing. You're not going to expose me and risk exposing yourself. You admitted as much a few minutes ago."

"I'm also not going to let anyone get hurt on my watch." He straightened up. "Stay away from the Lewis woman."

"She needs to leave. I heard her at church last week. She's thinking about wandering around the property. That can't happen."

"She's a big-city woman. She'll leave eventually."

"And in the meantime, she might take a hike, stumble onto stuff best left undisturbed. If the fire doesn't scare her away, she'll need some more persuading."

"Leave her alone, Wayne." He used his sternest voice. The one most people listened to . . . and obeyed.

Didn't work with the man across from him.

"I'll tell you what—why don't *you* try to convince her to leave in a kinder, gentler way? I'll lay low for three days."

"How do you expect me to do that?"

"You're a cop. You know how to solve crimes. I bet if you apply those analytical skills to this situation, you'll come up with a plan."

"And if I don't?"

"Then I'll take care of the problem." He ran a finger over the blade of the knife. "But one way or the other, she needs to leave ASAP. Deal or not?"

"I don't make deals with lawbreakers."

"No?" Wayne dropped into an upholstered chair with stuffing spilling from a split seam. "That's pretty high and mighty, coming from a police chief who trespasses on private property and goes on midnight dives for what appear to be very suspect purposes. That kind of activity sounds an awful lot like lawbreaking to me."

The pain in Roger's temples intensified. This trip had been a long shot, but appealing to the man's better nature had seemed worth a try.

Clearly, however, there was nothing left of the idealistic preteen who'd hung around the station twenty years ago.

He turned away and walked toward the door.

"So do we have a deal or not?" Wayne's voice followed him.

At the threshold, he paused. "I'll see what I can do. But if I fail, and there's another incident at her place, I'm going to have to ratchet up the investigation. I can't keep blaming it on the town vandals, or my officers will get suspicious."

"Then you better not fail."

Roger pushed through the door, letting it slap closed behind him, and headed straight for his car without looking back.

It appeared that was how he was going to have to play this with Wayne too. Close the door to the past, do what had to be done, move forward—and don't look back.

Not an easy assignment for a man who had more than one award hanging in his office from the National Association of Chiefs of Police. Who'd always taken pride in his accomplishments and his record.

But if his part in any of this current mess ever became public, he'd be dealing with a whole different kind of record.

He slid into the driver's seat, gripping the wheel as thunder rumbled in the distance. It was possible this would all end well . . . if he played it right. He wasn't going to resort to the kinds of tactics Wayne had used, but he should be able to come up with a plan that would persuade Dana to leave—for a while, anyway.

As he twisted the key in the ignition and pulled away from the decrepit farmhouse, he mulled over his approach. Why not ask her to consider removing herself from the scene until they sorted out the vandalism? After all, she was isolated—and vulnerable—out there, and while it didn't appear there'd been any intent to cause physical harm *yet,* that fire could have gotten out of hand before help arrived.

Yes. That argument might work.

And once she was gone, why would she return? New York was about as far removed from Beaumont as you could get. No doubt sentiment had led to her extended visit after Leo's death—but a cabin in the middle of a national forest wasn't consistent with her lifestyle. She'd be going back to the city sooner or later. Why not make it sooner?

He pulled out of the drive, onto the main road, and accelerated toward the empty house he now called home. Fatigue pulled at him again, weighing him down like the diving gear he lugged to Leo's lake for his midnight visits.

All that effort—and nothing to show for it.

Could he have missed the ammo cans somehow? It was hard to conduct a methodical search in the dark water. He'd tried to work his way out from the middle of the lake's current configuration, but the murky depths were disorienting. It was possible he'd skipped a section on his mental grid.

Or maybe the cans weren't there at all.

He tightened his grip on the wheel. No. There was no reason to doubt the veracity of Len White's letter. All the other facts had checked out—and the gold had never been recovered.

It was there.

But the clock was ticking. In ten days, Leah faced eviction.

He sped up, foot heavy on the accelerator. He'd go to the lake earlier tonight so he could finish in time to log a few hours of decent sleep. Wayne already knew he was there, and he doubted Dana would wander around after dark. Not since the vandalism incidents. No reason to wait until midnight to begin.

And come tomorrow, he'd pay Leo's granddaughter another visit. Wayne didn't want her gone any more urgently than he did. If she left, he could take a few of his accrued vacation days and make some daylight dives, when it would be much easier to keep track of the areas he'd covered.

Plus, he only needed to find one of the ammo cans. A few gold bars would be more than sufficient to cover Leah's expenses. He could sell them one at a time—from his safe-deposit box at the bank in Potosi. At least that's the story he'd tell the buyer.

All at once, a deer appeared on the shoulder of the road in the deepening twilight. After a millisecond hesitation, it bounded out of the woods.

Right in front of the patrol car.

Roger jammed on his brakes.

The car skidded, grazing the hind quarters of the deer, which stumbled . . . righted itself . . . and continued on its way.

Exhaling, he straightened out the car and moved on at a more sedate speed. How many close encounters with deer had he had on these woods-rimmed roads through the years?

Too many to count.

And 99 percent of the time, the deer escaped unscathed, despite their risky behavior.

He could only hope the odds would be as favorable to him in the dicey days to come.

—14—

"Just checking in, as promised." Finn propped the phone against his shoulder and slipped on his shades to cut the glare of the noonday sun reflecting off the lake.

"It's been a week since you called." Mac sounded disgruntled.

"Sorry. The days got away from me."

"Right."

That cryptic response was the very reason he'd called Mac instead of Lance. The middle McGregor brother would have been all over him about Dana. Mac had always been more discreet about . . .

"Time does fly when there's a beautiful woman close by." Amusement sniggered through Mac's addendum.

Scratch discreet.

"She works every day. I don't see her that much." He slanted a guilty glance toward the cabin. Not quite accurate. He'd gotten into the habit of showing up during her lunch break, and their evening spins around the lake were becoming routine. Not to mention their trips into town for church or pie at the Walleye.

None of which his brother needed to know about.

"I bet you manage to persuade her to take some breaks."

Finn huffed out a breath. "You know, if I'd wanted grief I would have called Lance. Besides, I have news." This should redirect his eldest sibling's thoughts. "I talked to Dad last night. I'm joining the firm."

"I knew you would." Mac's tone was nonchalant.

So much for his bombshell.

"How could you know what I was going to do? I only made the decision yesterday."

"Simple. It's an excellent fit for your skills, you like Atlanta, and family is important to you. Plus, you met a nice woman with potential who's making you realize the pluses of settling in one place."

"My decision has nothing to do with Dana." He turned away from the cabin.

"Think again."

Mac's I-know-more-than-you-do-because-

I'm-your-big-brother attitude rankled . . . as usual.

"I should have called Lance after all."

"He'd still be ragging you about Dana."

"And you're not?"

"Nope. Just pointing out the obvious—which you seem to have missed."

"Okay . . . I'll play along. Enlighten me."

"Simple. The right woman makes you view life differently. Once you meet her, that white picket fence starts to look more like a refuge than a reformatory."

"Move over, Confucius."

"Are there any other words of wisdom I can offer you, my son?"

"Ha-ha and no thanks. Besides, this is way too soon for such a serious discussion."

"Is it?"

The blue heron swooped into his usual spot near the bank, once more on the prowl. "Aren't you the one who always told me not to be impulsive—especially with women?"

"Yes. And I stand by that advice. But I've also learned that when you meet the woman you're going to marry, you know from the beginning she's different."

Hearing the *M* word verbalized sent a tiny tremor of panic spiraling through him.

"I didn't say I felt like that about Dana."

"Hey . . . chill. It's not *that* scary of a thought. And you didn't have to say anything. It's obvious.

Congratulations on your good taste, by the way. From what I saw, she could be a keeper."

"Since when have you gotten to be an expert on romance? Or even been tuned in to that kind of stuff?" Finn didn't try to hide his annoyance.

"Since I met Lisa. My wife has given me a new perspective on a lot of things. She told me to tell you she wants to meet Dana sometime."

Finn stifled a groan. Great. Now his brothers were talking to their significant others about his love life.

"You haven't mentioned her to Mom and Dad, have you?"

"No. I'll leave that up to you."

"Good. Because I'm getting ready to move to Atlanta—and Dana's from New York." Not that she planned to go back there. But Mac didn't need to know that.

"You'll find a way to make it work. You might have had your numbskull moments as a kid, but you were always inventive. Remember that time in London when you decided it would be cool to rappel down from our third-floor apartment?"

"That was Lance's idea."

"Yeah, but you were the one who figured out how to construct harnesses out of Dad's expensive leather belts."

"You're never going to let me forget that, are you?"

"Nope. The best part was when you got stuck

halfway down and the fire department had to rescue you. You're lucky Dad didn't put those belts to another use once they got you down." Mac's chuckle came over the line. "I'll have to share that story with Dana someday."

"I'm hanging up now."

"Stay in touch."

"I'll think about it."

Mac's laughter was still ringing as a screen door banged behind him.

Finn cut the connection and turned.

"I wondered if you were going to show up today." Dana waved at him from the porch, her smile of welcome sending a rush of warmth through him. For once, her hair was down instead of pulled back into its customary ponytail, the sun sparking the copper highlights among the light brown strands.

Man, she looked great.

And as he slid his cell back onto his belt and jogged up the slope, he had to admit Mac had nailed it.

From all indications so far, Dana Lewis was a keeper.

"Sorry. Were you on the phone?" Dana shoved her hands into the pockets of her jeans as Finn joined her on the porch.

"Nothing important." He touched her hair and smiled down at her. "I like it down."

The very reason she'd pulled out the elastic band and run a brush through it an hour ago—though she didn't share that nugget.

"And I like your shirt." She nodded toward the chest-hugging black number that said Baghdad Surf Team.

He dipped his chin, as if he couldn't remember what tee he'd grabbed this morning. For a instant his demeanor darkened. "Oh. Yeah. A birthday gift from a Ranger buddy. I just started wearing it again."

"Progress?" She reached for his hand, searching his face.

"I guess."

"I'm glad." She gave his fingers a squeeze. "I made some soup. Want to join me?"

"*Made* as in homemade?"

"Yep. Chicken and rice. Another one of Mags's recipes."

"When did you make that?"

"When I should have been working this morning. I had a visit from Chief Burnett that threw off my concentration."

"What did he say?"

"Let's talk while we eat."

He followed her through the door. Once in the kitchen, she gestured to a chair at the already-set table and continued toward the stove.

Two minutes later, after dishing up the hearty soup and setting a basket of French rolls on the table, she joined him, bowed her head, and said a short blessing.

"So what happened?" He spoke the instant she finished.

Her new friend might have many wonderful virtues, but patience wasn't among them.

She stirred her soup, her hunger evaporating. "He said he was concerned about my safety given the isolated location of the cabin and two back-to-back incidents. He more or less advised me to cut my visit short and consider coming back once they sort this mess out."

Twin grooves appeared on Finn's brow. "Does he have reason to think you're in danger?"

"Nothing specific. But I could tell he was worried. Based on what they found after poking through the remains of the shed, there's no question the fire was deliberately set."

"Why doesn't he send more patrols out this way?"

"I asked the same question. Insufficient personnel. The department only has three full-time officers and two part-timers." She continued to stir her soup. "What would you recommend I do?"

"What do you *want* to do?"

"I've never been the type to bow to intimidation —and I really don't want to leave yet." She poked at a piece of chicken with her spoon. "But I have to admit, after my New York experience

I'm not inclined to put myself in the line of fire if there's a serious risk."

Finn tapped a finger on the table. "I'll tell you what. Why don't you give it a few more days? There doesn't appear to be any issue in daylight. The chief said all of the vandalism incidents around town have happened at night. And as long as I'm around, a whistle will bring me here in minutes. Or I could sleep on your couch, if that would make you feel better."

The temptation to accept his offer was strong. He wouldn't even have to cram his six-foot-plus frame onto the sofa. Pops's bedroom was available.

But he *was* a whistle away, and uprooting him from his own place felt selfish.

"I appreciate that . . . but we've already put our makeshift security system to the test, and it works great. I'll be fine as long as I keep the whistle close at hand at night. And I've got the Winchester."

"Are you sure?"

"Yes." She did her best to appear—and sound—confident.

He studied her. "Okay. Let's go with that plan for now. In the meantime, I intend to enjoy every mouthful of this amazing soup."

"Mags was a super cook. I'm glad she left me all her recipes."

"And I'll be happy to sample any of them you're

in the mood to make." With a grin, he dived into the soup.

Finn kept the conversation lighthearted during the rest of the meal, and by the time he said goodbye with a kiss and a promise to return for their usual sunset row on the lake, she was more relaxed.

Yet as she watched him disappear into the woods . . . as an angry gray cloud dimmed the sun . . . she shivered.

Despite what she'd told Finn, the thought of spending nights alone in the cabin set off a flurry of butterflies in her stomach.

And until the vandals were found, she had a feeling the restful slumber she'd enjoyed since her handsome neighbor's arrival was going to be elusive.

Beep . . . Beep . . . Beep . . .

Beep. Beep. Beep.

BEEEEEEEP.

Roger froze, hovering suspended near the bottom of the lake, twelve feet of dark water above him as the distinctive alert from the metal detector came through his headphones.

This could be it.

Letting the detector rest on the bottom, he fumbled for the small telescoping rod on his equipment belt, pulled it open, and aimed his light at the spot that had caused the detector go berserk.

Nothing but silt—almost fifty years' worth.

But he was after what was underneath.

Heart pounding, he began poking the rod into the sediment.

It met no resistance.

He pushed harder, moving in a tight grid pattern.

Just when he began to wonder if the detector he'd paid big bucks for was defective, the rod hit a hard object.

His adrenaline surged.

Hand trembling, he closed the rod and put it back on his belt. After retrieving the six-inch drywall taping knife he'd dug out of his garage, he began to gently scrape the sediment aside.

Despite his slow, careful movement, particles swirled upward in the water, obscuring his vision. The guy at the dive shop had warned him about the difficulty of digging underwater, and he'd been right.

Roger peered at his air gauge. Ten minutes left, tops.

He couldn't wait for the sediment to settle.

Moving in closer, he went back to digging, working by feel now.

Through the neoprene gloves, his fingers came into contact with a solid object. He smoothed his hand over it, calculating. It was about ten, eleven inches long, maybe half a foot wide. The correct dimensions for a .50 caliber ammo can. And there was a handle.

He'd found the gold!

Grasping the can with both hands, he yanked it free of the sludge.

A cloud of sediment rose, engulfing him, but he never loosened his grip on the treasure.

With his air gauge dipping into the danger zone, he held fast to the handle with the rubberized palm of one glove and picked up the metal detector with the other. Then he kicked upward.

Once he broke the surface, he attached the detector to his belt and stroked one-handed toward the shore where he'd stashed his land clothes—the opposite side of the lake from the cabin, where lights always burned.

Did Dana Lewis never sleep?

But that wasn't a risk he'd have to worry about anymore, thank the Lord. Assuming this can held what he thought it did, his diving career was history.

Although his awkward cargo made for slow—and strenuous—going, he wasn't about to complain. The payoff would be well worth the herculean effort.

He was breathing hard when at last his feet touched bottom, and it took every ounce of his strength to heave himself and the can out of the water.

Near as he could tell once he pulled it free, the container weighed about twenty-five pounds. At current gold prices, that was close to half a million dollars—and consistent with what Len had said in his letter about the value of the gold they'd stolen and how they'd divided it into two cans.

For several minutes, Roger sat beside the lake, giving his energy and lungs a chance to recover—and to let reality sink in.

His money troubles were over.

Relief coursed through him, quivering through his muscles. Leah would have the care she deserved for as long as she needed it. He wouldn't have to break the promise he'd made to her long ago.

Should he send a thank-you heavenward?

No.

God might have allowed him to hit the jackpot tonight, but he wouldn't approve of his methods, no matter how good the intention. In the big picture, what he was doing was wrong.

Yet when he finally dredged up the energy to get moving, he didn't feel one ounce of remorse. You did what you had to do for the people you loved. Period.

He pulled off his flippers. Tugged on his shoes. Retrieved the backpack he'd hidden behind some scrub and shoved his diving equipment inside.

Not until after he bent to pick up the can did he realize he'd forgotten to kill his dive light.

His lungs balked, and he fumbled for the switch. Flipped it off.

That had been a stupid mistake.

But fatigue could mess with a man's brain . . . and he was dead beat.

He stood motionless, scanning the dark perimeter of the lake. An owl hooted, but there was no other sign of life.

His taut muscles slackened.

Only someone else with a suspect agenda would be wandering around on private property at this hour, and Wayne was lying low for the moment—assuming he was abiding by the three-day grace period he'd extended.

Still . . . it wouldn't hurt to get out of here ASAP.

Hoisting his equipment and the gold that would solve all his financial woes, he began the long trek back to his car.

Finn adjusted the hood of his dark sweatshirt and inspected the back of Dana's cabin, avoiding the soft glow spilling from around the shades in several windows. Apparently she still slept with the lights on . . . or had started to again after the vandalism incidents.

At least her screaming nightmares had subsided.

And all was quiet—as it had been on his previous three circuits during the hour and a half since beginning his patrols at ten-thirty.

Dana might have assured him again as they parted after their evening row that she'd be fine by herself overnight, but there wasn't much chance *he'd* get a lot of sleep with a drill-wielding, paint-toting pyromaniac running around. Might as well put the night hours to productive use. He could sleep tomorrow while she worked.

Staying in the shadows of the trees, he eased along the perimeter of the parking area toward the lake—and the spot he'd staked out earlier that offered him a concealed view of everything but the far side of her cabin. There was nothing to vandalize over there, though, nor any convenient access points. The windows were too high. But it didn't hurt to do a quick circuit every . . .

He froze as he rounded the cabin and got a full view of the lake.

Did a light just blink on the far side of the water?

It had come and gone so fast . . . could it have been a reflection from the full moon on the lake?

No.

His gut told him it had been an artificial light—and his gut had rarely let him down.

He swung his binoculars into position. Aimed them toward the area in question. Squinted.

Nothing.

He rotated a tad to the right.

Still nothing.

Switching direction, he swept the binoculars to the left.

Detected motion.

His pulse kicked up.

Someone was there.

Tucking the binoculars into the case on his belt, he took off at a jog, hugging the woods.

Once trees met water, however, the going got a lot more difficult—and it was a long hike to the other side of the amorphous-shaped lake, with its many little coves. Plus, the heavy underbrush forced him to slow down or risk alerting the trespasser to his presence. If the person or persons got wind of his approach too soon, they could take off before he reached them.

Although he forged through the gnarly undergrowth as fast as he could, it wasn't quick enough.

When he arrived at the spot he'd homed in on from across the lake, all was quiet. Nor were there any sounds of retreat in the surrounding woods.

Yet there was clear evidence someone had been here—matted ground cover, broken twigs on a low-growing bush, and mud at the edge of the lake, as if the person or persons had been in the water.

He frowned. That made no sense—unless Dana's uninvited visitors wanted to do some clandestine skinny-dipping. Perhaps a couple of teens had snuck in for some impromptu, late-night entertainment?

No.

On a hot July or August night, that might be a possibility. After all, this was about as far from Dana's cabin as you could get and still be at the lake. It was the kind of spot someone with that sort of agenda would choose.

With the cool April breeze chilling him even through his fleece hoodie, however, that wasn't a plausible scenario for tonight.

This felt planned—and devious.

Yet how was it related to the two previous incidents, which had both happened on the other side of the lake, much closer to the cabin?

The answer eluded him.

Giving up, Finn retraced his steps, did another security circuit around the cabin, and took up his sentry position again. No sense wasting time or thought on that question tonight.

Come tomorrow, however, he intended to go over the trampled area in the light of day with a fine-tooth comb.

And if there was any evidence to suggest who might have paid a late-night visit to Dana's lake, he'd find it.

—15—

At the knock on her front door, Dana jerked, sending the cursor skittering across the words on the screen.

Who would be visiting at eight-thirty in the morning—and arriving on foot?

"Dana, it's me."

Finn?

Her sudden swell of panic morphed to curiosity. Other than his daily lunch visits, he never interrupted her during the workday. Why break that pattern?

Pushing back from the kitchen table, she released her ponytail from its elastic band, finger-combed her hair as she crossed the living room, and opened the door.

Finn smiled at her. “Good morning.”

She gave him a quick head-to-toe. He was dressed in his usual jeans, his snug tee half hidden by a jacket, a day pack slung over his shoulder. With the sparkling lake in the background and the morning sun creating a swoon-worthy glow around him, he could have stepped out of an ad for extreme-sports gear. Potent masculinity oozed from his pores.

Dana gripped the edge of the door to steady herself. “You’re here bright and early. What’s the occasion?”

“An apology, an invitation, and a confession.”

“Wow. That’s a full agenda for a Tuesday morning. You want to come in?”

“The porch’ll do. First, the apology. Sorry for interrupting your work. Second, the invitation. Would you like to take a row with me to the far side of the lake?”

The man was full of surprises today.

“Now?”

"Yes—which leads me to the confession. I did a little surveillance here last night."

"You mean . . . while I was sleeping?"

"Yeah. Since I didn't figure I'd get much shut-eye with some weirdo showing up unexpectedly on your property, I decided to put my insomnia to productive use."

Another spike of alarm kicked up her pulse. "Did you see something suspicious?"

"Some*one*. But only from a distance."

She listened as he briefed her, digesting his discovery—and the personal implications—as he concluded his tale.

The man had stayed up half the night trying to protect her.

Her throat tightened.

Finn shifted the backpack into a different position. "I want to go back in daylight to see if I can spot any clues, and it's much easier to take the rowboat than trek through the underbrush. Since I knew you'd be suspicious if you noticed me on the lake, I decided I'd better 'fess up about my unofficial stakeout last night."

"Did you get any sleep at all?"

"Yes. I was in bed by one. I hung around for a while after I got back to the cabin, but all was quiet. I didn't think our culprit would come back twice in one night."

"But . . . what was he doing here to begin with? I haven't spotted any more vandalism today.

And why was he on the far side of the lake?"

"I'm hoping a short row might offer us some answers to those questions. Want to come along?"

"Yes." The manuscript she was working on could wait an hour. "Let me grab my jacket."

"I'll meet you at the boat." He did a one-eighty and clattered down the steps.

Dana detoured to the bathroom to dab on a touch of lipstick, then grabbed her windbreaker, jammed a thin pair of knit gloves in the pocket, and joined him on the dock.

"That was fast." He steadied the boat as she got in.

"I'm as anxious as you are to get to the bottom of this."

He put the oars to use at once, and silence descended as they skimmed across the lake. Finn was intent on his rowing, and it was no hardship to silently watch the early-morning sun shimmer on the water—and burnish his auburn hair.

As they drew close to the bank, he maneuvered the boat sideways, beside a tree. "Getting out is going to be tricky. If you can keep the boat in place, I'll grab that branch, swing out, and give you a hand up." He pointed to a sturdy, low-hanging limb that arched over the water.

"Or I can go first, since I'm closer. I was a jungle gym champ as a kid."

"A woman of many talents." One side of his

mouth hitched up, and he swept a hand toward the branch. "Have at it."

Trusting that jungle-gym climbing was like riding a bicycle, she stood, gripped the branch with one hand, and levered herself up. Once on solid ground, she latched on to a slender tree trunk.

"Very smooth." Finn let the boat drift down a couple of feet to give himself better access to the limb. "Can you secure this to a tree?" He tossed a rope up to her.

"Sure." She fingered the line, eyeing the slanted bank. Although she'd seen minimal evidence of the massive trauma to his leg, walking or going up and down steps was a lot different—and no doubt easier—than pulling a Tarzan stunt. "Is your, uh, leg going to be able to handle this?"

In answer, he followed her example and swung himself up in one smooth, lithe movement, all the while juggling the day pack.

"Never mind." She tied the rope to a tree, hoping he wasn't insulted by her query. "Your physical therapy regimen has obviously paid off. What's in there?" She motioned to the pack slung over his shoulder.

"Equipment I might need." He nodded to the left. "I found evidence of your uninvited guest about fifteen feet that direction."

He led the way, and she followed on his heels as he pushed branches aside to clear the path.

When he paused in a small clearing, she drew

up next to him. The scene was just as he'd described—matted vegetation and mud on the bank.

No question about it. Someone had been here last night.

"What are we looking for?"

"Anything the person might have dropped—or that might give us a clue to his identity."

"You're certain it's a he?" She shaded her eyes against the rising sun.

"Ninety-five percent. The kind of stunts he's been pulling usually have a male MO." He indicated the bank. "I'll see what I can find there. Why don't you search this area in about a six-foot radius."

"Okay—except I'm not going over there." She pointed to a brushy patch. "Poison ivy."

He gave it a quick perusal. "Your vision must be almost back to normal."

"Close. Besides, I learned to spot poison ivy the hard way. Pops took me on a what-to-avoid walk through the woods on my first visit, but the lesson didn't sink in until the next year, after I came down with the worst rash the local doctor had ever seen. I still have a few small bumps on my arm as a souvenir."

"In light of that experience, I'm surprised you ventured into the woods again."

"I didn't—on that visit. But Pops eventually convinced me to give it another try . . . and I learned that vigilance and precautions solved the problem." She swept a hand down her body. "Note the attire. No exposed skin. Plus these." She pulled out her gloves and waved them at him. "Final precaution? All of this will go in the washer the minute I get back to the cabin."

"Remind me to take you on my next scouting expedition."

She tugged on her gloves. "I'd have brought you a pair too, if I'd had any extra."

"No worries. I'm immune to poison ivy. After all the vegetation I've been exposed to in every kind of terrain you can imagine, nothing much phases me." He dropped to one knee and got up close and personal with the bank. "If you find anything, let me know."

She followed his instructions, working out from the center of the matted area in a gradually widening circle, but after he finished at the edge of the lake and joined her, she had nothing to show for her effort.

"I hope you had better luck than I did." She straightened up.

"Sad to say, no." He did a slow sweep of the woods surrounding the clearing. "That could be our man's point of exit." He indicated a spot at the perimeter.

"How do you know?" As far as Dana could see, there was nothing to distinguish that section of forest from any other.

Finn strode toward it, Dana on his heels. "See the broken branches?" He touched a few small twigs bent at an odd angle.

The man must have the eyes of an eagle.

"I do now. But even if my vision was normal, I doubt I'd have noticed them. They must give you Rangers some serious training in tracking."

"Enough." He pushed aside the broken branches. "Let's see if we can follow his path. Watch for anything he might have dropped or snagged on a twig or thorn."

They continued in silence, Finn leading the way. Dana followed a few feet behind, inspecting the ground and surrounding limbs as they passed.

When they at last emerged onto a one-lane, rutted dirt road, Finn stopped. "Any idea what this is or where it leads?"

"No. It's not on Pops's property, though. I tramped over every inch of it with him as a kid and there aren't any roads or trails other than the drive leading to the cabin. This could be a national forest service road. An unused one, based on all the potholes and weeds."

Finn walked along the edge of the overgrown byway, scrutinizing the ground. All at once he dropped to the balls of his feet. "It's being used now."

Dana walked over and bent down. Faint tire tracks were stippled on the dirt, along with partial footprints.

"I think he parked right here." Rising, Finn surveyed the narrow lane, then nodded toward some mashed vegetation on the shoulder, a dozen yards ahead. "That must be where he turned around. Let's search this part of the road and the shoulder on this side. If he was loading any kind of equipment in the car, it's possible he could have dropped something. Any clue, no matter how small, would help."

"I don't know if my eyes are up to the task of finding anything small."

"Two sets are still better than one. We'll both go over the whole area. Why don't you start on the left?"

They searched in silence for a few minutes, and in the end Dana was the one who found the one possible link to her midnight visitor.

Bending, she examined the semi-matte black object nestled among the blue blossoms of a wild phlox. It appeared to be some kind of latch or fastener—and given its precarious perch, it couldn't have been there long.

"Finn! I might have something."

He jogged her direction and hunkered down to examine it. "Huh."

"Care to explain that cryptic comment?"

He opened his backpack and dug out a small plastic bag along with a man's handkerchief. "It's a buckle."

"So?"

"Do you recognize the brand?"

She squinted at the lettering, just able to make out the unfamiliar name. Cressi. "No."

"They're one of the largest manufacturers of water-sports equipment in the world." He retrieved her find with the handkerchief and dropped it in the plastic bag. "This looks like a fin buckle."

She blinked. "You mean fin as in scuba diving or snorkeling?"

"Yes. Based on the mud at the edge of the lake, there was obvious water activity there. It fits."

"But . . . why would anyone want to dive in my lake? Especially at night?" This was downright weird.

"The obvious answer? He's hunting for something."

"Like what? There's nothing in there except bass and catfish."

"That you know of." He weighed the buckle in his hand. "You told me your grandfather expanded the lake through the years. What was on the land he flooded?"

"Nothing but woods and fields."

Finn tucked the buckle into the day pack. "Did he ever suggest the lake held anything of value?"

"No."

"What about the original pond? Did he ever talk about that?"

"Only to say it was too small and too artificially round. He wanted a lake that seemed more natural and wove in and out of the woods."

"And there was never any local scuttlebutt or a rural legend to suggest the lake contained anything . . . mysterious?"

"Such as?"

"Your guess is as good as mine."

She tucked her hair behind her ear. "Pops never said a word about the lake other than to comment on how much he enjoyed the view and the fishing, along with the wildlife it drew." Dana furrowed her brow. "Besides . . . how does this new twist relate to the vandalism?"

"If someone *is* searching for some item of value in your lake, they might prefer not to have any witnesses."

A shiver of unease rippled through her. "So he might be trying to drive me away."

"That's one explanation."

"Meaning the damage at my place may not be related to the vandalism at the picnic grounds."

"Maybe not."

A raindrop plopped on her nose, and she raised her face to the heavens as a low rumble of thunder rolled through the forest.

He settled the day pack into position on his shoulder. "We better start back or we could get caught in a storm."

"I'm right behind you." She followed him

toward the woods, mulling over the latest discovery. "So what happens next?"

"I want to have another talk with the chief. There may be a print on the buckle."

"You really think they have the resources to investigate such an obscure clue?"

"It's not hard to run prints through the national database."

"If there are any."

"True." A gust of wind whipped past, and he surveyed the sky again. "Let's try to pick up the pace."

She increased her stride as he led her back through the woods, toward the lake. The return trip went much faster, and they made it to the boat and back to the dock before the storm rolled in.

But as Finn gave her a quick hug and set off at a jog for his cabin, she had a sinking feeling that while they'd escaped this storm, an even bigger one was brewing.

It was done.

Leah's future care was secure.

Roger passed the Welcome to Beaumont sign and exhaled, loosening his grip on the wheel. The whole trip had gone much smoother—and faster—than he'd expected, the pieces falling into place like the plot of a well-constructed novel.

The visit to the safe-deposit box room at the

bank in Potosi, the three ten-ounce gold bars heavy in his pocket.

The meeting with the bank manager afterward, who'd sympathized with his need to sell an old family holding and offered to phone a reputable dealer in St. Louis—who, in turn, was interested in purchasing the bars at a fair price.

The promise from the dealer to wire the money to his account in the bank as soon as the gold was in hand and authenticated.

With that meeting set for nine-thirty tomorrow morning, the money could be in his account within forty-eight hours.

So on the drive back from St. Louis tomorrow, he'd stop at Woodside Gardens and let Alan Landis know Leah's bill would be paid in full by Friday.

For the first time in weeks, the tightness in his shoulders eased—followed by a rumble in his stomach. It was early for lunch, but nerves had quashed his appetite this morning. Why not swing into the Walleye and grab a bite before reporting for duty?

Two minutes later, he pulled into the parking lot, glanced in his rearview mirror—and froze.

Wayne's pickup was on his tail.

And based on the man's grim demeanor, it wasn't a coincidence.

Stomach knotting, he parked and hauled himself out of the car. The man wouldn't be tracking him down publicly unless there was an urgent need for them to talk. And it wasn't about police business, or he'd have used his cell.

Wayne swung in next to his car. Looked around the lot, which, as usual, held only a few cars at midmorning. Rolled down his window.

"Meet me at my place."

"What's the . . ."

Without giving him a chance to finish his question, Wayne cranked his window up, backed out, and took off down the road.

Roger watched him go, his brief burst of positive energy—and his appetite—evaporating.

Dread pooling in his belly, he slowly climbed back into the car. Put it in gear. Pulled out of the parking lot.

Wayne was long gone already . . . but the man was pacing beside his truck ten minutes later when Roger reached the end of the dirt-and-gravel road that led to the rundown farm.

The instant he stopped the car and slid out, Wayne was in his face.

"I thought you were going to get rid of the girl!"

"I'm working on it."

"Not fast enough." A muscle ticced in his cheek. "She and that neighbor of hers are wandering around the property. They came within twenty feet of my lab this morning. Twenty feet!" His nostrils flared, tension quivering in the air between them. “If they hadn’t been talking as they approached, and if I hadn’t gotten quiet real fast, they might have heard me and come to investigate. That is *not* an outcome any of us want—trust me.”

No, it wasn’t, based on Wayne’s angry flush and cold eyes. Nothing was more important to the ex-lead-smelter worker than protecting his lab and accruing the money he thought would buy him a new life.

Nothing.

Wayne would do whatever was necessary to achieve his misguided dream—even if that meant hurting people who got in his way.

The knife in Roger’s gut twisted.

“I warned her not to roam around.” He tried without much success to keep his voice steady.

“It didn’t work. I want her gone.”

“I can’t force her to leave, Wayne.”

The man’s mouth tightened. “Then I’ll take care of it.”

“How?”

“You don’t want to know.”

Roger drew himself up to his full height, buying him a scant one-inch advantage. “I’m not going to protect you if anyone gets hurt, Wayne. I already warned you about that.”

“And I warned *you*. Say one word about my operation, do one thing to shut me down, and my photos are going straight to the highway patrol.”

In the taut silence that followed, Roger debated his next move. Wayne's photos would raise questions—but they contained no proof of any illegal activity other than trespassing . . . and he was done with that. Yet trying to explain why he'd been scuba diving on Leo's lake at night was a tricky proposition. No matter what justification he came up with, the photos would damage his reputation and his credibility. Maybe even cost him his job.

And that was all he had left.

"Look—can't you suspend your operation for a few weeks?" He hated the subtle plea in his tone, but he was running out of options. "Leo's granddaughter isn't going to stay here forever."

"No, I can't! I busted my butt building a network of smurfers and brokers. If I don't come through for them on a regular basis, they'll move on and I'll have to start from scratch. I'm too close to the end to do that. Either you convince her to leave . . . or I will."

"Fine. I'll try again." What else could he say?

"You better succeed. Fast."

Roger turned away, retook his seat behind the steering wheel, and shut the door.

There *was* one other option. Now that he had the gold, he could cash in some more of it, pay Wayne off.

But he'd vowed to use the gold only for Leah's care—and even that had pushed him way past his moral boundaries. Using it to pay blackmail to a drug dealer? He couldn't go there.

As he pulled out, Wayne was standing where he'd left him.

Still holding all the cards.

And unless he convinced Leo's granddaughter to bid Beaumont farewell, the biggest loser in this nasty game could end up being Dana Lewis.

Finn pushed through the door of the Walleye, lifting a hand in greeting when Hazel waved at him from across the café.

"I'll be with you in a sec." She finished writing on her order pad and bustled over. "You here for a late breakfast or an early lunch?"

"Neither. I just need a coffee to go."

"You certain I can't tempt you? Chuck got in the mood to concoct fajitas today, and they're delish." She smacked her lips.

One corner of his mouth twitched. "I might swing by to sample them later. But I need to go see the chief first."

"He's not in."

How could the woman know that?

"You sure?"

"Ninety-nine percent. He pulled into the parking lot here twenty, twenty-five minutes ago, but after he exchanged a few words with Wayne Phelps, the two of them took off thataway." She waved toward the south, away from town.

Finn grinned. "You ever think of becoming a private eye? With observation skills like that, you'd make a fortune."

"These eyes don't miss much, that's a fact." She winked and nudged him with her elbow. " 'Course, I can't always make heads or tails of what I see."

"Such as?"

"I can't imagine what the two of them could be up to. It's not like they're best buds." She pursed her lips. "I wonder if Wayne had some damage at his place. There's a wave of vandalism going around, you know."

"Yeah, I know."

"I don't think that's it, though. Wayne couldn't have said more than a few words to him. Not enough to report a problem." Her brow puckered. "I hope he didn't drag him on some kind of wild goose chase. The chief is worn to a frazzle, what with trying to do his job and deal with his wife's illness."

"Sounds like he's juggling a lot of balls."

"That's the truth. And it's taking a toll, let me tell you. The other day, his hands were so shaky his coffee sloshed out onto the table. He joked about me filling the cup too full, and I went along, but it was nerves, pure and simple."

Finn could sympathize with the man's plight—and the buckle in his pocket was going to add one more chore to his full plate. Couldn't be helped, though. Dana's safety was his top priority.

"Well, if he's not around . . ."

"Wait." Hazel leaned around him and peered through the picture window at the front of the café. "This is your lucky day. There he goes now—in the direction of the station. At least wherever he went was a short trip." She straightened up. "You still want that coffee to go?"

Finn was already heading for the door. "I'll take a rain check. I might be back later for those fajitas too."

"You won't be sorry." She waved good-bye as the door shut behind him.

He covered the distance to the station in four minutes flat, and sixty seconds after that, he was standing in front of the woman at the main desk.

"Good morning. Is the chief in?"

She gave him a once-over. "Yes. Let me see if he's available." She rose.

"The name's Finn McGregor."

Lynette tossed a smile over her shoulder. "I know. I've heard all about you from Hazel at the Walleye and Marv at the hardware store . . . and several other people. Welcome to small-town life. Hang on a minute."

As she disappeared down a hall, Finn folded his arms. The town grapevine must be thriving if that many residents were aware of his presence—and knew his name.

Which raised an interesting question.

If everybody in town knew so much about everybody else, why was the police department having such difficulty nailing whoever was disrupting Dana's life?

One more mystery to add to his growing list.

But perhaps the next few minutes with the chief might throw some light on the puzzle.

—16—

"You have a minute, Chief?"

Roger swiveled his chair away from the window, scooted into his desk, and tried to conjure up a smile for Lynette. "I can always spare a minute."

"Well . . . to be honest, this might take longer than that. The good-looking guy who's renting the Busch place is out front. He wants to talk to you."

Finn McGregor was here?

Another piece of bad news.

His visit had to be related to the incidents at Leo's place. Based on how he and Dana had looked at each other Sunday during the button handoff, McGregor had more than a neighborly interest in the girl next door.

How could a day that had started out on such a high note deteriorate so fast?

"What does he want?"

"He didn't say, I didn't ask. When a hot guy

like that shows up, my brain stops working." She fanned herself.

Any other time, Roger would have been entertained by her theatrics.

Today apprehension trumped amusement.

"You want me to find out, send him back, or tell him you're busy?" Lynette tugged at the collar of her turtleneck as she continued to wave her hand in front of her face.

Roger tapped a finger on his desk. Despite the unsettling currents in the air, it was possible this visit was nothing more than a follow-up to the button discussion.

But no matter the reason for the man's appearance, perhaps he could use it to his advantage. If he could recruit McGregor to help him convince Dana it would be safer to vacate the premises, she might be more inclined to leave Beaumont.

It was worth a try, anyway.

"Go ahead and send him back."

Instead of leaving at once, Lynette pinned him with the same scowl she used on her sixteen-year-old son whenever he messed up. "Did you eat today?"

"I'm going to drop by the Walleye after this meeting."

"That's not an answer . . . or maybe it is." She harrumphed. "I'll call Hazel and tell her to save you a couple of Chuck's fajitas. They're on special today."

As she disappeared out the door, he tried to erase thoughts of spicy food from his mind. Unless his stomach stopped churning, he'd have to settle for a late breakfast of poached eggs and toast.

Sixty seconds later, McGregor walked in.

He rose and held out his hand. "I didn't expect to see you again so soon." The man returned his firm shake. "Have a seat and tell me what I can do for you today."

"I wondered if the button produced any leads." Dana's neighbor folded his long frame into the chair across the desk, his posture relaxed.

But his laid-back pose was a pretense. Nothing about this man was relaxed. His eyes were sharp. Probing. Intense. Leashed energy radiated from his pores. If the need arose, he'd be ready to rumble in a heartbeat.

Watch your step with this one, Burnett.

"I'm afraid not. As I mentioned on Sunday, it's a very common button. Plus, as I suspected, there were only fragments of prints on it. Not enough to run through a database."

"Hmm."

What was that supposed to mean?

Since he had no idea, Roger remained silent.

After a few seconds, Finn reached into his pocket and pulled out another plastic bag. "You might have better luck with this." He set it on the desk.

As Roger stared at the buckle, the air jamme in his lungs.

Stay calm. Keep your expression neutral. You'v never seen this before, remember?

Masking his shock, he tipped forward in hi chair and pretended to inspect it. "Is that som kind of clasp?"

"Yes. From a swim fin."

The man *would* have to know what the buckl was used for.

"Where did you find it . . . and why is i important?"

"This morning. On the side of a road in th national forest, near Dana's property."

As he proceeded to fill him in, Roger had to us every ounce of his self-control to mask his panic

Finn McGregor had spotted him last night— all because the excitement of finding the gol had addled his brain and he'd forgotten to switc off the stupid dive light.

Even worse, his fingerprints would be all ove the fin buckle.

"So I'm assuming our man is searching for som item of value he thinks is in the lake," McGrego concluded, lobbing the ball into his court.

Roger folded his hands on his desk to hide th quiver in his fingers. "That's an interesting theory But it seems unrelated to the vandalism at he place."

"Not necessarily. As I told Dana, if our dive

prefers to keep his search secret, he may not want to risk any witnesses. Diving in the middle of the night can't be very efficient, however. He could be trying to make her so nervous she leaves, giving him daylight access."

McGregor thought the *diver* was the one trying to spook Dana?

That was rich.

He was the one trying to *protect* Leo's granddaughter.

"I suppose that might be possible." He imbued his tone with as much skepticism as he could. "But I'm having difficulty wrapping my mind around the notion that Leo's lake could contain anything worth going to so much trouble to get." That, at least, was true. Or had been until he'd held the gold bars in his hands last night.

"That's what Dana said too." Finn crossed an ankle over his knee. "Maybe you'll find some prints on the buckle that will give us a lead—and shed some light on the issue."

"It's worth trying, I suppose." He picked up the plastic bag and examined the buckle.

"Have you had any success tracking down your other vandals?"

At the slight emphasis on the word *other,* Roger appraised him. "You think this is a separate operation?"

"Don't you, based on what I saw last night and what we found today?"

Every instinct screamed at him to say no, t
attribute Dana's difficulties to the same perpe
trators who were playing havoc with the picni
grounds. To dismiss this as nothing more tha
an extension of those pranks.

But even if he *didn't* know every intimate detai
of what was happening at Leo's place, he'd b
drawing the same conclusions as the man acros
from him. There was a big disconnect betwee
picnic grounds graffiti and the stuff going on a
the lake. To pretend otherwise would rais
suspicion.

He needed to play this as professional as h
could—and try to get McGregor on his side i
the campaign to send Dana packing.

"Yes, I do—and to tell you the truth, it worrie
me. I have a very small department that's alread
stretched thin. Trying to catch the picnic ground
vandals is hard enough. I can't park an office
there every night, all night. The Lewis place i
even more of a challenge." He shook his hea
and frowned. "We have less chance of catchin
someone in the act there, given the isolate
location—and that fire could have had a lot mor
serious consequences than it did."

"I'm aware of that." McGregor's jaw hardened

Ah. Telling.

He and Dana had obviously become *much* mor
than neighbors.

That gave him an angle to exploit.

Forearms on the desk, he leaned forward. "You know, I'd feel a lot more comfortable if Dana wasn't out there by herself while this situation is unresolved. You two seem to have become friends. Is there any chance you could persuade her to go to Leo's house in St. Louis for a couple of weeks until we straighten everything out?"

McGregor rested his elbows on the arms of his chair and steepled his fingers, his eyes shuttered. "You think you might have the case solved by then?"

"It's possible. We have this"—he lifted the bagged buckle, which would be of no help since it wouldn't contain any prints thirty seconds after McGregor walked out the door—"and we're keeping our ear to the ground. We'll get a break eventually."

"Yet you haven't had a break with the other vandalism incidents, and those began when?"

"Early April—but there's been no activity for the past ten days or so. That's why I thought they might have moved on to the Lewis place . . . until this." He tapped the plastic bag, silently cursing his carelessness. If it hadn't been for the buckle, he could have continued attributing the hits at Dana's place to the same perpetrators . . . and deflecting suspicion from the real culprit.

"Early April. Three weeks and no leads."

At the hint of censure in McGregor's voice—and the implication he wasn't doing an adequate job—Roger straightened up. This might be small-town police department, but he knew ho to work with limited resources, to find innovativ ways to get information. No one had a right t impugn his professionalism.

“As a matter of fact, I have my suspicions. M officers and I cultivate a good relationship wit the citizens. They talk to each other—and to u We’ve earned their trust, and they pass o information. We’re also tuned in to the grape vine. This isn’t public knowledge, but we hav two suspects we’re watching closely. It’s only matter of time before we catch them.”

“I suppose community gossip and scuttlebu can be a useful tool in crime solving.” McGrego studied him.

“Very.”

“Yet it hasn’t helped you identify any suspect in Dana’s case.”

Blast.

He’d walked straight into that one.

Backpedal, Burnett.

“Every case is different.” He managed to pul off a calm, cool, composed tone. “The incidents a her place are very recent. Plus, it’s an isolate location. There may be just one person involved meaning less chance of leaks. That’s why I thin it would be safer if she cut her stay short. Ha she said anything to you to suggest she migh be thinking about doing that?”

"No."

"Do you have any idea how long she plans to stay?"

"The original plan was indefinitely."

Not what he wanted to hear.

Roger scratched the back of his left hand. "Well, I'll beef up patrols out there as much as I can—but it may not be sufficient to prevent another incident."

Instead of responding, McGregor glanced at his hand.

Instantly, Roger stopping scratching. Looked down.

An angry red rash had appeared on his skin sometime in the past few hours.

Wonderful.

He must have brushed against some poison ivy last night in the woods.

McGregor lifted his gaze—but his eyes were hooded. "Dana was telling me just this morning how she got a bad case of poison ivy on her first visit to her grandfather's place."

Once again, Roger knitted his fingers together on the desk, brain firing on all cylinders. Had Dana and her neighbor discovered a patch of poison ivy somewhere in the vicinity of her late-night visitor? And if so, was McGregor beginning to wonder if the strange goings-on were connected to a certain police chief?

No. That was a stretch—and jumping to conclusions could lead to panic . . . and more mistakes.

Besides, no matter what kind of theories the man across from him might concoct, they'd go nowhere. The one piece of evidence McGregor had produced that could identify the mystery diver was in a plastic bag on his desk. Under his control. And he wasn't going back to Leo's property again for illegal purposes. His personal mission there was finished.

"Poison ivy is common in these parts." Pretending the rash was anything else would be foolish. Based on past outbreaks, in another few hours there would be no disguising it. "I picked up a touch of it myself, as you can see. It likes to hide in the weeds along the back of my property."

McGregor let a few moments of silence tick by, then stood. "I won't keep you from your work any longer. You'll let me know if you find anything on the buckle?"

"Of course."

The man eyed it—almost as if he was having second thoughts about leaving it and wished he could snatch it back.

Not going to happen.

Roger rose, picked it up, and set it on the credenza behind his desk. "My first priority after you leave."

After a brief hesitation, McGregor held out his hand. "Thanks for your time."

"That's why I'm here." Roger returned his firm shake, remaining on his feet as the man disappeared out the door.

Only after he heard Dana's neighbor exchange a few muffled words with Lynette did he lower himself into his chair.

The meeting had not gone well.

Not only had he failed to win McGregor over as an ally in his quest to convince Dana to leave, but her neighbor had seemed suspicious—and the poison ivy had added fuel to the fire.

He scratched his hand again. The calamine lotion and Benadryl in his medicine cabinet at home would take care of the itchiness.

Too bad he couldn't as easily produce a remedy for his other problem.

Namely, Wayne Phelps.

Shoving back his chair with more force than necessary, Roger rose and began to pace. If it wasn't for Wayne, he'd be home free. He could pay Leah's bills at Woodside Gardens, get more than a handful of hours of sleep each night, throw out his bottle of Tums.

Silently he cursed the man who had complicated his life in ways he could never have imagined.

Too bad the local market garden farmer couldn't fall off the face of the earth.

And too bad a small-town police chief who'd

already strayed from the straight and narrow wasn't the type to take matters into his own hands to nudge that wish along.

But while his conscience was already pinging a persistent red alert, he wasn't directly hurting anyone. Yes, he was looking the other way with the meth lab, but the people who bought Wayne's product were choosing to inflict harm on themselves. Besides, if Wayne didn't supply it, someone else would.

You're rationalizing, Burnett.

Maybe.

Still, he wasn't taking chances with people's lives, like Wayne had with that fire he'd started in the shed near Dana's cabin.

And Roger had no doubt the danger would accelerate if Dana didn't leave.

He stopped in front of his most recent award certificate and massaged his forehead. If the National Association of Chiefs of Police knew what he was up to, they'd nullify every one of the citations lining his walls—as they should. He didn't deserve them. Not anymore. Protecting a lawbreaker was dead wrong.

Bad as that was, though, his culpability would be far greater if Dana got hurt. Keeping law-abiding citizens safe was the most basic duty of a police officer.

And he didn't intend to fail at it.

That left him only a handful of options . . .

assuming he didn't sell more of the gold to pay off Wayne.

He could—and would—continue to lobby her to leave.

He could—and would—do some night patrolling himself, try to intercept any further threat. If Wayne showed up . . . if he refused to listen to reason and insisted on carrying out whatever dangerous plan he came up with next . . . well, law enforcement officers were obligated to protect the public. The use of deadly force wasn't encouraged, but neither was it condemned when a life was at stake.

Roger rested his hand on his holster. In all his years as a police officer, he'd drawn his gun less than a dozen times. And he'd never had to fire it.

But if Wayne gave him just cause?

He could—and would—pull the trigger.

"Knock, knock. I come bearing fajitas from the Walleye."

As Finn's voice wafted through the open front window, Dana hit save and pushed her chair back. After their early-morning row across the lake, the best she'd hoped for was a quick evening drop-in. If this kept up, she'd be burning the midnight oil making up lost time on the current manuscript.

Hmm. Sleep versus a bonus visit from Finn.

No contest.

She crossed the living room and pulled open the door. "This is a surprise."

"I want to fill you in on my visit with Chief Burnett. There were some interesting vibes during our meeting. I know I've already eaten into your workday, but I promise this will be a fast lunch. Hazel told me these are great." He hefted a white sack.

"Sold."

"That wasn't hard." He grinned.

"I'm hungry."

"You want to eat on the dock? It's a perfect day."

"Works for me."

She grabbed Pops's sweater off the back of a chair in the living room and followed him down the slope.

At the end of the wooden platform, he sat and let his legs dangle over the edge, removing two sodas and two wrapped bundles from the bag while she got comfortable beside him. "I asked them to assemble these so they'd be less messy. I hope you like them with the works."

"I do."

"Then dive in." He handed her one of the parcels, along with several napkins. "I said less messy—but messy and fajitas go together."

"And they're well worth it." She unwrapped the white paper and inhaled. "Mmm. Yum. So tell me what happened with the chief."

She listened as he recounted their exchange, eating steadily while he talked.

After he finished, she cocked her head. Whatever had raised Finn's antennas during the meeting eluded her. "The conversation sounds like it was pretty straightforward."

"It was. But the undercurrents . . . different story."

"How so?"

"I'm not an expert on body language, but several things struck me. One, he tried hard to hide it, but I could tell he was shocked by the buckle. Two, Hazel told me his hands have been shaky lately. Three, he tried to enlist my help to get you to leave the cabin. Four, there was a brief spark of panic in his eyes when I told him about my theory that the lake holds something of value. Five—and this is the clincher—he has what appears to be a new outbreak of poison ivy on his hand."

Dana stopped eating. "Are you suggesting *he* might be behind the vandalism here?"

"I'm not suggesting anything yet . . . just keeping an open mind."

"But . . . he's been the chief here forever. Pops thought he was a great guy. He's respected in town. And I heard he's won a bunch of awards."

"I saw a lot of them on his office walls—but people can change."

Dana took a bite of her fajita, watching the

blue heron come in for a perfect landing in his usual spot. "I know he's been under tremendous stress with his wife. That could account for his shaky hands."

"True. Factoring in everything else, however, it all strikes me as more than coincidence—and I'm not discounting my instincts. They've saved my hide more than once."

She scooped up a piece of red pepper from the wrapping paper and stuck it back in her fajita. "Is he going to check the buckle for prints?"

"So he says. But I doubt he'll find anything."

"Why?"

He shrugged.

She stared at him. "You think he might tamper with evidence?"

"If he has anything to hide, he might—and that's a topic worth exploring." He finished off his first fajita and picked up the second. "Are you working late tonight to catch up after our hike this morning?"

"Why?"

"I'm going to take another trip into town with my computer and get some pie at the Walleye. And while I'm there, I might do some googling on our friendly police chief. You never know what a little surfing will uncover."

Dana watched the motionless blue heron suddenly lunge forward to snap up an unsuspecting fish or frog.

She had a feeling the tenacious man beside her would exhibit the same total focus and quick decisiveness when the chips were down.

Thank goodness he was on her side.

"Are you inviting me to go with you?"

"If you can spare the time."

"For a piece of the Walleye's chocolate cream pie?" And another hour in his company? "Always."

"How does seven o'clock sound? I'd like to go after the rush is over and we can get a quiet, out-of-the-way booth where we won't be disturbed."

"Fine with me." She moved on to her second fajita too. "But if Hazel's there, she might be in a talkative mood. In case you haven't noticed, she's taken a shine to you."

"Must be my Army Ranger charisma." He winked.

Her lips twitched. "Must be."

"A moot point, in any case. She won't be working tonight unless she puts in twelve-hour shifts. She was there midmorning. To be honest, though, I wouldn't mind having another chat with her. She's a font of information—possibly better than Google for our purposes, if we steer the conversation."

"You have a point. She does seem to have her finger on the pulse of everything that happens in Beaumont."

They finished their lunch in companionable silence . . . until Dana worked up the courage to broach the subject she'd been thinking a lot about in recent days.

"So when are you leaving for Atlanta?" She tried for nonchalance—and somehow managed to pull it off.

He finished chewing his last bite, wadded up the paper, and shoved it back in the white sack. "I'm booked at the cabin through the thirtieth."

Eight short days from now.

She played with a stray piece of grated cheese. "Are you starting work right away?"

"The sooner the better, if my dad has his way."

"I can understand why he'd be anxious for you to get on board." She dropped the piece of cheese into the water. It was gone a moment later in a flutter of fins. "But can I be honest? I wish you had another month here."

"Hey." He touched her arm, and she looked over at him. "We'll deal with the long-distance challenge, okay? Besides, I doubt you'll stay here forever, unless I've misread your cues."

"No. Much as I love this place, and much as I needed to be here for these past few weeks, I don't see myself living in the country year-round. I'll keep it as a getaway, though."

"Sounds reasonable."

"As for where I want to call home on a more permanent basis . . ." She shrugged. "That's still up in the air."

In response, he stood, gave her a hand up—and

didn't let go. "I know you don't want to go back to the kind of life you led in New York, but would you consider living in another big city?"

Her lungs locked. "Such as?"

"What about Atlanta? It sure would beat a long-distance courtship."

"Courtship?" Not the sort of language she'd associate with an action-hero type. "Isn't that kind of an old-fashioned word?"

"I'm kind of an old-fashioned guy."

"Yeah? That's not the image I have of hotshot Army Rangers."

"I'm not a Ranger anymore."

"Hmm. That implies the old-fashioned guy is actually new-fashioned." She put a teasing spin on the comment—but Finn must have picked up her underlying concern because all at once he got totally serious.

"No. It's the way I was raised. I'll admit I did my share of partying while I was in college and in the Army, but my core values never changed. And they're solid—just like my brothers' are. Translation? Now that I'm out of the service, I'm ready to look for exactly what they found . . . someone to share my life with. I didn't expect to meet a woman like you quite this fast, but as my mother always reminds me, God's timing isn't always ours."

Wow. That was direct.

She reached for his other hand. Twined her

fingers with his. “I’d have pegged you for the strong, silent type who always keeps his emotions to himself—except you’ve blown that stereotype too.”

One side of his mouth quirked up. “Do me a favor—don’t ruin my image with my brothers. They give me enough grief as it is.”

“It will be our secret.”

“So what do you think about Atlanta?”

Her first instinct was to throw caution to the wind and promise to jump on a plane next week. Finn McGregors didn’t come around every day.

But relocating was a big decision.

He narrowed his eyes as the silence lengthened. “Am I rushing you?”

“A little. We met less than three weeks ago. What if we decide in a few months this isn’t going to work out? I’d have to uproot myself again.”

“My gut tells me that’s not going to happen.”

“Mine does too . . . but hormones can play havoc with normally sensible people.”

He blew out a breath. “Are you always this logical?”

“Sad to say, yes.”

“So what do you suggest?”

“My first preference would be to stay here for another few weeks, then head to St. Louis and get Pops’s house ready to put on the market. St. Louis wouldn’t be a terrible commute, would it?”

He made a face. “It’s not like meeting for dinner after work every night.”

“Every night?”

“Why not? You have someone better to spend your evenings with?” He stroked a gentle finger along the curve of her jaw.

She had to force her brain to keep working. “You’re building a very convincing case.”

“I have other persuasive techniques too.”

“Such as?”

He pulled her close and proceeded to demonstrate.

When the kiss ended, she kept a firm hold on him until the ground beneath her stilled. “Okay. I’ll think about it.”

“That’s a start, anyway. I’ll keep working on it. We Rangers are nothing if not persistent when on a mission.”

“Is that a promise?”

A husky chuckle rumbled deep in his chest. “Count on it. Walk me to my car?”

He took her hand again, his grip strong . . . sure . . . confident. Strange how a simple touch of his fingers could make her feel special—and safe. None of the other guys she’d dated had had that effect on her.

Once they rounded the cabin and said their good-byes, she lingered in the parking area until the last motes of dust from the departing SUV floated to the ground. Then she turned and ambled toward the door. Work was calling.

But much as she'd always enjoyed editing love stories, it was going to be very tough to concentrate on fiction when a real-life romance was playing out in living color in her own backyard.

—17—

"Well—welcome back! And with a lovely lady on your arm this trip."

As Hazel called out her greeting from across the dining room at the Walleye, Finn leaned toward Dana. "Does she live here or what?"

"I don't know . . . but as you pointed out earlier, this could work to our advantage if Google doesn't come through."

He had to lean down to hear her murmured response—and the fresh, sweet scent of her hair tripped his pulse up a notch.

"How were those fajitas?" Hazel beamed at them as she hustled over.

"Great. Thanks for the recommendation." He transferred his laptop from one hand to the other so he could inch closer to the woman beside him. "I can't believe you're still here, though."

"Not *still* here. Here again. I worked a split shift today."

Ah. That explained it.

"We're in the mood for some pie." Finn

motioned toward the counter, where several offerings were displayed under glass domes.

"Then you came to the right place. The chocolate cream is to die for. It's a particular favorite of a certain book editor, as I recall."

"You have an amazing memory." Dana smiled at the waitress.

"Only about important things like food . . . and handsome men—like your date." She gave him a nudge with her elbow.

"Do you think we could have that corner booth?" Finn stepped in, fighting down the blush that was the bane of his existence as he motioned toward the secluded booth he'd chosen the morning he'd googled his neighbor. Perhaps a similar dramatic discovery was waiting to be unearthed tonight.

"It's yours for the evening. The dinner rush is over. If you don't want the chocolate cream pie, we also have apple, pecan, and cherry. What'll it be?"

"Tough choice . . . but I'll go with your recommendation and Dana's favorite."

"Smart man. Coffee?"

"Yes. The high-octane stuff for me." Finn deferred to Dana for her choice.

"Decaf tea for me, please."

"I'll have it over in a jif. You two make yourselves comfortable."

Taking Dana's arm, Finn guided her toward the

booth. "Let's share one side so we can both see the screen." He motioned toward the bench facing the café, which would allow them to google in private.

"Mmm . . . very smooth. The suggestion sounds practical, but it gets you up close and personal with your date. Does it work with all the girls?" She grinned and slid onto the seat.

"I don't know. I've never tried it before." He joined her and set the laptop on the table. It *was* a little tight—but cozy. Very cozy.

"I bet you have a bunch of tried-and-true lines countless women have fallen for."

"Ancient history." He opened the laptop and booted up as Hazel approached with their mugs. "Impeccable timing. Saved by the java."

Dana elbowed him. "I'll let you off the hook, since I'm more interested in what's ahead than in what's behind."

"A smart philosophy for many aspects of life." Hazel set the mugs down, along with a pitcher of cream. "As my mother, God rest her soul, used to say, if you spend too much time looking back, you could miss the fork in the road that would have led to an amazing future."

"She must have been quite the philosopher." Dana dunked her tea bag.

"Yes, she was—and she had a saying for every occasion. Birthdays, weddings, new babies, graduations . . . I have a whole stack of—"

Across the room, the plate of pie in front of a five- or six-year-old hit the floor. The youngster immediately began wailing and poking her older brother with her fork. He let out a shriek. Both parents dived into the fray.

"I better go see if I can help salvage that family outing." Hazel tut-tutted. "You two in a hurry for your pie?"

"No. Don't rush on our account. We'll keep ourselves entertained." Finn motioned to his laptop.

"You know . . . there are better ways to entertain yourself in a secluded booth like this." Eyes twinkling, she took off on her mission of mercy.

"I never realized Hazel had such a romantic streak." Dana sipped her tea, amusement tickling the corners of her mouth.

"Is she married? I don't see a ring." Finn typed Roger Burnett's name into the browser.

"Briefly. From what Pops told me, she had a whirlwind courtship with some Army guy she met while spending a few weeks with an aunt in Kansas when she was eighteen. He shipped overseas a month after they got married and disappeared off the face of the earth. Hazel, being Hazel, picked herself up and got on with her life."

"The experience didn't seem to sour her on romance."

"Other people's, anyway. I wonder if she'd be as sweet on you, though, if she knew about your Army background."

"Also ancient history. And for the record, I'd never take off on the woman I marry. I'm a till-death-do-us-part guy."

"Nice to know."

"Keep it in mind." He flashed her a smile, then motioned toward the screen. "Not a lot of hits on our man. I'll scroll through, and if you spot anything interesting, stop me."

She leaned closer, her silky hair brushing his jaw, that sweet fragrance invading his pores again.

He sucked in some air through his teeth.

"What's wrong?" She tipped her chin up and searched his face, the gold glinting in her irises.

Man, she was beautiful.

"Finn?"

He blinked. "What?"

"You made an odd sound."

No kidding.

"That was . . . adrenaline." *Keep breathing, McGregor.* "Let's just say that if you get any closer, my brain is going to totally short-circuit."

"Oh." She backed off a few inches. "Sorry."

"No apology necessary. I enjoyed every minute. But I don't want to be distracted and miss some important piece of information."

Forcing himself to focus on the task at hand, he let the page roll up, skimming the headings and dates. A lot of the hits were old, many of them related to awards the chief had received or news stories containing a quote from him.

"That one might be worth reading." Dana pointed to a header from the *Columbia Missourian* that had caught his attention too.

He clicked on what sounded like a feature story about outstanding small-town chiefs of police dated three years ago.

They read it in silence. The reporter highlighted the chief's many awards; included quotes from the Beaumont mayor, the man's pastor, and other citizens praising his stellar personal qualities and professional abilities; and offered the chief a chance to explain in his own words how he viewed his role in the community.

> Police work isn't just a job for me. It's a calling—and a sacred trust. My parents instilled in me a love of justice and honor and truth, and since the day I was sworn in as a police officer, I've tried to bring those values to life in the world of law enforcement. To do less would go against everything I believe.

Dana leaned back as she read the last sentence. "That doesn't lend a lot of support to your theory. The man sounds like a Boy Scout."

"Yeah." He closed the article and continued to scroll down the browser until the hits began to peter out. Finally, he, too, gave up. "Not so much as a whiff of impropriety. This was a total bust."

"Maybe all those things you noticed in the interview *were* coincidental."

"No. There's a big disconnect between what's here"—he motioned toward the computer screen—"and what I observed."

"We could always tap into our other source." Dana looked at Hazel, who was setting a fresh plate of pie in front of the little girl at the now-placid table.

"It's worth a shot—and here comes our chance."

Hazel returned to the counter, cut two more slices of pie, and hurried over. "Sorry for the delay."

"No apology necessary. I have a feeling this is worth waiting for." He tapped the dessert plate.

"It is."

"I see calm has been restored over there." Dana pointed her fork toward the table occupied by the young family.

"Yes, thank goodness. I'm glad their evening out wasn't ruined."

"You know them?" Finn cut off a generous bite of pie with the side of his fork.

"Of course. They're the Langes. New in town. The father, Jeff, took a job in Potosi with some manufacturing company so they could raise their children—Vicky and Elias—in a small community. Marta—that's Jeff's wife—wasn't too keen on the idea at first, but she's taken to life here real fine. Joined the women's club at church, and now she's thinking about starting a knitting club."

As she finished her report, Finn slanted a glance at Dana. Based on her expression, she shared his conclusion.

If anyone knew anything useful about the chief, it would be Hazel.

Now he just had to get her talking.

"I can see the value of living in a small town." He picked up his mug and cradled it in his hands, using his best shoot-the-breeze tone. "It's kind of like an extended family."

"Bingo." Hazel aimed her index finger at him. "We're here for each other through thick or thin."

The perfect opening.

"Speaking of that—I'm impressed by how you all watch out for Chief Burnett. He's had some tough breaks."

"That's a fact." Hazel swiped a rag over a speck on the table, forehead furrowed. "I don't know how the man keeps going, to tell the truth. Having to watch the love of your life slowly become a stranger . . . that has to be heart-breaking."

"I imagine it is. Doesn't seem fair for such a nice guy to have all that grief dumped on him."

"Isn't that the truth? Makes you wonder what the good Lord's thinking sometimes, that's for sure." She sighed and shook her head. "The poor man doesn't have a spare minute to himself these days, not that he's ever been much of a

TV-watcher or hobbyist. Except once, years ago, when he and Leah got a notion to try scuba diving. Had the whole town talking for weeks, I'll tell you."

Finn almost choked on his pie.

"Goodness, did that go down the wrong way, honey? Here, take a sip of water." Hazel scooted the glass closer to him.

He complied, risking a quick peek at Dana. She looked as shocked as he felt.

Who'd have thought a noteworthy nugget like that would drop into their laps with so little effort?

He took another gulp of water. The evidence might be circumstantial, but given this latest piece of information, he'd be willing to bet six months' salary the chief was the one searching Dana's lake. And that meant he was also somehow connected to the dock incident and the fire.

But that didn't jibe with the stellar picture of the man painted by the townspeople and the media. The pieces weren't fitting.

He needed more information.

"I was just chowing down too fast on this great pie. My mother always told me not to gobble my food." He gave a self-deprecating shrug. "Anyway, I can see why a scuba-diving hobby in this neck of the woods would raise a few eyebrows."

"And how. 'Course, they do teach scuba over at the Bonne Terre mine, but mostly city folks take those classes. I think Leah talked him into it, to be honest. Had to drag him to the classes, from what I heard. They were planning a trip to some island in the Caribbean for an anniversary, and she thought it would be fun to try an off-the-wall activity. Funny thing was, she didn't care for it much. I think she only stuck it out because she was the one who'd insisted they try it. The chief, on the other hand, took to it like a duck to water."

"Does he still dive?" This from Dana, who had found her voice at last.

"Mercy, no. I think he went a few times after that trip, but Leah was done. And in recent years, he hasn't had a spare minute for anything much but taking care of her and doing his job—especially these past few months." The bell over the door jingled, and she shifted sideways for a better view. "Another latecomer. You all give me a holler if you need a refill on that coffee."

Finn waited until she was out of earshot before turning to Dana.

"I can't believe it." She angled toward him, her eyes wide.

"I'm struggling with it too, after what we know about the man. But it puts the coincidence theory to rest."

"Assuming he *is* the diver, what on earth could he be after?"

"I can't imagine." Finn felt as flummoxed as Dana sounded.

She poked at her pie, puzzlement etching her

features. “I’m at a total loss. Where do we go from here?”

“I think some surveillance is in order.”

“You’re already doing that.”

“I’m talking about watching the chief, not your cabin.”

“You mean like tailing him?”

“Yeah.”

“Do you think you can pull that off without being detected?”

Good question. Staying undercover while tracking an enemy was part of Ranger training, and in a war zone he’d have no difficulty. In a small town like Beaumont, however—where everyone seemed to notice everything—it would be much tougher to remain invisible.

“I hope so. It sort of defeats the purpose if you’re spotted.”

“Wouldn’t it be just as effective to continue what you’re doing at my place? If he shows up there, you’ll see him.”

“I’d like to see where else he goes too.”

“That sounds like a 24/7 assignment.”

“Not quite—but close.”

She sighed. “I’m sorry this has become a full-time job for you. Some vacation, huh?”

He wrapped his fingers around hers under the table and gave them a reassuring squeeze. “The perks have made it well worth my while.”

“Thanks for being such a good sport.”

"Hey—I have a vested interest in clearing this up too, you know."

"Nice to hear." She squeezed his fingers back, then propped her elbow on the table and cupped her chin in her palm. "You know, if this isn't resolved by the end of the month, I'm thinking of taking the chief's advice and hightailing it back to St. Louis."

"I hope we'll get some answers before I have to leave. But if not—I agree with your decision. I'd rather not have you here alone at night."

"That's more or less what the chief said—and now we have a strong suspicion why." She fiddled with her fork, and when she spoke again, there was a slight quiver in her voice. "The only glitch in your surveillance plan is that if you're following the chief, no one will be within whistling distance of my cabin."

If he wasn't reasonably certain the man was the source of Dana's trouble, he'd be concerned about that too.

Yet he *was* a little worried. The disconnects in the whole scenario bothered him, and he couldn't shake the niggling feeling they were missing some vital piece of the puzzle.

There was a simple solution that would ease both their minds on the safety score, though.

"Why don't you stay at my cabin at night? It has two bedrooms, one of which is unoccupied. I won't even be there much if the chief is engaging in nocturnal activities, as we suspect."

She bit her lower lip. "I hate to impose . . . but that *would* make me feel more secure."

"It's not an imposition—and it would give me more peace of mind too. Consider it done. You can grab an overnight bag when we get back, and I'll run you by my cabin."

"You're going to start the surveillance tonight?"

He wished he could erase the twin grooves of worry on her brow—but only finding out what was going on and putting a stop to it would do that.

His first priority during the remainder of his stay in Beaumont.

"No reason to delay. If he's after something important enough to send him as far off the straight and narrow as it appears, he could be planning another dive this evening. Now what do you say we put the mystery aside for a few minutes and enjoy our dessert?"

"I vote for that." She picked up her fork again. "This is too delicious to waste." Giving him a smile that seemed a bit forced, she scooped up a bite of the creamy filling. "So tell me about growing up with two high-achieving older brothers."

Perfect. If she was after distraction, tales of some of the McGregor boys' escapades fit the bill.

He told her several yarns, embellishing them

here and there, and by the time he finished the one about Lance getting stuck in a drainage pipe after accepting a double dare to explore it, her pie was gone—along with most of the tautness in her face.

"How did your mother ever survive the three of you?"

"As you told me once early on, Southern women are strong and resilient—though she does attribute the bulk of her gray hairs to us." He inspected his empty plate. "Do you think anyone would notice if I picked it up and licked it?"

"I would—but I won't tell a soul."

Instead of lifting the plate, however, he used his fork to scrape up what he could of the remnants of chocolate. "I'll be couth—in your honor."

That earned him a soft chuckle.

Hazel buzzed back over to their booth, check and coffeepot in hand, as he finished. "Refills?" She set the slip on the table.

"Not for me. Dana, would you like some more tea?"

"No thanks."

Finn pulled out a twenty and set it on the table. "Keep the change."

"My." Hazel eyed the bill. "That's the best tip I've had all day. Make that all month." She sent Dana a meaningful look. "You hang on to this one. Generous tipping is the sign of a generous character and giving heart. After all these years in the waitressing business in a town where everybody knows everybody else, I can vouch for that."

"I'll keep that in mind."

"On that note . . ." Finn slid from the booth, computer in hand.

Dana followed him out.

"You two drive safe going home." Hazel picked up the money. "Those deer are a real menace at night."

"We'll be careful." Finn took Dana's arm and led her toward the door.

And as they exited into the cool spring air . . . as he pointed the SUV toward her cabin . . . he intended to abide by that promise for much longer than their return drive on the winding, wooded road.

Because whatever was going on at Dana's place was dangerous. He knew that in the marrow of his bones. There might not have been a direct attack on her—yet—but the fire had come much too close for comfort. Whatever the motivation that had driven the chief to take such drastic measures, it was formidable. And people who got in the way of his goal could wind up hurt . . . or worse.

He wasn't going to let that happen to Dana. Moving her to his cabin at night should be sufficient protection while he tried to get to the bottom of this. The Busch place didn't appear to be of interest to anyone, and no one had bothered her during the day on her own property.

However, if there was no resolution by the end of the month, he had no intention of leaving her behind when he winged south to Atlanta. He wanted her safe in her grandfather's house in St. Louis.

He darted her a quick glance as the SUV traveled down the dark road. At least convincing her to do that shouldn't be too tough. She was already thinking along those lines, and she'd latched on to his suggestion about bunking at his place. She was seriously spooked by the odd goings-on at her place.

Small wonder, after everything that had happened to her in New York.

His gut clenched as he thought about those crazed robbers holding her at gunpoint. One wrong move, she could have been dead.

But that wouldn't happen on his watch.

He'd keep her safe.

And no matter what Roger Burnett was up to, if push came to shove, the Beaumont chief of police wasn't going to best an Army Ranger.

—18—

As the first rays of sun peeked around the drawn shades in Finn's spare bedroom, the smell of sizzling bacon teased Dana awake.

Her host was cooking breakfast after getting in at who knew what hour last night?

Guilt crashing over her, she sat up and swung her legs to the floor. While she'd enjoyed the soundest sleep she'd had in months, Finn had spent most of the night huddled in a chilly, dark forest. The man had to be operating on fumes. The least she could have done was get up and make breakfast.

Moving at warp speed, she dressed, ran a brush through her hair, swiped on a touch of lipstick, and headed toward the kitchen.

Although her sport shoes were noiseless on the wood floors, Finn turned from the counter the instant she appeared on the threshold.

Either the ex-Ranger had exceptional hearing or he was always on alert for a stealth approach. Perhaps both.

"Good morning." He smiled over his shoulder as he stirred scrambled eggs in a frying pan.

"Morning." She assessed him as she entered the room. How could he look so wide awake after so little slumber? "When did you get in last night?"

"About two."

She tapped her watch. "Four hours of sleep isn't enough."

"I'm used to functioning on much less. Hungry?" He lifted the pan of eggs.

"I am after getting a whiff of that bacon. But I'm not eating your breakfast."

"I made plenty for both of us. I was going to put yours in the oven. I could still do that if you'd rather get a few more minutes of shut-eye."

"No. I'm up for the day. What can I do to help?"

"There's juice in the fridge, if you'd like to pour us each a glass." He set the plate of bacon on the table and began to dish up the eggs.

"So tell me about last night. Did the chief show?"

"Yep."

She froze, fingers locked on the handle of the fridge. "So we were right."

"Not entirely. Go ahead and sit."

She moved to the table, poured the OJ, and took her seat as he joined her. "You're going to explain that, I assume?"

"Uh-huh. He came about eleven." He doused his eggs with a liberal sprinkling of pepper. Added several dollops of ketchup. Topped everything off with a healthy dash of tabasco sauce.

The back of her throat began to burn.

"To dive?" She unglued her gaze from his plate and gave her own eggs a scant sprinkling of salt.

"No. I was in my usual place in the woods by your cabin, but I kept an eye on the far bank through my binoculars. All was quiet there. I spotted him at the dock end of the lake. After he prowled around for a few minutes, he settled in near your cabin, not far from my position." Finn forked up some eggs.

"What did he do?"

"Nothing."

Dana squinted at him. "What do you mean, nothing?"

"I mean nothing. He just sat there, like I did. At first I thought he was making sure the coast was clear before proceeding with whatever nefarious deed he had planned for the night. But he never budged. Finally, about one-thirty, he left."

Mental gears churning, Dana did the math—and came to a startling conclusion. "Do you think . . . it sounds like he was doing what you were doing. Waiting for the vandals too."

"That's my take."

"Wow." She sat back, trying to absorb this new development—and its implications. "So his diving and my vandalism aren't related."

"I'm not certain about that . . . but I *am* fairly confident the chief isn't the one who damaged your property."

"So what do we do next?"

He continued to chow down. "I assume he went

home to sleep after putting in a full day at work and spending hours hunkered down in the woods. The man has to get *some* shut-eye. But I want to tail him today. Hazel told me he made a trip south of town yesterday on the heels of a Wayne Phelps. That name ring any bells?"

She ran it through her mind. Came up blank. "No."

"Hazel seemed to think it was odd. That may have no bearing on our case—but I want to see if he goes anywhere else today that could be suspect." He swiped his napkin across his mouth and stood. "I'd like to be in position near his house before he takes off for the day. Could you be ready in five minutes? I'll drop you at your place before I drive into town."

"Yes." She scooped up the last of her eggs, finished off her bacon, and washed it all down with a gulp of orange juice while he tidied up the kitchen.

Less than ten minutes later, he was pulling in behind her cabin.

"I'll swing by late this afternoon or early evening to give you a ride back to my place. I don't know exactly what time; it will be whenever I get a window of opportunity to take a break."

"You're going to be exhausted." She took the overnight bag he retrieved from the backseat.

"No worries. I can keep this pace up for several days without feeling much of an impact." He took her arm and guided her toward the cabin. "Give me a minute to do a quick walk-through."

She unlocked the door and waited inside while he moved from room to room, then followed him to the porch. From there he walked the perimeter of the cabin and went down to the dock.

"All quiet." He rejoined her. "Since our guy—or guys—like the dark, you should be fine here today. Keep the doors locked as a precaution, though."

She shoved her hands in the pockets of her jeans, fighting back a sudden surge of unease.

Don't be a wimp, Dana. Finn's an expert at detecting danger. If he thought there was any reason to be worried, he wouldn't let you stay here alone. He'd have suggested you haul your computer equipment over to his place and work there.

"I like that you have nearby access to cell coverage from here." He spoke as if he'd read her mind. "You wouldn't have that at my place. Plus, I've seen no indication there's any danger here during the day. If I had, I'd be urging you to move to your grandfather's place in St. Louis immediately."

His calm, reassuring tone quieted the butterflies in her stomach.

She summoned up a smile. "It's kind of spooky, the way you're able to read my mind."

"Not spooky. More a sign that we're simpatico—and meant to be together."

"I like your spin."

He touched her face, his fingers a gentle whisper against her skin. "If you want to pack up and relocate to St. Louis now, though, I'll take you there."

For a brief moment she considered that option. Rejected it. If she left, she'd be giving up what meager time they had left to spend together before Finn flew off to Atlanta.

Better to cope with a case of nerves than make that sacrifice.

"No. I trust your judgment."

The hint of a frown flashed on his brow, but it was gone so quickly she wondered if she'd imagined it.

"I appreciate your confidence—but if anything at all spooks you, I want you to promise to call for help."

"Who? 911 calls get routed to the station here."

"Call my brother Mac." He pulled a piece of paper out of his jacket, jotted a number down, and handed it over. "I'll alert him to the situation. He's a detective with St. Louis County and can get someone here fast from the highway patrol or sheriff's department. Not that I think it will come to that, but it's a safety net."

"Okay." She kept a tight grip on the slip of paper. "Good hunting."

"Thanks."

He leaned down. She rose on tiptoes to meet him. And as his lips closed over hers, all of her worries evaporated for a few blissful seconds.

Too bad he couldn't stay within touching distance all day.

But as he drove off in a cloud of dust to search for answers, Dana forced herself to relax. He'd be back in a few hours, and she wasn't going to worry while he was gone.

If Finn thought she was safe, that was good enough for her.

So Burnett wasn't going to see his wife, after all.

Keeping a moderate distance between the SUV and the chief's car, Finn stayed on the man's tail as they passed the turnoff for Woodside Gardens and continued north.

Curious, too, that he was dressed in his civvies and driving his own car on a Wednesday morning, when he should be in uniform and at work.

As they traveled north on Highway 21, Finn punched in Lance's number. He owed him a call; no reason not to make his drive do double duty.

"What's up, Finn?"

His brother's clipped tone didn't bode well for a long conversation.

"You busy?"

"You might say that. I'm on a stakeout."

"Then I won't keep you. I was just following up on my promise to stay in touch."

"Wait! Don't hang up yet. How's your neighbor?"

He would home in on that.

"Fine."

"You at her lake now?"

"No. I'm actually heading your direction."

"You're coming to St. Louis and didn't tell us?"

"It's an unplanned trip. Besides, I don't know that I'm going to end up in St. Louis."

"Huh?"

"Long story." Finn switched lanes to keep Burnett in sight. "I'll tell it to you sometime."

"How about Saturday?"

He frowned. "Why Saturday?"

"I know you're distracted by that neighbor of yours, but Mac's birthday is Sunday, remember? I thought the three of us might meet in St. Louis for lunch. He and Lisa have plans for Sunday."

Oh, man. How could he have forgotten his big brother's birthday?

"Yeah, I can do that. Text me the place and time."

"Will do. I'd invite you to bring Dana, but this is a guy event."

"Understood."

"So are you two going to stay in touch after you move to Atlanta?"

"That's the plan."

"Think she'd come to a going-away party your

last night here? Christy wants to fix dinner for you."

"No kidding?" Finn eased back on the gas pedal as Burnett slowed behind an over-the-road truck. "That's nice of her."

"Yeah. She's a real nice woman. That's why I married her."

"I can understand that. What baffles me is why she said yes."

"Ha-ha."

Finn grinned. "Anyway, tell her I said thanks. And I'll ask Dana—despite your ulterior motive."

"Which would be?"

"You all want to size her up."

"I'll follow Mac's example and plead the Fifth."

"Doesn't matter. I'm on to you guys. But believe me, she'll pass any test you throw at her." He picked up speed again as the truck turned off the highway and Burnett lengthened the space between them.

"Hmm. Am I detecting the scent of smitten here?"

"Go back to your stakeout, bro."

"As a matter of fact, I will." The clipped inflection was back. "We might be about to see some action. I'll be in touch."

The line went dead.

Finn slid the phone back onto his belt. Typical Lance. A jokester one minute, all business the next if the situation demanded it. The FBI gig suited him to a *T*. And Mac had turned out to be a stellar detective. Amazing how they'd both found perfect careers in their post-special-forces life —and lucked out in the romance department as well.

Best of all, if the spark between him and Dana continued to sizzle, he'd be following in their footsteps in the not-too-distant future.

Feeling more content than he had in a long while, he propped an elbow on the open window and continued to guide the SUV north.

One hour and twenty minutes later, on the outskirts of St. Louis, the Beaumont police chief arrived at his destination.

As the man pulled into a parking spot and entered a building, Finn read the sign above the door.

Midwest Gold & Coin

Interesting.

Even more interesting was the tagline underneath.

We buy and sell treasures.

Hmm.

If the chief had been in search of treasure on his clandestine dives, his visit here suggested two things.

First, he must have found whatever he'd been seeking.

Second, he was in a sell mode, not a buy mode.

But why would the man resort to covert—and

likely illegal—activity if his wife's family money had left him with a nice cushion, as Hazel had confided?

He puzzled over that for fifteen minutes, until Burnett reappeared, got back behind the wheel, and began to retrace his route south.

Finn followed at a discreet distance, pulling out his phone after they left the city behind and the heavier traffic thinned. Mac might be able to find out the reason for Burnett's trip to the city today. Cops often cultivated relationships with reputable dealers of gold and jewelry, and the place the chief had gone to was in a respectable part of town. Knowing what business the man had conducted could be helpful.

It was possible that Hazel's information, for once, wasn't accurate. Perhaps the man did need to raise some cash. Woodside Gardens had to be expensive. He might be feeling the financial strain of some hefty extended-care bills.

Whatever the reason for Burnett's clandestine activity, though, they were one step closer to getting some answers—assuming Mac came through for him with the gold and coin shop.

His next order of business.

Keeping one hand on the wheel, he punched in his eldest brother's number. Waited while the phone rang once . . . twice . . . three times . . . then rolled to voicemail.

Finn left a succinct message. Knowing Mac,

he'd return the call before Burnett hit Potosi again. Especially after their conversation earlier, when he'd given him a quick briefing and alerted him that Dana might call if she sensed any trouble.

And in the meantime, he was going to stick close to the chief. Today had already been profitable—who knew what else he might discover?

"You have a nice morning off, Chief?" Hazel poured a mug of coffee and pushed it across the counter.

Roger slid onto a stool at the Walleye and set his uniform hat beside him. "How did you know I took a half day of vacation?"

"I have my sources." She smiled and propped a hip against the counter. "In this case, it was LouEllen Bradshaw. She was driving back from Potosi after visiting her sister and passed you heading the other way. She said she waved, but you didn't notice her."

No, he wouldn't have. His mind had been on the pending transaction in St. Louis.

He stirred some sugar into his coffee. "It wasn't vacation in the usual sense. I had some business to take care of, and after that I stopped in to visit Leah."

Hazel's expression softened as she patted his hand. "How's she doing?"

"Not great." Far from it. In truth, today had been one of her worst days. He'd no sooner stepped into the room than she began screaming for him to leave. Accusing him of imprisoning her. Screeching how much she hated him.

Even though he knew the words weren't coming from the heart of the woman he loved, they never failed to wound.

He picked up his coffee and took a sip, praying the caffeine-laced liquid would squeeze past his constricted throat.

"Well, you sit here for a spell, take some deep breaths, and have a nice lunch. You know everyone in the community is behind you. That's one of the beauties of small-town living, as I told Dana Lewis and that handsome young man who's renting the Busch place. They stopped in for pie last night and we had a nice chat. They might not be locals, but they're real sympathetic to all the tribulations you've had."

"You talked about me?" He tightened his grip on the mug.

"Oh, not in the way you mean. I've never been one to gossip, you know that. They were just sorry to hear about all you've been through. I didn't say anything personal except that you don't have a minute to call your own these days—and everyone in town already knows that."

He took another careful sip of the hot coffee. "I don't mind being busy. It's not like I have any other obligations that require my time."

"Nor hobbies either, like that model railroading

Marv obsesses over. I don't know how the man keeps the hardware store afloat, with him running all over the place to those train shows. But you could use a diversion once in a while. Too bad you gave up scuba diving."

He jerked, and the coffee sloshed out of the mug, searing his fingers.

"My word, your poor hand! First a nasty case of poison ivy, now a burn." Hazel scurried over to the ice bin, wrapped a handful of the cubes in a towel, and pressed it against his fingers. "You hold that there for a few minutes. It'll take away some of the sting."

Stay calm, Roger. Just because she mentioned your scuba diving doesn't mean there's anything to worry about.

"I'll be fine. It was only a quick splash. The mug must've slipped." Hard as he tried to control it, a slight quiver vibrated through his words.

"I hope it wasn't wet when I gave it to you. I did grab it out of the dishwasher."

"No. It was my own clumsiness." He adjusted the ice on the burn. *Keep it casual and conversational, Roger.* "Funny you should mention scuba diving after all these years. What made you think of it?"

She twirled her pencil. "I don't rightly know. It must have been on my mind from that nice chat I had last night with Dana and her neighbor. I mentioned it to them."

As her words registered, his skull began to pound with the pulsing beat of a supercharge rock band, drowning out the lunch buzz in the café.

Finn McGregor knew he was a scuba diver.

Knew he'd pretended ignorance when confronted with the fin buckle.

Knew he most likely was Dana's midnight diver.

This was a disaster.

"Chief? Chief? Are you okay?"

Hazel's concern managed to penetrate his panic.

Pull yourself together, Burnett. See what else you can find out. You could be overreacting.

He attempted without much success to force up the corners of his lips. "Yes. A little tired is all."

"And no wonder." She patted his uninjured hand. "You need a vacation. A real one, not half a day to take care of business."

"I'll have to give that some thought. Some place where I could refresh my scuba skills might be nice."

"Now you're talking. White sand, blue water, a tropical breeze—that would help you relax."

As if his budget would allow even a weekend trip to Lake of the Ozarks. He might be willing to use that gold to help Leah, but he'd never spend a penny of it on himself—or anything else.

Holding on to the mug with both hands to prevent another spill, he took a cautious sip of coffee. "I bet Dana and her friend were surprised to hear someone in Beaumont had taken up an unusual sport like that."

"They did seem a bit taken aback, like we all were. But I told them you took to it like a duck to water."

The knot in his stomach coiled tighter.

"Did you also tell them it was years ago?"

"My, yes. You haven't had a spare minute for a hobby in ages. Excuse me a minute, Chief. Harvey and his cronies are trying to flag me down."

As soon as she walked away, Roger dug out a couple of bills, set them on the counter, and stood, praying his shaky legs would hold him up. He needed to go to his office, close the door, and try to figure out where this whole mess Wayne had created stood—and what, if any, damage control he could do.

One thing he did know, though.

He'd gone to far too much effort to let anything—or anyone—jeopardize Leah's future.

Burnett wasn't going to come through for him.

Back resting against the rough bark of an oak tree, Wayne lowered the binoculars and regarded the Lewis cabin. There'd been no outside activity—but Leo's granddaughter was still there. After sitting here for two hours, he'd finally spotted her passing by a window.

Muttering a curse, he picked up a rock and hurled it into the woods.

He needed to cook . . . and he needed privacy to do that.

Meaning he'd have to take matters into his own hands.

As he stowed the binoculars in their case, he mulled over next steps. More vandalism was a possibility, but if it hadn't worked on the first two tries, there wasn't much chance a third attempt would produce different results. Besides, that muscleman from next door was hanging around too much. For all he knew, the guy could show up some night and catch him in the act.

No, it was too risky. He was done with vandalism.

Besides . . . maybe it wasn't necessary.

Other than the one hike she and her beefy neighbor had taken in the woods, and their evening rows on the lake, neither had wandered from her cabin over the past few days—and his lab was pretty far off the beaten path. That's why he'd chosen the location. It was a fluke they'd come as close as they had on that hike.

So why not get on with his cooking—preferably in the daytime, as he used to do before Dana Lewis showed up—but take a few precautions to make sure no one stumbled onto his operation?

After one last scan of the cabin, he rose and started back through the woods, the plan solidifying in his mind. It wouldn't be hard to find out how to take care of interlopers. Meth makers were used to dealing with them, and there was plenty of information about their methods on the net. Some of the tactics they used were meant to warn . . . some to scare . . . some to hurt.

The choice of which approach to take deserved some serious thought. Catching a daytime visitor who got too close while he was working would require a different setup than catching one at night when no one was at the lab.

Based on the pattern of activity he'd observed to date, however, there wasn't much chance anyone would be roaming around back here in the dark, other than the chief. A daytime scheme might work best . . . but he'd rig up a few nighttime surprises too—just in case.

He pushed aside some scrub and continued toward his parking spot on the unused forest road. The same road where he'd spotted the chief's car the night he'd taken the photos that had proven to be very valuable. Except he parked in a different, more secluded spot now. No one passing by would notice his car tucked in the dense undergrowth.

If he was lucky, no one would notice his lab, either.

But if they did . . .

Wayne touched the hunting knife stuck in his belt and skirted a bramble patch, staying clear of the thorny branches that tried to snare him. He didn't want to hurt anybody. He just wanted a ticket out of this sorry town. A chance to live a life where he didn't have to scrabble in the dirt for every buck. The kind of life every decent human being deserved. What was wrong with pursuing that dream? And if someone got hurt because they stuck their nose in his business . . . well, that wasn't his fault, was it?

You know what your daddy and mama would say to that, Wayne Phelps.

Quashing the rebuke from his conscience, he clamped his jaw tight. Yeah, he knew. But they were gone. He was on his own. And he wanted a real life. Maybe if Sue Ann hadn't ditched him two years ago for that suit-wearing guy at the savings and loan where she worked in Potosi, he could have been content here.

Maybe.

But not anymore. He was done with rising at dawn, and dirty fingernails, and trucking produce north for city folks who picked over his offerings with their noses in the air. Oh, he'd keep up the pretense for a while as a cover, but no matter how hard he worked the land, his market garden wouldn't get him out of here.

Meth was the key to his dream.

So he had to protect his lab, no matter what.

It wouldn't be that difficult to do, either. An hour or two of simple research should give him the tools he needed to keep it safe.

All he had to do was google booby traps.

—19—

Gripping the wheel of the SUV with one hand, Finn pulled the vibrating cell off his belt with the other.

Mac.

Finally.

He put the phone to his ear, keeping Burnett in sight. "I thought you forgot about me."

"Hello to you too."

"Hey—I have a lot on my mind. Did you find out anything from the gold and coin place?"

"I didn't . . . but one of my colleagues who's dealt with the owner of that shop in the past did. A lot of stolen stuff gets fenced through places like that."

"You don't say."

Two seconds ticked by.

"I'll attribute your sarcasm to worry about Dana and cut you some slack."

Finn opened his mouth to protest. Closed it. If Mac was trying to bait him, he wasn't biting.

A chuckle came over the line. "Congratulations on your self-restraint. The kid must be growing up. Anyway, my colleague was tied up yesterday on a case and didn't have a chance to put in a call until this morning. Seems your guy had some gold bullion to sell. To be specific, three ten-ounce bars worth close to forty thousand dollars in today's market."

"Wow." Finn hung a right in Burnett's wake.

"There's more. The owner said the gold bars appear to be old. He couldn't date them, but they were definitely not of recent vintage."

"Did your guy ask the owner if Burnett told him where he got the gold?"

"Yeah. Burnett didn't offer any information, but the sale was arranged through his bank. The bank manager called the shop on Tuesday to see if they'd be interested in buying some gold Burnett had in his safe-deposit box. He said Burnett needed to liquefy some long-held family assets to cover medical expenses for his wife. Does that fit with what you know?"

"Too well." Finn eased back on the gas pedal as the chief pulled into the picnic grounds at the edge of town. Another police cruiser was already on the scene, the officer talking to two lanky teens. "But it doesn't explain his extracurricular activities at Dana's lake."

"Maybe he's not after anything of monetary value there."

"What else could it be?"

"I don't know. All I can say is I'm glad it's your case instead of mine."

"Thanks a lot."

"Anytime. You still coming to lunch Saturday?"

"That's the plan." But truth be told, the notion

of leaving Dana alone at the cabin and driving almost two hours north wasn't sitting well, not with the situation at her place so up in the air.

"Stick to it. I want to see you. And if you're worried about Dana being by herself, I can ask Lisa to organize a girls' lunch with Christy."

Strange how Mac had always been able to read his brothers' minds. Must be a purview of eldest siblings.

No matter. Unless he was close by to run interference he had no intention of subjecting Dana to the third degree by a female police chief and a woman skilled at handling tenacious media types.

"I'll think about it." The cop up ahead held up what looked like a paint can and proceeded to load the two teens into the back of the police car. The case of the picnic grounds vandals had apparently been solved.

"If you're worried, I'll tell Lisa to leave the interrogation spotlight and cattle prod at home." A hint of laughter lurked in Mac's words.

"Very funny."

"*I* thought so. Need anything else today?"

"If I do, I'll be in touch."

"The Acme Detective Agency stands ready to meet your every need."

At his brother's atypical jocularity, Finn narrowed his eyes and swung down a side street as the chief returned to his car. "What's with you today? You're in unusually high spirits."

"Must have something to do with impending fatherhood."

Finn's mouth dropped open, and he jammed on the brake. "Lisa's pregnant?"

"Yep."

"Man. That's . . . wow! Did you tell Mom and Dad?"

"Earlier today."

"I bet they were over the moon."

"You might say that. Mom's already planning a baby shower for Lisa."

"That sounds like her." Out of the corner of his eye, Finn caught the chief's car passing the side street. He executed a quick U-turn and zipped back to the main road. "We'll make Saturday a double celebration. Congratulations—and give her my best."

"Thanks, I'll do that. See you Saturday."

As he slid the phone back in its holster, a slow smile tugged up the corners of Finn's lips.

Mac—a father.

What a kick.

And that would make him an uncle.

Uncle Finn.

Not bad.

He picked up speed as the chief accelerated back toward town. Hard to believe a new generation of McGregors was on the way.

And if all went as he hoped with Dana, he might

not be too far behind making his own contribution to the family line.

"Good morning." Dana turned from the stove in Finn's cabin as he entered the kitchen.

"Morning. Thanks for getting up to cook breakfast."

"My pleasure. I wanted to do it yesterday, but you beat me to it—again."

"I was awake early yesterday—again." He wandered over to the coffeepot and poured himself a cup. "Need any help?"

"No. I have it under control. Why don't you sit and enjoy your coffee?"

He followed her suggestion without protest.

Hmm. That was revealing—as were the faint lines etched beside his eyes and the shadows beneath his lower lashes.

Finn might think he could survive on limited sleep forever, but after four days, it was taking an obvious toll.

Worst of all, despite the considerable effort he'd put into solving the mystery of Lewis Lake, they were no closer to answers now than they'd been when he'd begun watching the chief. Burnett kept showing up each night at the cabin . . . but nothing ever happened.

"You know, I'm beginning to think the vandals are through at my place." She set a plate of pancakes in front of her host.

"That thought's crossed my mind too." He opened the bottle of syrup and squirted some on the stack. "But the chief hasn't stopped watching for them yet."

"I expect he will soon, don't you?"

"Depends on what he knows that we don't."

"He didn't dive last night, did he?"

"No. There hasn't been any more diving since the night I spotted him on the far side of the lake."

She joined him at the table with her own plate in hand. "Do you think the gold he sold is somehow related?"

"I don't see how. The bank manager said he retrieved it from his safe-deposit box, and it's common knowledge in town that Burnett's wife came from money." He raked his fingers through his hair, frustration scoring his features. "None of the pieces are fitting."

"Do you think we might be complicating this too much?" She used the tip of her knife to slide a pat of butter over her top pancake, watching it slowly dissolve. "He might be hanging out here hoping to catch the vandals himself. We know the department doesn't have the personnel to do a stakeout, and he strikes me as a dedicated guy who'd be willing to put in extra hours to solve a case. As for my vandals, they could have gotten tired of their games."

"True. Except that doesn't explain Burnett's

diving. And if he was planning to do night surveillance at the cabin, why not tell you?"

"Both valid points." She speared a bite of pancake. "But if he wasn't involved in the vandalism, and the vandals are gone, I should be safe, right? I agree the scuba diving in my lake is odd, but do we really need to find out why? He didn't hurt anyone doing it. Maybe we should let it go."

Based on the firm set of Finn's jaw and his obstinate expression, letting go wasn't part of his DNA.

His next words confirmed that.

"I don't like loose ends or unanswered questions. I'm thinking of following a hunch and trying a different tack today."

"What?"

He forked a piece of pancake and chased some syrup around his plate. "I want to check out Wayne Phelps. Hazel gave me the impression the brief conversation Burnett had with him in the parking lot at the Walleye was out of character. Even stranger, according to her, was that they both took off in the same direction—out of town."

"Why was that strange?"

"She didn't offer any specifics then—but I asked a few questions about him when I dropped in at the Walleye yesterday while I was following Burnett. She said Phelps lost his job a few years ago and now earns his living with a market garden, selling his organic vegetables and herbs at farmers' markets and to restaurants. According to Hazel, he used to be a nice boy who loved his daddy something fierce—her words—but her opinion of him has deteriorated in the recent past."

"Did she say why?"

"Not directly. But she isn't impressed with how he's let his folks' place go downhill since they died—and she used the words *loner* and *surly* to describe him."

"Hmm." Dana wasn't about to discount Finn's instincts . . . but homing in on Phelps? Seemed like a stretch. "Do you think it's worth spending a lot of effort on such a wild card?"

"It can't hurt. I've gotten nowhere with Burnett."

"What about today's birthday lunch with your brothers?"

He shrugged and finished off his pancakes. "I may bail."

"No." She set her fork down and sat up straighter. She was *not* going to let her troubles interfere with such an important family event. "You can't not show up, especially now that you have two things to celebrate. I'd feel terrible if I was the reason you missed it."

He studied her over the rim of his mug. "I'm running out of time to solve this, Dana. My last day in Beaumont is Wednesday."

As if she didn't know that. It was circled in black on her calendar.

"You could check Wayne out after you get back from St. Louis."

He took a sip of coffee. "I'll tell you what. Let's compromise. Lance scheduled a late lunch, so I'll work the Phelps angle this morning, show up for lunch, and see if I can pick up his tail after I get back. Sound reasonable?"

"No. With that agenda, you'll end up putting in another eighteen- or twenty-hour day."

"I can catch up on sleep in Atlanta."

"Hah. I bet your father is chomping at the bit to get you on board and up to speed at the firm."

"He'll cut me some slack for the first few days after I explain what went on here." He drained his coffee. "You want to stay here today or go to your place?"

"I'd like to work while you're gone. If I get a little ahead, I'll have a few more hours to spend with you before you leave—assuming we solve our mystery soon so your schedule frees up."

"No arguments from me on that." He twisted his wrist to examine his watch. "It's early, and Phelps isn't too far away. If he's in the market garden business, he's probably long gone to some Saturday farmers' market. That will give me a chance to poke around his place."

"You're going to trespass?"

He gave her a look of mock indignation. "That would be illegal. I'm just going to stop by for a visit. If no one answers the door, who would blame me for taking a walk around the place to see if I can find him?"

"Remind me never to get on your bad side."

He grinned and guzzled the last of his coffee. "I wouldn't worry too much about that if I were you."

She sighed and propped her elbow on the table, chin in hand. "You know what I wish? I wish our plans for the day included a leisurely spin on the lake, a picnic on the dock, and pie later at the Walleye."

The fine lines at the corners of his eyes crinkled. "I like how you think. I propose we implement that plan at the first opportunity—at the very latest on Tuesday."

"Your last full day here."

"But the prelude to lots of days in a new chapter of our lives."

Warmth filled her heart. "As you said a moment ago—I like the way you think." She squeezed his hand, rose, and began clearing the table.

He joined her half a minute later, working with his usual quiet efficiency.

Twenty minutes later, with a kiss and a promise to stop in before eleven with a report before he drove to St. Louis for lunch, he disappeared down her drive.

She closed the door, flipped the locks, and strolled over to her computer. Her neighbor had tenacity, she'd give him that. Unable to discount his negative vibes about what was going on in Beaumont, he was wearing himself out trying to keep her safe.

But as she booted up her computer, she felt more secure than she had in weeks. While lots of unanswered questions remained, everything had been quiet at the cabin for days. Why not let the mystery rest?

Given her druthers, that's what she'd choose.

Because if no one had gotten hurt yet despite plenty of opportunities to inflict harm, was there really any reason to think danger might still be lurking in the shadows?

Talk about perfect timing.

As Finn's GPS guided him to the access road to Wayne Phelps's farm, a small, nondescript pickup truck pulled out, Phelps at the wheel. He wasn't an exact match for the photo in the news article about Washington County market gardeners that Google had unearthed—his hair was longer, and he sported a scruffy beard—but it was him, no question about it.

Now he could be certain the place was unoccupied.

However . . .

He tapped a finger against the steering wheel. It was late to be leaving for a farmers' market. Most of the Saturday events started at seven, seven-thirty.

Follow him—or use the window of opportunity to poke around the farm undisturbed?

Finn slowed, grateful he'd opted for dark-tinted windows and generic black when he'd ordered the vehicle. The SUV had the power he wanted without attracting attention. There were countless vehicles like his on the road . . . including a couple in Beaumont.

Phelps's truck passed him going the opposite direction.

Decision time.

Follow him.

Sound advice. If Phelps ended up at a farmers' market, he could come back and nose around while the man was hawking his produce.

Without further deliberation, Finn reversed direction and accelerated.

He caught sight of Phelps's truck again as he rounded a bend, keeping it in view as it traveled through Beaumont. Passed Dana's drive. Continued north.

Frowning, Finn backed off on the gas. The next town of any size was Potosi, home to the county farmers' market. If Phelps hadn't stopped in Beaumont, that was probably his destination. Was it worth a drive all the way there just to watch him unload his new-age vegetables and . . .

Wait.

The pickup slowed.

Finn reduced his speed again.

Thirty seconds later, the truck veered right and disappeared into the woods.

He squinted. Was there even a road there?

Approaching the spot at a crawl, he scrutinized the overgrown ground as the pickup's receding taillights flickered in the woods. Yes, faint tracks were visible—as if this had once been a road.

Like a forest road, perhaps?

They *were* on national forest land now.

Land that adjoined the Busch and Lewis property.

His pulse took an uptick. Hard to say for sure what Phelps was up to—but one thing was certain.

He wasn't going to a farmers' market.

Finn swung onto the road. If this was the same byway where they'd discovered the buckle, there were spots wide enough to allow a vehicle to turn around. If it wasn't—if he met Phelps coming back the other way—he could claim he'd been looking for a hiking trail and gotten lost.

Lame—but if the man had nothing to hide, the excuse would be irrelevant.

And if he did . . . Finn rested his fingers against his Beretta, tucked inside the top of his jeans in its concealed carry holster.

He was prepared for any contingency.

Peering through the trees as he jounced over the rough terrain, Finn managed to keep the man in sight thanks to the small cloud of dust billowing in the truck's wake.

But once that cloud remained stationary, Finn braked as well. If Phelps had arrived at his destination, he needed to squeeze the SUV into one of the niches along the road and proceed on foot.

When the haze of dust stayed in one place and began to settle, Finn picked up his binoculars from the seat beside him and aimed them that direction. Even with his trained eye, it took him a few moments to locate the vehicle. Phelps had pulled off to the side of the road and tucked his truck behind some brush. If the man hadn't been moving around, he doubted he'd have seen it.

Very suspicious.

If this was some sort of innocent outing, why not leave the truck in plain view?

He watched as Phelps withdrew a large, overstuffed backpack. The kind people took on several-day treks into the wilderness.

But he'd lay odds Phelps hadn't come out here to commune with Mother Nature.

After hoisting the backpack into position, Phelps crossed the road and disappeared into the woods.

Toward Dana's property.

Finn's adrenaline surged.

Tucking the binoculars onto his belt, he slid out of the SUV and jogged down the overgrown road toward the concealed truck. The man might already have melted into the trees, but it wouldn't be difficult to track him. For one thing, the large backpack would slow his progress. For another, a man carrying that kind of bulk would leave clear evidence of his route through the overgrown woods. And finally, he wasn't making much effort to conceal his presence. As he approached the truck, Finn had no trouble picking up the sound of Phelps's movements in the quiet forest.

Once he reached the man's point of entry into the woods, Finn shifted into stealth mode.

And as he followed the market garden farmer toward Dana's property, he had a feeling the answers to all their questions were only a short hike away.

—20—

Roger adjusted his glasses, smoothed a hand over the single sheet of lined yellow paper, and reread what he'd written while sipping his Saturday morning coffee on the back porch. It wasn't perfect, nor did it right any of his wrongs—but it was the best he could do.

Leaning back, he exhaled and lifted his gaze to the cloudless sky, where a hawk soared, wings outstretched, letting the air current set his course. Someday, once he was gone and long after Leah had passed on to her reward, the gold from

Len White's decades-old crime would at last be returned to its rightful owner.

Most of it, anyway.

Shoulders drooping, he picked up his pen, signed the handwritten document, and slid it into the envelope containing White's letter to him. He licked the flap, sealed it, and with a hand that wasn't quite steady, wrote nine words across the front.

To be opened upon the death of Roger Burnett.

On Monday, he'd drop the envelope off at his attorney's office in Potosi. The man would be curious—but he wouldn't ask any questions, and he could be trusted to deal with the matter promptly at the appropriate time.

Leaving the envelope on the kitchen table, he pushed himself to his feet. He should have slept in this morning instead of getting up at the crack of dawn to weed Leah's flower beds. Lord knew he needed some shut-eye after crouching in the brush at Dana Lewis's place until the wee hours for nights on end. Plus, every muscle in his body ached. His close-to-retirement-age bones weren't up to that kind of punishment anymore, not like in the old days when he could go twenty hours at a stretch without feeling any ill effects.

Yet sleep was as elusive as the hummingbirds that would soon be flitting around Leah's feeders, coming almost within reaching distance but always darting away before they could be grasped.

And he had Wayne to thank for his insomnia.

While acid from the java gurgled in his stomach, he pushed through the door into the kitchen, empty mug in hand. The man might be lying low for the moment, but the threat hadn't gone away. He was up to something.

Roger opened the fridge and inspected the contents. He ought to have some breakfast. A man needed to eat whether he was hungry or not. An egg, maybe. Or toast and jam. Or a bowl of oatmeal.

But nothing tempted his taste buds.

No matter what he fixed for himself, it wouldn't come close to the great Saturday-morning breakfasts Leah used to whip up for him and John, back in the happy days when his family was intact and laughter rang around his long-empty table.

What little appetite he had evaporated.

Why not go back to bed for a while? Even if he didn't sleep, he could rest. Or try to. Otherwise, he could end up drifting off during the long night to come at the Lewis place. Wayne might be biding his time, but he'd been clear about his intention to remove all risks of detection.

Especially one named Dana.

Who knew what he'd try next?

Ditching his mug in the sink, Roger trudged back toward the bedroom.

Halfway there, the strains of Beethoven's "Ode to Joy" trilled from his cell phone.

He stopped. Looked like sleep wasn't going to be on his agenda after all. No one would call him on an off-duty Saturday morning unless there was some sort of emergency.

Pulse picking up, he returned to the kitchen and plucked the phone from the charger on the counter. Hopefully this crisis wasn't related to Leah, like the one two weeks ago after she'd fallen and bruised her knee while trying to run away from the staff at Woodside Gardens.

He scanned the screen. Hmm. No caller ID.

That was odd.

Punching the talk button, he called up his official voice. "Burnett."

"We have a problem."

It took him a second to place the voice. "Wayne?"

"Yeah. You need to get out here."

"Where? Your farm?"

"No. To my other, more profitable business. Park in your usual spot—and make it snappy. I'll meet you there."

"What's going . . ."

The line went dead.

Slowly Roger slid the phone onto his belt, dread roiling in his gut. He didn't want to go anywhere near the man's lab. The whole mess sickened him—especially his role in it.

Tension began to throb in his temples, and he wiped a hand down his face. Too bad that lab hadn't blown up, as many of those volatile operations did. And if Wayne had happened to be inside . . . well, that's the chance you took if you made meth.

But he couldn't get that lucky.

Instead, the man was sucking him deeper into his illegal operation.

Roger drummed his fingers on the counter, the caffeine he'd ingested adding to his jitters. If only he could wish this whole nightmare away.

Since that wasn't possible—could he at least ignore this summons?

No.

The answer came fast and definitive. Wayne wouldn't have called him unless there was a serious issue—like Dana had stumbled across his lab.

And if that had happened, her life could be in danger while he dillydallied in his kitchen.

Heart pounding, he stuffed his off-duty pistol into a holster. Shoved some plastic restraints into his pockets. Grabbed his car keys.

He might not want any part of whatever was happening on Leo's property, but if Dana was involved—and Wayne was offering him a chance to help find a solution that didn't involve bodily injury—he had to take it.

Finn had no trouble identifying the taste on his tongue.

It was blood.

Everything else, however, was fuzzy.

Letting his Ranger training kick in, he methodically ticked off the items on his capture checklist.

Keep your eyes closed and remain motionless. Check. Not that he had much choice, with his hands and feet bound and a gag stuck in his mouth. But it was always better to get the lay of the land before alerting anyone who might be watching that you were regaining your senses.

Regulate your breathing. In. Out. In. Out. Slow and steady. Check. A change in respiration was a signal to a captor to be more vigilant—but trying to breathe normally with a cat urine/rotten egg/fertilizer smell invading his nostrils was a challenge.

Compartmentalize the pain. Check. That was a lesson he'd learned long ago, during the brutal Ranger training. Suppressing the familiar but intensified pain in his leg and the new, pulsing throb in his head wasn't difficult. The predicament, not the pain, demanded 100 percent of his attention. His life could depend on the choices he made in the next few minutes.

Assess your situation and develop an action plan. That was the most difficult item to implement. How could you assess and plan if you couldn't remember what had happened?

Forcing himself to concentrate, he rewound his memory to what he *could* recall—the hike through the woods on Phelps's trail—and moved forward from there.

The man had been a piece of cake to follow, as expected, so there had been no need to get too close. The sound of him slogging through the brush had carried clearly in the quiet forest.

After about a quarter mile, the sound had stopped—suggesting he'd arrived at his destination. By Finn's calculation, they had been on or near Dana's land.

At that point, he'd gone into super stealth mode, creeping forward until he was close enough to get a view of the man through the trees.

He'd spotted the well-concealed shed within thirty seconds—and watched as Phelps removed assorted paraphernalia from his backpack, including blister packs of over-the-counter cold and allergy medications, charcoal lighter fluid, drain cleaner, coffee filters, and matches. The dead spots in the foliage around the area suggested toxic material had been dumped there, leading him to the obvious conclusion.

Phelps was operating a meth lab.

That also explained the noxious scent now assailing his nostrils.

And it wasn't some thrown-together shake-and-bake setup, either. This operation was much bigger.

As for how he'd ended up busted and all trussed up . . . that memory came back too—in painful and embarrassing detail, even if it *was* a testament to his well-honed covert reconnaissance skills.

He'd edged in close and hidden himself among the underbrush, intent on his surveillance. The deer nibbling upwind on some foliage hadn't seen him—nor had he spotted the deer—until the doe finally lifted her head and they found themselves almost nose to nose. It was hard to say who had been more startled.

But once the deer got a whiff of him, the situation had gone downhill fast.

The doe had reared back, then bounded away—straight toward the lab.

Phelps had jerked their direction.

As the doe crashed through the brush, Finn had scrambled to distance himself from the deer and dive for cover, hoping the man would assume some innocuous annoyance had frightened the easy-to-spook animal.

Too bad he hadn't seen the trip wire that had triggered a blinding, choking discharge of tear gas or some similar irritant.

Before he'd been able to recover enough to see, his head had exploded—and the world had gone black.

Gritting his teeth, Finn struggled to steady his respiration and corral the urge to lash out and kick something. After surviving attacks from extremists, roadside bombs, and high-risk reconnaissance missions behind enemy lines in the Middle East, this had not been his finest hour.

If nothing else, though, he did have some answers. Wayne Phelps was operating a meth lab on Dana's property—and ten chances to one he was the perpetrator of the vandalism. The man wouldn't want to risk her stumbling across his operation. They'd been correct in their conclusion that someone had been trying to chase her away.

But how and why was the chief involved?

That, however, was a mystery to solve later. His top priority at the moment was to get himself out of this mess.

After several more minutes passed with no sign of Phelps nor any sound to suggest he was close by, Finn half opened his eyes.

Everything was dark save for a faint horizontal band of light a few feet away, at ground level. The bottom of the door to the shed he'd spotted, perhaps. Phelps must have stashed him in the makeshift lab.

He continued to listen, straining his ears for any sound that suggested the man was nearby, but all was quiet. It was possible he'd gone to retrieve more supplies while his unexpected visitor was too out of it to be a threat.

Whatever the reason for the man's absence, he'd take it. He needed every minute he could get to free himself from the ropes binding his wrists and prepare for his next encounter with the market-garden-farmer-turned-meth-cooker.

Because a man who booby-trapped the approach to his operation . . . who set a fire that could have had fatal consequences . . . who knocked out an unwelcome visitor and secured him in an unstable area prone to dangerous explosions . . . wasn't likely to think twice about taking much more drastic measures to keep his business secure.

Up to and including murder.

So before Phelps stuck his head back inside his lab, Finn was going to do everything in his power to be ready and waiting to give the man a welcome he'd never forget.

Roger pulled in behind Dana's cabin, set the brake on the cruiser, and drummed his fingers on the wheel.

Should he have gone directly to meet Wayne, as the man had demanded?

No.

If he could confirm Dana was safe first, whatever crisis had freaked out his unwanted partner in crime might be more manageable. As long as lives weren't at stake, and no witnesses were able to identify either of them, they ought to be able to deal with whatever had come up.

Dana appeared in the window as he slid from the car, and he held on to the door to steady himself as his legs went shaky with relief.

Yes!

She was okay.

When he lifted a hand in greeting, she waved back—but instead of opening the door, she raised the sash a few inches.

"Good morning, Chief."

"Dana."

"What can I do for you?"

Even if her behavior hadn't already communicated her caution, the wariness in her features—and in her tone—screamed distrust and apprehension.

McGregor must have shared his suspicions with her.

Not unexpected, given how those two seemed to have hit it off.

"I thought I'd swing by on my way to Potosi, make certain everything was okay." He summoned up a stiff smile. "No more visits from the vandals, I take it?"

"No." She leaned her forearms on the windowsill. "I heard you caught the two teens who've been hitting the picnic grounds, though."

"Yes."

"Then maybe all will continue to be quiet here."

She was baiting him. McGregor didn't think the vandals were one and the same, and he'd surely shared that theory with Dana.

"I think we're dealing with a different set of perpetrators here. So we're keeping this on our radar. We'll get a break one of these days." Roger kept his manner casual and conversational. "Have you thought any more about temporarily relocating to your grandfather's place in St. Louis?"

"I'm considering it, once Finn leaves next week."

That was the best news he'd had all day.

If he could help Wayne deal with whatever crisis had come up and convince the man to hold off on his cooking a little longer, perhaps everything would smooth out and life could get back to normal.

Or what passed for normal these days.

"I think that would be wise. I can keep you apprised of any developments by phone."

"Thanks."

"Well . . ." He gave the cabin and surrounding area a sweep. "As long as everything here appears quiet, I'll get out of your hair. Enjoy your Saturday."

"You too."

He returned to his car, put it in gear, and crunched back down the road, feeling more upbeat than he had in weeks. Dana was safe—and seriously thinking about vacating the premises in a few days. Wayne should be able to push off his customers that long.

Whatever crisis had prompted him to call this morning, they'd find a way to deal with it.

After all, Dana had been the major threat all along. If she wasn't the problem, how bad could this be?

• • •

Dana waited until the chief's car disappeared in a cloud of dust, then let the curtain drop back into place.

That had been strange.

She wandered over to the sink to get a glass of water, fingering the whistle around her neck. Since the dock incident, he'd kept his distance—except at night. What had prompted a daytime visit?

Too bad Finn wasn't around. It would be interesting to get his take.

She glanced at the clock over the table as she sipped her water. Ten-forty-five. That meant he'd be here soon to give her the promised report on his morning before driving north for lunch with his brothers.

Chances were, though, it had been a total loss. The whole Wayne Phelps theory seemed like a long shot.

Still . . . Finn wasn't the type to waste time or effort on wild goose chases. If he thought Phelps was worth investigating, it was possible he was involved somehow.

Chief Burnett remained a wild card too. Pops had trusted the man implicitly, and she'd always held him in high esteem. But now . . . some nuance about Burnett felt off. Strange vibes continued to waft through the air in the wake of his surprise visit.

Thank goodness he hadn't hung around or asked to come in. That would have really freaked her out.

Suppressing a shiver, she dumped the rest of the water in the sink and started back toward the table to resume her editing.

At her chair, however, she hesitated. Prickles of apprehension continued to vibrate in her nerve endings. Maybe she was overreacting, but why not take a page from Finn's playbook and follow her instincts?

Without further debate, she detoured to the living room and picked up the Winchester from beside the door. Carried it back to the kitchen. Propped it beside the table as she took her seat. With Finn away, the whistle wouldn't be of much use. Having the gun close at hand should give her a bit more peace of mind.

Though truth be told, any peace of mind it did produce could be a sham. Yes, she knew how to load and shoot the rifle. And yes, she'd once been a very accurate shot.

But shooting at empty soda cans was a whole lot different than shooting at a person.

And no matter how critical the situation, she had no idea whether she'd be able to pull the trigger on a real live human being.

She could only pray it wouldn't come to that.

—21—

He almost had the cord binding his wrists loose enough to slip off. Another twist . . . another . . . one more . . . there!

His hands were free.

Finn shook off the rope and flexed his fingers to restore circulation, ignoring the burning in his wrists where he'd rubbed the skin raw.

As soon as his hands were functional, he ripped out the gag and went to work on the rope around his ankles.

That was dispensed with much faster.

Once on his feet, he patted himself down, sucking on his cheeks to activate his salivary glands and lubricate his parched mouth. Cell phone, binoculars, wallet—all gone. As was his Beretta, of course.

First order of business: find a weapon.

Prowling through the dim lab, he assessed the equipment. Big plastic buckets. Gas-grill-sized propane tank. Coffee filters. Duct-taped piping. Plastic tubing.

He homed in on the tubing.

That could work.

Moving in close, he peered at the setup in the darkness. He was no meth expert, but as far as he could tell, nothing was cooking.

Based on all the stuff Phelps had hauled in today, however—and was perhaps continuing to haul in at this very moment—that was about to change.

Working more by feel than sight, Finn managed to secure a length of the flexible tubing without making much noise. Once he had it in hand, he crossed to the door, groped for the handle to determine which direction it opened, and put his ear to the wood.

Now he could pick up movement outside. It sounded agitated. Angry. As if someone was striding around, trying to work off restless energy—or a head of steam.

Too bad he couldn't crack the door to see what was going on. But if Phelps spotted him, realized he was no longer tied up, the man would get the upper hand.

Not going to happen again.

Finn wanted the advantage on his side this round.

So he'd have to sit tight and wait for his captor to enter the lab, no matter how much the delay taxed his patience.

And if the element of surprise worked as he hoped it would, Phelps would get the shock of his life.

Finn should have been here by now.

Giving up any pretense of working, Dana rose

from the computer and began to pace. He'd said he'd be back by eleven, and it was ten after. He might cut things close after living on the edge for years as a Ranger, but he'd never once been late for any of their scheduled get-togethers.

Could he have had a flat tire?

Hit a deer and skidded off the road?

Run into some serious trouble at Phelps's place?

Her heart stuttered at the last possibility. What if Wayne Phelps *was* involved in the vandalism at her place? A guy who did that kind of damage—and took chances with people's lives—was dangerous. And while Finn seemed well able to take care of himself, there was always a chance something could go wrong . . . like on the mission where he'd almost lost his leg.

She sucked in a breath, fighting back a sudden wave of panic. If she kept this up, she was going to hyperventilate.

Calm down, Dana. Don't overreact. He might be in the middle of some critical surveillance and doesn't want to leave yet. If he's within cell range, it's possible he's already alerted his brothers he's going to be late. He may even have left you a message and expects you'll check your voicemail if you don't hear from him.

Her breathing smoothed out.

Better.

And it stayed better until the clock hit eleven-thirty and her little pep talk wore off.

Time to ramp up her cell.

After retrieving her phone from the charger, she opened the front door and peeked out. Save for the chirp of birds, all was quiet, as it had been the entire morning. A quick trip down to the lake in broad daylight should be safe.

Convincing her thumping heart of that as she jogged down the incline toward the water, however, proved impossible.

Once on the dock, she kept an alert eye on her surroundings as she punched in her voicemail passcode.

Nothing.

No text, either.

Finn hadn't tried to contact her to explain why he was delayed.

The red alert began to flash with increased urgency in her mind. He wasn't the type to cause anyone he cared about to worry—and he knew by now she'd be fretting and anxious.

She tried calling his cell number.

Instead of ringing, it rolled immediately to voicemail—as if he'd turned his phone off.

Not like him, either.

She wiped the palm of her free hand down her jeans. Calling 911 wasn't an option—but she did have Mac's number stored in her phone. Why not touch base with him, see if he'd heard from Finn?

Fingers trembling, she scrolled through until she

found the number Finn had given her. Placed the call. Tapped her foot as it rang.

Once.

Twice.

Three times.

Please don't roll to voicemail!

"McGregor. Leave a message and I'll get back to you as soon as I can."

She closed her eyes and expelled a frustrated breath.

"Mac, this is Dana Lewis. I know Finn's supposed to meet you and Lance for lunch, but he said he'd stop by here first. I haven't seen or heard from him, and I wondered if you had." She went on to give him a quick recap of Finn's plans for the morning. "I hope that was coherent. As you can probably tell, I'm worried. I only get reception down at my lake, so I'll hang around here until I hear from you."

After ending the call, she pocketed the phone and sat on the edge of the dock, dangling her feet over the edge. Faint traces of orange paint lingered on the wood despite Finn's diligent effort to remove them—just as whoever had defaced her property was still lurking out there somewhere.

She took another nervous look around. While a slight fuzziness continued to cloud her distance vision, her eyesight was much better than it had been even three weeks ago. And as far as she could tell, the only other sign of life close to the lake was the ubiquitous blue heron, claiming his usual spot in the shallow water near the bank.

Leaning back against a post, she held tight to her phone . . . and counted off the minutes while she waited for Mac to return her call.

All the while praying that wherever Finn was, he was in control.

He needed to get this situation under his control—no matter what it took.

Keeping a firm grip on the coil of tubing in his hands, Finn shifted position slightly inside the dark lab to take the weight off his aching leg. Given the level of pain, he must have done a number on it when Phelps tackled him in the woods, while he was blinded. Maybe caused some serious damage.

Not great news.

The last thing he needed was more hospitals and rehab.

Reality check, McGregor. The last thing you need is to be stuck in a meth lab trying to escape with your life.

Right.

He could worry about his leg later.

The footsteps in the brush outside moved closer, and he tensed.

This might be it—and he couldn't blow it. He was only going to get one chance to overpower Phelps, and while he had no doubt he could mop the floor with the guy under usual circumstances, his bum leg and that blow on the head were going to give his adversary a distinct advantage.

All he had on his side was the element of surprise . . . and some muscle power.

The footsteps stopped on the other side of the door.

The knob jiggled.

Finn's adrenaline spiked.

An instant later, the door swung open and Phelps inched inside, the blade of a hunting knife glinting in his hand.

He froze. "What the . . ."

Before he could finish his sentence, Finn sprang forward and looped the tubing around his neck. Yanked it taut.

Phelps dropped the knife and clawed at the loop of plastic that was crushing his windpipe and cutting off his air supply.

Finn kicked the knife out of the way, increased the pressure, and kneed the man in the kidneys.

He groaned, legs crumpling.

So far, so good. Now all he had to do—

"Phelps? You in there?"

At the summons from a familiar voice outside, Finn swung around, loosening his grip on the tubing for an infinitesimal second.

But it was long enough for Phelps to jerk away and break his hold. They both lunged for the knife.

Phelps got there first, but Finn was on top of him in a millisecond, grappling for control of the weapon. As his fist connected with the man's nose, Phelps abandoned the fight and rolled toward the door.

While Finn grabbed the knife and regained his footing, Phelps disappeared outside.

"It's about time you got here. What took you so long?" Phelps hissed out the words.

The response was too soft to hear, but Finn had already identified the new arrival.

Chief Roger Burnett.

Unfortunately, it didn't appear the man was here in his official capacity.

"I *did* plan to meet you on the road," Phelps continued his tirade, "but I got a little tied up here, as you can see. And yes, the SUV you saw belongs to Dana Lewis's neighbor."

Finn shoved the knife into his boot. If fate was kind, Phelps would forget all about it.

But what to do now?

As if he'd heard the question, Burnett called to him, his words tinged with weariness. "Come on out, McGregor."

What choice did he have?

Trying to psych himself up for whatever curve they were waiting to throw him, he stepped into the sunlight.

Phelps gave him a venomous glare, spat out a mouthful of blood, and swiped his sleeve across his lips. The man was a loose cannon.

But Finn was more worried about Burnett. The chief's eyes were cool, composed . . . and resigned.

Plus, he had a Sig.

And as Finn stared down the barrel, as the cold reality slammed into him, his insides turned to ice.

They were going to kill him.

"Why couldn't you have stayed out of this?" What appeared to be genuine remorse softened the chief's features.

Hmm.

Finn's mind clicked into analytical mode. If the man was a reluctant participant in the nastiness going on here, that could give him a tactical advantage. Guilt and shame were strong emotions —and he might be able to exploit them.

"I told you this could happen if you didn't get rid of the girl!" Phelps scowled at Burnett and started to pace. "If you'd pressed harder after I set that fire, she might have left."

So Phelps was definitely the vandal.

But why was Burnett protecting him?

"I tried."

"Not hard enough." Phelps stopped inches from the chief, fury etching his features. "I should have sent those diving pictures straight to the highway patrol."

"Then I would have given them mine."

As Finn listened to the exchange, the pieces began to click into place.

Burnett had protected Phelps because the man was blackmailing him. Whatever his reason for diving in Dana's lake, Burnett didn't want anyone to know about it—and he'd countered Phelps's blackmail threat with one of his own.

"Fine. So we're stuck with each other. That means we have to get rid of the boyfriend—together."

"We're not getting rid of anyone, Wayne. It's over."

"Over?" The man gaped at him. "Are you crazy? I'm not giving up everything I worked my butt off to get for the past two years. And what about you? I don't know what your scuba diving is all about, but it can't be legal—and your career will be toast once I show those photos to the highway patrol. Who knows? You might end up behind bars yourself."

Some of the color leeched from Burnett's complexion.

So his diving *was* related to some illegal activity.

As the two men faced off, the left side of Finn's brain began to crank at warp speed. While Phelps would kill him in a heartbeat, Burnett didn't appear to have the stomach for murder. However, if backed into a corner, Burnett might panic . . . and everything would hit the fan.

He needed to make his case. Now. Phelps's patience was clearly running out.

"There might be another solution."

Both men swiveled toward him as he spoke.

"What are you talking about?" Phelps squinted at him.

"Shut down the lab. Dismantle it. No one ever comes back here, anyway. Take the money you've made and leave town. The chief's not likely to track you down, based on whatever arrangement you two have, and I'm leaving next week. My memory could fade very fast."

Phelps's eyes tapered to slits. "Why would you walk away? Don't you work for the government?"

"Not anymore." He tried for a reasonable tone, praying they'd buy his argument. "Look, if you erase all evidence of your lab, it would be my word against yours. Unless you've left a clear trail, which I doubt, there wouldn't be enough evidence to convict you of anything."

"It's a good solution, Wayne." Burnett appeared to be receptive to the idea—but his gun didn't waver.

Was he amenable—or working some other angle?

Impossible to tell.

"No, it isn't. I'm not finished here yet." Although blood continued to drip from Phelps's nose, his chin rose a notch. "I need more time."

"You're out of time, Wayne." Burnett's voice hardened. "Take the deal the man is offering."

"No! There's a better solution. If we kill him and bury the body back here, no one will ever find him."

"That would never work. If he disappears, people will look for him."

"Who? You? This is your jurisdiction. Make sure the investigation goes nowhere."

Finn's pulse took a leap. The situation was deteriorating fast. He needed to get that knife in hand and be prepared to rush them if necessary, despite the long odds. Otherwise, he'd be a sitting duck.

"I can't do that, Wayne." Slowly Burnett swung the gun toward Phelps.

Finn didn't move a muscle.

"What are you doing?" The man's eyes widened.

"Putting an end to your games."

"What? You're going to shoot me?" Phelps managed to infuse his tone with derision, but fear dilated his pupils.

"Not unless you do something stupid."

"Like what?"

"Like resist arrest."

"You're *arresting* me? What about my photos?"

"I have a feeling I can find them as part of my investigation into your illegal activities."

"This is insane!"

"Yeah, it is. It has been for weeks."

"You need to shoot *him,* not me!" A note of hysteria raised Wayne's pitch.

As the meth cooker pointed his direction, Finn's fingers began to tingle. One way or the other, this was going down.

Now.

"I'm not shooting him, Wayne."

"Well, if you won't, I will!"

With that, Phelps dived for Burnett's legs. The two hit the ground, wrestling for control of the gun.

Finn bent down to pull out the knife.

And then the forest exploded with a single shot that shattered the stillness—and changed everything yet again.

—22—

Someone was firing a gun on her property.

As the shot ripped through the air, destroying the peaceful stillness . . . as the blue heron launched itself skyward with a noisy flap of its enormous wings . . . Dana scrambled to her feet, pulse hammering.

That had been close.

Too close.

And unless the shooter was hunting illegally, he or she wasn't aiming at animals. Nothing was in season in April, as Pops had told her on a long ago spring break visit when she'd been worried about hunters and stray bullets.

The events of the morning strobed across her mind in quick succession. An odd visit from the chief . . . Finn missing . . . a gunshot on her property.

Those pieces fit together somehow—and while the emerging picture remained unclear and confusing, it was scary.

Very scary.

Cold fingers of fear squeezed her throat.

She needed to get someone to investigate.

Now.

Tension vibrating through her, she tried Mac again.

The call rolled to voicemail.

Again.

After leaving another abbreviated message, she hung up.

Now what?

She shoved her hair back, massaged her forehead, and tried to organize her chaotic thoughts.

Finn had said Mac would be able to round up help from the highway patrol or sheriff's department in an emergency. She could try to do that too—except even if she explained everything in minute detail, they might write her off as a nutcase. Casting aspersions on a respected police chief? Panicking over a man who'd missed an appointment by less than an hour? Worrying about a stray gunshot on private forest land that could be nothing more than someone doing target practice?

Still, what choice did she have when she knew, deep in her soul, that bad stuff was happening on the far reaches of her property?

After googling the number for the highway patrol, she punched it in. Paced as she slogged through the prompts. Finally got a woman who would listen to her story.

But she had to go through a bunch of name/address/phone number questions before she could get to the meat of her call.

Once she finished what she hoped was a concise, coherent recap of the situation, there was dead silence on the line.

"Um . . . the Beaumont Police Department would be the appropriate agency to deal with your concerns, ma'am. I'd be happy to place a call to them for you."

Had the woman listened to one word she'd said?

"I told you . . . I think the chief may be involved in whatever is going on. I don't want to call there."

"All right." The woman's tone became placating. "Let me see if we have an officer in your area. Hold, please." The woman was gone before she could respond.

So Dana held . . . and held . . . and held some more.

Just as she was about to hang up, the woman came back on the line.

"Our closest car is in Farmington, but the officer is dealing with a major traffic accident. I can get him there in about an hour."

Not fast enough.

"Isn't anyone else available?" A note of desperation wove through her words.

"Let me put you on hold again while I—"

"No! Wait! Contact a detective named McGregor with St. Louis County. He'll verify my call is legitimate. I'll leave a map of the property on my back door for your officer, pinpointing my best guess about the location of the shot I heard. I'm going to check this out myself."

"Ma'am, it would be safer to wait for professional help to arrive."

She didn't doubt that—in terms of her own well-being.

But if shots were being fired and Finn was missing, his safety took top priority.

"I'll be careful. Please . . . call McGregor at County and get someone over here ASAP!"

Without waiting for a response, she punched the end button and took off for the house.

Once inside, she snatched up a piece of paper and drew a crude map of the property, putting an X in the vicinity of the shot. After taping it on the back door, she exchanged her Stanford sweatshirt for a dark green sweater, then veered back into the kitchen. To the Winchester propped against the kitchen table.

Only then did she hesitate.

This was a weapon that could kill—just as the handguns her abductors had held to her head in New York could kill. A single bullet was all it took to end a life.

Stomach twisting, she retreated a step. The advice from the woman at the highway patrol was sound. It would be better to leave this to the professionals.

But if the situation is life-threatening, they could arrive too late. Do you think Finn would sit around waiting for reinforcements if he thought you *needed help?*

No.

He'd dive into the thick of the action.

Clenching her teeth, she picked up the rifle, the weight of it heavier than she remembered. Finn might be better trained than she was, but thanks to Pops, she knew every inch of this property. Knew how to use this gun. Knew how to listen to the sounds of the woods and distinguish natural ones from those produced by humans. Knew how to spot wildlife and creep in to get an up-close-and-personal look.

Mouth firming, she strode to the spare bedroom and grabbed a dozen cartridges from the box she'd showed Finn. Stuffed them in the pocket of her jeans. Headed for the front door.

Wait.

She jolted to a stop.

If there was bad stuff going on across the lake, someone could be watching the cabin for anything to suggest the suspicious activity had been noticed. Better to follow Finn's example and keep a low profile on approach.

Reversing direction, she moved toward the back of the house and slipped out the rear door. After melting into the woods, she began to press through the brush around the lake, toward the far side—the area where she and Finn had hiked the day after he'd spotted the chief diving.

She had a feeling it wasn't a coincidence that the shot had come from that general vicinity.

As for what she'd find in the bowels of the forest—her fingers tensed on the rifle. If Finn was in trouble, she'd do her best to come to his rescue as he'd come to hers the night he'd raced through the woods in response to her screams.

And during this hike she'd pray for the strength to use the gun if that's what it took to keep him safe.

"Have fun with Lance and Finn."

Turning, Mac gave Lisa a lazy smile and propped a shoulder against the doorframe that separated the kitchen from the garage. "Want the truth? I'd rather stay here with you."

"You'll have me all to yourself tomorrow—and I have plans. Big plans."

"Yeah? Better than this morning?" He waggled his eyebrows.

She gave him a playful shove. "Get out of here before I drag you back inside."

"Is that a threat or a promise?"

"You're incorrigible."

"Nope. In love."

Lisa's face softened, the way it always did during their tender moments, lightening his heart and reminding him how blessed he'd been the day he'd strolled onto her crime scene as a wet-behind-the-ears County detective.

Fortunately, she hadn't held his foot-in-mouth disease that morning against him.

She leaned close and brushed her lips over his. "I know. That's why you were going to leave without this." She held up his cell phone.

He felt around on his belt. Yep. Missing.

Only she could make him forget his tether to the world.

"Thanks." He slid it into place.

"Aren't you going to turn it on?"

"After I'm on the road. I have to take care of some more important business first." He pulled her close to demonstrate.

"Mmm. I like your priorities." She smiled up at him, then eased out of his arms. "But you need to get moving if you want to stop at the range before you meet your brothers."

"Yeah." Somehow, shooting at paper targets

held zero appeal this morning. Necessary, though, if he wanted to keep his skills sharp. "I'll be back by three."

"Don't rush on my account. I have Tally to keep me company." She bent down to pat the golden-haired stray she'd rescued a couple of years ago.

"A poor substitute for a handsome husband . . . but at least I don't have to be jealous." He winked and gave Tally a rub under the chin himself. "See you later."

She stood in the driveway, waving, until he disappeared around the curve of the drive. Only then did he activate his cell.

Once he emerged onto the two-lane country road, he scrolled through email and text messages. Nothing urgent. He could deal with all of them later. But he did have three new voicemails.

The first one was an auto reminder about an upcoming department meeting already on his calendar. He erased it.

The next two, however—both from a concerned Dana—set off alarm bells.

Finn appeared to be MIA.

And shots were being fired on her property.

Unless he'd misread his brother's neighbor during their brief introduction, she wasn't the type to push the panic button without cause.

He tapped in her number, keeping tabs on the traffic as he drove.

The call rolled to voicemail.

Dana hadn't waited at the lake for him to respond—and unless she went back down there, she wouldn't have cell coverage. Who knew when they'd connect?

But if she was sufficiently worried to call and ask him to send the highway patrol, he wasn't about to defer rounding up the troops until they touched base.

Within five minutes, he'd been put through to someone with authority at the highway patrol, learned Dana had already called—and discovered that her request was in a queue to be dealt with ASAP.

He got her bumped to the top of the list. Fast.

His next call was to Lance.

"Hey . . . I know you're anxious for us to buy you lunch, but you didn't have to remind me. It's on my calendar." Lance's yawn came over the line.

Mac hung a fast right onto the main road and accelerated. "Lunch may not happen." He gave Lance a quick download. "I'm southbound as we speak. Do you want me to swing by and pick you up?"

"I'll be ready in five." Lance's grim tone matched his own mood.

Ending the call, he increased his speed again. But even if he kept his foot pressed to the floor during the entire drive, their optimal ETA was an hour and twenty minutes.

Too long.

Because a boatload of bad stuff could happen in far less time than that.

This wasn't how it was supposed to play out.

He wasn't supposed to die before Leah.

Roger leaned his head back and gripped the wound in his arm, watching Phelps jiggle the gun he'd managed to grab after it had discharged during their scuffle.

A gun that was now trained on both him and McGregor as they sat side by side, backs propped against adjacent oak trees in the small clearing.

Beads of sweat trickled down his temples as his lungs parsed out meager breaths—but his condition had nothing to do with the superficial wound in his arm.

It was due to the crushing pain in his chest.

He was having a heart attack.

All the signs pointed to it—and during his many years responding to emergencies, he'd seen plenty of them.

One other fact was also clear.

He was going to die if he didn't get medical assistance fast.

And the odds of that happening were slim to none.

The pressure in his chest increased, and he let out a soft moan. What would happen to Leah once the truth was revealed about the source of the funds that had paid off her bills at Woodside Gardens?

Wayne marched over, his features twisted with fear . . . anger . . . desperation. Who knew? "Stop with the groaning! If you're trying to get sympathy, it's not working."

"He needs medical attention, Phelps."

As McGregor spoke, Roger dipped into his waning reserves of energy and twisted his head toward the other man. Their gazes met—and in the man's razor-sharp eyes, he glimpsed understanding. McGregor was smart enough—or experienced enough—to know a simple flesh wound shouldn't produce the kind of symptoms he was experiencing.

"Yeah, well, too bad." Phelps's chest heaved, and sweat beaded on his brow too.

For very different reasons.

McGregor clasped his hands loosely around his upraised knee. "You have to know you're not going to get away with this, Phelps."

"Shut up!" His finger twitched on the trigger. "I need to think."

As Dana's neighbor regarded the gun, Burnett managed to wheeze two words his direction. "I'm . . . sorry."

"I said, shut up!" Phelps stomped closer, swinging the gun back and forth between his two captives.

McGregor didn't respond—because he was

afraid of setting Phelps off, or because he didn't believe the Beaumont chief of police truly felt remorse?

Perhaps both.

After all, why *should* he think the apology was legit? There was no reason to trust a law enforcement officer who'd drifted to the dark side.

Moisture clouded his vision, and Roger closed his eyes. Everything had gone so wrong with the plan that had seemed simple, straightforward, and safe in the beginning. The only person who was supposed to have been at risk was him.

Now, McGregor's life was at stake too.

And what about Dana?

A cold chill swept through him. If anything happened to the man beside him, she wouldn't rest until she got answers. And if Wayne had been willing to go to extremes to keep her from discovering a meth lab, he'd be twice as ruthless about eliminating anyone who tried to connect him to murder.

Lord, how could this disintegrate into such a colossal mess? And what am I supposed to do now?

The desperate question poured from his soul, startling him. How long had it been since he'd turned to God for guidance—or help?

Since before he'd found the gold, that much he knew.

But now, as his strength ebbed, he reopened the conversation.

Lord, I've made a lot of mistakes. You know I wanted to honor my promise to Leah to provide for her. You know I would never have used a dime of the money from that gold for myself. I thought I could control the situation, make certain no one got hurt, but instead I got tangled in a web of deceit that's literally sucking the life out of me. Please forgive me. Please watch over Leah after I'm gone. And in the little time I have left, please give me a chance to help those I've wronged.

"Hey." The toe of a shoe nudged his leg. "You still with us, old man?" Wayne's voice seemed to come from far away as he struggled to open his eyelids. "Yeah. I see you are."

He stared up at the gun-toting man. "Get right . . . with God . . . Wayne."

The man's jaw dropped. Then he gave a harsh laugh. "You're kidding, right? Let me tell you . . . after God took away my job and my girl and stranded me in this dump of a town, he should get right with *me*."

"The chief has a point." McGregor sounded relaxed and composed, as if they were all having a chat around mugs of coffee at the Walleye. "It's not too late to have second thoughts. Yeah, you made meth, but as far as I know, you haven't killed anyone—yet. Once you cross that line, though, there's no going back."

"There's no going back now. I'm this close"—

Wayne spread his thumb and index finger an inch apart—"from having what I need to ditch this place and start over."

"So what are you going to do about us?"

He stalked over to McGregor, almost within lunging distance . . . but not quite.

"I'm thinking about it. But if you don't shut up, you're going to end up with another gag stuffed in that smart mouth of yours."

He backed off, gun aimed their direction, and Roger once again rolled his head toward McGregor, willing the man to read what was in his mind.

I'll help you overpower him in any way I can.

For several beats, Dana's neighbor studied him. Then, as if he'd gotten the message, he gave a slight nod. Slowly reached down to scratch his leg. And when the sudden flutter of a bird in the trees distracted Wayne for a second, he slid his pants leg up to reveal a hunting knife tucked in his boot.

Wayne's, based on the carving in the handle.

McGregor must have wrestled it from him during their skirmish in the lab.

Unfortunately, Wayne could realize at any moment that it was missing.

Meaning this needed to wrap up soon—for a lot of reasons, not the least of which was his failing heart.

McGregor let his pants leg slide back down as

Wayne swung toward them, but he didn't break eye contact.

The pressure in his chest increased, and Roger swallowed past the pain, struggling to breathe. He had no idea how he could help McGregor when the man made his move, but he'd do whatever he could.

Warmth seeped down his arm, and after a slight nod of his own, he dropped his chin. The bullet wound continued to bleed, the dark stain on his dark green shirt widening with each minute that passed.

If he had the physical strength, he'd take the initiative. Rush Wayne, take another bullet, to buy McGregor a window to pull out the knife and have a fighting chance against the man. Wayne couldn't deal with both of them at once.

But sooner or later, he was going to recognize that vulnerability and tie them up.

McGregor had to know that too.

So unless he was way off base, the man sitting next to him wasn't going to wait much longer to implement whatever plan he was undoubtedly concocting to flip this situation on its head.

—23—

Dana slowed her pace, carefully picking through the underbrush as she swiveled her head back and forth, listening for any sound or movement that suggested the shooter was nearby. She had to be getting close—but it was difficult to keep her bearings with the thick vegetation obscuring the lake and the sun at its high-noon apex.

High noon.

If she wasn't scared out of her mind, the irony of the timing would be amusing.

But with the rifle in her hands and the very real possibility of a shootout looming ahead, nothing about this situation held the remotest trace of humor.

She stopped to peer into the dense underbrush and do a slow, three-sixty rotation.

Nothing.

The woods were as quiet as they'd been the day she and Finn—

"Shut up!"

At the muted, barked command somewhere to her left, she jerked. Fumbled the gun. Managed to grab it before it crashed to the ground.

After giving her heart a few seconds to regain its rhythm, she crept toward the voice. She couldn't identify the person, but the emotion was clear.

Anger.

And anger could prompt people to make bad choices.

Her palms grew damp—and her hands began to shake.

Steady, Dana. You can do this. Just remember what Pops taught you about the woods. Approach quietly. Observe. And don't forget what he said during those target practice sessions with the soda cans—always take the safety off before firing.

The showdown was about to begin.

Finn watched as Phelps strode over to the moaning chief. The man's nostrils flared as he pointed the gun at Burnett's chest. "I said, shut up!"

"He's dying, Phelps."

"That's a lie." Their captor's mouth twisted into a sneer. "I barely nicked his arm."

"He's having a heart attack." Finn let that sink in for a minute. "A simple flesh wound wouldn't turn his skin gray or make him sweat like that or glaze his eyes or disrupt his breathing."

Phelps backed up and inspected the semi-conscious Burnett, twin crevices denting his brow. "I've known him my whole life. He's never had heart problems."

"He does now." Finn clasped his hands around his knee again, positioning his fingers within touching distance of the knife. He couldn't wait much longer for a window of opportunity. Phelps was becoming more agitated by the minute . . . and agitation could prompt a person to do crazy things.

Like pull a trigger.

He had to lure the man close and pray for a distraction of some kind. A second or two, that's all he'd need to take him down.

"Hey . . ." Panic flitted across Phelps's face as he felt around on his belt. "Where's my knife?"

Finn stiffened.

Unless some sort of miracle occurred, he was hosed.

"You have it, don't you?" Phelps's eye twitched.

The chief turned his head—and it was clear from his grim demeanor he realized this was the do-or-die moment.

It was also clear, in the silent communication that passed between them, that he'd do what he could to help.

Unfortunately, he was in no condition to assist at this stage.

Finn swallowed. Whatever happened next was up to him . . . and God.

When he didn't respond to Phelps's question, the man edged closer.

Perfect.

"Stand up." He motioned with Burnett's pistol.

Finn eyed the gun. One slight bit of pressure,

a bullet was going to blow a hole in his chest.

He stood.

"Strip."

At the unexpected command, he blinked. "What?"

"Strip. Down to your skivvies. Now. And do it fast."

The man was smarter than he'd thought. Watching as his prisoner shed his clothes would allow him to keep his distance and verify whether a weapon was concealed anywhere.

Not so perfect.

So . . . how to play this? Hand over the knife Phelps was going to discover anyway, or take off his clothes as slow as possible and buy himself another couple of minutes that probably wouldn't make much difference?

Better to stall. A brief delay might not help—but it couldn't hurt.

He pulled out the tail of the Oxford shirt he'd planned to wear to lunch with Mac and Lance and worked the front buttons loose, drawing out the task as long as he dared before turning his attention to the ones at the cuffs.

"I said do it fast!" Again, Phelps waved the gun.

Ignoring that directive, Finn finished the job at his own pace and shrugged out of the shirt, leaving only his tee covering his torso.

He needed Phelps closer.

As if on cue, the chief began to wheeze and clutch his chest.

Phelps didn't spare the man more than a quick glance. Far too short to risk a lunging tackle. But maybe he could draw Phelps in by using what he assumed was a ploy by the chief.

"Do you have any water?"

Phelps frowned at him. "What?"

"Water. For the chief. If you won't get him medical help, at least ease his suffering." And then he played his trump card, praying Hazel's assessment of Phelps's relationship with his father was accurate. "If your dad was around, what do you think he'd say about all this?"

A spasm of pain tightened Phelps's features. "You shut up about my daddy!"

"I heard he was a good man."

"Better than you . . . or him!" He waved the pistol at Burnett, eyes blazing.

"If that's true, I bet he'd want you to give the chief a drink of water."

Several tense beats ticked by as they held a staring match.

In the end, however, Phelps backed away, toward his pile of supplies.

Yes!

Finn maintained an impassive expression, but every muscle in his body tightened, preparing to spring into action. There wasn't much chance Phelps would come close enough to hand the water to Burnett—though that would be ideal. More likely he'd toss a bottle their direction.

And that scenario could work too . . . especially after he glanced at the chief and the man opened his fist to reveal a rock, then tipped his head toward the trees. It was too small to cause any damage . . . but it would create a great distraction if lobbed into the woods.

All he had to do was lunge for the bottle after Phelps tossed it, blocking the man's view of the chief. Fumble with the container to give Burnett a window. And wait for their captor to react to the noise in the woods from the thrown rock.

Once he had the guy on the ground, this would be over fast. That brief scuffle in the lab had told him all he needed to know about the man's physical condition. Despite a sore leg and the mother of all headaches, he could take him in a heartbeat.

Gun trained on his prisoners, Phelps dug through his backpack with his free hand.

Finn took several long, slow breaths, praying he and the chief were on the same page.

But whether they were or weren't, this was going to end in less than a minute—for better or worse.

As she watched from her concealed position while the guy she assumed was Phelps rummaged through his backpack, Dana took the safety off Pops's rifle—and made a decision.

If she and Finn got out of this alive, she was moving to Atlanta.

ASAP.

Lollygagging—to use one of Mags's favorite words—was foolish when your heart already knew the best course. Only the fear of making a mistake had held her back from agreeing at once to his suggestion.

That fear, however, was nothing compared to the terror now coursing through her veins.

Heart banging against her rib cage, she looked back at Finn. He was standing beside the chief, his posture relaxed, thumbs hooked in the pockets of his jeans.

But that laid-back stance was an act.

He was gearing up for an attack. She could sense it, even if Phelps couldn't. They might be new friends, but there was a powerful, intuitive connection between them.

Another reason to follow him to Atlanta.

And another reason not to delay making her move. She'd been here long enough to get the gist of the situation—and to know it was volatile. No matter what Finn was planning, Phelps had the gun . . . a huge advantage. Burnett already seemed to be wounded, based on that dark stain on his sleeve, and she doubted a man who'd fired at a police chief would hesitate to pull the trigger on a civilian.

Phelps retrieved a bottle of water from his backpack. Began walking toward Finn and the chief.

This was it.

Stepping out from her cover, she pointed the Winchester at him. "Drop the gun."

He halted but continued to aim his pistol at Finn as he jerked her way.

Finn lunged his direction—but Phelps swung back toward him and pulled the trigger.

As slivers of oak bark spewed into the air from the tree behind him, Finn froze and Dana almost lost her breakfast. Another few inches to the left, the bullet would have lodged in his brain.

Oh, God, please help me! The silent plea ripped from the depths of her soul. *I am so out of my element here!*

Although she could feel Finn's gaze burning into her, she kept her focus on Phelps. "I said drop the gun."

After sizing her up, his lips curled. "I don't think so."

He was calling her bluff.

That's when she realized her tactical error. She should have let him get as close as possible to Finn before stepping out from her concealed position. That way, Finn would have been able to complete the tackle he'd attempted.

Too late for second thoughts now, though. She had to work with what she had—and her number one priority was clear: convince Phelps she was serious. If she did, she could cross to Finn, hand him the rifle . . . and let him finish this job for which she was so ill-suited.

Diverting the barrel a hair to the right of Phelps, she prayed her aim was as accurate as it had once been, thanked God her midrange vision was back to normal—and pulled the trigger.

She absorbed the recoil as Pops had taught her and reloaded the bolt-action rifle in one swift, smooth motion as the spent casing ejected.

"The next one goes in you unless you drop the gun." Much to her surprise, her words didn't waver a fraction.

But Phelps did. A touch of uncertainty glinted in his eyes. He might not be convinced she'd follow through on her threat—but he wasn't sure she was bluffing, either.

Please, God, let him back down!

He started to lower the gun.

But instead of dropping it, he yanked it up and aimed her direction.

The next sequence of events happened so fast, Dana couldn't even sort out the order.

A shot was fired.

She squeezed the trigger.

Booms resounded through the forest, shattering the stillness.

Finn dived for Phelps, who crumpled into a motionless heap on the ground.

A uniformed officer strode onto the scene, pistol in hand.

And as fast as it all began, the whole thing was over.

Shaking worse than the leaves fluttering in the breeze around her, she lowered the rifle. She was still standing, so Phelps had missed her . . . right?

"Dana!" Finn croaked out her name and limped toward her. "Are you okay?" His hands grasped her shoulders—strong, warm, reassuring.

She tried to speak. Failed. Settled for a nod.

He crushed her against him, nuzzling her hair.

It felt like heaven.

Far too soon, though, he ended the embrace. "Sit here while I see to Burnett." He urged her down, keeping a firm grip on her until she was on solid ground.

After exchanging a few muted words with the uniformed officer who was dealing with Phelps, he lowered himself beside the chief, laid the man flat, pressed his fingers against his neck.

Dana forced her lungs to keep inflating and deflating. Managed to slow her pulse from furious to fast. Then crawled over to see what she could do to help with what appeared to be a serious medical emergency.

". . . radioed for assistance."

"We might need to begin CPR if . . ."

". . . thready, and color is . . ."

The words ping-ponging over his chest faded in

and out, but Roger knew the discussion was about him.

If he had the strength, he'd tell them not to fret. There was nothing they could do to save him. After all his years in the field, he knew it was too late.

He was dying—and the kind of help he needed would never arrive in time.

The voices grew more distant. Muffled. As if a door was slowly closing. The hard ground beneath him also fell away, and he began to drift, suspended between earth and sky. Like the moment on that high jump at the pool when he was a kid, after he took the leap and hovered for an instant between air and water.

He tried to hold on, to keep from falling, but it was futile. His fingers were weak, and there was nothing to grasp but air.

Expelling a final breath, Roger let go with a simple prayer.

Please, Lord, take care of Leah.

And have mercy on my soul.

"He's gone." Finn looked across the chief's body at the highway patrol officer on the other side, who'd helped him administer CPR.

"Yeah." The man sat back on his heels. "I think it was a lost cause from the beginning, to be honest. If we could have gotten an EMT team here sooner, he might have had a fighting chance."

"I don't think so. He's been in severe cardiac distress for quite a while."

The trooper scowled at Phelps's body. "No thanks to him."

"No." Finn eased the weight off his throbbing leg, trying not to wince.

But Dana picked up on his pain, moving in from the sidelines where she'd retreated as the two men worked in unison to try to keep the chief alive. "You're hurt."

"I'm okay."

The trooper homed in on his temple. "You have a big bump on your forehead. Did you lose consciousness?"

"Briefly."

"The EMTs can check you out. You may have a concussion."

"What about your leg?" Dana touched his arm.

"It's not an issue." He shot her a let's-not-discuss-that-now look.

She fell silent.

"Do you feel up to telling me what happened?" The trooper rose.

"Yeah. Why don't we talk over there?" He indicated a shady spot away from the two bodies.

Without a word, Dana stood and reached down to offer him an arm.

He took it—and needed a lot more help than he wanted to admit to regain his footing.

The trooper led the way, and Dana slipped her arm around him in a subtle invitation to lean on her as he limped after the man. He took it.

By the time they'd answered all the trooper's questions, the distant sound of sirens wove through the forest.

"The reinforcements have arrived." He pocketed his notebook.

"Do we need to hang around?" Finn shifted his weight, hissing out a breath. What he wouldn't give for a Vicodin. Or two.

"You might want the EMTs to do a quick assessment."

"Not necessary."

"Finn . . ." Worry pooled in Dana's eyes. "It might not be a bad idea."

"I'll be fine." He managed a smile. "What I need is to sit down next to you on the porch with a glass of lemonade and chill."

"Your call. I assume I can find you there if I have any more questions?" The trooper slipped on a pair of dark sunglasses.

"Yes." He tugged Dana closer and draped his arm over her shoulders. "Let's go."

She wrapped her arm around his waist as they left the scene, not once looking back toward the lab and the bodies. When they met a bevy of troopers and a paramedic crew thrashing through the woods, they paused only long enough to point them toward the crime scene.

But once they were alone again, Dana stopped. "I have an idea."

"I do too."

Ignoring the pain shooting up his leg and radiating through his head, he pulled her close and gave her a kiss so thorough and fierce it left them both breathless.

"Wow." She clung to his tee, the fabric bunching in her fingers.

"When I saw you standing there with that gun . . ." His voice hoarsened. "You could have been killed."

She swallowed—telling him she was as aware as he was about how close they'd come to tragedy. "But I wasn't . . . despite my slightly off timing. I should have let Phelps get closer to you before I stepped out."

"You're being way too hard on yourself." He brushed the hair back from her forehead. "What you did was amazing . . . and brave . . . and incredible. Now what's your idea?"

"I liked yours better." She squeezed his fingers, then angled toward the lake. "We're almost to the place on the bank where you spotted the chief diving that night. Why don't you wait there and I'll go get the boat? Treat you to a row across the lake."

A refusal sprang to his lips, but he bit it back as common sense took over. The mere thought of fighting through the overgrowth on the circuitous route around the lake was daunting. Dana's idea had merit. She wouldn't get lost, the place was safe now, and he could row them back. His ego might take a hit, but it was a logical choice. And no one but he and Dana ever need know he'd reached his limit.

"That'll work."

Her eyebrows rose. "That was too easy. You must really be hurting."

"I've hurt worse."

She looked as if she wanted to say more . . . but instead transferred her attention to the lake. "You want me to help you over there?"

"No. Go ahead and get the boat. I'll be waiting."

He remained where he was until she disappeared . . . but as soon as she was out of sight, he grabbed a nearby tree limb to steady himself. Okay, maybe he was hurt a little more than he'd let on. But why worry Dana? If he still felt rocky after they sat on her porch for a while, he could always ask her to have one of the Beaumont police officers drive her to fetch his SUV, then take him into the city. She was planning to get behind the wheel again next week, anyway.

But for now, he just wanted to sit by a placid lake, breathe—and thank God the two of them had survived an explosive situation that could easily have cost them their lives.

—24—

As Dana emerged from the woods on the cabin side of the lake, a vehicle roared up the drive, spewing gravel in its wake.

Must be more law enforcement people arriving. Perhaps they were using her place as a staging area.

But as she approached the dock, she knew the two men who appeared around the corner of the cabin weren't here in an official capacity.

They were here as brothers.

The instant Mac and Lance spotted her, they broke into a jog.

"Did you find Finn?" Mac was a step ahead of his brother.

"Yes." She briefed them on the events of the morning, watching their expressions morph from grim to ominous. Thank heaven she was on their side; otherwise, she'd be downright intimidated.

"So I'm going to row over there now and get him." As she concluded her story, the furrows on Mac's forehead deepened.

"How badly is he hurt?"

"I don't know. He's upright, but the bump on his temple is big and he's limping. He refused medical attention, though."

"Yeah? We'll see about that." Mac marched toward the dock.

"Wait! I promised I'd pick him up." Dana trotted after him, Lance at her side. Finn did *not* need a take-charge big brother pushing him around—no matter Mac's good intentions.

"You've had plenty on your plate today already. Plus, I can get there faster."

"I'll go too." This from Lance—and the determined jut of his jaw said that point wasn't negotiable.

"There's no room. It's a small boat." Dana jogged after them onto the dock.

Mac was on board, oars in hand, before Lance could protest. "Where am I headed?"

Dana gave up the fight. No way were either of these McGregor men going to let her row across the lake alone. "On the far side, straight across. You'll see a very small clearing as you approach."

"Got it. Lance, take care of Dana."

"I'm fine." Not exactly true. Her legs felt like rubber after her trek around the lake—not to mention all the trauma. But she didn't need anyone to take care of her.

Except maybe Finn.

"Then he'll keep you company." Mac untied the mooring line and pushed off. "We'll be back in a few minutes."

With several strong strokes, he pulled away from the dock.

"You want a glass of water or . . . something?" Lance watched the rowboat skim across the water.

"No thanks. I'll wait here."

"Yeah. Me too." He folded his arms, adopted a wide-legged stance, and directed a fierce look at the far shore. "And even if I have to drag the runt to the hospital by the hair, he's going to get checked out. ASAP."

Dana didn't argue. Nor did she take issue with Lance's concern.

But it was doubtful Finn would agree—and he didn't like being bullied.

Sighing, Dana dropped down onto the dock, let her legs hang over the edge . . . and prepared for another round of fireworks on this Saturday that had started out so peaceful and quiet.

Squinting at the approaching rowboat, Finn pulled himself to his feet.

Why was Mac manning the oars instead of Dana?

Plus, when his oldest brother looked over his shoulder, he had that don't-mess-with-me demeanor—hard jaw, flat mouth, steely stare—Finn had seen too often to count.

It was never a positive omen.

Mac locked gazes with him when he reached the bank, then gave him a thorough once-over. "You okay?"

"Yeah. Where's Dana?"
"Waiting on the dock with Lance."
Oh, great. *Both* of his overprotective brothers were on hand.
"What are you guys doing here?"
"Dana left me a voicemail. It sounded like trouble was brewing." He steadied the craft against the bank with an oar. "You need a hand?"
Finn eyed the boat. Considering the pain in his leg, the odds of boarding gracefully were miniscule.
But he was *not* asking for help.
"No thanks."
"Then get in."
He edged closer. If he distracted Mac, it was possible his brother wouldn't notice the sure-to-be-awkward maneuver.
"Did you talk to Dana by phone before you drove down?"
"No. When I returned her call, she was out of range."
"How come you didn't answer her call, anyway? I thought that cell phone of yours was permanently attached to your body."
Mac gave him a shrewd appraisal. "Why are you stalling? Is your leg hurting that much? Are you dizzy?"
How much had Dana told his brothers about his condition?
"I'm not stalling."

"Then get in the boat."

"I'll get in if you answer my question." Another attempt at the best-defense-is-a-good-offense strategy might be worth trying. "This wasn't the most opportune day to decide to disconnect from the world, you know." He stepped into the boat with his sturdy leg.

Mac sent him a level look. "Lisa and I were getting an early start on my birthday presents, okay?"

"Oh." Not much he could say in response to that.

Gritting his teeth, he swung his other leg in. It banged against the edge, setting the boat rocking, and he sat down fast. Too fast. He had to grab the edge of the seat to steady himself.

Not the most convincing proof his leg was sound.

"We need to get you to a hospital." Mac aimed the boat back toward the cabin and picked up speed with a few powerful thrusts of the oars.

"I'm fine."

"Right."

The remainder of the trip passed in silence.

But as they approached the dock and Lance's rigid shoulders came into view, Finn geared up for a second blitz.

Not that he took issue with their logic. It was their high-handed approach that rankled. Would they ever realize he was grown up and could make his own decisions about stuff like this? He already had a plan in place; if his leg and head didn't feel a lot better in an hour or two, he'd get medical help.

First, though, he needed some downtime with Dana to take a deep breath and unwind.

Maybe if he explained that to them in a calm, reasonable tone, they'd back off.

The boat nosed into the dock, and Mac tossed the line to Lance. "Help him out."

"I don't need help."

After sending him a disgusted look, Mac vaulted onto the deck and nodded to Lance. An instant later, they both leaned down, grabbed his arms, and hauled him out of the boat in one swift, smooth motion.

Once he was on his feet, Mac kept a tight grip on him.

"Are you okay?" Lance repeated the thorough scrutiny Mac had given him.

"Fine."

"Not." Mac glared at him. "And stubborn as ever."

Forget about calm and reasonable.

"Look who's talking about being stubborn." Finn slammed his arms over his chest.

"Dana." Mac was clearly holding on to his temper by a fast-fraying tether. "Would you talk some sense into him, please? We'll give you five minutes. Come on, Lance." Grabbing their middle brother's arm, he tugged him toward the porch, Lance protesting all the way.

She waited until they were out of earshot, then moved close and spoke in a soft voice, her hand on his arm. Where it belonged. "Sorry about that. They kind of ganged up on me. Your brothers are . . . formidable."

"No kidding."

"But I think they're also right." She laid her fingers beside the bump on his temple. Despite her light touch, he cringed. "This needs attention. And after all you went through to get your leg back in shape, why take chances with it now? If there's any damage, wouldn't it be better to address that as soon as possible rather than let it get worse? I know you don't want that limp for the rest of your life."

Funny how her soft touch, tender tone, and caring manner were a thousand percent more persuasive than his brothers' overbearing high-handedness.

"I can't argue with a word you've said. I just wanted a few minutes alone with you first." He surveyed his brothers. Both had their arms folded and were in a deep, heated discussion—about him, no doubt. He exhaled. "Doesn't seem like that's going to happen for a while, though."

"Look on the positive side. You have family that cares enough to be upset if you're hurting or need help. That's a blessing."

Her gentle tone didn't contain one iota of criticism, but guilt gnawed at his conscience. Once again, she was right. During her recent trauma, there'd been no one to rant and rave at her about taking care of herself. She'd been on her own. Mac and Lance—not to mention his parents—did tend to overreact when it came to his well-being, but it was hard to fault zeal prompted by love.

"Thanks for the perspective check." He laced his fingers with hers and gave them a squeeze.

"Does that mean you'll let the EMTs look you over?"

"Better than that." In his gut, he'd known it would come to this sooner or later. Much as he hated doctors and hospitals, there was no sense delaying the inevitable. "I'll have Mac and Lance drive me over to pick up my car, then Mac can take me to St. Louis while Lance follows in the SUV. The doctor I've been going to for my leg has all my records, and I'll have them drop me at the ER where he's on staff."

"Want some company?"

"It could be a long day."

"It's already been a long day. But sitting here, waiting for word, will make it longer. I'd rather sit with you."

"Sold." He gave Mac and Lance a quick inspection, shifted position to block their view in case they decided to eavesdrop, and leaned in close for a quick kiss. "That will have to do for now."

"As long as there's more to come." Her words were a whisper of warmth against his jaw.

Sweet.

"Count on it."

He held her for a few more seconds, at last forcing himself to step back and call out to his brothers. "You win."

Mac gave Lance an I-told-you-so smirk. "I figured Dana would have more luck than us getting through that thick skull of yours. Let's go."

"Not so fast." Finn outlined the plan. "Then, once we get to the ER, you guys can drop me off and be on your way."

Lance snorted. "Like that's gonna happen. We're sticking with you until we get the all clear from the doc."

"But after that, we'll leave you two to your own devices," Mac amended. "Let's roll."

The two brothers flanked Finn, forcing him to relinquish Dana's hand. But in view of the fact his leg was beginning to *really* hurt, he didn't argue. They'd have time together later.

And once he was back on his feet—literally—he intended to make the most of it.

Dana surveyed the group assembled in the ER examining room and tucked herself farther back in the corner, buying herself a few more inches of personal space. This room was *not* designed to accommodate three muscular ex–special forces operatives, a girlfriend, and a nurse.

And it got even more crowded once the tall, stocky doctor joined them—but no one except the nurse left. They all just rearranged themselves around the equipment.

“You have quite a pit crew.” The doctor edged around all of them to join Finn, who was propped up on the bed—and growing more impatient by the second. If the man hadn’t shown up within the next five minutes, Dana had a feeling the patient would have bolted.

“What’s the word?” Finn cut to the chase.

“The word is good overall. As far as we can tell, no concussion. But over the next twenty-four hours, you need to watch for any symptoms that could suggest complications. Drowsiness, dizziness, nausea—”

“Confusion, double vision, headache. Yeah, yeah, I know the signs.” Finn dismissed the warning with a flip of his hand. “What about the leg?”

“Based on my exam earlier and the MRI, it doesn’t appear you did any serious damage. All the hardware your surgeons installed is fine. Your orthopedic doctor, who reviewed the scan remotely, agrees. We’re classifying the injury as a Grade II quadriceps strain—to the rectus femoris, if you want specifics. I'm not seeing any signs of severe tearing, though. Given your general physical condition, and assuming you don't push yourself too hard, you should feel back to normal in a week to ten days."

"What does he need to do?" Mac muscled in, ignoring Finn's dark look.

"Cold therapy is important for the first forty-eight hours. We'll give you detailed instructions on discharge. A stretching and strengthening program might also be helpful. You can discuss all that with your doctor next week."

"So I can leave?"

The doctor's lips twitched. "Are you tired of us already?"

Finn glanced her way, and at the heat in his eyes, Dana's heart missed a beat. "I have plans for this evening."

"Then I'll try to expedite your paperwork." The doctor angled toward Mac and Lance. "Are you two hanging around until he's free to go?"

"No."

"Yes."

As Finn and his brothers spoke in unison—and with equal vehemence—Dana tried not to smile.

"It might be wise to take advantage of their upper body strength to get you home, unless you want to resort to crutches or weigh down your friend here." The doctor dipped his head toward her.

Despite his obvious frustration, Finn capitulated. "Fine."

"You're welcome." Lance propped a shoulder against the wall and shoved his hands in his pockets. "And since you're being so gracious about our generous offer of bodily assistance, you should also know that Christy is preparing our guest room for you as we speak."

"On that note, I'll leave you all to work out the particulars." The doctor wove through the crowd and disappeared out the door.

"I'm not moving in with you guys." Finn crossed his own arms. "You're practically still on your honeymoon."

"We've been married for almost two months—and you'll only be gracing us with your presence for a few days. I'll kick you out if you try to stay too long."

"Trust me, that won't be an issue. I have to be in Atlanta next week, remember?"

"Nope." Mac flanked him on the other side of the bed. "I talked to Dad and Mom while you were getting the MRI. He's delayed your start date a week. And they expect a call later today."

"Also, Christy's leaving some dinner for you. Enough for two, Dana." Lance winked at her. "We're going out to eat."

The nurse bustled back in, cutting off the possibility of a response. "You guys must have pull. We never get discharge papers signed this fast."

Once she was done with her business, Mac and Lance moved into position and steadied Finn as he stood. Then they walked him out to the drop-off area, where Lance had created his own parking spot.

At the passenger door to the SUV, Mac released his hold. "Don't forget to call Mom and Dad."

"I won't." Finn kept a firm hold on the doorframe. "Sorry about ruining your birthday lunch."

Mac shook his head. "Ruined would have been never getting the opportunity to reschedule." His voice rasped, and he pulled his kid brother into a hug. "Take care of yourself."

"I will. But I think I might have some help with that too." He aimed the half-question at her over Mac's shoulder.

"You will." Dana smiled at him.

Mac released Finn and gave her his full attention. "Thanks for all you did today."

It was Dana's turn to be engulfed in a bear hug.

Then, with a mock salute, Mac strode off toward the parking lot.

"Are you getting in or are we going to stand around here all day?" Lance elbowed Finn.

With his help, Finn swung into the front seat while she clambered into the back.

Forty-five minutes later, after meeting Lance's wife, helping settle Finn on the couch in the living room with an ice pack and ottoman for his leg, and waving good-bye to his brother and sister-in-law, Dana rejoined him in the living room.

"Sit." He patted the couch beside him.

"Don't you want to eat first? Christy left a nice dinner, and breakfast was hours ago. You must be hungry."

"I am." He gave her a slow smile that set her heart racing, patted the couch again, and laid his arm across the back. "Sit."

She sat.

"Better." He pulled her close. "I thought they'd never leave."

She snuggled in and shifted toward him . . . just in time for his lips to meet hers.

The kiss was a continuation of the one they'd shared in the forest—intense and passionate, fierce yet tender—but much longer.

When he at last eased back, he didn't go far. He simply rested his forehead against hers.

She had to verify her lungs were still working before she could speak. "That was . . . incredible."

"An excellent description."

"Mmm." She inhaled, long and slow. The hospital smell continued to cling to him, but beneath the whiffs of antiseptic, the scent was all masculine—and all Finn. "The one piece of upbeat news to come out of today is that you have an extra week in St. Louis."

"I agree. That gives me seven more days to

ramp up my campaign to convince you to move to Atlanta."

She'd been waiting for hours to address that very subject.

Backing off a bit, she draped her arms around his neck. "We don't need to waste the week on that. I've already made my decision. I'm coming to Atlanta."

He blinked. "Seriously?"

"Seriously. As I was tramping through the woods today toting that rifle, I realized I was letting fear dictate my choices. Yes, moving to Atlanta carries some risk. Our relationship might not work out. I might end up having to relocate again in three or four or six months. But you know what? An ex–Army Ranger who races through the woods to rescue a woman in distress, fixes docks, takes me for moonlight rows, treats me to homemade pie, gives up sleep to watch over me—and who kisses like a superhero—is worth taking a chance on."

A slow grin spread over his face. "You know what?"

"What?"

"I don't think you're taking all that big of a chance. Because my instincts tell me the electricity between us isn't some freak lightning storm. It's the real deal. As in till death do us part."

Dana's breathing hitched. "That almost sounds like . . . like a proposal."

"Would you say yes if it was?"

"I wish I was that brave—but even moving to Atlanta this fast is taking me light-years out of my comfort zone."

"That's what I thought. So I'll bide my time. And since I don't have to spend the next week convincing you to relocate, I'll get to work on my next mission."

"And what would that be?" She stroked the thick hair at the base of his neck, trying to control the temptation to pull him close again and claim another one of those amazing kisses.

"It's top secret—but the code name is Operation Persuasion."

"Mmm. I like the sound of that. Can I help in any way?"

"Oh, I'm counting on it. Starting right now."

And as he leaned down to launch his campaign, Dana met him halfway—and gave him her full cooperation.

—Epilogue—

That was the best Thanksgiving dinner ever. Great job, Mom." Finn carefully dabbed his mouth with the fancy heirloom linen napkin and set it beside his empty dessert plate. One more bite and he'd burst.

"Finn McGregor, haven't I told you and your

brothers for years not to be afraid of those napkins? They're sturdier than they look, or they wouldn't have survived three generations of this clan." His mom demonstrated by giving hers a thorough workout. "But I'm glad you enjoyed the meal."

Lance snorted. "If he'd enjoyed it any more, the glaze would be off the plate."

"Hey . . . who are you to talk? I saw you scrape the crumbs from the bottom of the pie tin." Finn scowled at his middle brother.

"Now, boys . . . no fighting at the table." His dad stood, a touch of amusement mitigating the reprimand. "But at least no one threw food this year."

Mac snickered. "Yeah. Remember the Thanksgiving Lance and Finn started tossing rolls at each other in the middle of the meal? Where were we living then?"

"Cameroon. We couldn't find a turkey and had to compromise with beef kabobs. Not a popular choice with this family, let me tell you. I remember that day very well." His mom arched an eyebrow at Mac. "And as I recall, they only launched into those shenanigans after you double-dared them to."

"Ah-ha. So you were an instigator as a kid." Lisa nudged her husband. "This is a side of you I've never heard about before."

"Thanks a lot, Mom." Mac draped his arm

around his wife's shoulders. "Keep that up, you'll ruin my knight-in-shining-armor image."

"Man, it's getting deep in here." Lance plucked at his pants leg.

"On that note—shall we let the ladies retire to the living room while we men take over the cleanup? A family tradition, Dana—and don't let Finn forget that down the road."

Beneath the table, Finn captured her hand. Thank goodness all the high-spirited banter and teasing hadn't intimidated her. His family could be a handful when they all got together. But she'd breezed through the meal like a pro, even joining in here and there on the lighthearted jabbing.

In other words, she fit into the McGregor clan perfectly.

The very reason he wasn't inclined to follow tradition today. He had much bigger plans for the next hour or two than scrubbing dirty dishes.

After giving her fingers a squeeze, he rose, drawing her up with him. "You know I normally pull my weight at these family shindigs, but I'd like to stretch my leg. It's feeling kind of cramped after sitting for two hours. Do you guys mind if I skip out this year and take a stroll around the block with Dana?"

Lance narrowed his eyes as he began to gather up plates. "Convenient timing."

"Yeah. You made it through an extra piece of pie without complaining about your leg." Mac shot him a disgruntled look.

"It's okay, Finn. Go ahead. I'll pitch in if they need an extra set of hands." Christy winked at him.

"Me too," Lisa offered.

"No, you won't." Mac gave his wife a stern glance. "The doc told you to stay off your feet as much as possible for these last few weeks. And while a baby on Thanksgiving might be memorable, I'd rather spend the day here than in the hospital."

"Then let your brother off the hook. Dana deserves a break from this rowdy bunch, and I'm sure Finn will find a way to distract her." Lisa sent him a knowing smile.

Interesting how his sisters-in-law seemed to have intuitively picked up that more than an evening stroll was at stake, while his brothers' well-honed instincts, though keen on the battle-field, left them oblivious to kinder, gentler undertones.

"Thanks." He urged Dana toward the door before Mac and Lance could resume their ribbing. "Let's grab a jacket."

Three minutes later, after he'd pulled on a sweater and she'd donned a fleece hoodie, they stepped into the cool, late-afternoon air.

"Is your leg really bothering you?" Dana tucked

her hand in his arm as he guided her down the front walk and turned left.

"Not much . . . but I thought you might need a break from the McGregor clan. One-on-one, we're manageable—sort of. Put us all together, we can be overwhelming. I think we almost lost Lisa the first year she came to a big family gathering."

"You aren't going to lose me. I enjoy being around your parents, and your sisters-in-law help tone down some of the testosterone that zips around whenever you and your brothers converge." She squeezed his hand. "Are we heading for the park?"

"Yeah." One spot in particular, near a fountain, surrounded by gardens. Their favorite spot to stroll after having dinner with his parents. Best of all, the manicured pocket park in the subdivision was deserted more often than not . . . and very private.

Just the kind of place he had in mind for today.

They strolled for a few minutes as Finn mentally rehearsed his speech . . . until he realized the silence had stretched too long. Dana wasn't the kind of woman who needed to fill every quiet interlude with conversation, but as a rule she liked to chat after a social event.

He gave her a swift perusal—and frowned at her pensive expression. "Everything okay?"

She squeezed his hand. "Yes. Sorry, I didn't

mean to zone out. I was thinking how blessed we are, and how much we have to be thankful for—which is the point of Thanksgiving, after all. Things could have ended so differently last spring." A slight shudder rippled through her.

"Have you been having nightmares again?" They'd plagued her for weeks following the traumatic events in the woods, though she'd only admitted that after the fact, when the shadows under her lower lashes had become too dark to mask with makeup.

"No. They're gone . . . forever, I hope. But if I never hold a gun again, it will be too soon." She let out an unsteady breath. "I can't seem to erase the memory of the moment I aimed that rifle at Phelps and p-pulled the trigger."

"Hey." He paused and turned her toward him, his free hand kneading her shoulder. "You don't have to feel any misplaced guilt about that. The man had murder on his mind. It was self-defense, pure and simple. Besides, the state trooper's bullet ended his life, not yours. You just nicked his shoulder." It was the same reassurance he always gave her when the subject came up.

And she gave him the same response. "I know. But I *could* have killed him."

Finn pulled her into a hug. It didn't take a genius to understand why a woman with Dana's kindness and empathy, who spent every workday dealing with happy endings in those books she edited, would be distressed by the knowledge that she possessed the ability to kill.

But he hated that she had to wrestle with undeserved remorse or self-reproach.

At last she eased back. "You think I'm being oversensitive, don't you?"

"No." His denial was immediate—and firm. "I think you're being Dana . . . and I wouldn't change a thing about you. Your sensitive heart is one of the reasons I fell in love with you."

She exhaled and relaxed against him. "The feeling's mutual, in case there's any doubt."

"Nice to know." Especially tonight. "Shall we continue to the park?" He took her hand again.

"Sure."

As they ambled toward their destination, Finn tried to redirect the conversation. But when his attempts were met with monosyllable answers, he gave up. Ignoring the elephant in the room wasn't going to make it go away.

"You're still thinking about what happened, aren't you?"

"Yes. About Chief Burnett, actually. I know what he did was wrong—both keeping the gold a secret and staying quiet about that meth lab—but I can't help feeling sorry for him. It's hard to fault someone for wanting to take care of a person they love."

As far as he was concerned, wrong was wrong . . . but he could appreciate the nuances that troubled Dana. If he was in a situation like Burnett, desperate to provide for a loved one, who knew what lengths he might go to, what kind of compromises he might consider? He'd like to think he'd stand firm on his principles and take a higher road . . . but pressure could bend even the strongest person. That didn't make it right, nor was it an excuse, but it happened.

Sometimes with fatal consequences.

And the chief had definitely paid the price for his deception.

At least he'd redeemed himself somewhat in the end by doing what he could to help thwart Phelps.

"The situation was messy, no question about it. And you do have to admire his loyalty to his wife." He could concede that much.

"I agree. I'm glad the company that owned the gold offered to pick up her bills after it was returned to them. Setting some funds aside as a reward and applying them to her care was a generous gesture."

"Good PR too."

She nudged him. "Cynic."

"Realist. Besides, it didn't cost them that much."

"That's true. Everyone in town said she'd been slipping, but I think they were all surprised when she died five months after the chief."

"Uh-huh." They were approaching the park, and

he didn't want one millisecond of sadness to mar the surprise he had planned. Time to lift the somber mood. "Our bench awaits." He guided her to their usual spot.

"Yes . . . and the pansies are beautiful despite the chilly nights. In New York, most of the flowers are gone by Thanksgiving." Her tone was more upbeat now—as if she, too, was anxious to leave heavier subjects behind.

Excellent.

"Does that mean you're liking it here in Atlanta?"

"Yes. The city has many attractions." She sat.

"Such as?" He joined her.

"Hmm." She leaned back, her expression speculative. "Warmer weather than New York, reasonable access to beaches, Southern charm, fabulous ethnic food . . . let's see, am I leaving anything out?"

Finn reached into his jacket . . . took a deep breath to steady his nerves . . . and pulled out a small square box. "They have great jewelry stores too."

Her gaze dropped to his hand. Darted back to his face. Dropped again.

He flipped up the lid to reveal a marquis-cut diamond in a platinum setting that the clerk had assured him would dazzle any woman.

Based on the sudden sparkle in Dana's eyes, the man hadn't overstated his claim.

"Is there a . . ." She stopped. Swallowed. "Is there a speech to go with that?"

"Yes—if I can remember it. Being around you has a tendency to muddle my brain."

"I'll take that as a compliment."

"You should." He tried to coax up the corners of his mouth, formulate a witty response, but for once his ability to lock down his nerves in stressful situations failed him. He couldn't manage either the grin or the comeback.

Giving up, he gripped her hand and launched into his speech instead. "Being around you also makes me smile—more than I ever have in my life. And it makes me want to be the kind of man you'll always be proud of. It also reminds me of what's important in life . . . and how precious every single day is. You bring out the best in me—and you help me notice things I never appreciated before. The pleasure of a gentle touch. The joy of shared laughter. The sweetness of simple moments spent together. Just by being part of them, you make ordinary days extraordinary."

A sheen appeared in Dana's eyes, and she reached up to swipe her fingers under them. "If you keep this up, Finn McGregor, you're going to ruin my mascara."

"Then get your makeup kit handy, because there's more." He extracted the ring from the box—a far harder task than he expected, thanks to the tremors in his fingers. "I love you, Dana. I love your courage and kindness, your sense of humor and intelligence, your empathy and caring. I love the way you look at me right before I kiss you, how your eyes get soft and that little pulse beats in your throat. I love how you make me feel like the luckiest man in the world. And the truth is, that's what I am. Or I will be if you answer this question with a yes. Will you marry me so we can end every day in each other's arms and greet every morning with a kiss?"

"Yes." Her acceptance came out in a soft rush of air as she lifted her hand and held it out.

His lips finally agreed to curve up. "I guess all those roses and candlelit dinners and classic movie nights at my condo paid off."

"They helped seal the deal—but you want the truth? I think deep inside I knew almost from the first day we met that you were destined to be the one." She wiggled her finger. "Whenever you're ready."

Without further delay, he slipped on the ring.

And as he slid the shiny band into position, elation surged through him, just as it used to after finishing a high-risk mission, when all was well and he was heading home.

Except this time he was heading home *forever*.

The sooner the better.

With the ring firmly on her finger, he grasped both her hands. "I have one other question. How fast can we get married?"

"Anxious?"

"Close enough." And a more polite way of phrasing it.

"What would you think about a Christmas wedding?"

One month away.

He could wait that long.

Maybe.

"I think that would be the best Christmas present I ever got."

"Then let's shoot for that." She fingered the edge of his crew-neck sweater, the brush of her knuckles against his jaw driving him crazy. "Too bad you're new on the job, though. If you had more vacation accrued, we wouldn't have to settle for a long weekend somewhere after the wedding."

She thought he intended to take an abbreviated honeymoon?

Ha.

"Oh, I have some pull with the boss. I think I can wrangle a few extra days off. Is there any specific place you'd like to go?"

"No . . . although I'm partial to privacy and palm trees and white sand."

"That gets my vote too. And I know the perfect spot. Have you ever heard of Cayo Espanto?"

"No."

"It's in Belize. A private island resort with coconut palms, empty beaches, and great food.

They only have a handful of individual, secluded villas."

"Wow! That sounds exotic—and very expensive."

"Worth every penny to get you all to myself."

"Have you been there?"

"No, but I've done some research on honeymoon destinations. I had several possibilities in mind, depending on your geographic preference."

"Is there anything to do there other than eat and be a beach bum?" Her eyes began to twinkle.

"Oh yeah. I have lots of activities in mind. Shall I give you a preview?"

"By all means."

She lifted her chin.

He leaned down.

And in the instant before their lips met, he sent a silent thank-you heavenward.

For the sweet love of this special woman who would bless his days for always.

For the grace that had led him from the darkness of battlefield demons to the light of hope.

And for absolute proof that happy endings didn't only happen in books.

Not again.

Adam Stone slammed the door on his decrepit Kia, expelled a breath, and surveyed the damage.

The rustic, one-room cabin he called home appeared to be untouched this go-round. But it would take some serious sanding to get rid of the profanities spray-painted on the small out-building that housed his woodworking shop.

At least the vandals hadn't broken any windows this time.

But where was Clyde?

Breaking into a jog on the gravel drive, he scanned the surrounding woods that offered peeks at the pristine Oregon beach and choppy April sea a hundred yards away.

"Clyde!"

No response.

"Clyde! Come on out, boy. It's safe."

Silence, save for the distinctive trill of the sandpiper that gave this secluded cove its name.

He clamped his jaw shut. Damaged property, he could deal with. But if those thugs had done anything to . . .

A soft whimper came from the direction of the workshop, and the swinging door he'd rigged up for the adopted stray gave a slight shimmy.

Adam switched direction, digging out the keys to the shed as he goosed his jog to a sprint.

"I'm here, boy. Hang on." He fumbled the key as he inserted it in the lock, tremors sabotaging his fingers.

Clenching his teeth, he tried again. It was crazy to worry about a dumb mutt who hadn't had enough sense to move out of the path of a car.

Letting yourself care for anyone—or anything—was an invitation for grief.

And he didn't need any more of that.

Yet walking away from a hurt, defenseless creature hadn't been an option on that foggy day by the side of Highway 101 when he'd found the injured pooch barely clinging to life.

The lock clicked, and he pushed the door open.

From the corner of the shop where he'd wedged himself behind some scrap wood, Clyde poked out his black nose. He whimpered again, his big, soulful brown eyes filled with fear.

Adam exhaled, his tension whooshing out like CO2 being released from a soft drink can.

Clyde was scared—but okay.

Hunkering down, he held out his hand and gentled his voice. "You're safe, boy. Come on out."

Clyde didn't budge.

No problem.

Adam sat cross-legged on the rough-hewn floorboards and waited. Pushing any creature to trust if they weren't yet ready to do so could backfire—no matter how well-intentioned the overture. The small white scar on his right hand from the night Clyde had mistaken a friendly reach for a threat proved that.

But these days, it didn't take long for the mangy mongrel to emerge from a hiding place.

Less than fifteen seconds later, Clyde crept out

and inched toward him, limping on his bad leg.

As the dog approached, Adam fought the urge to pull the shaking mass of mottled fur into a comforting embrace.

Instead, he remained motionless until Clyde sniffed around, stuck a damp nose in his palm—and climbed into his lap.

All forty-three pounds of him.

Only then did Adam touch the dog.

"No one's going to hurt you, fella. Everything's fine." The last word hitched as he stroked the mutt. "I'm here, and I won't be leaving again until I go to work tomorrow morning. We'll spend the rest of Sunday together. I might even grill a burger for you too, instead of making you eat that dog chow the vet recommended. How does some comfort food sound?"

Of course the stupid dog had no idea what he was saying—but his soothing tone seemed to calm the canine. Clyde's shakes subsided, and when their gazes connected, the mutt's eyes brimmed with adoration.

A sudden rush of warmth filled Adam's heart—but he quickly squelched it. How pathetic, to be touched by a dog's affection.

Besides, it was all an illusion.

Dogs didn't feel emotions.

Without breaking eye contact, Clyde gave his fingers a quick, dry lick. As if to say, *Yes, we do. And I think you're great.*

Pressure built in Adam's throat as he smoothed a hand over Clyde's back, his fingertips feeling every ridge of scar tissue that had been there long before their lives had intersected sixteen months ago, when both of them had been in desperate need of a friend.

Okay. Fine.

Maybe he was reading too much into the dog's reaction.

Maybe he was being too sentimental.

But for today, he'd let himself believe the abused pooch *did* have deeper feelings.

Because while he'd made a few friends in Hope Harbor during the year and a half he'd lived here, the only one waiting for him in Sandpiper Cove at the end of each day was Clyde.

And without the canine companion who'd claimed a wedge of his heart, his life would be even lonelier.

"Happy Monday, Lexie. How's your week starting out?"

Hope Harbor Police Chief Lexie Graham leaned a shoulder against the side of Charley's taco truck and considered the man's question as she gave the picturesque wharf a sweep.

Planters overflowing with colorful flowers served as a buffer between the sidewalk and the sloping pile of boulders that led to the water. Across the wide street from the marina, quaint storefronts adorned with bright awnings and flower boxes faced the sea. A white gazebo occupied the small park behind Charley's truck, where the two-block-long, crescent-shaped frontage road dead-ended at the river.

All was peaceful and predictable . . . as usual.

Just the way she liked it.

"So far, so good. Everything's been quiet."

"I don't know. Looks can be deceiving. You ordering for one today?"

"Yes." She studied the taco-making artist, who hadn't changed one iota in all the years she'd known him. Same leathery, latte-colored skin. Same long gray hair pulled back into a ponytail. Same kindly, insightful eyes.

It was comforting to have one unchanging element in a world that liked to throw curves. The town sage and wisdom-dispenser could always be counted on to offer sound advice and brighten her day.

But his looks-can-be-deceiving comment didn't leave her feeling warm and fuzzy.

Squinting, she took another survey of Dockside Drive. Nothing amiss in town, as far as she could see. Nor did there appear to be any issues meriting attention on the water. The long jetty on the left and the pair of rocky islands on the right that tamed the turbulent waves and protected the boats in the marina were as unchanging as the sea stacks on the beach outside of town.

Everything seemed normal.

Maybe Charley's comment had just been one of those philosophical observations he liked to throw out on occasion.

Whatever the impetus for his remark, she didn't intend to dwell on it.

"What kind of tacos are you making?"

"Cod's the star today." He pulled a handful of chopped red onions out of a cooler and tossed them on the griddle, alongside the sizzling fish. The savory aroma set off a rumble in her stomach. "Enhanced by my grandmother's secret lime cilantro cream sauce."

"Sounds great, as always."

"We aim to please." He flipped the fish and sprinkled some kind of seasoning over the ingredients on the griddle. "So did you find any clues out at Adam's place?"

At the non sequitur, she blinked. "What are you talking about?"

"The vandalism at Adam Stone's place yesterday." He stirred the onions. "Didn't he report it?"

"Not that I know of." And she would know if he had. Every crime report landed on her desk.

"Hmm. That surprises me, seeing as how this is his second hit."

There'd been *two* incidents of unreported vandalism inside the town limits?

"Well, I can't solve crimes if people don't report

them." A prickle of irritation sharpened her tone.

"I suppose, given his history, he might prefer to stay off law enforcement's radar. You do know Adam, don't you?"

She called up an image of the man she'd seen only from a distance. Six-one or two, lean, muscled, dark hair worn longish and secured with a black bandana, bad-boy stubble, usually attired in jeans and a scuffed black leather jacket. She wouldn't be surprised if he sported a few tattoos too.

In other words, a guy who'd feel at home in a motorcycle gang—and who fit the hard-edged name everyone in town except Charley called him.

Stone.

"I know who he is." When an ex-con came to town, the police chief did her homework. "But we've never spoken."

"Is that right?" Charley set three corn tortillas on the counter beside him. "He's a regular at Grace Christian. I assumed your paths had crossed."

They might have if she still went to church.

Not a subject she was inclined to discuss over fish tacos on a public street.

Interesting that the guy went to services, though. She wouldn't have pegged him as a churchgoer.

"No. I work a lot of Sunday mornings." Like all of them. On purpose.

"Well, I hope you get a handle on this vandalism before it escalates to a lot worse than spray-painted graffiti, a few broken windows, and some uprooted flowers." He gestured to the planters along the wharf as he began assembling the tacos. "Rose and her garden club members spent hours salvaging what they could of the flowers after the last incident. And quite a few of the planters are damaged. They're being held together with spit and prayers."

"We're working the case as hard as we can, but whoever is doing this is picking times when no one is around. With our small force, we can't be everywhere at once 24/7."

"I hear you." He wrapped the tacos in white paper, slid them into a brown bag, and set them on the counter in front of her. "It's a shame about Adam's place, though. He's had too many tough breaks already."

"Not much I can do if he doesn't bother to file a report." She dug out her money.

"But there might be a clue out there." Charley counted out her change and passed it over.

And maybe you should check that out.

Charley didn't have to say the words for her to get his message. The man never pushed, but he had a gentle way of nudging people in directions he thought they should go.

Lexie sighed and shoved the coins into her pocket. "I suppose I could swing by his place."

"Couldn't hurt. But he won't be home until later."

Right.

He and the rest of BJ's construction crew were in the middle of building Tracy and Michael's house out at Harbor Point Cranberries. Given the small-town grapevine, showing up at the farm out of the blue to talk to him might not be the best plan. Who knew what people would think if law enforcement tracked him down? And a man who'd paid his debt to society didn't need any more hassles.

"I could stop by on my way home." Not that there was much chance she'd find a clue lying around a day after the fact. "How do you know what happened out there, anyway?"

"Adam came by for tacos after church yesterday. I think it's his weekly splurge."

An order of tacos from Charley's was a splurge?

The man must not be saving much of the money he earned working for BJ.

Then again, if you were starting from scratch after spending five years in prison, it could take a while to refill the well.

"Thanks for lunch." Lexie picked up the bag, the tantalizing smell tickling her nose.

"Enjoy." Charlie grinned, gave her a thumbs-up, and greeted the next customer in line.

Bag in hand, Lexie eyed the tempting benches arrayed along the curving wharf . . . but resisted the impulse to linger. There was a mound of paperwork waiting on her desk, and she'd procrastinated too much already.

She picked up her pace. Maybe after dinner tonight she and Matt could come down and watch the boats for a while. He always enjoyed that—and it would be a pleasant end to the day.

Especially if her official visit with police-shy Adam Stone turned out to be less than cordial.

Acknowledgments—

It's always with mixed feeling that I finish the final book in a series. Typically, I'm ready to move on . . . yet I know I'll miss the characters I've spent many months getting to know. From the FBI buddies in Heroes of Quantico, to my dynamic siblings in Guardians of Justice, to the former college roommates and ex-law-enforcement operatives turned PIs in Private Justice, all of my heroes and heroines hold a special place in my heart.

The Men of Valor series has been no different. The McGregor brothers were amazing.

At the same time, I'm excited about my next series, Code of Honor, which features three childhood friends. Book 1 will release in fall 2017. I hope you'll join me then for another thrilling ride.

In the meantime, I'll be heading back to my charming seaside town of Hope Harbor on the Oregon coast—where hearts heal . . . and love blooms. I invite you to travel there with me in *Sandpiper Cove*, coming spring 2017.

As I wrap up this series, I want to once again thank all of the experts who took time out of their busy schedules to answer my technical questions. I couldn't have done this without you.

A special thank-you also to the amazing team at Revell; to my mom and dad, the world's best parents; to all the readers who buy my books and allow me to tell my stories; and to my husband, Tom—my real-life leading man.

—About the Author—

Irene Hannon is a bestselling, award-winning author who took the publishing world by storm at the tender age of ten with a sparkling piece of fiction that received national attention.

Okay . . . maybe that's a slight exaggeration. But she *was* one of the honorees in a complete-the-story contest conducted by a national children's magazine. And she likes to think of that as her "official" fiction-writing debut!

Since then, she has written more than fifty contemporary romance and romantic suspense novels. Irene is a seven-time finalist and three-time winner of the RITA award—the "Oscar" of romance fiction—from Romance Writers of America. She is also a member of that organization's elite Hall of Fame. Her books have been honored with a National Readers' Choice award, three HOLT medallions, a Daphne du Maurier award, a Retailers' Choice award, two Booksellers' Best awards, two Carol awards, and two Reviewers' Choice awards from *RT Book Reviews* magazine. That magazine has also honored her with a Career Achievement award for her entire body of work. In addition, she is a two-time Christy award finalist.

Irene, who holds a BA in psychology and an MA

in journalism, juggled two careers for many years until she gave up her executive corporate communications position with a Fortune 500 company to write full-time. She is happy to say she has no regrets! As she points out, leaving behind the rush-hour commute, corporate politics, and a relentless BlackBerry that never slept was no sacrifice.

A trained vocalist, Irene has sung the leading role in numerous community musical theater productions and is also a soloist at her church.

When not otherwise occupied, she and her husband enjoy traveling, Saturday mornings at their favorite coffee shop, and spending time with family. They make their home in Missouri.

To learn more about Irene and her books, visit www.irenehannon.com. She is also active on Facebook and Twitter.

Center Point Large Print
600 Brooks Road / PO Box 1
Thorndike, ME 04986-0001 USA

(207) 568-3717

US & Canada:
1 800 929-9108
www.centerpointlargeprint.com